The Secret Dead Drops

of Paris and London

By Susan Jane Denman

D1416788

This book is dedicated to the memory of my father:
Alan C. R. Howard.

A thoughtful and intelligent man who always ensured
I wanted for nothing.

Sadly, he endured much suffering, before his life was cut short
by Parkinson's Disease in April 2020.

"One can't have everything in this world;
be content with the greatest of joys: health."

–Frédéric Chopin

1

Clarissa Belmonte elevated her face. The rain was falling fast. Cold water hit her eyes and ran into her mouth, but she didn't care. She didn't care about anything anymore.

The water drummed onto the cars in the Hoops Inn carpark. A distant tangle of music hummed amidst the evening birdsong. A faint sound like air escaping from a punctured tyre suggested the presence of distant traffic.

His words were still resounding in her head.

'Let's face it. We're done,' he'd said, not forty minutes ago, unable to look her in the eye.

They were cruel words. Clarissa had shivered involuntarily as if she'd experienced a sudden exposure; the words seemingly stripping her of something she hadn't been aware she'd needed until now. She'd taken the blow well; she'd even tried to smile. 'Yes,' she'd found herself saying pragmatically. 'I was about to say the same thing.' It was nothing but a defence mechanism.

He'd asked her to meet him at 7 p.m. on Sunday 10th March at the Hoops Inn in Perry Green. She now realised he'd arranged the rendezvous in order to terminate their relationship.

He'd grown increasingly distant over the last couple of months. Clarissa was a flight attendant based at Stansted (short haul only). They each had their own flats – hers in Bishop's Stortford, his in St. Albans. They had their own circle of friends, their own lives. When his calls became less frequent, she'd put it down to his work schedule. But then, when he did ring, he hardly spoke. It was as if the spark that had ignited them had diminished – for reasons unknown.

They'd met in the sky. He'd been returning from a conference in Paris; she'd attended to him on the plane. He'd been smooth and refreshing, like a gin and tonic on a hot summer's evening. He'd made her laugh, and she soon realised that she'd been aching to laugh like that for some time. After he'd asked for her number three times, she'd written it on the back of a paper coaster, handing it to him with his coffee. He'd called her the following day.

She used to play the piano. She liked Chopin. She'd discovered a Chopin CD boxset in his flat even before she'd revealed to him her love of the great composer. It was a connection.

But he was always working. He checked his phone constantly. He had money, seemed to know people in high places, but she was unable to shake a sneaking suspicion that he was somehow involved in the criminal world. He had a safe in his flat, he kept his desk locked, and he made mysterious calls in the middle of the night when he thought she was asleep. He never, *ever* discussed his work, and he kept a loaded Beretta 9mm handgun in the drawer beside his bed.

She watched as he emerged from the Hoops Inn, his slick city suit getting wet. She was painfully aware that soon after this moment, he would no longer be part of her world.

He looked uncomfortable. The air smelt redolent with cut grass and soft earth. Muted birdsong seemed to be dissolving around them like sugar granules tipped into a cup of strong espresso. Why add sweetness to a drink celebrated for its bitterness? Supposedly, for the same reason you would dump someone in a place of natural beauty, surrounded by birds and flowers.

'I thought you'd left,' he said.

'I needed some air,' she said.

They regarded one another awkwardly.

'Well, I suppose this is it,' he said with a sombre nod of the head.

'I suppose it is,' she echoed feebly.

'Good luck, baby,' he said.

There was a faint glimmer of warmth in the ephemeral smile he used to accompany his valediction, and possibly a wink as well

– it was difficult to tell, as rain was coming down and a drop could easily have got into his eye.

Clarissa felt herself flinch at his use of the word *baby,* not because he'd just broken up with her, but because in the eleven months they'd been together, he'd never once addressed her as anything other than Clarissa. It just wasn't a word she'd come to expect from him, and yet there it was. *Baby.* And even stranger, as he'd said it, his voice had cracked just slightly, and she couldn't help attributing this to an involuntary sentiment of ruefulness.

'Oh, I almost forgot,' he said, regaining his steely composure.

Reaching into his jacket pocket, he produced the key to her Bishop's Stortford flat. It was still attached to the padded love-heart keyring she'd given him three months ago. The sight of it in the palm of his hand getting wet in the rain caused her own heart to lurch. She took it, wincing afresh at its symbolistic relevance – he was rejecting her heart; the gesture seemed to make things worse. The absence of a reciprocation on her part – she had never been given a key to *his* flat – only added further insult to injury.

He started to walk towards his Audi.

'Charlie?' Clarissa heard the desperation in her voice.

He turned to stare at her, as if she were a stranger, as if they had not been having a relationship for eleven months.

Raindrops were suspended in his hair, still a rich blond at thirty-six. He screwed up his blue eyes and waited for her to speak. His lips were full and slightly parted; they weakened her.

She did not have any words to utter. There was nothing that she could say to make this any better, after all.

'Are you okay?' he said. It came out devoid of any compassion.

She nodded, suppressing the deluge of tears that she would no doubt relinquish later, but had no desire for him to bear witness to. The effort it took surprised her; any attempt to speak was rendered temporarily impossible.

He nodded again, before getting into his car and starting the engine. So it really is over, she thought.

She watched him drive off down the road.

With her green coat dripping and her blonde hair darkening, Clarissa allowed the rain to pummel fiercely into her. Unexpectedly she felt the urge to vomit, as if the shock had been writhing around her insides for too long now, as if she had absorbed a poisonous chemical that she was now ready to expunge.

Deserted vehicles stretched towards a narrow lane that wound round to the inn's rear entrance. Clarissa found herself walking back there absently to the white brick building with its red tiled roof. There was a multitude of small-paned windows. The one to the left of the door was shining a glossy black, watery beads descending obliquely across it, when a bird smacked into it and fell to the ground.

She had become surplus to requirements. Like the bird, she'd believed she'd been heading in the right direction with Charlie. *Smack*.

No sufficient explanation had been offered to account for his decision, so she hadn't sought one. She wouldn't fight to stay with someone who didn't want her. It hurt, but surely the pain would not last? She would allow herself to be absorbed by her work. She would apply her makeup, pin up her hair, and smile at the passengers on her flights as she attended to their needs. Her memories of him would soon fade. *Wouldn't they?*

She looked at the bird on the gravel and thought she saw it blink.

Shortly after this, the rear doors of the inn flew open purging three happy, giggling couples with alcohol-inebriated bodies. Clarissa turned her attention to them. Two hours ago she would have associated herself *with* these people: late twenties/early thirties, attractive, relaxed, comfortably off financially, only a small step away from settling down and getting married, only a small step away from planning families; now, she felt as out of place next to them as a starfish tossed into a hot desert.

'Mind the bird!' shouted one of the men with a thick cockney accent; exposing many teeth, but no smile.

For a moment Clarissa thought he had been referring to *her,* instead of the bird on the ground.

'Shucks!' retorted a woman with long blonde hair and a skirt that looked as though it were restricting her stride. 'Poor thing!' she cried with her American accent, as she teetered drunkenly past it on stilettoes. The woman *had* been referencing the bird, but again, Clarissa took unexpected comfort from this small display of compassion.

The six of them stopped to notice her collectively.

'You all right, love?' said a man who was wearing less than the others; just a white dress shirt in fact, his top button undone, its thin cloth filling up fast with rain splats.

'I'm fine, thank you,' replied Clarissa politely, forcing a tight smile to reside upon her lips. Then she hurried back to her mint Fiat 500 and let herself into its dry shell.

She sat in her car and waited. She wasn't sure what she was waiting for, but it helped just to sit there for a few minutes, examining the pattern in the steering wheel through her fingertips.

Suddenly a fist starting pounding on her window. She jumped. She saw a man's muscular arm sporting a black watch with an orange display. She read the numbers: 20:20. It belonged to the man wearing the white dress shirt.

'Are you sure you're all right?' he asked. He looked older close up. She could see the lines around his brown eyes when he smiled.

She tried to lower the window, but of course it wouldn't work without the ignition, so she opened the door.

'I'm fine,' she said. 'Thank you.'

The man was getting soaked. She wished that he would go.

'It's just that you don't look all right,' he said.

She forced herself to smile so that she did look all right. 'I'm fine,' she said again. 'I'm just waiting for someone, that's all.'

'Okay,' came the man's reply. 'You take care, now.'

She shut the door. She wanted to drive away at once but all the windows had steamed up, so she started the engine and switched the de-mister on.

She saw the man climb into a dark blue Jaguar. He appeared to be alone and she began to think that perhaps she'd been mistaken about him belonging to the group she'd just seen coming out of the pub. She watched him lower his window. For a moment, she thought he was going to say something else to her, but his hand emerged clutching a cigarette, and a thin wisp of smoke curled into the air as his car reversed in a spray of gravel. Then he sped away.

Clarissa waited for her windows to clear completely before she turned the key in the ignition.

Pulling out of the Hoops Inn car park, she drove along a narrow road flanked on either side by rich green fields. The sun was starting to set, and she began to feel an odd sensation that she attributed to resisting the urge to cry.

She had driven for about a mile, trying to come to terms with her new predicament, when she saw Charlie's black Audi TT on the road ahead of her – she recognised the plate: "CJD 1010" for Charles James Davenport, born on the tenth day of the tenth month. But as she slowed down, she saw something that alarmed her. The driver's door was open – not just ajar, but *fully* open – and Charlie was not there.

She knew that this meant that something was wrong, but she wasn't sure if an ex-girlfriend, freshly dumped, should care about such matters.

Pulling into a clearing about a hundred yards further down the road, she locked her Fiat and hurried back to the TT.

On reaching the Audi, Clarissa scanned its interior. The "open door" alarm was pulsing and she didn't like the way the keys were just hanging there in the ignition. As the daylight diminished, she stared into the black trees by the side of the road tentatively and called out his name.

'Charlie?'

Instinctively, she found herself removing the keys and immobilizing the car. Then she began to encircle its periphery in a state of panic.

There was nothing to see. No damage to the vehicle, no flat tyre. There was no obvious place to run to either; a thick line of bushes encased the road on the opposite side, a double layer of trees and undergrowth separated the Audi from the field beside it.

As Clarissa started to head back alongside the trees in the direction of the Hoops Inn, she was able to make out a clearing allowing her access to a field.

On reaching it, she found herself looking out over a dense patch of brown mud. She heard the crack of a branch followed closely by what sounded like the hoot of an owl. She thought about the Beretta and wondered if Charlie was carrying it.

Suddenly a rabbit darted out in front of her making her jump; she felt her heartbeat quicken and caught her breath.

Then she had an idea. Pensively, she pulled her mobile from her pocket and called Charlie's number.

She heard his ringtone.

It was coming from the muddy field.

The black expanse of land was growing darker by the minute but on she trudged following its tune, her heeled shoes squelching in the thick clay.

She found Charlie's phone lying face up in the earth. As she plucked it out, her tears began.

Clarissa spun around under a sky the colour of a livid bruise. As night descended upon her, she found herself frantically searching for a sign of him. She emitted the torch on her phone and checked for footprints. There was some sort of trail moving deeper into the field, as if he had been crawling, or maybe even dragged.

She wanted to call out his name again but instinct seemed to suggest that she should remain silent. She began to think that if Charlie *had* been attacked by someone, that *someone* might still be lurking around.

Shadowy shapes loomed about her on all sides, amorphous and equivocal, but she proceeded to follow the tracks in the sticky field.

Then they just stopped.

Consumed by anxiety, Clarissa felt she had no choice other than to return to her car; so this she did, slipping and sliding back through the mud, wet and shivering as the rain tapped the foliage all around her.

She had climbed inside, but had yet to close the door, when she saw them; two men in suits in her rearview mirror, arguing by the side of the road. It was as if they had appeared from nowhere.

Hurriedly, she killed her interior light and shuffled further down into her seat, leaving her door ajar in order to hear them; trembling with fear, in case they were to hear *her*.

Their conversation was fragmented, but she could just make out the words:

'...back to his car!'

'...bloody impossible...towards the field!'

'...how did he get away?'

The men disappeared as suddenly as they had come.

Panic-stricken, Clarissa closed the door, switched on her headlights, and pulled away.

Progressing up through the gears, she hurtled along the narrow country road, her heart thumping like a drum. She braced herself for a further surprise, half-expecting to see someone else or catch a glimpse of the vehicle these men had arrived in, but there was nothing but trees and fields.

Clarissa embarked on her journey back to her flat in Bishop's Stortford with an awful feeling in the pit of her stomach.

She drove nervously at first, scouring the landscape for any sign of Charlie, but she saw no indication of movement at all. She glanced in her rearview mirror expecting to be followed, but the road was as deserted as the fields. She intended to pull over and call the police at the earliest opportunity, but as soon as she passed a golf club, she drove as fast as she could, too scared to stop the car even for a minute.

The B1004 was not busy. She was home in less than half an hour.

Once she was safely inside her flat, she stood against the door panting like an animal. Then she pulled her eyes back into focus and stared at her piano, immediately opposite her through the open living room door. She wanted to feel comfort from looking at the grains in the wood, but instead she saw an envelope on the music rack, an envelope *she* had not put there. Approaching it, her heart-rate quickened – the writing on the front was in Charlie's cursive hand:

Good Luck, Baby

She ripped it open with trembling fingers, dried mud covering it like pepper. The note said:

By the time you read this, they will have taken me.
Please do not call the police.
I will try and get a message to you.
Nocturne, Opus 9, No.2.

Clarissa felt her body freeze. This can't be real, surely?

She removed her muddy shoes and coat as if she'd been transported into a dream world. She placed Charlie's phone and keys on the coffee table by the door. She thought: If I have his car keys, his house keys and his phone, what does he have?

She sat on the floor and said: 'Alexa, play Chopin's Nocturne, Opus 9, Number 2.' She was familiar with the piece.

As the melody emerged, limpid and clear, its flow and form unassuming like crystals hanging in a light wind, Clarissa tried to make sense of everything.

Then Charlie's mobile rang, as shrill and unexpected as a hawk bursting in through the window.

'Alexa, music off!'

Consumed by an overwhelming sense of confusion, Clarissa grabbed the phone from the coffee table. The display on the screen was flashing: "S calling". She didn't know whether she should answer it or not. The phone seemed to ring forever while she decided, the sweat from her fingers turning brown from the mud. Finally, she swiped the screen right and accepted the call.

'Hello?'

2

Silence.

'Hello?' repeated Clarissa.

'...Who the hell are you?' said a man's voice, dry and brittle, like a nail scraping metal. 'Is Charlie there?'

'He's asleep.'

'Then wake him up! Tell him Roland Steed's on the phone. It's urgent!'

Clarissa chewed her lower lip as she considered her response.

'I'm afraid I can't do that,' she said impassively. 'Is there a message I can pass on to him?'

'You can't do that?'

The man's incredulity was expressed by a low mirthless laugh that seemed to echo through the phone like gravel caressing the inside of a barrel.

'Why the hell not? Out cold, is he? Been a bit of a naughty boy, has he?'

Clarissa swallowed hard. 'I'm sorry, is there a message for him or not?'

'Listen, love. There's no need to get your bloody knickers in a twist. I'm a friend of Charlie's. A friend who's growing a bit concerned for his safety, if you know what I mean.'

He paused. She imagined him taking a drag from a cigarette; mid-fifties in age, thick-set, balding; slouched in a leather chair shrouded in smoke.

'Perhaps you can tell me where he is,' he said. 'Or where you are? Or where my fucking brother is?' The words emerged like small incisions puncturing a sheet of aluminium; rhythmically serene but at the same time charged with danger.

'…Just a little outside London,' said Clarissa cautiously.

'Good enough.' The man coughed. 'I'm "just a little outside London" myself. Perhaps we're in the same place, who knows? But I've got the feeling we're not about to find that out. So, the message I would like you to depart to our mutual friend is this: What the hell is he doing there, when he should be here? Perhaps he'd be good enough to call me back with an answer to this question. When it's convenient for him, of course.'

The line went dead.

Clarissa was left staring into the mud-speckled glass of Charlie's smartphone (a device she no longer had access to without a password) confused.

Her suspicions that Charlie was involved in something of a "criminal nature" were, as far as she was concerned, as good as confirmed.

Slowly, she sank back into her blue sofa, its plush pile imbibing the water from her hair, and considered what she knew:

1. Charlie had planned a meeting with Roland Steed directly after their rendezvous. *Why?*
2. Charlie had feared someone coming for him. *What had he done? Who was after him? And why had he seen it necessary to make sure she was informed of this?*

She read his note again, looking for answers, but it offered her so very little in the way of an explanation, she wondered why he had bothered at all. She knew that his reference to the Nocturne had to hold some significance here too, but its relevance was not obvious. Then absently, she turned the paper over. There was something she'd missed, on the back, written in small capitals:

I PRAY THAT YOU WILL FIND IT IN YOUR HEART
TO FORGIVE ME.

The paper crackled as she fingered it. The note appeared to be personal, but it was not. Front and back, it provided her with nothing other than an instruction not to call the police, the promise of a further message, and the suggestion that her forgiveness for dumping her out of the blue *had* meant something to him after all.

But there was no real affection here, just capital letters.

Clarissa thought about the Audi abandoned in Perry Green. She wondered how long it would remain there without the police being notified. She knew that as soon as it was discovered, the authorities would try to contact its registered keeper and in no time a report would be generated declaring Charlie as a missing person. The note may not have told her much, but it did give her explicit instructions *not* to involve the police.

She got up and went into the kitchen to consult her work roster. By an absurd stroke of luck, she found herself off-duty for the next two days. The rest of the week, her time would be swallowed up by work: two days on stand-by, followed by three earlies, starting with a 5:30 a.m. flight to Charles de Gaulle Airport, France.

She planned to retrieve the TT first thing in the morning. She would drive it back to Charlie's flat, let herself in with his keys, and take a look around.

Clarissa took a shower, still in a state of shock. Roland Steed left her alone. Her own mobile stayed silent. She pressed her forehead against the tiles in the shower cubicle and cried as she washed the mud from her hair.

She slept.

When she awoke the next morning, yesterday's memories arrived in her head like low black clouds at a birthday picnic. Charlie's disappearance seemed to have engendered in her an anxiety that she could almost feel as a physical presence swimming around her body, threatening to break her usual composure at any time. She did her best to ignore it by attending to her external appearance as usual, but she was unable to shake off the inherent bite of the sensation.

In her bathroom mirror Clarissa made up her eyes with her usual makeup, but she couldn't help noticing that they looked different somehow. She had not imagined that "fear" could be so clearly defined in one's face.

Clarissa's mind swam with confusion. She wondered if she should confide in her best friend Donna, but quickly discarded the idea. She didn't have time for conversation. She had to move quickly.

Once dressed, she arranged for a taxi to collect her at 9 a.m. and take her back to Perry Green.

The cab was ten minutes early.

To evade suspicion, she babbled inconsequentially to the driver about meeting up with an old friend, and asked him to drop her about half a mile from the Audi's location.

'*This* is the house!' she exclaimed after catching a glimpse of a small farm nestled in the open countryside. It was not too far from Charlie's car, but far enough to avoid any association with it. 'I haven't been up here in years!' she said, sighing deeply to add credibility. It was a good subterfuge, but she thought the driver still eyed her with suspicion.

The taxi smelled odd. Clarissa detected the high notes of a sweet pungent vanilla – possibly jasmine – beside a metallic, eggy infusion she attributed to the driver's breath. He was a small, jovial man with a calm disposition and spoke with an indeterminable accent – she guessed Middle Eastern, possibly Turkish? She refused the suggestion he'd made of taking her up to the farm's gates, by protesting that this would ruin the surprise element to her visit, and paid him a reasonable tip so that he would drive away with a smile on his face. But when she slammed the door of his Toyota Prius shut, he lowered his window and said: 'I hope he's worth it!'

Clarissa smiled wanly and watched his taillights recede. Red blurry dinner plates in the grey air.

The birds were here with her again, but the rain, thankfully, was not, even though the threat of it was in the sky.

She thought the breeze blew cold for March and the atmosphere seemed eerie – she couldn't shake the feeling that she was being watched – but she tried to channel all her energy into finding the Audi.

It took her longer than she'd expected, but the car was there, exactly as she'd left it. It gave her the creeps.

She walked around a bit, identifying the field where she'd found the phone, but was unable to locate the exact spot she'd pulled it from the mud. Everywhere looked the same, a vast expanse of nothingness stretching on to infinity.

Clarissa headed back to the Audi and unlocked it remotely with Charlie's keys. To help conceal her identity, she'd put on black leather gloves to prevent her fingerprints from being found on the wheel and a black hat to hide her hair. She climbed into the driver's seat nervously and applied sunglasses to her eyes. She felt like a thief. She had to remind herself that whilst taking a car without its owner's permission was a criminal offence, she was *returning* the vehicle to the owner's property, which had to cancel out any impropriety.

Satisfied that no one had been assigned to watch the car and follow it if it moved, Clarissa started the engine.

She had travelled in the TT many times, but had never actually driven it herself.

Clarissa managed to manoeuvre the car back onto the road fairly easily then off she went, to Charlie's flat.

She estimated that the car contained enough fuel to get her to St. Albans. She drove it okay, although she was a little surprised at how loud the engine sounded. The traffic was bad, which increased her journey time, but she was comforted by the thought that her body was pressed into the same leather *his* had occupied yesterday; the vestiges of his scent triggering a welcome fizz in her veins.

When the clean, white, rectangular apartments of Gabriel Square came into view, Clarissa prayed that she would find Charlie at home there waiting for her – even though she knew the chances of this actually happening were minimal.

She took the Audi to the private residents' carport located in the belly of the building, below street level, and tapped in the pin-code that Charlie had given her a few months ago.

Her access was permitted.

Once the TT had been dutifully parked, she climbed out of it self-consciously. She could hear a faint grinding sound, but apart from that, nothing.

She glanced about suspiciously, expecting to bump into one of the other residents, but no one else appeared.

Whilst navigating her way up a narrow staircase to Charlie's flat she saw a young couple talking on a balcony, a man leaving his apartment with a phone glued to his ear and an elderly woman with red lips cleaning a nearby window. None of them looked at her.

As she walked, Clarissa pulled out Charlie's mobile along with her own, to check for missed calls or messages; but no one had called; no one had rung.

Her breathing quickened as she reached the door of his apartment. The air, suffused with bleach and lemon polish, was all too familiar. She knocked once, then a second time to be sure, but when there was no response, tried only to focus upon the code Charlie had previously given her to turn off the alarm.

Click.

She was in, but the silence prevailed.

It soon became apparent that the alarm had already been de-activated, and looking around in horror she saw that the place had also been completely trashed.

Clarissa's eyes searched the debris frantically as she crept through the apartment.

In the living room, dust motes were dancing in a shaft of sunlight that was striking the metal of Charlie's safe, its door wide open. Apart from an empty red folder that protruded from its cavity like a tongue, the safe had nothing inside it but air.

As she moved into the bedroom, stepping over slashed sofa cushions and mounds of flattened books and CDs, the ringtone of Charlie's phone suddenly burst from her rucksack. This time the screen was flashing: *"Prof. Chloe Ward calling"*.

She swiped the screen to accept the call. 'Hello?'

'Good morning. It's Professor Ward from the Royal Academy of Music Museum here. I just wanted to confirm our meeting for tomorrow at 4:30 p.m.?' A strong voice, tightly clipped, professional; annoyed.

'The meeting,' said Clarissa.

'Yes, this *is* Charlie Davenport?' The woman made no attempt to conceal her irritation; and there was no surprise that Charlie Davenport was female.

'…Yes.'

'I wanted to make sure you'd received my email. I didn't get a reply from you. This is the second time I've called. Considering the unique nature of the subject of our correspondence, I expected a little more…determination on your part to get back to me.'

Clarissa heard herself audibly gulp in response to this. It sounded like Charlie had been exchanging emails with this woman, but they'd never actually met, which was lucky for her.

'Yes. That was inexcusable of me,' Clarissa said in her most apologetic voice, her heart beating faster. 'I am *so* sorry. I've had a few…unexpected problems recently.'

A sudden image saturated her mind of the men she'd seen arguing by the abandoned TT, Charlie's stolen laptop in their hands, the meeting with Professor Ward already clocked, the intention to turn up at the previously proposed time already planned.

'Do you know what?' Clarissa began. 'Tomorrow's good for me, but is there a chance you could make it any earlier?'

She held her breath; no part of her seemed to know what she was doing, but impersonating Charlie in order to arrange a meeting with this stranger felt like the right step to take.

At first, Professor Ward didn't sound too keen on changing her plans. But then she paused and said: '9:30 a.m.?'

'That's perfect,' Clarissa replied. 'And the location?'

'I'll meet you at the main entrance.'

'Great. Thank you,' said Clarissa, relieved. 'The main entrance to the museum?'

'Yes, of course.... I must say,' Professor Ward lightened her tone, 'I'm surprised. From your emails, I was expecting –'

A man?

'Somebody more...*resolute.*'

Clarissa scoured the demolished contents of Charlie's bedroom with disbelieving eyes. 'Professor Ward, I can assure you that at this moment, I have never felt more resolute about anything in my life.'

This seemed to please her.

'Excellent,' said the professor. 'I have some information I think will prove most beneficial to you! I look forward to seeing you then.'

Their connection went dead.

Clarissa's gaze landed upon the glass door that opened out onto the balcony overlooking the development's communal gardens. She focused on the mirrored sculpture, positioned within a square of green grass at the garden's core, and remembered the last time she had surveyed the same view two weeks ago: They had just got out of bed, and Charlie's mobile had rung. He had walked into the living room to take the call. His entire conversation had been muffled and unclear, but four sentences had separated themselves: *"...Royal Academy of Music Museum. I haven't met this one yet. Liszt was one of his peers, for God's sake, Max! It's the closest we're going to get."* And later in the same conversation: *"...and you wonder why I keep a loaded 9mm Beretta beside my bed!"*

Clarissa backed away from the light and moved towards the drawer by the bed where Charlie kept his gun. Unlike every other drawer and cupboard in the flat, it was closed. She pulled it open tentatively, not expecting the Beretta to still be inside, surprised to find that it was.

Carefully, she removed it. It was the first time she had ever touched it; it was the first time she had touched *any* weapon. It was cold and heavy in the palm of her hand. She slid the gun into her handbag for safe-keeping, along with the phone charging cable that was lying beside it, thinking that if Charlie made contact, they might prove useful.

Next, she tried to find Charlie's laptop, but it was nowhere to be seen. She suspected that it had probably been one of the first things they'd gone for.

Finally, she returned to the safe to examine the solitary red folder hanging from it, and found just that, nothing more. One word had been neatly handwritten on its cover: *"Chopin"*.

There was paperwork everywhere, and most of it seemed ordinary: household bills, car maintenance documents, receipts, that sort of thing. She suspected that sieving through it all would prove futile. It was obvious that anything significant had already been removed.

It was also starting to became clear that whoever had rifled through Charlie's possessions had done so with a degree of calculated precision. There was nothing haphazard about the carefully sliced food packets or the neatly peeled and dissected sections of kitchen worktop; so it didn't make sense that these people had left the gun. She could only assume that they'd found what they'd been looking for and exited the premises before they'd seen it.

Clarissa locked up Charlie's flat at 12:40 p.m. and walked to the railway station, which she knew was close by. She intended to get a train to Euston, where she would take a connection to Liverpool Street and return to Bishop's Stortford from there.

When she arrived at St. Albans Station, she bought a ticket to London from the machine, followed by a sandwich and some water on the platform.

She listened to a high-pitched clicking sound as she waited for her train, feeling the weight of the gun in her bag.

The man standing next to her would not stop fidgeting. It wasn't long before the small shuffling movements he was executing escalated into agitated pacing; the upgrade compounded her anxiety.

She tried not to stare at him – young, oversized textured sunglasses, tight clothes, shaved head, a crawling insect tattooed at the stem of his neck; aggressive. But he suddenly turned to her and said: 'When did they ban smoking on train platforms? It's a fuckin' joke!'

Other than shrugging and shaking her head sympathetically, Clarissa could think of no response for this, so she just continued to wait for her train, hoping not to be addressed by him again.

'I can't remember the last time I was at a fuckin' station, d'you know what I'm saying?' the man went on. 'I wouldn't be here if it wasn't for that bloody bitch anyway. When you're waiting, you need to be able to put your hands somewhere, d'you know what I mean? If you…it's all very well them saying "get a drink", but how can you get a fuckin' drink if you haven't got the right change for the machine?'

Clarissa stood on the platform trying to concentrate on the clock; large yellow numbers on a black background adjusted themselves slowly. She didn't know if she was imagining it, but the man seemed to be getting closer to her. While she waited, she was aware of only two things: *him* and the *gun*, and the thought of what might happen if the two were put together.

When the sound of the engine vibrating through the tracks finally reached her ears, Clarissa sighed with relief.

The train slid to a satisfying halt.

She watched its passengers disembark messily before she joined one of the queues to board, ensuring she entered the train via a different route to the tattooed man, just to be on the safe side.

She also made doubly sure he wasn't in her carriage, before seating herself at one of the table seats beside a window.

As the train pulled away, Clarissa was soon soothed by its chugging rhythm. The woman opposite her didn't even look up from her newspaper. This was the sort of company she was hoping to keep.

Clarissa checked both phones again, and saw that nobody had messaged either.

Ten minutes in, an inspector appeared asking for tickets and as Clarissa reached into her bag, her fingertips brushed past several objects – including the gun – before she located hers. The reminder of the presence of a loaded killing tool in her possession caused her to shudder involuntarily.

She handed her ticket to the inspector with a strained smile and he scrutinised it with comical eyes. She waited, taking in his wild curly hair and old, red face. He was breathing heavily. He smelt of tobacco, and oddly, of honey.

'I thought all you youngsters preferred to go digital nowadays!' A smoker's laugh snuck out of him. She guessed he was referring to her paper ticket.

'At least I still get to use "the beast" occasionally,' he said, removing his silver ticket cutter from the pocket of his jacket. 'This will probably be in a museum this time next year.'

Clarissa smiled. She could have told him that she normally used digital downloads along with the majority of the population, but she suddenly felt too tired to speak. Her day had been a long one, and all she wanted to do was get home.

It was only after he'd returned her ticket to her – clipped with a fresh hole – that she noticed a small smear of blood across the word "Euston".

Looking down, Clarissa saw that she had cut one of her fingers.

Searching through her bag for an explanation, she came across the padded keyring attached to her spare door key (the one Charlie had returned to her outside the Hoops Inn) and noticed, for the first time, that a sharp piece of metal was protruding from the heart.

She tugged at it.

Something had been sewn inside.

Carefully, she unpicked the thread. To her surprise, she pulled out a USB memory stick. Suddenly she understood the significance of the capital letters on the back of Charlie's note. The sentence had been spaced deliberately:

I PRAY THAT YOU WILL FIND IT IN YOUR HEART TO FORGIVE ME.

Clarissa clutched the small nugget of metal in her hand like it was a precious stone. Unfortunately, she would have to endure the monotony of her train journey home before she could read its contents on her laptop.

3

C larissa stared at the file icon on her computer screen. It had been given a one letter name: "C". What it stood for was anyone's guess: *Clarissa? Charlie? Chopin?*

Her fingers trembled as she guided the small black arrow that sat on her screen over to it, via her touchpad, and clicked.

This is what she read:

C,

On the 11th February 2019 I was hired to transport a valuable piece of sheet music from Paris to London. If anything happens to me, I am entrusting this manuscript to you.

If you are reading this, I am expecting to be caught imminently. My car and flat will be searched, but nothing will be found. They'll soon move on to everyone I've been in contact with since the 11th February, which includes you. I've left a trail that will make them think I've been unfaithful to you. I have not. They'll believe this to be the reason for our split.

They'll probably still search your car and flat in case I have hidden the manuscript there. I have not.

I've planted a series of 8 USB memory sticks (of which this is the first) that will lead you to the manuscript's hiding place. The remaining seven have been buried as Dead Drops (USB sticks that have been partially cemented into walls or kerbs). All the sticks have red sheaths and are located in either Paris or London. You will find them if you know your Chopin, and you do. Once you have the manuscript you must take it to Professor N. Kowalski of the Chopin Society, London.

Ensure you destroy/wipe each stick after you have read its contents, including this one.

I must ask you again not to get the police involved under any circumstances.

You must not take any time away from work as it will arouse suspicion. I have placed the Drops to fit in with your work roster.

I am hoping that you are reading this before you fly to Paris on Friday 15th March.

Eternally yours,

C.

Stick No.2: 46 B.S.London. Commutateur!

As Clarissa tried to comprehend the words that appeared on the screen, she felt herself recoil from the enormity of the task that Charlie had entrusted to her.

Slashed sofa cushions, rolled up carpets, piles of strewn clothing, heaps of paper – Clarissa's head was spinning with it all;

but she wasn't imagining Charlie's flat, she was looking at the state of her own.

She'd got off the train at Euston and travelled to Liverpool Street as intended. During her journey to Bishop's Stortford, Charlie's phone had revealed the beginnings of a text, barely gracing the screen long enough for her to determine any more than its first line before it was sucked out of reach into the forbidden pin-only realm: *"Message from Max – Where are you? I saw Cla –".*

With mounting frustration, she'd tried to unlock Charlie's mobile once again to read the rest of it, with no success.

She'd always assumed Max had been one of Charlie's work colleagues; she'd heard the name a few times during his "night calls". She'd imagined the remainder of the text ran something like: *"I saw Clarissa coming out of your flat this morning."* She wondered if Max had known her (by sight at least) even though they'd never been formally introduced. She wondered how long Max would leave it before he phoned, and intended to intercept the call and fill him in on the details of Charlie's disappearance when he did.

Arriving at her hometown at 3:15 p.m. she'd exited her train and hired a taxi to get back to her apartment on Chantry Road. As soon as it had pulled into the carpark of the old Edwardian schoolhouse conversion, she'd noticed it. Her mint Fiat.

She'd found it unlocked, its upholstery slashed. There were several 'C' shaped lacerations buried in the carpet, the contents of her glove box had been transferred to the floor, and two oval incisions glinted at her from the dashboard like the eye-holes of a skull.

She'd gone on to find the front door of her flat ajar and an arm belonging to her sofa appearing five metres before the rest of it – its extraction so neat, the fabric hadn't even frayed.

To her relief, her piano had fared better. It looked as though a gentle decapitation along a manufacturers' join had been enough to allow an adequate inspection of its innards; the damage – she assured herself – was perfectly repairable with a runnel of wood glue and a steady hand.

Seated on the floor amongst the debris, Clarissa had lodged Charlie's memory stick into her laptop with the sort of sinking feeling that could only be associated with the expectation of inexorable devastation. She watched its light pulse gently before igniting scarlet.

What she had read had left her stunned. She tried to take comfort from the fact that at least she didn't have to worry about *them coming*. The job had been done. Both her flat and her car had been searched. And the way Charlie had ended his communication: "Eternally yours" suggested the craziest possibility that her "dumping" had not been genuine. But even so, somehow the idea that he still wanted her seemed as inconceivable today, as the idea that he no longer wanted her had done yesterday.

Clarissa typed: *"original handwritten Chopin music scores"* into the internet and found that a few still existed. Many were locked away in the Chopin Museum in Warsaw, Poland. A small number had been auctioned at Sotheby's; an autographed working manuscript of the opening of the first Ballade in G minor, Opus 23 had been sold by a private collector to the museum in 2016 for £200,000.

The clue she had been given for the 2nd USB stick: *"46 B.S. London"*, when entered into the web, brought up: *"The London School of Economics and Political Science"*, which didn't seem to connect to Chopin in any obvious way. But while she considered other possibilities for the significance of Charlie's clue, she was convinced that *"46 B.S. London"* had to represent the first line of an address that she was expected to visit.

As she typed various versions of addresses into her laptop, she observed that her flat not only looked different but it *smelt* different too. It felt stained, contaminated, and she soon began to feel stifled by it.

Her garden, she thought, would provide a better space for her to undertake this research, so she ventured out into the small sanctuary that she had created on the other side of her back door in the hope that at least *there* she would not have to be surrounded by such a devastating mess.

On this, she had been wrong. The blue bench on which she liked to sit in order to catch the afternoon sun had been upended, and the majority of her border plants had been torn from their beds. There were numerous mounds of earth beside corresponding holes, and her lawn had been sliced open with some sort of sharp implement. On closer inspection, however, she was pleased to see that all she really needed to do to fix this was complete one enormous jigsaw puzzle.

Clarissa set to work at once, resurrecting both the bench and the lawn. She then proceeded to shovel the soil back into the holes and replant her flowers. To her surprise, she found she could almost deposit her forget-me-knots, hyacinths and tulips back into the exact crevices they'd been extracted from, as neat clumps of earth remained clinging to their roots. At least the vandals responsible had seen fit to leave the wall that ran around her garden's periphery intact, she thought. That would have proved a far more complicated repair.

Half an hour later, she returned to her bench with a tea in one hand and her laptop in the other, connecting to the internet again as the breeze pulled at her hair.

After researching addresses for Chopin in London, she discovered that he'd been the guest of a family called the Broadwood's at 46 Bryanston Square, Marylebone in 1837. She also realised that this address was so close to the Royal Academy of Music Museum, it would be possible for her to visit it directly after her meeting with Professor Ward in the morning.

Next, she carried out an internet investigation of Professor N. Kowalski (member of the Chopin Society and Charlie's chosen confidant). She discovered him to be a Professor of Music at King's College, London. His photograph on the college's website depicted him as a man in his fifties with greying hair and thick black-rimmed spectacles; his eyes were smiling, but his lips were tightly closed. His email address was also advertised. Clarissa wrote to him immediately.

11.3.19, 3:45 p.m.

Dear Professor Kowalski,

I have been given your name by my friend Charlie Davenport. He is insistent that I pass some information on to you regarding a musical manuscript connected in some way to Chopin.

Can we possibly meet to discuss?

Kind regards,

Clarissa Belmonte (BMus RCM)

At 6:15 p.m. Clarissa was about to fix herself something to eat when her good friend and fellow cabin crew member, Donna Rossini's number flashed up on her phone.

'Donna!'

'Hi, hun! How ya' doing?' Donna's sweet, exuberant voice swelled with emotion – she was half-Italian, half-Egyptian, but as she had lived in New York for the majority of her life, spoke with a full-blown American accent.

'How are you?' said Clarissa. 'I hope you're having a better day than me.'

'What's up, sweetie? You sound fed up. Had a bad one?'

This was an understatement to top understatements, but she had to move the conversation past this; it seemed the best way forward. 'Oh, I'm just tired. You know how it is.'

'Listen. Do you fancy meeting up tomorrow? I could use an ear,' Donna asked, expectantly.

'I'd love to, really. But I can't,' replied Clarissa, fighting back the temptation to tell Donna everything. 'I've arranged to meet up with an old college friend. Sorry.'

Donna made no attempt to disguise her disappointment. Clarissa tried to get her to talk some more, but this was only met with protestations. Donna ended their conversation abruptly with the words: 'Got to go. Woody's just arrived!'

Woody (not his real name) was a pilot that Clarissa detested, but pretended she didn't. "Intelligent", "charismatic" and "handsome" were words often used to describe the first impressions he made (on women in particular). After two years of flying with him, Clarissa had replaced these with: "deceitful", "arrogant" and "BASTARD". He was seeing Donna behind his wife's back, but refused to leave his oblivious spouse for her. This had been going on for five months. In the meantime, Clarissa had witnessed him openly flirting with every member of the crew (apart from Justin, the male steward). His recent promotion to captain had only made him worse. He had even touched *her* thigh once, mid-flight, stroking her flesh with hot, spidery fingers, exonerating himself by saying he had mistaken her for Donna. She had been positively disgusted.

After dinner, Clarissa did not leave it long before she retired. She wanted to get to the museum in good time for her meeting with the professor tomorrow. She was nervous, but determined to go through with it. She knew about music, having studied at the Royal College, so that had to help. But she knew she would have to be careful not to portray an insider's perspective here. Charlie Davenport was not a musician.

Baker Street Tube Station was bustling. Hot metal and black dirt described the smell. A lone rat darted across the sunken track; the warm air a serious threat to her makeup. She'd dressed as if she were attending a job interview: black suit, white blouse – in this case over-dressing seemed preferable. She wore her hair in a chignon (flight attendant style), but her heels higher than regulatory cabin crew recommendation (four instead of three inches) as the occasion seemed to warrant it.

She had got off the train beside some Sherlock Holmes tiles. His image, in profiled shadow, complete with deerstalker hat and curved pipe, assuaged her; she had always liked the detective.

Clarissa was caught up in a sea of people, a stream of bodies moving around a network of corridors to piano music. It seemed inconceivable under the circumstances, but it sounded like somebody was playing Chopin.

It could be heard even from the bowels of the station; a repeating note (A-flat) was constant in the background of the piece. Clarissa recognised it at once: Opus 28, number 15 (Chopin's longest Prelude).

Its significance chilled her, for she had once had a personal connection with the Prelude, its melody so deeply rooted in her past life as a concert pianist, its connotations caused her to smart like she had just received an electric shock.

The tune was melancholic; it spoke of loss, desperation. For a moment, she imagined herself back in the mud field again, bending to retrieve Charlie's phone from the wet ground, a sickening feeling forming in the pit of her stomach.

As she neared the base of the escalators, she could at last see where the music was coming from. A busker was sitting on the floor, his back residing against a wall of white cracked tiles, an electric piano on his knees.

The pianist looked as though he was in his early twenties. He had short dark hair with an asymmetrical fringe; attractive, but serious. He was dressed completely in black. He kept his eyes closed for most of the performance, feeling his way through it. He'd generated quite an audience. He was putting everything he had into it.

Clarissa joined the people watching him. He really was quite spectacular. The direction the music took trickled around his face as eloquently as his fingers found the right keys to play it.

As the piece gained momentum, money began to accumulate in a bag alongside him. Passersby seemed to be throwing it in rhythmically, like dancers in a performance.

Clarissa waited for her favourite part: "the crescendos", a gradual build up almost to the brink of explosion, when the score finally hits the chord of E and B. When it came, it was so well executed, it seemed to strike a secret nerve deep within her soul. Then she listened for "the bridge", where the most expressive part links back to the delicate melody used at the beginning – the hardest section to play, in her opinion – but the busker tackled it expertly and took the piece to its final codetta most adeptly.

As soon as the piece concluded, a blast of applause echoed through the high tunnel, and a broad smile arrested the busker's features. Clarissa watched him measure the atmosphere. A group of people were bobbing around him appreciatively, and as the money and praise kept coming, he nodded along with their chatter, looking up modestly through his hair. Suddenly his eyes snagged her own.

The two of them stared at one another for one long, charged moment.

When the crowd began to disperse, she felt compelled to speak to him.

'How can you play Chopin like that?' she enquired.

An Irish voice replied – it was unexpected: 'Admittedly, it *is* a bit painful on the old knees, but if I'd brought the stand, then *I'd* have to stand (as I can't really manage the stool as well) and I *have* to sit down. I have difficulties standing whilst playing. That sounds as if there's something wrong with my legs. There's nothing wrong with my legs! I just prefer to sit down when I'm playing. Anyway, I have a penchant for Chopin.' He beamed at her with hazel irises, glinting like jewels under the harsh lighting.

'That's not what I meant,' said Clarissa, amused. 'You're...very talented.'

'Thank you,' he said, looking slightly embarrassed.

They continued to stare at one another.

Self-consciously, Clarissa took a handful of coins from her pocket and threw them into his bag.

'You're rewarding me for making you cry?' he asked, unable to ignore Clarissa's wet cheeks.

She attempted to dry her eyes without smudging her makeup; it wasn't easy.

'A death. Unrequited love. A battle with an incurable disease,' said the busker, matter-of-factly.

'*Excuse me?*'

'The top three reasons why a person might cry in response to Chopin. In my experience anyway.'

'Aren't they just the top three reasons why a person might cry in general?' said Clarissa.

The busker cut her a resigned glance and shrugged. 'I can't argue with that! Don't worry. I won't go so far as to ask what *your* reason is. You play the piano yourself, I can tell.'

Clarissa produced a small smile. '*How* can you tell?'

'Hold out your hands.'

She wasn't in the mood for games, she had to get on, she had to get to the Royal Academy of Music Museum in less than twenty minutes.

'You can't tell by looking at a person's hands!' she said dismissively.

'Did I say I was going to *look* at your hands? I don't intend to look at your hands. I just asked you to hold them out. Only a pianist would respond with such a riposte! *That's* how I can tell. I'm right, am I not? You *are* a pianist?'

Clarissa felt her lips curl at the edges. It was involuntary. She didn't want to engage in flirtatious conversation with this stranger but it seemed to be happening anyway, of its own accord. 'Okay,' she admitted, 'you're right. I graduated from the Royal College of Music in 2012.'

The pianist's grin was now so big, it seemed to change the shape of his face along with his perception of her. 'I knew it! I'm at the Royal Academy of Music. Final Year. What did you do after graduating?' He pulled his slanted fringe away from his left eye, and adopted an expression of genuine interest. 'Are you teaching?'

Clarissa produced a wan smile. She realised that he must be at least six or seven years younger than her. It made her feel old. 'I'm not even playing,' she said. The admission seemed to fill her with a sense of sadness. 'I chose to do something else entirely.'

'Why? What happened?' he asked.

She had never really talked to anyone about what had happened, it was too painful. 'It's complicated,' she said.

'It always is,' he said.

'Listen,' said Clarissa tentatively. 'Do you mind if I ask you a question?'

'Sure.'

'When you think of Chopin. Does: "46 B.S. London" mean anything to you?'

The pianist threw his head back and laughed. 'What's that? A crossword clue or something?'

Clarissa made a small noise of indifference.

'And I thought you were going to ask me if I fancied going for a coffee. I've got to admit it, I'm more than a little disappointed!'

Clarissa looked at her watch and frowned. 'Listen, don't worry about it. I've got to be somewhere,' she said, edging away – it was worth a shot, but the busker had just stared at her blankly, after the laughter. So she allowed herself to be swept back into the moving crowd once again. She couldn't risk being late for her meeting with the professor.

'Wait! I'll think on it! How can I let you know my answer? Don't go yet, I don't even know your name!' The busker looked distraught. 'I'm Ralph, by the way. Ralph Valero!'

Clarissa called out her name from the ascending escalator. Ralph looked confused, then angry.

'Are you coming back this way again?' he cried. 'CLARISSA! COME AND WATCH ME PERFORM TONIGHT AT THE RAM AT 7 P.M.!'

He was staring at her face, imploring her to confirm attendance.

'I'M SORRY, I WON'T BE ABLE TO MAKE IT!' she called back. 'I HAVE TO SLEEP. I HAVE TO GET UP EARLY FOR WORK!'

She saw him cup his ear, as if he hadn't heard what she'd said.

They continued to stare at each other as she was lifted away. Then his face was lost in a sea of others.

A woman, clad in a crumpled ivory raincoat and beige culottes, was waiting at the top of the steps of the Royal Academy of Music

Museum between two ivory pillars. She looked like a smaller, thinner version of the pianist Martha Argerich; but younger, possibly in her forties, with a premature mass of grey, frizzy shoulder-length hair.

She smiled as Clarissa approached her.

'Miss Davenport?' she enquired, tucking the stack of folders she was carrying adroitly under her left arm, while her right arm flew forwards.

Clarissa, interpreting the gesture as an invitation to shake hands, offered hers willingly. 'Professor Ward?' she said, as if there was some doubt to her identity; as if it were possible that someone else could have addressed her as Miss Davenport.

'Pleased to meet you!' said the professor, nodding once, before gripping Clarissa's hand and pumping it avidly.

'I understand you have some news for me?' asked Clarissa.

'Yes. Please. Come this way,' replied Ward, releasing Clarissa's hand and ushering her into the museum.

Clarissa followed the professor through a long chamber, their heels resonating sharply on the wooden floor; it was a comforting polyrhythm. As they walked, the most beautiful violins appeared in glass cases along the way like mystical objects suspended in gas, but Clarissa couldn't help comparing them to corpses floating in transparent coffins; once alive, now dead.

'They're sometimes still played by the students, you know,' Ward declared, as if she could read her mind.

'I'm glad to hear it,' said Clarissa, suddenly struggling to keep up with the professor's pace.

It was working. There was no awkwardness. There was no suspicion here.

Not yet.

But everything was about to change. Her plan was about to be compromised. It was a powerful sentence, like a blade. It was enough to cause her confidence to peel away, like the skin of an orange left out too long in the sun.

Professor Ward turned to her, almost cheerily, and said: 'Come. Your colleague Max Siskind is waiting for us in my office.'

4

4 6 Bryanston Square, Marylebone.

She had gone straight there, running through the streets like a hunted creature; with the Georgian townhouses – raw umber with white cornices and window frames – looming majestically before her. On the other side of the road was a park, its tall trees flexing their fronds in the March sky.

There were four steps to a pair of black doors, a pillar on either side, and iron railings from which the basement windows could be seen. The first two layers of the building were white, freshly-painted, resembling a cake, iced upside-down.

Clarissa searched for the Dead Drop.

As she checked the kerbs on both sides of the road for a cemented memory stick, she thought about Chopin. She imagined him emerging from his carriage in 1837, impeccably dressed, his flared frockcoat whipping in the wind. She could almost conjure up the smell of his freshly stretched beaver hat, a slither of gold dancing from a pocket-watch given to him by his lover, Madame Dudevant (a.k.a. the writer George Sand).

There were no Dead Drops here. Perhaps she had misunderstood the clue. She wondered if the Irish busker had come up with anything different.

Clarissa was still staring at the tall trees, watching their dancing leaves, when Charlie's phone rang: *"Max calling"*.

She lifted the phone to her ear. 'Max?'

'…Why didn't you come in?' said a woman's voice, Geordie accent. 'I was expecting you. I knew you weren't Charlie, you know.'

'Who's *this*?'

'It's Max Siskind.' There was a pause.

So Max is a woman?

'Don't tell me. You were expecting a man?'

'Yes. I suppose I was,' said Clarissa, more than a little shocked, taking a moment to reflect on the irony of the situation; she was, after all, impersonating a man herself.

'The name's Maxine,' said the voice in the receiver, 'but I prefer Max. The name gets taken for a gadgie quite often, like.'

'I see,' said Clarissa. 'Do you know who I am?'

'Yes, Clarissa. I know who you are. What did you say to get out of the meeting, then?'

'I said I had to make an urgent phone call.' Clarissa's voice was small and faint, drowned out by a passing red London bus.

'Where are you now?' Max demanded.

'…Not that far away.'

'Do you want to meet us for a drink, like?'

A small busy café in Marble Arch. Max's choice.

On her approach, Clarissa experienced a sudden rush of nerves.

A woman, attractive but unsmiling, clad in a designer jumpsuit, rose from a silver table immediately inside the door on Clarissa's arrival. She could have been any age between twenty-five and forty. She beckoned to the empty seat beside her. Then she pushed back a wisp of dark hair from a knot at the top of her head and shook Clarissa's hand.

So this was Max.

'Sit down, Clarissa.'

The woman had already taken the liberty of ordering two coffees – a fancy latte for herself, a flat white for Clarissa – although it was soon evident that the gesture, ostensibly for solicitude, was nothing more than a pre-requisite for interrogation.

'What's happened to Charlie?' said Clarissa with sharp insistence, pressing herself awkwardly onto the edge of a small red chair.

Max took a sip from her tall glass, drinking through whipped cream laced with caramel, fitting it carefully back into its saucer before continuing with the conversation. 'Relax, pet. Have some coffee and tell us what happened. I need to try and piece things together.'

Clarissa felt the speeding thump of her heart underneath her jacket; she was so ravenous for answers, her whole being seemed to tremble from the proclivity. 'How do I know you are who you say you are?'

Max smiled for the first time, her lips stained maroon, wet and thick. Her eyes were sharp and the darkest shade of brown. 'Are you joking?' she said. 'Don't worry, Clarissa. You can trust us. Charlie's told me all about you. I wanted to be an air hostess when I was at school too. Although, I understand you had another career in mind when you were little. Didn't you train to be a concert pianist but things didn't turn out quite as you'd expected? You see, I know all about it!'

Clarissa experienced a sensation like ice tingling down the length of her spine. She wanted to say: *No one knows all about that, not even Charlie!*

'Clarissa, you look propa scared, like!' Max went on, amused, as if the whole thing was a joke. 'There's really no need for it, you know. Charlie and I work together, so we talk sometimes, it doesn't mean anything. He told me you were a right canny lass and I've no reason to doubt him. Now, if I can trust *you,* surely you can trust us, can't you?'

'Thanks for the coffee,' said Clarissa, deciding to place Max firmly in the "late thirties" age category after *this;* convinced that no youngster would ever speak to her in this way.

'You're welcome, Clarissa. Now, loosen up and giz us a chance,' said Max. 'Despite what they say, I generally don't bite, you know!'

Clarissa attempted a smile, but failed. Despite being immaculately turned out herself, she was uncomfortable next to Max. She felt too neat, too dutiful, definitely in the flat-white category – Max had got that one right – the mere suggestion of a lavish topping, wholly inappropriate and unnecessary. She saw herself as a servant reporting to a wild action heroine. Max, she imagined, was the sort of woman who didn't mind getting her hands dirty; the sort of woman who could pull the trigger of a Beretta with the intent to kill and not be fazed about getting blood on her designer clothing. Clarissa closed her eyes briefly and tried to imagine *this* version of "Max" working alongside *her* version of Charlie.

She could not.

'Clarissa?' Max's brash Geordie voice cut through her thoughts. 'You need to tell us what you know, so that I can understand what happened.'

'…Err…of course,' said Clarissa. 'Well, he disappeared Sunday night.'

'And that's the last time you saw him, like?'

Clarissa nodded.

'How come you've got his phone?'

Clarissa cleared her throat.

'We went out for a drink Sunday evening. Charlie left the pub before me. Then I found his car abandoned by the side of the road, but *he* had vanished. I went on to discover his phone lying in a nearby field. When I got home he'd left me a note instructing me not to call the police if he disappeared suddenly. It was like he'd been expecting it.'

Clarissa watched the woman's reaction to this carefully, trying to ascertain whether or not she should trust her.

Max's face was as rosy as if she'd just returned from a stint of hay baling, but her eyes, they seemed to tell a different story; they had an almost savage quality to them.

Max shook her head, concerned. 'Whoever it was must have tricked him into stopping his car.'

Clarissa agreed.

They drank in unison.

Suddenly, the Geordie's phone buzzed. She reached for it instantly, primally, like a cat digging its claws into the warm flesh of a mouse. And as Clarissa watched her lower her eyes and read its illuminated screen, she decided that she would tell her only the bare minimum here, working on the premise that if Charlie had wanted *Max* to know about the Dead Drops, he'd have left them for *her* to find.

'And this meeting with Professor Ward?' Max asked her, arching her chin slightly. 'How did that come about, like?'

'She called Charlie's phone,' said Clarissa, her voice ringing out like cut glass amidst the clattering of plates and cutlery in the café. 'She thought *I* was Charlie. She said that she had some news and I thought it might be important. How did *you* manage to get invited?'

'Oh, I must have called her immediately after she'd come off the phone to you, like,' said Max, waving her hand dismissively. 'She told us she'd just arranged to meet Charlie, but when she referred to him as a "she", I knew something wasn't quite right, so I tried to ring him. When I couldn't get hold of him, I drove straight over to St. Albans. That's when I saw you coming out of his flat.'

Clarissa nodded. This account certainly fitted in with the text she had seen rolling across Charlie's smartphone yesterday morning.

'So, if you suspected from the start that *I* might turn up to the meeting instead of Charlie,' began Clarissa, 'why didn't you try to ring Charlie's phone to give me some forewarning?' She glared at the Geordie fixedly.

A thin smile danced across Max's lips. 'Howay, man! I didn't think you'd actually go through with it now, did I?'

Clarissa took another gulp of her coffee, the acrid taste of the flat white rolling across her tongue.

'You had some guts to arrange to meet her as Charlie, though,' Max went on. 'If your nerves hadn't failed you, and you'd gone through with it like, I'd have backed you all the way!' She threw her phone back into her handbag and it landed with a thud.

'It's a pity I didn't know that at the time,' said Clarissa, with a hint of sarcasm in her voice. 'I take it, Professor Ward gave you the information she'd promised?'

'She did,' said Max, beaming with satisfaction.

'Well, at least *some* good came out of it.'

'Are you not going to ask us what it was, then?'

By the woman's smile, she sensed that Max was playing with her a little now. She was not amused.

'Would you tell me if I did?' Clarissa snapped.

Max laughed, short and sharp like a bird.

'Where is he, Max?'

'Clarissa, if I knew that, do you think I'd be sitting here with you, like?'

'But you must have an idea?'

As Max leaned in towards her, Clarissa detected her scent: apples and cigarettes. She said: 'You *have* told us everything, haven't you, pet?'

'Why would I hold anything back from you? I'm as anxious to find him as you are!'

The two of them regarded one another carefully.

Then Max assumed a feline expression again, her eyes glowering with a recondite slyness. 'Listen to us, Clarissa. If Charlie has told you anything else, *anything at all,* it would be wise to tell us about it now. If I'm going to find him, I'll need to know everything.'

'But I told you what his note said,' retorted Clarissa.

'I know,' said Max irritably. 'But have you been approached by anyone since Sunday evening? Has anyone called his phone? Somebody *must* have called him since Sunday night, man!' She rolled her eyes. 'Here, giz us a deek at it, I'll check it out for myself!'

'Bit pointless right now,' said Clarissa, imagining this would result in her losing the phone for good. 'I'm afraid it's just run out of charge.'

There was a disquieting silence.

Max reached for her own mobile and pressed its screen a couple of times. Directly afterwards, Charlie's phone began to ring from the inside of Clarissa's bag.

'I'd prefer it if you didn't lie to us,' said Max, aggrieved.

'All right,' said Clarissa resignedly. 'Someone did call him, Sunday night, around ten.'

'Go on.'

'A man called Roland Steed.'

She saw the way Max flinched as the syllables rolled off her tongue.

'And what did "Roland Steed" have to say?'

'He wanted to know why Charlie wasn't with him. He seemed really angry about it. He said he couldn't find his brother either. You know who he is, then?'

Max sat back and sucked her teeth.

'Roland and George. The infamous Steed brothers,' she said derisively. 'I believe Charlie had some business dealings with them.'

Clarissa baulked. '*He* had some business dealings with them, but *you* didn't? But you work together, don't you?'

Max shot her a trying look.

'Yes, Clarissa. We work together, but the Steeds were not involved,' said Max disdainfully. 'Those brothers have danger running through their flesh like sticks of rock, man!'

'Is Charlie in danger?'

'Charlie can handle himself.'

Charlie doesn't have his gun, she thought.

'So, did he tell you anything else then?' said Max, growing exasperated all of a sudden.

'Only that he'd been hired to transport a manuscript from Paris to London.'

Max stared at her with renewed interest.

'He didn't tell me what it was,' said Clarissa. 'But I gather it has international historical importance.'

'I knew you had to know,' said Max, getting the measure of her. She drank some more of her coffee. 'We were both hired for the job. Our task was to authenticate the document and transport it to London.'

'And how did *you*…well, get into this line of work?'

Max grimaced. '*Why*? What's it to you, like?'

'Well, you don't seem…You don't seem to fit the stereotypical "historical document handler" profile.'

The Geordie threw back her head and laughed. 'Because I don't have a plum in my mouth like you, you mean?'

'No, of course not,' said Clarissa, diplomatically. 'You just seem an unorthodox choice. That's all.'

Max leant in close to her across the silver table.

'I'm a businesswoman Clarissa, I manage projects for private clientele and I'm good at what I do. I get hired because I don't stand on ceremony. People like that about us. What they see is what they get, like. Now, I'm gonna take a wild stab in the dark here, and guess that Charlie's told you something about where he's hidden the manuscript?'

'No! Absolutely not!'

It was obvious that Max disbelieved her repudiation.

Clarissa rocked her cup of coffee within the confinements of its saucer impatiently. 'Who was the client who hired both of you?'

'Two words: "Client Confidentiality",' said Max.

Clarissa sighed. 'Fair enough. But does this person know that Charlie's disappeared?'

'Not yet.'

'So it wasn't the Steed brothers, then?'

'I told you before, I don't have any dealings with the fucking Steed brothers. I try to keep away from them, and you'll do the same, if you know what's good for you!'

'Caveat noted,' said Clarissa. She sat back in her chair. She had certainly heard enough to think twice about answering anymore calls from Roland Steed, that was for sure.

The conservation dwindled after this. Clarissa was forced to recount her last evening with Charlie a couple more times, but when Max could extract no more from her, the Geordie got up to leave.

'I'm clamming for a tab, man, I'll see you later,' she said, throwing her bag over her shoulder. She couldn't have been more abrupt if she'd tried. But just before she departed, she scribbled her mobile number on a loose receipt she found in her bag, and urged Clarissa to ring her if Charlie made contact.

Once Max had gone, Clarissa sat reeling from the experience. Max was about as far removed from her expectations as she could be. She was glad to return her attention to the problem of "46 B.S. London" for a respite.

This *had* to be the location for Charlie's second USB stick, she thought. So why couldn't she find it? She wondered again if the busker had come up with any ideas, and set off to find him with eager anticipation.

Mozart's Allegro. It was a definite change of mood. Clarissa rode the escalator down into belly of Baker Street Tube.

Ralph Valero stopped playing the moment he saw her.

'So you came back to get my answer?' he said, visibly delighted.

She smiled. 'You've worked it out?'

'46 Bryanston Square!' he said triumphantly.

She nodded, relieved.

So they were on the same page after all.

'Yes. It's what I got too,' she said, nodding more frantically. 'But I've just come from there and there was nothing. I just don't understand it.' Her tightly clipped accent seemed to resonate through the tunnel, amplifying her disappointment.

Ralph Valero looked deflated. 'Correct me if I'm wrong now, Clarissa, but I think there's something I'm missing here?'

'But we can't both have got an incorrect answer,' Clarissa went on, as if she were talking to herself. 'I can't have searched properly.'

'Just what is it we're *searching for*?' asked Ralph. She watched the happiness in his features morph to consternation.

'Clarissa?' Ralph ran his fingers across his keyboard sharply, causing her to start.

She really had no idea just how much of all this she should disclose.

'How can I help you, if you don't confide in me?' he said, imploring her to release a bit more of this strange puzzle to him.

Clarissa thought about it. Would it be unwise to give him some more information? After all, he *had* taken the time to work out the clue. What if he could assist her further? Perhaps she should give him a chance.

'A USB stick,' she said suddenly. 'We're looking for a USB stick with a red sheath, partially buried in a wall or kerb.'

Ralph smiled. 'So it's a Dead Drop location?'

She stared at him open-mouthed. 'You mean you've actually *heard* of them?'

'Sure. Aram Bartholl's got quite a large following on social media.'

'*Who?*'

'He's the conceptual artist behind the Dead Drop Manifesto. He's German. He released it some time ago now, about ten years back, I think.'

'*Dead Drop Manifesto*? So this thing is some sort of phenomenon?' said Clarissa, surprised. 'I thought it was something Charlie had dreamt up.'

'Who's Charlie?' said Ralph.

'I'll explain later.'

'So, it *is* a Dead Drop location then?'

Clarissa nodded. 'Yes, but it's not one of Aram Bartholl's Dead Drops. Charlie must have used his idea, he's obsessed with Conceptual Art.

Ralph looked intrigued.

'Something's wrong though,' said Clarissa, starting to move away from the busker. 'I thought I'd followed the clue in as many ways as I could think of, but the Drop wasn't there. I should get back and take another look around.'

'Hey, listen! Before you disappear again,' Ralph pulled the long part of his asymmetrical fringe back with a clenched fist. 'Consider letting me go back there with you. I could help you find it!'

'But you're working.'

He grinned at her. 'You're joking, right? The chief benefit of busking is you're sort of in charge of your own shifts,' he said, tidying a mound of notes and coins into a bag. 'You can pretty much start and stop when the need takes you, if you follow my drift?'

Clarissa stared at him, weighing things up.

'Okay,' she said after a pause. 'Why not?'

Ralph got to his feet. 'There's a condition, mind,' he said quietly.

There would be, she thought.

'If I find this Dead Drop for you, you'll have to do something for me in return.'

She looked at him questioningly.

'Buy me a drink and tell me why you gave up on your dreams!'

'Fine,' snapped Clarissa. 'But let's just stick to the drink part. My dreams aren't relevant here!'

'Fair enough,' said Ralph.

'What about your –' Clarissa alluded to his piano with a slight upward tilt of her chin.

'Oh, I'll just leave it here. I've a tendency to drop everything for a beautiful woman!' He smiled with a fierce twinkle in his eye. 'Don't worry, I'm only messing with you! I have a bag for it. It's no problem, I can wear it on my back.'

She watched him fit the instrument snugly into its soft case and pull up the zip. She looked enviously at his worn leather trainers as he crawled around on the floor adjusting things (her feet had started to ache from her choice of inappropriate footwear). Then the two of them proceeded to climb the ascending escalator, Clarissa leading the way.

'I must warn you though,' said Ralph, moving aside to allow some Japanese businessmen to pass. 'If this thing goes pear-shaped, I'm likely to try and sue you for loss of earnings!'

'Are you always like this with complete strangers?'

'I'm not sure I know what you mean. Listen, you're not going to run off again are you? Because I'd never be able to keep up with you with this thing on my back!'

'Err…Have you seen the shoes I'm wearing? If we had a race now, you'd win hands down!'

Ralph glanced at her feet and smiled, his eyes glinting with what looked like fresh hope.

When they emerged from the Underground, the air felt cold. Clarissa led Ralph along Marylebone Road. Traffic of all shapes and sizes roared past them, revealing the distinctive shape of a red London bus every few minutes.

'Your fella too busy to assist you today, then?' said Ralph, dubiously.

'Something like that.'

'So you *do* have a fella, then?'

'I do,' said Clarissa, praying that her new friend wouldn't probe any further.

'And this fella, he wouldn't happen to be called Charlie, by any chance would he?'

'Look. We really have to get back to this Dead Drop location,' said Clarissa, shrinking away from the question.

As she marched on, her heels resonating loudly on the pavement, she stared resolutely ahead of her, giving every impression of a woman on a mission. She remained fully focused on her task, but occasionally, she turned to look at him; this *Ralph Valero*. She couldn't help being fascinated by the very bones of him.

To a stranger hurrying past, Clarissa thought the two of them could easily pass for the same age (even though she knew she had to be at least five years older than her companion). He was tall, well over six feet she guessed, but in her heels, they walked at the same height. They had both trained in classical piano at prestigious London music schools (although Ralph's image seemed to suggest that he belonged to the world of Alternative Rock – she had assumed a similar identity at college herself). But despite their similarities, Ralph appeared to have something that *she* didn't: a belief in his own capabilities; a belief in his music. It was a quality that allowed him to bristle with a passion only possessed by the young.

And for that, she envied him.

'Where do you live?' he said, after they'd been walking for a few minutes.

'Bishop's Stortford.'

'Nice place?'

'It used to be,' replied Clarissa. 'I'm not so sure anymore,' she added, alluding to her recent break-in. 'Yourself?'

'Kentish Town. I share a house with four others. It's all right. The landlord advertised for music students. He's a Royal Academy of Music alumnus, so he's sympathetic to our needs. These days he composes scores for films. There's even a John Broadwood and Sons' piano downstairs we can use.'

'*Really?*' said Clarissa, impressed. 'It sounds wonderful!'

'Aye, I was lucky to have found it, I suppose.'

As they passed row upon row of towers, the ground floor of each occupied by various businesses: an office supplies shop, an internet café, a couple of banks, a dental surgery, Clarissa began to bitterly regret her choice of footwear. Her right ankle was really throbbing now.

'What will you be performing this evening?' she asked.

'Chopin. The Etudes. Opus 10, numbers 1 to 4.'

Clarissa stopped walking. Her eyes grew wide. 'Rather you than me! Number 4 has to be one of the most difficult pieces to play on this earth!'

Ralph smiled at her. He was wearing a chunky silver herringbone chain around his neck; the sun ignited it briefly. The effect was bordering on celestial.

'Now, if I thought like that, I wouldn't be able to play a note of it, would I?' he quipped. 'I've been living and breathing the Etudes for the last six months. Once you reach a certain point, you should be able to freefall through it without thinking. You *enter* the piano. Join forces with it; *become it.* You must have got that feeling before yourself?'

'Well…I've never heard it put quite like *that*,' said Clarissa, intrigued. 'Maybe you experience something I don't?'

'But you must know what I'm talking about?'

Clarissa smiled weakly. 'Yes. I think I do, but it's not quite like that for me.'

'So what's it like for you?'

'I don't know how to describe it, really.'

When they reached a zebra crossing, a black cab skidded dangerously around the corner in order to make the lights. A car hooted. Clarissa felt Ralph's protective arm stop her from stepping out in front of it.

'BLOODY EEJIT! The Jo Maxis think they own the road in this town!' He cut her a sidelong glance. 'Are you all right?'

'Yes,' said Clarissa, catching her breath. 'Thanks for that. It's not much further now.'

After they'd walked a bit more, Ralph said: 'It's a shame you can't make the performance tonight. What is it you have to get up so early for anyway?'

'I'm cabin crew. I have to be at Stansted at 4:30 a.m.'

'You're a *trolley dolly*?'

'Err…didn't that term become extinct in 1989?' said Clarissa, mildly offended.

'You know, I was *not* expecting you to be an air hostess,' Ralph said animatedly, ignoring her objection to his poor use of phrase. 'But now that you come to mention it…you know, I can see it! Now, where would you be flying off to tomorrow?'

'I don't know yet. I'm on standby. It could be anywhere. Basically I'm relieving anyone who's sick or late for work.'

'And what happens if nobody's sick or late for work?' he countered.

'Well, I just wait in the crew member's lounge, until my shift is over.'

'What? You just have to sit there waiting? Isn't that a bit tedious?'

'It's just part of the job,' said Clarissa, who'd become accustomed to this sort of questioning over the years. 'It's why you never fly without a full crew.'

'I see,' he said politely.

They walked past Marylebone Library with its ribbed concrete columns.

'So, were you a child prodigy?' Clarissa asked him. 'You're so relaxed with a piano.'

'When you get to know me better, you'll laugh at that statement!'

'What do you mean?'

'Let's just say, I've acquired my confidence…over time.' He looked into the stream of traffic anxiously, and Clarissa watched his smile dissolve like butter in a hot pan.

They walked on in silence for a while, and she sensed that she'd inadvertently opened a wound in him.

'You okay?' she asked tentatively.

'Aye,' he replied, in a disconnected sort of way. 'But you've got to tell me something I've been longing to ask you since we left Baker Street.'

'What's that?'

She felt his eyes stroke her legs.

'Why didn't you slip a pair of trainers in that bag of yours before you left the house? Your feet must be killing you in those shoes! Am I right?'

She cut him a look. 'Hindsight's such a wonderful thing, don't you think?'

'I knew it!' He grinned. 'Not that you don't look hot though,' he added through his teeth.

They trudged on.

The buildings on Upper Montagu Street were private residencies, generally four stories, the occasional business nestled amongst them. When they turned down Montagu Place and past the red and white flag of the Switzerland Embassy, Bryanston Square began to creep into view.

Clarissa led Ralph to house number 46 and looked at him intently.

'46 B.S. London. 46 Bryanston Square, London. Now, I've tried 46 steps from the front, 46 steps from the back, 4 steps right and 6 steps left and 6 steps right and 4 steps left.'

'I'm surprised you haven't been arrested!'

'Very funny. Can you think of any other combinations?'

'Wait a minute. What did the clue say? *Exactly*,' asked Ralph in a serious voice. 'How was it written?'

'46 B.S. London. Commuter. With an exclamation mark at the end.'

'*Commuter*? You didn't tell me about that bit before.'

'Well, it was spelt incorrectly, I'm assuming it was *meant* to say "commuter". There was a mistake.'

Ralph's eyes began to gleam excitedly. 'There's no such thing as a mistake in a Dead Drop clue. Think, Clarissa. How was it spelt, exactly?'

Clarissa reached into her bag. 'Just a minute, I wrote it down.'

She pulled out a piece of paper and handed it to him.

'It says "*commutateur*",' said Ralph. 'It's French.'

'French?'

'It means "switch".'

Clarissa suddenly experienced a lightbulb moment.

'Of course! How could I have been so stupid?' she cried. 'It's not number *46*…,' she smiled.

'It's number 64!' they both said in unison.

Clarissa began to run up the road in the direction the numbers ascended. Ralph followed close behind her, the piano rolling around on his back comically.

Number 64 Bryanston Square wasn't quite as grand as number 46. There was just a single door entrance at the top of five stone steps crowned by an iron archway. A small lantern was hanging from its apex.

Clarissa stood at the base of the steps, her green eyes dancing furiously. Slowly, she walked to the kerb and bent down between the two cars that were parked there. There was plenty of congealed dirt and she watched a pink and yellow sweet wrapper drift by serenely. Then her eyes snagged on something else.

There was some sort of curved rubber buffer protruding from the side of the road – it looked like it had been made from a section of a tyre. She jostled it and it came away in her hands.

And there it was!

Cemented between two lumps of kerb-stone, silver and glinting like a mouth. The Dead Drop was real and in front of her. All she had to do was attach her laptop to it and Charlie would speak.

Ralph caught up.

'Now you're suckin' the diesel my friend!' he shouted triumphantly.

Clarissa flashed him a grateful smile before reaching for her laptop. She plugged in the stick with some difficultly as she could only just squeeze in between the two vehicles, and once she had made sure she had downloaded it correctly, she deleted its contents (as per her instructions). She intended to read it later, when she was alone.

Hurriedly, she fitted the rubber protector back over it again, and sprang to her feet.

'Ralph Valero, you're a genius!' she cried, running back along the road.

She could hear his voice behind her. 'Hey! Wait up! My drink, remember?'

The café was small, unassuming. Clarissa had stretched to buying Ralph lunch to show her gratitude.

'You're right by the way, my feet *are* killing me,' she told him, as they seated themselves at a table by the window.

Ralph smiled. 'I could always rub them for you, if you like?'

'I'm fine,' she said, a little more haughtily than she'd intended.

They ate toasties while jazz music dipped and rose in the background.

'So do I get to know what this is all about now?' he said, his eyes frantically searching hers for an explanation.

She hesitated. 'It's complicated.'

'I'm listening.'

She sighed. It wasn't that she distrusted Ralph, it really wasn't. She just wanted to wait until she *knew* she could trust him.

She poured herself some water and glanced at the rain that had started to tap the glass behind her. She sensed him watching her. He was sitting opposite her facing the street, the passing traffic casting reflections in his eyes. He took a moment to frown at the weather.

'Let's exchange mobile numbers in case I need you again,' she said briskly.

He grinned, surprised. 'That was easier than I thought.'

'I'm not asking you out on a date. I just thought you might be able to help me find the next Dead Drop location.' She glared at him.

'So there's *another* one? What's the clue?' Ralph checked his watch. 'I could help you now, if you like?'

'We can't, not now.'

'Why? Do you have to be somewhere? I don't have to be back at the Academy until four.'

She couldn't help but smile at his enthusiasm. 'No, it's not that. The next one's not around here.'

'So where is it?'

'Paris.'

'Paris, *France*?' Ralph looked shocked.

She nodded. 'But thanks. And thanks for putting me straight on the last clue. I couldn't have found it without your help.'

'It was no problem at all, Clarissa!' said Ralph, his Irish accent elevating the inflection. Suddenly his eyes were drawn to the window. She watched his expression change from "content" to "panic stricken" in three seconds.

'What is it?' she asked.

'I don't believe it! *Jesus, no!*'

'Ralph? What's the matter?'

Clarissa turned around.

5

When the two men burst into the café, Ralph immediately leapt to his feet, his chair crashing to the ground.

Some diners exclaimed in surprise.

The intruders, mean-looking men wearing leather jackets and biker boots, hauled some chairs over from another table and seated themselves between Ralph and Clarissa impertinently.

Clarissa, suddenly finding her body taut and alive with adrenalin, reached instinctively for her laptop, which was lying on the floor beneath her, and with one skillful scoop of her feet, the device was secured between her ankles.

The ugliest man, sporting a neck as fat as his head, bared yellow teeth as he complained about the weather. Then he looked backwards and forwards between Ralph and a very startled Clarissa, and said: 'Now, what have you two been up to, then?'

Clarissa saw Ralph glance at the door.

'Don't even think about it, Valero. I've got someone at the back as well as the front,' growled the other man, thinner, more wasted-looking. He then attempted to smile whilst chewing gum, and Clarissa watched a gold tooth appear briefly at the side of his mouth like he was sucking on a bullet.

The mastication then resumed with fresh gusto.

'How we doing then, old chum?' he continued with a dirty cockney accent. 'Are we any further forward with our little arrangement?'

The busker went to reach inside his jacket pocket. This seemed to prompt the fat-necked one to raise a hand to Ralph's throat.

'I'm getting you the money, man!' protested Ralph.

'Got it here with you today, have you?'

'Tone it down a bit, Silas. You're scaring the customers!' said the wasted-looking one, glaring around at the café's surprised clientele.

The hand promptly fell from Ralph's neck.

'Yeah, tone it down a bit, Silas!' said Ralph, adding a mocking tone to his Irish accent. 'Do you want today's takings or not?'

Clarissa's mouth fell open as Ralph tipped the entire contents of his money bag onto the table. Coins clattered noisily, small pieces of paper lay scattered amongst them: the blues and browns of five and ten pound notes.

'Now, what the fuck am I supposed to do with all that shrapnel, eh?' said Silas irritably. 'But the notes, I'll take!' he said greedily, plucking at various parts of Her Majesty's face.

'Fifty-five pounds,' said Silas, after he had smoothed all the notes out onto the table. 'Write that down.'

To Clarissa's horror, a small note-book was proffered, and the value recorded.

'How much is owing now, Slim?'

'Six thousand, four hundred and twenty pounds,' came the reply. 'Better think of a few more ideas, other than just busking eh, Valero? Or this thing is going to go on forever!'

Slim shot Clarissa a quick glance, before returning his gaze to Ralph.

'Nice bit of skirt, Valero! Morgan know about this little rendezvous, does she?'

'Just take the money and fuck off!'

Ralph was grabbed by the collar of his jacket.

'You want to step outside and say that?' demanded Silas. 'It's high time you had a lesson in manners!'

'Any time!' shouted Ralph. 'ANY TIME!'

Slim got up. 'Come on, Silas. No physical damage, remember? Nothing to compromise his playing.'

'Physical damage!' Silas scoffed. 'He doesn't know the meaning of the words.' He leaned in towards the busker, and Clarissa heard him whisper: 'When this thing is over, Valero, I swear, I'll teach you a thing or two about fucking *physical damage*!'

As they left, Ralph's blazing eyes peered at them reproachfully through a screen of hair.

Once the door had closed, Clarissa excused herself and went to the ladies, where she tried in vain to regain her composure. When she got back, the owner of the café approached their table and asked them to leave.

As Ralph escorted her back to Baker Street Tube, Clarissa discovered to her absolute horror that she was shaking.

'Are you all right, Clarissa?' Ralph asked her, concerned.

'*What* just happened?'

'I'm sorry you had to see that.'

'What on earth did you do to get on the wrong side of them?'

'Ah, yes, well. It wasn't me, you see.' Ralph hesitated. 'It was my girlfriend, Morgan.'

'Really,' said Clarissa.

'She's sort of gone and got herself in a wee bit of trouble.'

'A bit? They were monsters!' said Clarissa, stopping dead in the street, the light rain making her squint. They'd reached the Swiss Embassy; the roads were heavy with traffic and the dark sky gave the impression that it was far later than it was.

'It's complicated,' said Ralph, wrapping his head with his hands in a dejected manner.

'It always is,' said Clarissa, with a half-smile.

A few minutes later Ralph said: 'I guess you won't be needing my help in finding anymore Dead Drops now?'

Clarissa shot him an incongruous glance: 'Well, are you going to tell me what your girlfriend's done, or not?'

'You're pissed off because I didn't tell you I had a girlfriend aren't you?'

'Don't be so ridiculous!'

'I'm sorry about that, really I am.'

'Why should I care if you have a girlfriend? I don't care if you have a girlfriend! I was going to offer to help you!' shouted Clarissa, frustrated.

Ralph laughed. 'I don't mean to sound ungrateful or anything, Clarissa, but you don't look like the sort of girl who can pull a punch, or perhaps you have a spare £6420 you could let me borrow?'

'You're asking me to lend you money? I've known you for what? Five minutes?'

'Then how can you help me, Clarissa? How can *you* help *me*?'

Clarissa considered her reply. She didn't know why, but as infuriating as this man was, she felt an overwhelming desire to keep him close to her. She attributed this to the initial mesmerising effect his musical ability had generated within her. An effect that, try as she might, she felt unable to disentangle from the other lesser qualities the man was unfortunate enough to possess.

'Listen, when those men burst in like that, my first thought was that they were after *me*.'

'After you? Now why on earth would men like that be after you, Clarissa?'

'Because I'm in a "wee" bit of trouble myself, you see.'

'You've got to be kidding me!'

'Believe me, I wish I was.'

'What about this fella of yours, isn't he sorting things out for you?'

Ignoring the question, Clarissa suddenly stopped walking, pulling a bemused Ralph towards a window advertising bank loans.

'You're suggesting I should get a loan?' he said pushing his damp hair away from his cheek, displaying perfectly exaggerated brows.

'No. That's just coincidental,' she replied dismissively. 'I'm checking to see if we're being followed.'

'...By my lot, or your lot?' he asked, with a smirk she didn't appreciate.

'Just stand here a while and pretend to be interested in the content of the window.'

Ralph couldn't repress his amusement. 'Now, what sort of trouble could you have possibly got yourself into? Let me guess. Swindling the Duty Free trolley? Smuggling someone onboard without a passport?'

She rolled her eyes irritably. 'You think I'm joking?'

He looked at her more seriously.

'I can't tell you here,' she said. 'Come with me.'

After a few minutes she began to walk briskly and he followed. Deciding it was best to engage him in some form of conversation to alleviate the silence, she said: 'So, your girlfriend. Is she at the RAM too?'

'What, Morgan? Jesus, no. She's a...dancer. But she works as a barmaid during the day.'

Clarissa looked at him dubiously. 'What sort of dancer?'

'Oh, you know, the sleazy kind: strip-tease, pole dancing. That's what you're thinking aren't you? *Jesus,* your face! She works the theatres in the west end!'

'Very funny. Is that how you met? Through the theatre?'

'No. I met her at a party in Camden.'

A group of school children trotted past them with raised voices and excited smiles. She waited for the whole group to pass before she continued.

'And how did she get involved with Slim and...the other one?'

'She met them in Joe's bar, where she worked,' said Ralph. 'They soon became regulars. I used to notice Slim watching us from along the bar sometimes. Little did I know, he was checking us out. One night he must have followed me. I caught sight of him when I was leaving the RAM after a performance. He knew who

I was; he knew what I did. He must have put a similar surveillance on Morgan. More to the point, he knew we were both poor. We were the perfect bait. Or rather Morgan was.'

They navigated another zebra crossing. Amidst the bleeping sound, came Clarissa's voice: 'Bait for what?'

'He knew the nights I visited Joe's. He knew the nights I didn't. He began to strike up conversation with her on the nights I was absent. She thought nothing of it at first. She talks to a lot of punters. Then he asked her if she wanted to make some easy money. A hundred quid for passing a package from one punter to another. Now, I know what you're thinking. How could she have been so stupid? How could I have let her do such a thing? She was desperate for money, that's how, and she must have done it five or six times before I knew anything about it! Anyway. It was all going fine until one day…'

'What happened?'

'She was seen,' Ralph went on, 'by her landlord. It resulted in her losing her job. Instant dismissal. But she was fired whilst in possession of a packet containing a large sum of heroin. This was confiscated by the landlord, who eventually turned it in to the police, but Morgan wasn't implicated. The landlord just told her to leave and not set foot in the place again. So Morgan doesn't have a criminal record, but she does have Slim and Silas serially demanding the value of the heroin back on a weekly basis. She has another job now, in another bar, but she can't earn enough to satisfy them. It's the reason I busk. On a good day I can make quite a tidy sum.'

Clarissa looked horrified. 'So, *you're* having to pay them back as well as her? That doesn't seem right to me. You must really love her.'

'Love her? The woman's RUINED MY LIFE, SO SHE HAS!'

Ralph stopped walking to adjust the weight of his piano.

'So what's she like, this "Morgan"?' asked Clarissa, with genuine interest.

'Would you like to meet her?'

'Now, why would I want to do that?'

'If you're asking if she's extremely talented or stunningly beautiful, the answer's "no" on both counts. If you're asking if I'm in love with her, again the answer's "no".'

'Then why are you helping her?'

They started to walk again.

'Because I'm in love with my music, Clarissa! I need to play the piano and if I don't help her get their money back to them, my career is as good as over!'

Clarissa thought back to what she'd heard in the café.

'They've been threatening you?'

'Look, put it this way, if I don't play for them, they'll see to it that I *can't* play, if you get my drift! I comply, so I don't get my head kicked in. It's also the reason I'm still with Morgan.'

Clarissa looked at him. She realised she was half-expecting him, to say: "I'm only messing with you!" But when he didn't, she began to see him in a whole new light.

'So, now you know I'm not this altruistic pianist with a heart of gold, do you still want to tell me your plight?' he said provocatively.

Clarissa surveyed him afresh, with his bellicose stance and supplicating eyes. Although his story had been unexpected, she found it could not occlude her interest in him.

'I think we might be able to help each other out,' she replied diplomatically. 'But what I'm about to tell you is confidential and must not be discussed with anyone. I cannot stress this enough.'

'Discretion is one of my greatest attributes!' Ralph declared avidly, and she could not help but be affected by his obvious excitement.

Clarissa concluded that as far as problems went, Ralph seemed to be burdened with more than his fair share. But she was starting to look upon Charlie's task as too complicated for one person to manage effectively – she was already exhausted by its demands – and Ralph's potential to assist her was proving impossible to resist.

'Come on,' she said. 'Let's find somewhere quiet.'

As she trudged back with him through the London streets, she felt the damp air cling to her skin, and with it came a distrust of her emotions. She liked Ralph, but she couldn't allow herself to grow to like him more than was necessary. She knew his help would be invaluable in finding the Dead Drops. She was sure the esoteric nature of the clues would appeal just as well to him as it did to her. But she could also see the way he was looking at her, and she had to make it clear that she was interested in nothing other than his mind.

On reaching Baker Street Underground Station, they came upon another café. Clarissa stepped inside without a word and Ralph followed. He insisted on buying them both a drink with what remained of his busking change, and they positioned themselves at the back of the establishment in silence while she found a safe spot for her laptop and his piano.

Once settled, Clarissa took off her shoes and sipped her coffee before launching into the story. But she had to admit, it sounded a little different from the last time she told it.

'My boyfriend is a thief,' she said. 'He's stolen a valuable piece of script music and hidden it. He's since disappeared, but he's left me a trail of Dead Drops to guide me to the manuscript's location.'

Clarissa waited for Ralph to respond to this with some sort of wisecrack, but he didn't. He just sat there staring at her, expressionless, waiting for her to deliver the rest of it. So she went on.

'I believe the manuscript to be a handwritten score by Chopin.'

Ralph smiled at this, but still managed to hold his tongue.

'I'm flying to Charles de Gaulle on Friday. I will go after the next Dead Drop then.'

Ralph pulled his hair back savagely: 'You've already looked at the next clue haven't you? And you're flummoxed. That's why you're telling me all of this. You want me to work it out for you, to help your "boyfriend".'

Distracted by his ability to read her, Clarissa lifted her laptop onto the table shakily.

'I'm not asking you to do it for my *boyfriend*,' she said crisply. 'I'm not even asking you to do it for *me*.'

Ralph mimicked indifference.

'I'm asking you to do it for Chopin!' she said defiantly. 'If there's a secret handwritten manuscript by Chopin floating about, surely it's our duty to find it?'

Ralph indicated his fidelity with a serious nod.

Clarissa opened her laptop gently, as if it were a precious silver shell. She began to press some buttons on her keypad.

'It's not like the previous Dead Drop clue,' she said, fighting to mitigate her passion; she hadn't meant to speak so fervently. 'But you're right,' she admitted, 'I took a brief look at it in the ladies in the café and it makes absolutely no sense to me.'

She opened the file and presented the screen to Ralph. This is what he saw:

Stick No.3: 32 S.P. CON E NOT F, 1ST PP. Paris.

Ralph took out his phone and pointed it towards the laptop.

'What are you doing?'

'I'm sorry,' he said. 'Please permit me to take a photo of the clue, so that I can think it over.'

'Certainly not! No photos. No technology that can be traced. That's why he's used Dead Drops! You can write it down with a pen and paper instead.'

Clarissa removed a page from her notebook. She wrote her phone number at the top of it before she passed it to Ralph, along with the pen.

He smiled again and copied out the clue. Then he wrote his phone number down for her and tore it off.

Clarissa put it in her bag. 'Thank you,' she said.

'Thank *you*,' said Ralph, getting up. 'Now, I'd better get back to the Academy. I need to rehearse for tonight's performance.'

'Well, good luck!' said Clarissa.

'With the performance or the clue?'

'With the clue, of course!' said Clarissa curtly. 'You don't need "luck" for the performance, you should be able to freefall through it, remember?'

Ralph's eyes sparkled with unfettered optimism. 'I'll be in touch when I've worked it out. I'll be sure to do it before Friday.'

She nodded. 'Thank you. No texts, remember. You'll have to call.'

'That's grand,' he said placing his piano on his back. 'And it's been a real pleasure meeting you, Clarissa. I'll be sure to call.'

6

Dressed smartly in her blue uniform and pillbox hat, Clarissa braced herself for takeoff with a degree of trepidation. Ordinarily, she would have acknowledged this procedure with an accustomed sense of familiarity, but over the last couple of days she'd developed a head cold and her ears hurt, so she knew that her shift would be an uncomfortable one.

It was Friday and Clarissa was onboard her 5:30 a.m. flight to Charles de Gaulle Airport on the outskirts of Paris. Having carried out her safety checks and strapped herself into her jump seat, she stared resolutely ahead, determined to get through the day. Disappointedly, she had not heard from Ralph or Professor Kowalski (her Dead Drop quest was going nowhere fast). And to make matters worse, Donna had seen fit to blank her during their pre-flight briefing; and since they'd now been assigned to opposite ends of the aircraft – Donna, economy, and Clarissa, first class – there could be no reconciliation between the two friends for at least an hour and a half.

As her plane finally lifted from Stansted's runway, she thought of Charlie, alone, being held against his will; being subjected to a violent interrogation about the Chopin manuscript. She wondered how far his captors would go to obtain the document, and whether they'd hurt him for it. It was difficult to grasp the level of danger he was in.

Clarissa's "standby" days had passed uneventfully. On Wednesday, her services had been utilised to board only one flight due to a crew member getting stuck in traffic, but she had not been required to travel. Subsequently, she had spent the rest of that day in the crew member's lounge on her laptop trying to decipher the clue to the Paris Dead Drop, and getting nowhere. On Thursday she had flown to Greece and back twice, covering for a crew member with food poisoning, but the weather had issued some delays, and on returning home later than anticipated, Clarissa had immediately taken to her bed with a temperature, leaving her flat wreckage unsorted and the Dead Drop clue unsolved.

As the plane completed its climb-out, Clarissa swallowed repeatedly to manage the pain but a continuous high-pitched squealing in her right ear was bringing tears to her eyes.

Soon, Woody's lethargic voice came over the tannoy to announce their designated cruising height, and Clarissa waited for him to wrap up so that she could begin her initial combing of first class. But when his monotonous voice finally disconnected, her fellow cabin crew member, Vanessa, whispered in her ear: 'Look hard. I'm flying to Denmark in three weeks.' (Flight attendant's code for "Take a look at the passenger in seat 3D").

When Clarissa turned her head to get a better view of the seat's occupant, she found a broad-shouldered man with white hair grinning back at her. She took him to be in his mid-sixties; he was dressed well – navy suit, gold handkerchief in his breast pocket, tanned face, abnormally white teeth – but he kept as still as porcelain, in a way that seemed to award him the highest status of formidability, like a dangerous animal about to snap the neck of an oblivious bystander.

'Anyone you know?' asked Vanessa inquisitively, rolling her eyes.

'I don't think so.'

'Well, he hasn't taken his eyes off you since he boarded. You might get some attention from him later, just to warn you. Do you want me to take the left this time, or do you want to face the music?' said Vanessa, referring to the side of the plane they would take care of.

'No, it's okay, I'll face the music,' said Clarissa impassively.

Used to this sort of exchange, she wouldn't normally have worried about some man taking an interest in her. But in the light of recent events, she found she'd raised her guard.

When the seatbelt light flicked off, the cabin crew stood up to begin their duties.

As Clarissa smiled and began to work her way down the plane, the man in 3D, who was occupying an aisle seat, put his hand out to prevent her from walking past.

'Hello, Clarissa,' he said. 'Do you remember me?'

Clarissa flinched with the realisation that she did indeed know who this man was, for she had heard his voice on the evening of Charlie's disappearance.

'Roland Steed,' said the man sanctimoniously. 'Delighted to make your acquaintance!'

'Hello,' said Clarissa, so shocked she continued to ask him if he was comfortable and if she could do anything for him, as she would have done any other passenger.

'There *is* something you can do for me, as a matter of fact,' he said, lowering his gravelly voice. 'How about you tell me where Charlie is. Or my brother George? Has he been in touch?'

Clarissa bent down closer to him. 'I don't know where Charlie is. And I've never met your brother.'

'I don't believe you,' said Steed defiantly. 'A girlfriend, not knowing the whereabouts of her boyfriend is most unlikely.'

'I agree,' said Clarissa. 'But you see,' she lowered her voice to a whisper: 'He isn't my boyfriend anymore. He ended our relationship.'

'Oh?' replied Steed dubiously. 'You expect me to believe that? Why would a man walk out on someone as lovely as you, Clarissa? Either he's lost his mind or you're lying to me.'

'Actually, he was seeing someone else,' she replied in a low voice, so convincingly in fact, she almost believed it herself. She added in an angry whisper: 'Not that it's any of your business.'

She watched Roland Steed's smile falter for a moment, before she moved on to another passenger, trying not to catch his eye again. But thirty minutes later, when she had to serve him with the trolley cart, he grabbed her wrist.

'Remember, my presence, my dear, and be most careful. When we arrive in France, every move you make will be observed. Oh, and I'll have a tea, please, with plenty of milk!'

Clarissa poured him his drink and forced her mouth to produce a smile. 'Then your time will be wasted,' she said eventually. 'I am doing nothing but work. Enjoy your tea.'

During the flight, Vanessa grew concerned. 'Are you all right, Clarissa? Is that guy in 3D giving you a bit of trouble? I saw him grab your hand earlier.'

'Oh, it's nothing I can't handle,' she said, shrugging it off. But in reality, the encounter had shaken her to the core. The thought that this man knew not only what she did for a living, but that she'd be working on this particular flight disturbed her a great deal.

Later, while they were separating the recycling in the food preparation area, Vanessa, sensing that something was bothering her colleague, attempted to lighten the mood with a bit of small talk: 'How did you enjoy your days off, Clarissa? Did you get to spend some quality time with your boyfriend?'

Now due to the pain in her ears, her distress at Donna's avoidance, Ralph's indifference, and Roland Steed's aggression, Clarissa found herself incapable of producing a simple retort to such a question. Her response: 'Actually, my boyfriend dumped me over the weekend,' was immediately regretted.

Vanessa stopped what she was doing and her eyes seemed to enlarge in response. 'Oh, God! I'm so sorry! Are you okay?'

'I'll be fine, really,' said Clarissa, wishing the statement could somehow be retracted, noticing a hole in her plastic recycling bag and tying it quickly before its contents burst out over the floor. 'I just need to concentrate on my work. I really don't want to talk about it. Sorry.'

'Of course!' gushed Vanessa, with genuine concern. '*I'm* sorry. I had no idea you two had even been fighting.'

But we haven't, thought Clarissa. That was the weird thing about all of this, having to keep up with this ridiculous pretence, for Charlie! If it wasn't bad enough, being forced to play the detective, trying to work out these ridiculous clues in order to locate pieces of metal scattered across two countries, she found herself unwillingly saddled with the role of "actress" as well; an actress, she realised, who was starting to believe the strength of her own lies.

When they touched down at Charles de Gaulle Airport, Clarissa felt like she was trapped in a vacuum; a repeated clicking prevented her from hearing what Vanessa was saying to her, and Woody's words were just a discordant noise, like a wasp dancing inside her brain.

Then later, whilst seeing her passengers off the aircraft, Roland Steed, simply said in passing: 'Goodbye, Clarissa. Until we meet again.' But the sentence managed to produce in her the unnerving effect of extinguishing her smile and upsetting her demeanour, as thoroughly as if he'd just issued a curse.

Shortly afterwards, with the cabin crew assembled to leave, Woody and Lianne (the first officer) exited the flight deck, and Clarissa saw Donna exchange a glance with the philandering pilot that told her something was wrong between them.

Once they had retired to the Crew member's lounge, Clarissa made her way to the ladies. When she emerged from the cubicle, she found Donna already there waiting for her.

'Hi, babe. What's up?' It was one of Donna's customary greetings, but her eyes were abnormally red-rimmed and her dark skin uncharacteristically shiny, making Clarissa immediately concerned.

Realising they were alone, Clarissa seized the opportunity to apologise: 'Listen, about the other day, I'm sorry if I –'

'I'm pregnant,' said Donna.

The news emerged like a bullet.

Clarissa touched her friend on the shoulder. 'Oh, God.'

'My career is over,' said a devastated Donna, her eyes welling up afresh.

'Are you sure? Have you done a test?'

'I've done three.'

'Does Woody know?'

Donna nodded.

'What was his reaction?'

'He wants me to "terminate the pregnancy".'

'*The bastard*! What are you going to do?'

'I don't know yet.'

Following this exchange, Clarissa watched in silence as Donna make a sterling effort to apply fresh make-up to her face for their 10:55 a.m. flight back to Stansted.

This was the last thing she'd been expecting. She couldn't believe her friend had found herself in this predicament.

'Did you not…have something on you then?' asked Clarissa quizzically. 'You're normally so careful. Whenever we've talked about it, you've –'

'I *know*!' cried Donna, rummaging around inside her make-up bag and tending to her face with such over-defined gestures, Clarissa found it disquieting. 'You don't need to tell me what I'm normally like. We got carried away.'

Clarissa flashed her friend a disapproving look.

'Oh, come on! Don't tell me it's never happened to you?' Donna glared at her. 'It's called passion!'

I thought it was called *adultery,* Clarissa wanted to retort, but bit the words back into her mouth; the idea of reprimanding Donna in this way suddenly seemed unfair.

There was an uncomfortable silence while Donna applied a fresh coat of crimson lipstick to her cupid's bow lips.

'Look. I'm sorry, sweetie. I don't mean to take this thing out on you,' she said gently, trying to smile.

Clarissa produced a nonchalant shrug and pressed her hand to her forehead. Donna's flash comment was reverberating like a turbine. *It's called passion.* Passion. For the first time, Clarissa considered the possibility that her "careful" intimacy with Charlie had only been possible because of a lack of it.

Donna snapped the lid back on her lipstick with a loud click and threw it forcefully into her make-up bag.

As they prepared to leave the restroom, Donna said: 'Vanessa seems to be under the impression that you and Charlie are no longer together. Is that true?'

'Yes,' said Clarissa, baulking at the very sound of it.

Donna mumbled something to herself in Italian. 'Were you *even* going to tell me?'

'Of course! Your news seemed a bit more important, that's all.'

'But what happened, hun? I thought you two were air-tight?'

'Yes, well. It turned out, we weren't,' said Clarissa, succinctly.

It would have to do for the moment, she thought. She had every intention of confiding in her friend eventually, but it wasn't the right time, in between flights, during work. The real explanation would have to wait.

'Hey, do you fancy some breakfast?' said Donna.

'Sure.'

Donna smiled and marched off towards the door.

When they emerged into the crew member's lounge, Clarissa turned to her friend.

'Donna?'

'Yeah?'

'Do you find the label "trolley dolly" offensive?'

Donna pulled a face. 'Not really. I guess I've always thought of it as a bit of a term of endearment, really. Why?'

'No reason.'

Charles de Gaulle Airport was pulsing with activity. Its tangle of escalators set in transparent tubes suspended over the central atrium was packed. Amidst the swelling crowds, Clarissa followed Donna through the network of glass passages down to the second floor where the restaurants and shops were located.

As they marched in their heels, Clarissa caught a reflection of the two of them in a window. They were identically dressed in their blue uniforms with their pillbox hats, and perfectly in step with each other, wheeling their small cases in sync behind them. In fact their figures were so similar, from behind, they were indistinguishable. Then Clarissa thought about the baby growing inside Donna, and realised that if she went ahead with this pregnancy, the two of them would not be mistaken for one another for much longer.

The friends were about to enter a café, when Clarissa heard music. Piano music, to be more precise; the melody so arresting, she felt her whole body freeze in response to it. Sensing an absurd desire to run to its source like some sort of conditioned animal, she stopped dead to make sure her ears weren't deceiving her. Yes, she concluded. She wasn't mistaken. She could really hear Chopin's Etude, Opus 10, No.4.

'Donna, I'm so sorry…but I'm feeling a bit unwell,' Clarissa found herself saying waveringly. 'I'm going to need to use the toilet again.'

'Oh hell,' said Donna.

'Don't wait for me, get yourself some breakfast!' cried Clarissa, as she sped away into the crowd.

Clarissa despised herself as she ran. She knew that she was letting Donna down when she really needed her. She would certainly have a lot to do to make it up to her after this.

Ralph cannot be *here* at this airport, she thought, as she hurried on through the terminal, navigating her way around groups of animated passengers talking in different tongues. How can he be *here*?

But she could think of no other explanation for what she was hearing. The Etude could only be played by a limited number of skilled pianists. Herself, excluded.

Up ahead she could see a large group of people assembled in front of her.

As Clarissa broke through the throng of onlookers, she gasped in astonishment. For there, in front of her, sitting on the floor in one of the airport's seating areas, an electric piano upon his knees, was Ralph, playing Chopin.

He was partially obscured by a cluster of passengers (predominately children in school uniform clutching instrument cases). Skillfully, he took the piece through to its conclusion with no errors, whilst everyone watched him in complete awe.

Pushing her way to the front, Clarissa realised that Ralph's ability was not only extraordinary, it was also unsurpassed – she was quite sure she hadn't come across a talent even remotely like his in all her time at the Royal College. The speed at which he played was breathtaking.

Once the piece had finished, she watched him scan the sea of faces in his audience. On locating hers, he beamed at her. Then he passed the piano to the boy next to him, addressing him in French, before making his way towards her amidst the clapping and cheering.

'What are you doing?' she cried, in utter shock.

'Calling you. Without using traceable technology. Just like you asked me to,' he said, with a smug smile on his face.

Clarissa felt a burst of laughter threaten to explode, but repressed it.

'Well, it's resourceful. I'll give you that!' she said.

'The uniform looks good on you, by the way,' he said. 'I like the hat.'

Clarissa rolled her eyes. 'Did you try calling my phone? I don't think I got any missed calls.'

'I've been trying to ring for a while, but I couldn't get a decent enough signal,' said Ralph. 'This was a sort of impromptu thing. I saw a kid with a piano case and took full advantage of the situation.'

'You *do know* it's illegal to busk in an airport, right?' said Clarissa, still trying to digest her shock.

'It's illegal to busk on the London Underground,' Ralph pointed out, 'but the fuzz tend to turn a blind eye. I figured they'd have the same attitude here. We're musicians, not criminals!'

They walked away from the school children.

Clarissa thought Ralph looked so self-satisfied, she decided not to lavish yet more praise on him for his competence with the Etude. She also noticed that he didn't seek her opinion regarding his performance, and this display of modesty impressed her almost as much as his rendition had.

'Have you worked out the clue?' she asked fervently, trying to concentrate instead, on his reason for being there in the first place.

'Jesus! Why else do you think I'm here? Of course I've worked out the clue!'

'And you're sure? You're absolutely *sure* you've got it?'

'There's no doubt in my mind.'

Clarissa couldn't believe it. She had turned the clue inside out, but absolutely nothing had come to her.

Their conversation was suddenly interrupted by a French announcer listing the flights that were currently boarding.

'Listen. I've got about two hours,' said Clarissa, removing her hat. 'Where are we going? Train access is this way.' She beckoned to her left.

'I think we should take a taxi,' said Ralph, adding: 'I'll pay.'

'Then we'll need to go up a floor,' she said, leading Ralph towards the ascending escalator.

When they reached the third floor, they exited the terminal, the cold air lashing at them like a whip. Clarissa watched Ralph hail a taxi, scraping his hair back from his face savagely in that determined way he had, revealing his fierce, hazel eyes and long, smooth forehead, and she felt what could only be described as a wave of grateful affection.

'Thanks!' she said suddenly, with an uncontrollable burst of gratitude. 'For coming, I mean. It means a lot.'

'I'm doing it for Chopin, you understand,' said Ralph. 'He's done a lot for me over the years.'

'Of course,' said Clarissa. 'We're both in the man's debt!'

'*Où aller?*' asked the taxi driver, once they'd both got into a cab.

'*9 rue Cadet s'il vous plait,*' said Ralph.

'How long do you think it will take to get there?' Clarissa asked the Frenchman, who shrugged his rounded shoulders and thought it over.

'Err….About fifty minutes,' he replied in English.

'Fifty minutes? I'll never make it back!' she said to Ralph.

'Just how important is this?' he asked her.

Clarissa knew that to drive away from the airport with Ralph was not only foolish, it was also highly irresponsible. In a worst case scenario, if she failed to make it back in time for her next flight, she could very well lose her job.

'I'll just have to risk it!' she declared, and the taxi driver seemed to understand and pull away.

'Rue Cadet. Where is that exactly?' Clarissa asked Ralph as they joined the A3, fifteen minutes into their journey.

'It's north of the Seine. Opera Quarter. Ninth arrondissement.'

'But how on earth did you come to *that* location? I was looking for "S.P." roads and number "32's".'

'So was I, at first. But then I realised that in this instance, "S.P." doesn't stand for the name of a road. It's an abbreviation for Salle Pleyel.'

'The concert hall? But that's in rue du Faubourg Saint-Honoré.'

'Aye, it is *now*. But in 1832 it wasn't.'

'So "32" is a year! "S.P." *Salle Pleyel.* "Con" has to be *Concerto.* And "E NOT F 1 ST PP?"'

'Chopin's first performance in Paris was at the Salle Pleyel in 1832,' said Ralph excitedly. 'It's well documented that Chopin played the concerto in E minor, but what a lot of people don't know is that it was originally intended to be played in F minor. Hence: "E NOT F 1S T". "PP": *Performance* in *Paris*!'

Clarissa found herself nodding furiously, her eyes creased in the occupation of deep thought. 'You're right. You've got it!'

She felt exhilaration surge through her like an ocean wave, but when she turned to smile at Ralph, she found him staring intensely out of the window, a worried expression on his face.

'Ralph?'

'I hate to be the bearer of bad news, Clarissa, but I'm pretty sure we're being followed,' he said grimly.

'*Est-ce l'argent* BMW?' said the taxi driver, unexpectedly.

'What did he say?' asked Clarissa.

'He said: "Is it the silver BMW?"'

Ralph leaned forward in his seat and addressed the driver. 'No. It's the taxi behind the BMW. Do you think you can lose him, my friend?'

'*Pas de soucis, mon ami! Dites à la dame de bien tenir*!'

'Did he say he could?' asked Clarissa.

'I'm surprised you don't speak French!' said Ralph. 'You're an air hostess for God's sake!'

'Are you going to interpret for me or not?'

'He said: "Tell the lady to hold on tight,"' said Ralph, smiling with his eyes, adding in a low voice: 'preferably to the handsome young man sitting beside her.'

Clarissa flashed him a look.

7

The French taxi driver suddenly put his foot down and switched lanes. Clarissa strained to catch a glimpse of the figure residing in the cab behind them, but all she could see was the man at the wheel (young, with glasses and short brown hair), his passenger on the backseat heavily concealed.

As they hurtled towards Paris, weaving in and out of the traffic, Ralph's fears appeared to be confirmed as the taxi behind them replicated their trajectory.

'I could let him overtake us?' said the driver, helpfully.

'No, keep going!' said Clarissa. 'It would slow us down too much.'

The road consisted of four lanes, but two additional roads flanked theirs (one on either side) also streaming with four lanes, resulting in a tumultuous concentration of no less than twelve rows of vehicles.

With so many cars surrounding them, Clarissa looked to the periphery of her vision to find something else to focus on, but found only fields (save the odd warehouse). Occasionally a pylon, resembling a gigantic sewing needle stabbed the land, a monstrous triangular hole positioned at its head. Clarissa visualised a long length of red thread joining these needles together as they sped past them.

After ten minutes of high speed, Ralph said: 'Do you know who's tailing us?'

Clarissa shook her head. 'I can't see them properly.'

'But you have an idea who it is?'

'…Yes,' she said eventually. 'There was a passenger on the plane. He told me I'd be watched as soon as I got to France.'

'And you didn't think to mention this before?'

'It sort of escaped my attention, due to your little "surprise".'

'You should have let me text you,' Ralph ventured.

'You should have *called* me!'

'So you've been followed from London? Jesus, Clarissa! This manuscript must be something! And where did you say your boyfriend was again?'

Silence.

'I didn't.'

The car changed lanes on full throttle.

'Clarissa?'

'Charlie's being…held.'

'Held?'

Ralph produced a sort of forced smile as the taxi driver regarded him in his interior mirror. He lowered his voice: 'What do you mean he's being held? Who's holding him for God's sake?'

Clarissa grew distressed. 'Look, I really don't know! I can only presume it's somebody after the manuscript.'

Ralph shook his head in disbelief. He looked worried. 'These people, are they dangerous?'

Clarissa just sighed and continued to stare out of the window.

'Please Clarissa, I need to know what sort of company we're keeping here? I mean, I'm up for an adventure and everything, but they're not going to start pulling out revolvers and taking aim at us are they?'

Unable to rescind such a possibility due to the presence of the Beretta – now hidden safely inside the guts of her disemboweled piano – Clarissa flashed Ralph a supplicating look.

'I'm more than a little concerned that you're not answering me here,' said Ralph pensively.

'We're not in America,' said Clarissa, bracing herself as the car shifted its position again.

She finished watching a pink warehouse float past them on the horizon before she spoke: 'I don't know *what* they're capable of, exactly.' She looked at Ralph, her green eyes fearful. 'All I know is that they're so hungry for this manuscript, they've trashed my flat and cut up my car just to get their hands on it, and now I've got two parties following me in case I try to retrieve it from somewhere!'

Ralph stared at her, shocked. Then a short, sharp note accompanied by a buzz took them both by surprise and Clarissa watched Ralph pull out his phone and glance at the text he'd just received. He produced no expression.

'What do you mean by *two* parties?' he said, sliding the phone back into his jacket pocket.

'Well, there's the group holding Charlie,' said Clarissa taking another surreptitious glance at the passing traffic, 'but it looks like the manuscript is being sought by yet another group led by a man called Roland Steed, who just happened to be aboard the plane I've just crewed. I tried telling him that Charlie and I had broken up, but he refused to believe me!'

'Wait a minute, you and Charlie have broken up?'

'Yes...I mean, no! Charlie staged finishing our relationship to try and keep them away from me, but so far his plan hasn't worked.'

Ralph looked confused. 'So, your fella finishes with you, then you get a message from him asking you to follow the Dead Drop trail he's planted?'

She flashed him a sidelong glance. 'Yes.'

Ralph was silent for a minute, then he said: 'This manuscript. What do you know about it?'

'Only that it's by Chopin.'

'Mm.' She watched him push back his hair and look thoughtful. 'It must be worth a small fortune, going by the amount of people trying to get their hands on it. I wonder what it is.'

The taxi driver slowed the car to within the speed limit. 'I think I have lost him, Monsieur!'

Ralph smiled at Clarissa, who just nodded tenuously and reached for her bag.

Ralph thanked the driver in French, before turning back to Clarissa, who was hurriedly scrolling through her mobile.

'What are you doing? Are you calling someone?' he asked.

'No. I'm texting my friend,' she said, frantically tapping the glass of her smartphone. 'I need to let her know I'm all right. When I heard you playing, I sort of abandoned her.'

She typed: *"Sorry to disappear on you, hon. I'm ok. I've got myself in a spot of bother. I'll explain everything later. xx"* and sent the message to Donna.

'I interrupted something with your friend,' said Ralph. 'I'm sorry.'

'No, really, it's fine. You needn't apologise. You solved the clue. I can't believe I didn't twig that '32' was a year!' she said crossly, more to herself than to Ralph. 'Incidentally, did you know that it was also the year George Sand published her first novel?'

'"Lélia"?' said Ralph.

'"Indiana,"' said Clarissa.

'That's the one. So it was a significant year for both of them,' Ralph remarked. 'Chopin's first recital in Paris. Sand's first book. The year they both emerged as artists within Parisian society. When did they begin their affair?'

Clarissa's phone pinged. It was a text back from Donna. She opened it. The screen simply displayed an exclamation mark followed by three question marks.

Her eyes jumped from her phone to Ralph. 'Sorry. Now, let me see, Chopin and Sand's affair? 1835 or '36, I think.'

Ralph nodded. 'Sounds about right. A couple of years before their Majorca trip. The man was a genius! He didn't deserve the suffering he endured there. Fate certainly dealt him a cruel hand!'

Clarissa agreed avidly. Chopin's famous Majorca trip had always fascinated her. From the accounts she'd read, the general vibe seemed to suggest that he'd been turned away from all the hotels on the island because of his Tuberculosis. This, in turn, had forced him to take refuge in a Carthusian monastery in Valldemossa where he ended up writing the majority of the Preludes.

Clarissa adjusted her position on the back seat of the cab. 'Makes you wonder if the Preludes would be the work of such a genius if Chopin hadn't been so ill? He was compelled partly *by* his suffering, don't you think?'

Ralph pulled a face to show he was impressed by her thinking, then frowned. 'Pain *is* a powerful force, it's true,' he agreed. 'But, you know, some say Chopin was awarded his genius status at the age of seven when he first started composing his own symphonies – long before he was seriously ill – so it might not have made that much of a difference.'

'In this case, I disagree' said Clarissa, adjusting her gaze momentarily to take in the landscape, which was suddenly growing wide and flat as they had lost one of the adjacent roads. She looked at Ralph. 'Chopin was so ill in Majorca he could barely take the air into his lungs to breathe! A doctor at the time told him his death would be imminent. The Preludes were a direct expression of his pain and frustration!'

Ralph was looking at her like she'd just slapped him.

'What is it? Are you okay?' she asked.

'Creative expression is the best way to alleviate pain,' he said with unexpected emotion. 'You give it up, the pain only remains inside you.'

Clarissa tried to look as though these words hadn't sent a chill straight through her.

As they approached Paris, the graffiti began to appear. French words in bright greens and pinks marking the territory, turning walls and bridges into art.

They drove on in silence watching the scenery unfurl around them, all three of them intermittently checking for any sign of the taxi that had been following them; relieved of its continued absence.

As the architecture got grander, the street art diminished, giving way to majestic cream buildings with decorative iron embellishments, retail outlets dominating their base layers and cafés with outdoor seating springing up at intervals.

Clarissa followed the long balconies with tired eyes, their linear neatness making her conjure up Balzac's descriptions of Louis-Phillippe's Paris.

'Did you know that Chopin didn't dedicate even *one* piece of music to Sand?' said Clarissa pressing her head onto the glass of the window.

'Maybe not officially,' said Ralph. 'But I'd be very surprised if he didn't write *something* for her, he was in love with the woman, for God's sake!'

'How did you pay for your trip to France, Ralph? Did you busk?' said Clarissa suddenly, stretching and adjusting her gaze to the road ahead without looking at him. It was something that had been bothering her more and more since they had left the airport: how Ralph could afford to travel to France *and* pay for their taxi when he was desperately trying to manage Morgan's debt. It didn't make any sense. 'You must have spent a fair bit of money on your flight? Slim and Silas will be livid.'

'Well, Slim and Silas can fuck off!' said Ralph.

Clarissa smiled. 'You didn't answer my question.'

'Busking can bring in quite a bit of money on a good day, you know! You could pretty much live by it. Have you ever tried?'

'*Me*? You must be joking!'

'You're nothing but a snob!' said Ralph, smiling with his eyes, inviting her to contradict him.

The driver's radio suddenly bleeped and a French female voice said something inaudible. As the driver responded, Clarissa looked at her watch. 'We should be there soon.'

When the road sign confirmed their arrival at rue Cadet, Ralph unsnapped his belt and leant across to speak to the driver.

'Can you pull in here?' he said, realising that rue Cadet was a narrow pedestrian road, barely wide enough for a single car.

'Can you wait?' asked Clarissa. 'We'll only be five minutes!' The driver nodded in the affirmative and said something in French.

'*Merci, mon ami*!' said Ralph, placing a stack of notes in the driver's gnarled hands.

Clarissa grabbed her case and they leapt from the car. Ralph was trying to ascertain how close they were to number '9'.

'Come on!' he shouted. 'I don't think it's that far!'

This time Ralph was the one ahead. He ran so easily in his trainers, unencumbered by his piano, that Clarissa kept shouting at him to slow down.

Passing a pharmacy on a corner, they encountered a large café with street tables. Clarissa saw a copy of *Le Monde* snapping at the edges while a middle-aged couple re-arranged their breakfast in the breeze, the tantalising scent of coffee and warm croissants filling her nostrils as they hurried past.

A large hotel came shortly afterwards, then two rival opticians, then a bakery. Finally, they passed a butchers followed by a greengrocers, the smell of blood mixing with tropical fruit.

Counting out the little white numbers set in their blue squares, they came upon it suddenly. Number 9.

The plaque was positioned above an archway – a car parked snugly in its cavity – sandwiched between a bookshop and a café.

'Incidentally, the motion photographer Eadweard Muybridge had a connection with this address during the 1860s,' said Ralph. 'He's the man who proved that all four of a horse's hooves left the ground when the animal galloped.'

'Oh, yes?' said Clarissa. 'I know the photos. That's a bit of a coincidence.'

The pavement began to get peppered with rain. A few lone people were walking through. Only one couple occupied a table at the café next door. Clarissa eyed them suspiciously. They were in their late twenties, loquacious, sucking frantically on cigarettes and sipping coffee. The man was blond, with a thin face and unsmiling eyes. The woman: mixed race, pretty and well-dressed. Their conversation was growing aggressive.

'Can you hear what they're saying?' Clarissa whispered, reaching for Ralph's arm. 'Should we be concerned about them? We can't really look for the Drop properly with *them* there.'

Ralph pretended to do something on his phone while he listened to them. Then he bent in so close to her ear, she felt his lips touch her skin: 'She's angry because he's forgotten to take her mother something. But he's saying that her mother told him not to come so early. By the way, don't look now, but the Drop is in the kerb beside the woman's bag. Take a seat on the table next to them and I'll get us some coffees.'

Clarissa walked over to the small circular table beside the couple and proceeded to sit down on one of the wicker chairs tucked underneath it. Their animated conversation stopped briefly as she seated herself, but then resumed again when Clarissa took out her phone from her case.

Anxiously, Clarissa glanced at her watch. She was worried how long they would have to stay there; they had so little time. She took care to avoid looking directly at the couple's faces but secretly registered how much coffee they had consumed. The man had drunk half a cup. The woman had barely touched hers. The rain was increasing slowly.

When Ralph emerged from the café, Clarissa flashed him a frustrated glance and shrugged her shoulders.

He smiled at her briefly, placing two espressos on their table and sat down. A thin, grey canopy sheltered them from the rain falling gently above their heads.

'The driver will go without us if we don't return soon,' whispered Clarissa. 'What are we going to do?'

'Just leave it to me,' said Ralph confidently. '*Ah, excusez-moi, Mademoiselle. Et Monsieur*!'

Oh, God, he's speaking to them in French, thought Clarissa, trying to look like she knew what he was saying, wishing that she had paid more attention to the subject at school.

At first, the two smokers just stared at him blankly while he talked. Then they started contributing to the conversation with some interest. But just as the couple's austere expressions were beginning to lift, giving Clarissa a flicker of hope, the woman began to shrug and shake her head most aggressively, indicating that he'd blown it.

Then something unexpected happened. Ralph issued a sentence and without warning, the couple burst into uncontrollable laughter and began to smile at Clarissa most avidly – and a bit disturbingly if she thought too deeply about it – as if she were somehow playing a bigger part in this charade than she'd realised. Then they got up and left. Just like that.

Now, until that moment, Ralph's fluency in the French language hadn't really made that much of an impression on Clarissa, but after she'd watched him charm these two strangers into doing exactly what he'd needed them to do, she realised that he had, in fact, taken her breath away. Somehow, he'd managed to completely transform their mood, and he hadn't even used a piano to do it!

'What on earth did you say to them?' exploded Clarissa, once the couple had disappeared from sight.

'I'll tell you later. You need to download the Drop,' said Ralph impatiently, indicating the kerb with his eyes.

Clarissa nodded and removed her laptop from her case. She glanced around before bending down, but she was quite sure that there was no one observing them now. Her eyes were drawn to the little rubber buffer in the kerb.

She removed the protective shield and attached her laptop to the metal tip of the USB stick beneath it, the rain gently tapping the canopy above her head as she did so. Then as before, once she had transferred all its data to her device, she deleted its contents. She felt relief engulf her.

'It's done. Come on!' she said, slapping the lid of her laptop down definitively. 'Before the taxi leaves without us!'

As they ran out into the rain, Ralph removed his jacket and held it over them. 'Grab onto me!' he cried. 'We'll be able to move faster!'

Clarissa felt the warmth of Ralph's arm as he slipped it around her back, her skin reacting to the contact in a way she had not been expecting. As they ran, they both began to smile. This quickly turned to laughter as their taxi came into view, but stopped rather abruptly when they saw the woman leaning against it, waiting for them.

'Jesus!' Ralph cried, immediately disentangling himself from Clarissa. He stared at the woman distrustfully. In her skinny torn jeans, cropped top and tight biker's jacket, she wore the uniform of the youth, giving off the cocky self-assured stance of an eighteen-year-old student defying her parents. She was a redhead, tall and lithe. And in possession of the perfect dancer's physique, thought Clarissa.

'Well, isn't *this* cosy!' the stranger thundered, flicking back her wet hair, her eyes gleaming. 'I take it this is the *real* reason for your sudden change of heart about consenting to play in the production, despite Richard hounding you for months to join us!'

'Morgan, this is *not* what it looks like!' cried Ralph defensively.

'Well, I've got to hand it to you Ralph, you didn't actually *lie* to me, I'll give you that. But when you said you'd decided to accompany me to Paris to perform in the show because it would be "romantic" and "exciting", I was sort of under the impression you were referring to *me*!'

Morgan glared at Clarissa with disgust. 'Morgan Winterson. Ralph's *girlfriend.* I don't think we've met.'

'Hi. I'm sorry, but I need to get into that taxi,' said Clarissa with a detached air. 'Please stand aside and let me pass.'

As if on cue, the driver who had not long started up his engine, began to rev it furiously.

Ignoring them all, the redhead began to take in Clarissa's uniform. 'What *is* she? She looks like a flight attendant.'

Clarissa jumped as the taxi driver suddenly sounded his horn and shouted something in French at them out of the window.

'Look, please! If you would be so kind as to move out of the way, I really need to get in that cab!' cried Clarissa.

'Let her get into the car, Morgan,' said Ralph. 'I *swear* I'm not cheating on you! I can explain. Let Clarissa go, and we can go somewhere quiet and talk.'

Morgan looked defiantly at Clarissa. Brazenly, she poked an admonitory finger into her face. 'I want her to explain "this" to me! What business do you have with my boyfriend, *Clarissa*?'

'For God's sake, Morgan! You're acting like a bloody eejit! I was showing Clarissa where a building was, there was no more to it than that!'

Suddenly the taxi started to move. Morgan swore, and jumped away from the car. It was then that Clarissa noticed that another car had been forcing it out of the way. Clarissa ran to catch up with her cab. To her relief, the driver stopped and allowed her to climb inside.

As she pulled away, Clarissa looked at Ralph through the taxi's rain-splattered glass. Incapacitated, he stared back at her ruefully, ignoring the tearful Morgan, who was caught up in a paroxysm of silent screaming by the roadside. Clarissa watched him lift his hand in a valedictory wave. She mirrored his gesture from the cab. He smiled.

Once the taxi was safely caught up in a stream of moving traffic, Clarissa took out her laptop and opened the file she'd just downloaded.

The clue had been typed in a larger font than before – *in order to command more attention perhaps?* And its position, in the centre of the white screen, seemed to evoke in her what she could only describe as "a sense of vulnerability."

Stick No.4: 48.J.S.48.D.S.London

8

Two days and six flights later, Clarissa awoke on the morning of Monday 18th March on her day off (the first of three), exhausted and full of a cold.

She indulged in a long bath, sipped hot honey and lemon from her favourite mug, and called her parents for one of their customary chats. Tucked away in their country estate in Oxfordshire, she saw her mother and father less than three times a year, but still tried to maintain a weekly communication with them by phone, like any good daughter should. Her mother had suffered from anxiety and depression for many years and was heavily medicated for it. Due to this, Clarissa found her difficult to be around.

Clarissa told them nothing of her turbulent week, as her mother was psyching herself up for a hip operation at the end of the month and her father was having a bad time with his angina, so she decided to stick with the pretence that everything was carrying on in very much the same way as it had been before.

Thankfully, in some ways it was. For example, she still had her job. Needless to say, her frantic taxi race to return to Charles de Gaulle in time to meet and greet the passengers on her 10:55 a.m. flight to Stansted, had resulted in success. She could also still call Donna her best friend, although persuading her to join her for a bite to eat after their shift on Friday had not been easy. Once she'd agreed however, Clarissa had gone on to achieve its primary objective: to obtain the flight attendant's forgiveness for deserting her at the airport, and explain everything that had really happened regarding Charlie. Donna had been shocked of course, but had listened attentively. She'd also been relieved to talk about her pregnancy and her problems with Woody. Clarissa had tried to remain impartial throughout this unburdening, as it was still unclear whether or not her friend would keep the baby, but secretly she hoped that Donna would go ahead and have the child as she thought in this case, it was the right thing to do.

Two days had passed since their meal. It was enough time for Clarissa to start worrying about how her friend was faring. Subsequently, she found herself climbing slowly onto her blue sofa with her phone, making herself available in case Donna needed to talk to her again. (The reason she'd climbed slowly, was to ensure that she didn't disturb the line of wood glue she'd applied to the structure some twenty-four hours earlier in order to seal the thing back together; and it did seem to be working, so far anyway).

When Donna didn't ring, Clarissa reached for her laptop. She was aware that she had to make some more progress on solving the fourth Dead Drop clue, but before she knew what she was doing, she caught herself logging onto Instagram. She found that social media got you like that sometimes, emitting in her a slow but insistent impulse to check on her accounts at the most inappropriate times.

She stared at her profile picture. It was as if the photo depicted someone else, not her. There she was standing on Brighton Pier: happy, in love. Charlie had just thrown his arms around her waist, his face was partially buried in her hair. She was smiling with teeth, looking directly into her smartphone camera, a loose, blonde tendril sticking indiscriminately to her cheek.

Her last post on the site had been a photo she'd taken of a sunset behind the Queen's Walk lampposts bordering the River Thames, snapped on the 2nd March (eight days before Charlie had disappeared). Reluctantly, she scrolled through the other photos taken that evening. Charlie had obscured himself from the majority of them, but she'd managed to get one of him, on the Millennium Bridge. He was staring directly into the camera; he looked tense. She remembered how he'd protested: *"For God's sake! Don't take another one of me!"*

This display of disapprobation seemed to make sense, only now. He must have thought there'd be little point in her taking the shot when he'd be terminating their relationship in a matter of days. She wondered how much progress he'd made with the Dead Drop clues at the time the photo was taken, and how far he'd got with the colossal task of trying to bury them across the two cities.

Clarissa exited her Instagram account and logged into Twitter. Her last Tweet had been a response to a member of the Association of Flight Attendants who'd expressed grave concerns about aircraft emissions (a subject close to Clarissa's heart). Clarissa had posted an outline of the intentions of the International Civil Aviation Organization regarding their carbon offsetting reduction scheme. This had, in turn, generated a few remarks from her fellow cabin crew members.

After she'd taken a few minutes to read through these, she found herself navigating to the Royal Academy of Music's Twitter page, scrolling the feed for proof of the busker's identity. She was soon satisfied. *"Don't miss the performances of four of our most gifted piano students as they play Chopin on Tuesday 12th March."* Four portraits followed, one of them Ralph's; his face unmistakable, his name printed clearly beneath it.

Then she began to search for other internet references under the name: "Ralph Valero" and an Instagram account surfaced. Glimpsing at the profile picture: a black and white photo of four piano keys, she had no reason to suspect the account belonged to someone else.

'Alexa,' she said. 'Play Chopin's Etude, Opus 10, Number 4.'

The melody began, blasting at whirlwind speed through her flat, taking her back to Ralph's superb performance at Charles de Gaulle Airport. She smiled at the memory while she amused herself reading his feed. His posts made comments on classical composers, literature and art. He appeared to follow every classical music association she could think of. His opinions were interesting, intelligent and witty. She had been relieved to find no photos of Morgan.

When the Etude stopped, she found that she had little appetite for any more music and continued scrolling through the internet in silence.

Next, she called up Charlie Davenport's Instagram account, expecting to find it unchanged from when she'd last viewed it three days before they'd split up, shocked to find that this wasn't the case.

The first thing she noticed was that he'd changed his profile picture. The one she'd grown accustomed to (depicting the two of them nestled snugly on his expensive St. Albans' sofa) had been replaced by a shot of him, alone. Her absence, although explainable under the circumstances, stung her. In addition to this, four new photos had been added on the morning of Sunday 10th March (eleven hours before he'd disappeared). All of them had been taken at a party the night before at rather a grand house. There were two shots of a Rococo chair with some strobe lighting falling across it. In another, a white marble sculpture – not unlike

Michelangelo's David – had been debased by a cluster of partially filled drinking glasses at the statue's feet. The fourth image showed a grand white-tiled staircase furcating beneath a crystal chandelier – this could easily have been a common stock photo, if it hadn't been for the bottle of blue gin and Gucci handbag thrown onto the third step. These were typical of Charlie's photographs, merging the old with the new, the ordered with the haphazard; they were a sort of a preoccupation with him, and he'd take similar shots wherever he went. She was sure he would have had a good career as a photographer, if he hadn't followed whatever line of work he had chosen. But this party was news to her.

A few people had posted comments on the artistic qualities of the photos, but apart from these, there was nothing to suggest the party's location, or the identity of its host.

Clarissa typed: "Morgan Winterson" into her internet browser. Just *how* she had managed to locate both of them in Paris was still a mystery. And had she been the one in the BMW following them, all along? Or were there two cars on their tail? Clarissa had still not been able to work this out.

She had no problem finding social media accounts for the redheaded dancer. Clarissa discovered four, all sharing the same profile picture: a close up of Morgan's fully made-up face, her eyes large and glancing skywards like a demure little kitten. It looked as if she favoured her Instagram account though, as it was only here that Clarissa found evidence of her current show at the Théâtre du Ranelagh in Paris. As she scrolled through the photos, she noticed that the dancer had rejected some potentially interesting behind the scenes shots in favour of pure narcissism – her own face! Disappointingly, Morgan had chosen to document her time backstage through a series of selfies, in none of which did she smile. Her pictures occasionally depicted some of the cast and crew. Clarissa searched for a photo of Ralph. She found just one. He was staring at the floor, a shadow licking his cheek, a group of dancers adjusting their costumes in the background. He looked disinterested, detached and unaware of Morgan's presence. Clarissa realised that this was exactly the sort of image she'd been hoping to see.

Soon she found herself investigating another name: "Max Siskind". She was surprised to discover that the confident Geordie lass also possessed an open Instagram account. In her profile picture, a sultry-looking Max wore dark glasses and smiled tight-lipped. Her most recent photos proved very interesting as they appeared to have been taken at the same grand house as Charlie's. This was verified by a picture of a white staircase (from a different angle) but containing the same blue gin bottle and Gucci bag. Completely fascinated, Clarissa began to examine the rest of the party shots, hungrily searching for her boyfriend's image. Unlike Charlie's pictures, Max had favoured the wide-angled room shot, where gigantic be-jewelled chandeliers hung above partially shadowed faces.

It wasn't long before she spotted him.

He was off-centre and unaware that the photo was being taken, but there was no mistaking his grey suit and distinctive blue eyes. It was Charlie all right. He had his arm around a woman. He was smiling and she was nuzzling her head in his neck. The woman had long dark hair, a short black dress, and a hand on Charlie's thigh. As Clarissa slid through the rest of the images, another photo caught her eye. In this one, four friends were grouped together laughing, holding champagne glasses out to the camera, but Charlie and the woman were there in the background, kissing on the mouth. She zoomed in on them to be sure. But there was no doubt about it. It was Charlie.

She felt sick.

Clarissa closed the site and slammed down her laptop screen with shaky hands. The kiss had been captured on the day before he'd finished with her at the Hoops Inn. To cushion her pain, she recalled what Charlie had written in his first memory stick, the one that had been sewn into her love-heart keyring. She'd deleted the message (as instructed) but had remembered the exact words he'd used: *"I've left a trail that will make them think I've been unfaithful to you. I have not."*

Could this have been what he'd been referring to? Part of her wanted to believe that the shot had been staged. The Instagram feed could be viewed by anyone. Charlie's captors would have certainly seen it. But she had to admit, it looked *very* real to her. She wondered who the woman was.

Clarissa reached for Charlie's phone. He'd now acquired fourteen missed calls and seventeen unread text messages since his disappearance. So far, she'd failed to crack his pin, but she'd noted a list of her attempts and kept trying. She now suspected that at least some of these messages had come from this woman. She wondered if she should call Max to find out her identity.

Suddenly her phone rang.

Clarissa was so sure it was Donna, she swiped right to take the call without even looking at it.

'Hello.'

'Clarissa? It's Ralph.'

'Ralph….How's the show going?'

His Irish voice was upbeat and friendly: 'Good. Yeah. It's been okay….So did you make it back to the airport in time for your flight? I've been desperate to know.'

'I did, yes. Thanks.'

'I'm glad to hear it! Are you at work? Can you talk?'

'I'm on a day off. I'm at home. Are you still there? In Paris?'

'No. I'm back in London again….The show wasn't really for me.'

Clarissa was stunned.

'You quit a show at the Théâtre du Ranelagh after *two* days?' she exclaimed. 'I bet Morgan was livid! Did she come back with you?'

She froze, suddenly remembering that Ralph hadn't told her where they'd been performing.

'...You've researched the show?' he said.

Silence.

'Sorry. I sort of came upon it by accident on the internet.'

'There's no need to apologise. Look, I'll come clean with you, it was a way to get to Paris, so I took it. They paid for my flight. I had no intention of remaining in the production. And yes, Morgan's still there, thank God! And you needn't worry, I didn't tell her anything about the Dead Drops. Which begs me to question. Is there another one?'

Clarissa was still reeling from his confession. She could not believe that he'd gone to such extremes to help her. It made her feel strange, as if hundreds of tiny electrical impulses had shot through her in less than a second.

'Err.... Yes. There's another one,' she said, trying to sound as if what he'd just said had not affected her.

'And have you figured out the clue yet?'

'Not yet.'

'Do you want to hit me with it?'

'Are you sure Morgan would approve?'

'This has nothing to do with Morgan.'

Clarissa returned to her laptop and summoned the clue back on the screen. 'Sure. Are you ready?' She gave him the numbers and letters in sequence, taking care to insert the full stops as they appeared.

Another silence.

'Perhaps we can meet, in what? Four hours? There's some stuff I need to do first. Then we can go and find the Drop. This thing's become like a sort of addiction for me!'

'You make it sound like a game.'

'I –'

'It's not a game, Ralph.'

'I know it's not, but you could do with my help, right? Charlie hasn't exactly made the clues a piece of cake now has he?'

Clarissa found herself flinching with fresh pain at the mention of his name.

'No. I mean *yes*. Yes, I could do with your help,' she said hesitantly.

'Clarissa, are you all right?' said Ralph.

'Yes. Sorry. I've had a bit of an ear infection, but I'm getting over it now.'

The Royal Academy of Music sat majestically in front of her in the afternoon sun. As Clarissa approached the familiar Georgian building with its terracotta and white-bricked symmetrical façade, she couldn't help but pause to admire its arched entranceway with its beautiful black and gold ironmongery.

On entering the foyer of the oldest conservatoire in England, Clarissa realised that she was struggling to regenerate her former zest for solving Dead Drop clues. Her enthusiasm, she found, having undergone a sharp defection the moment she'd caught sight of Charlie with his lips pressed onto the mouth of the mysterious woman, was proving difficult to revive. This dreadful photograph forced her to conclude that she'd been mistaken all along about Charlie still having feelings for her. Perhaps he had just been using her to get the manuscript to a safe place?

And it was for this reason that she waited for Ralph with such anxiety. For she knew that she would be presenting a rather different version of herself to him now, not only physically – her tight jeans and leather jacket having been rescued from the back of her wardrobe and her blonde hair left down – but also mentally, as she had gone to meet him in London with her feelings for Charlie having changed rather dramatically.

Clarissa looked at the Royal Academy of Music's two reception desks, with their symmetrical wooden grids, glass tops, and integrated lights. She'd marvelled at these before when she'd been a student. Now, she was only aware of the fact that Ralph wasn't standing beside them, waiting for her as he'd promised.

She began to think about when she'd visited the place last. She recalled watching a Brahms' concert in the Duke's Hall nine years ago. She'd been in her first year at the Royal College, full of a sense of her own importance. Back then, she'd really believed she'd been destined for greater things. Correction; she *had* been destined for greater things. But she'd stopped it, because of what had happened to her. She'd cancelled her life. Forced to observe it from the outside, like she didn't belong in it at all.

She waited for twenty-five minutes. Then she found she could stand it no more. She had to get out of there before she exploded. She ran, in the direction of Regent's Park.

She found herself crying as she sped from the building. She cried for Charlie's absence and for his betrayal, but she also cried for the hole in her life that had once been filled by music.

When she came across a bridge, she stopped. She felt better. The effect of her tears had been cathartic. She was leaning over the balustrade staring blankly at the dank green water when she heard her name being called.

'CLARISSA!'

She turned to find Ralph jogging towards her and was taken aback. She'd no idea he'd even been there, behind her. He was wearing an orange and black striped jumper underneath a black high necked biker's jacket. Clarissa realised that she'd omitted to take in what he'd been wearing on previous occasions, but it must have been something dark and nondescript for this new image to arrest her senses in the way it did. He looked more bohemian. She approved. She watched him absorb the change in *her* appearance and smile, and she saw the relief in his eyes when she smiled back.

'Hey,' she said.

'Hey,' he said, gasping for breath. 'You move fast without your heels! Why did you run? Did you see someone hanging around?'

'No,' said Clarissa. 'Well, I don't think so, anyway.'

'I'm sorry I was late,' he said, eventually. '*Shit*! I should really exercise more. I got delayed after my recital. The bloody professor wouldn't stop talking!'

'It's fine,' she said.

'Are you okay?' he said, suddenly looking worried, and she remembered she'd been crying.

'Oh, I've had a cold,' she said dismissively, wiping her eyes with her hands.

'Aye, you said you'd had an ear infection. It can't have been easy flying,' he said, pressing his side hard underneath his jacket as if he were in pain.

'I imagine flying with morning sickness would be far worse,' she said absently. 'What's wrong, are you all right?'

'It's just a stitch. What do you mean? Who's flying with morning sickness?'

'My friend Donna,' she said.

'Ah,' he said, straightening himself up, unintentionally revealing a slither of naked torso.

Clarissa felt her cheeks flush red.

'What address did you get for the Drop?' she said, trying to avert her eyes from Ralph's body. 'I got 48 Dover Street.'

'Same,' said Ralph, his bare stomach becoming swathed in black and orange once again. 'So you didn't need my help in finding this one, after all!'

'We haven't found it yet,' said Clarissa. 'I've got the map ready on my phone. Looks like it's in Mayfair.'

'Okay' said Ralph. 'Lead on!'

'We need to take the Jubilee line south, to Green Park,' said Clarissa as they headed in the direction of Baker Street Tube.

'Do you want to talk through the clue as we go?' said Ralph, straining to be heard above the intense buzz of traffic on the Marylebone Road.

'Sure. You start,' said Clarissa, increasing her pace slightly. 'But we must hurry, it's coming up to rush hour, we don't want to get caught.'

'Right,' said Ralph. 'Okay, so this time the number "48" has been used twice. It denotes both a year *and* a house number. In 1848, Chopin lived at 48 Dover Street.'

'It was also rather significantly the year of the great French Revolution,' Clarissa chipped in – she'd been fascinated by this period of history at school, and had enjoyed researching an essay on the Second Republic overthrowing King Louis Philippe's rule.

'Aye,' said Ralph. 'Which is how Chopin came to be here in the first place. He'd fled France to escape to England, just like his king had done before him.'

'Didn't he spend a bit of time in Scotland as well?' she asked, suddenly remembering that Chopin had taught the wealthy Scottish aristocrat Jane Stirling to play the piano, many years after his affair with George Sand.

'Aye,' said Ralph, looking straight ahead of him as he walked. 'You're thinking of Jane Stirling, right?'

'Yes.' Clarissa was impressed that he knew about her; not many people did. 'I think it was probably Jane Stirling who introduced him to the cream of London Society,' she said. 'She could even have found him the place to live at 48 Dover Street.'

'I think you're probably right,' said Ralph. 'Chopin's final romantic liaison.'

'There's absolutely no proof of that!' countered Clarissa, flashing Ralph a quick glance as they crossed the road. 'Why is it that folks always assume that two people can't simply be "good friends" without talk of romance? Besides, Chopin was a very sick man by then, don't forget.'

Ralph smiled at her. 'Yes he was, but I'm going to have to disagree with you about his relationship with Jane Stirling,' he said. 'I think they were certainly more than just good friends! For a start, Chopin dedicated two Nocturnes to her, which is more than he ever did for George Sand. And secondly, she was the one he asked to take charge of his effects after his death. Your mysterious manuscript may even have started off in her hands! And in my experience, a heterosexual man and a heterosexual woman generally can't remain just "good friends". It's impossible! One would always end up desiring the other!'

Clarissa experienced a sharp physical jolt at his words.

'Hmm, possibly,' she said, trying to appear indifferent. 'But isn't it more likely that the manuscript didn't pass through her hands at all? I get the feeling that if she'd taken possession of it, it would have been virtually impossible for anyone to have stolen it in the first place!'

'Okay. I'll admit it, you have a point there,' said Ralph noticeably avoiding her eyes, but she was not remiss of the playful smile that had taken hold of his mouth.

When they reached Baker Street Tube Station, there were notably no buskers.

'Nobody's taken your slot,' she remarked.

'They will,' he said.

They descended the escalator in silence. Then Clarissa followed the overhead signs to find the Jubilee Southbound platform, leading Ralph through a maze of congested tunnels alongside hundreds of sweaty homeward-bound commuters.

The platform was warm, packed and dirty. Clarissa stared at the filthy silver tracks as they waited.

As their train came in, Ralph took her arm and they boarded it together, squeezing themselves into the packed carriage like sardines in a tin.

There was an awkward moment when the two of them grabbed the same part of the handrail; their fingers touching briefly, causing Clarissa to spring back and ostensibly arrange her laptop bag, allowing it to fall onto her front, where it lay between them like a shield. Then the doors bleeped and closed with a swish and a clunk and the train emitted a plaintive whine as it heaved away into the tunnel.

As Clarissa watched the bright platform disappear out of the window and dark smeary glass replace it, full of the distorted mirrored-images of its compressed passengers, the train seemed to squeal, like it was protesting to the mere weight of its load, and its repetitive chugging rhythm began.

Clarissa was aware of Ralph staring intently at her.

'I need to tell you something,' he said.

She looked at him questioningly.

'Back in Paris,' he said, 'when you sped away in that taxi, do you remember the car that was trying to force you out of the way?'

'I think so, yes,' replied Clarissa.

'Well, after you left, three men in suits got out of it. The first two, young. Then this old fella got out, grey hair, important looking –'

'Gold handkerchief in his breast pocket?' asked Clarissa, tentatively.

'Err…. Now that you come to mention it…yes! You know who I'm talking about?'

The carriage rattled suddenly and Clarissa felt her body collide with Ralph's. She adjusted her feet to brace herself better. *So, Steed had actually followed them himself!*

'His name's Roland Steed,' she said. 'I met him for the first time on Friday. He's got a younger brother called George apparently; perhaps he was one of the other men? Roland Steed was the guy I told you about, the one on the plane who said I'd be watched the second I set foot in France.'

'Jesus,' said Ralph. 'So he wasn't joking!'

'What did he do after I'd left?' asked Clarissa inquisitively.

'Not much. Just got back in the car and drove off. One of the men went with him, the other one stayed.'

The train squealed again. Clarissa caught a glimpse of the top of a woman's head behind a newspaper, a small flash of a pair of sunglasses, painted lips, dark hair. Then she realised that the middle-aged man sitting alongside this woman was staring rather lecherously in her direction and she was briefly shocked. A patch of light was glinting off his spectacles, and his chin, peppered with an uneven layer of grey stubble was wobbling to the motion of the carriage.

'Steed must have told one of the men to stay behind and follow you,' she whispered self-consciously.

Ralph nodded in affirmation. 'Aye. I didn't think too much of it at the time. But now I'm starting to think that's *exactly* what happened.'

The carriage seemed to be picking up speed. Clarissa could smell Ralph's neck: ginseng and musk. She could feel his breath beside her earlobe as he spoke: 'Clarissa, I've got to tell you something else. But before I tell you, you've got to promise me you won't freak out.'

'Go on,' she said, growing uncomfortable.

'You've got to promise me you won't freak out first.'

'Okay. I promise.'

'He's over there.'

'Who's over there?'

'The josser Steed sent to follow me in Paris. He's right over there, on our train.'

'*What?* Are you serious?' cried Clarissa, peering around suspiciously.

'Don't make it so obvious,' said Ralph.

'Sorry,' she said, turning back towards him.

'Behind you,' he whispered. 'Halfway down the carriage, next to the woman with the kid. Suit. Tan Briefcase. Brown hair. Reading the *Metro*.'

Clarissa turned around slowly. She saw the woman with her child. Then she saw the man in question. He was concentrating on his paper. He looked quite ordinary. He didn't look up.

'Are you sure that's him?'

The train made a noise like it was wailing.

'Aye,' said Ralph. 'I'm sure. Unfortunately for him, he's got a small scar under his left eye, shaped a bit like a fish. It gave him away.'

'What are we going to do?' said Clarissa, starting to panic. She was beginning to feel constrained by the train, oppressed by the heat, constricted by the surrounding bodies.

'What *can* we do?' said Ralph.

'Whatever we do, we can't let him see us download the Drop. He might grab the laptop and run off with it!'

'If that were to happen, I'd get it back off him, don't you worry. I could take him on!' exclaimed Ralph, a little too loudly.

As a result, Clarissa felt several pairs of eyes ensnare them with fresh interest. Inhibited by the attention, she bent in even closer to Ralph.

'For God's sake, keep your voice down. And please don't do anything like that, you could get hurt,' she whispered. 'He could be carrying a knife.'

'So could *I*, seeing as you put it like that!' said Ralph irascibly.

'And *are* you?' she retorted, horrified.

'Of course I'm not!'

'Well, at least that's something!'

When they approached Bond Street Station a few people got off. A few got on. This seemed to provide a brief respite from the tension, the doors producing a sound like a shot of exhaling breath. Clarissa considered dragging Ralph off the train there and then, but a second later the doors bleeped and sealed shut once more and she knew she'd missed her chance.

They started moving. Clarissa saw the man with the *Metro* glance up and stare directly at her.

'I can't stand this,' she said.

'You said you wouldn't freak out,' said Ralph.

'Well, I wasn't expecting you to say something like *that*. What are we going to do?' she repeated, more urgently this time, beginning to feel strangely like she was falling down a dark hole, the pain in her ears returning.

'Don't worry, I'm here,' said Ralph, using his best conciliatory tone.

The man with the wobbly chin was still leering at her. Roland Steed's spy's eyes were upon her. Everyone seemed to be staring in her direction; it was disquieting, suffocating.

'I can't breathe,' she said.

'You'll be all right.'

'No, really. I can't breathe! Everyone's looking at me. Why's everyone looking at me?'

'Hey, it's okay. You're hyperventilating, you need to focus on your breathing. Everyone's looking at you because you're a very beautiful woman. We're very nearly at our stop. You just need to concentrate on breathing slowly,' said Ralph gently, coaxing her. 'I'm right here. Concentrate on your breathing.'

Clarissa calmed herself down. She took a few deep breaths of what was mainly ginseng and musk. Then she realised that Ralph's hand was upon her shoulder, issuing a reassuring massage to her collarbone. She felt her panic subsiding.

'You okay?' he said.

She nodded, relieved that she seemed to be breathing normally again.

As the rhythm of the train started to slow, Ralph bent in towards her ear and said: 'Our stop's coming up. When we get off, I vote we run. Try and lose him. Do you feel you're up to it?'

9

It was their best option, to run, she knew that. Clarissa looked at Ralph. 'Let's do it,' she said. 'I'm okay now.'

'You sure?'

She nodded.

'Which way are we going when we leave the station?' he asked.

'Left,' she said. 'Then Dover Street is the second road on the left. It's literally two-minutes away.'

Ralph gestured a small response to this with his eyes.

Their train continued to slow.

'He's making his way towards the other exit,' said Ralph, as a multitude of blue and red "Green Park" signs began to spin furiously outside the windows.

Their train ground to a halt. The doors bleeped and slid apart. They got off.

At first, Clarissa and Ralph were forced to assume the pace of the crowd as they moved along the platform tediously, sluggishly, sandwiched between unknown bodies, helplessly looking for the correct exit.

'Clarissa,' Ralph instructed, 'as soon as we divert into the tunnel, we run. But don't turn around; don't look at him. Are you ready?'

'I'm ready,' she said, cutting Ralph an anxious glance.

Clarissa peered at the lit exit sign. She could hear the sound of her own breath. She could feel the heat coming off Ralph's body.

As they entered the tunnel she felt Ralph's fingers interlock with her own – a boldness she found both shocking and thrilling. For a moment, her hand remained inanimate, unresponsive, as if she were unsure how to react to him, then she tightened her grip and the two of them ran for all they were worth.

They skirted the narrow passage into the corridor. They raced up the left-hand side of the long ascending escalator with their hands still entwined, Ralph leading the way. They released hands briefly in order to swipe themselves through the ticket barriers, but joined them again on the other side, naturally, comfortably.

When they reached the road, they took a sharp left and ran past Regent's Park along Piccadilly. They crossed Berkeley Street and ran parallel to the Ritz hotel. Dover Street appeared shortly afterwards. There were no alleys to sneak down and no passages to duck into. There was a café on both corners, the Mayfair Club was on their left, then number "48" appeared in large brown letters on the side of the building next to it. Tacitly, they both acknowledged it, before crossing the road to the Clarence pub opposite. Ralph led Clarissa straight through its black and gold framed doors.

They only released hands on entering the pub, where they stood recovering their breath, looking through the glass in the doors for their pursuer.

The pub was surprisingly large and old and smelt of sweet ale and warm pies. The wooden floor had a shelf running along its left side, lined with stools, and five or six tables to the right, all occupied. The place was heaving. Deeper inside the premises, a long wooden bar curved around the corner upon a floor of black and white tiles. There were more tables at the back, most of them taken. People were talking animatedly, drinking, laughing, shouting, eating. Fast paced music was thumping away in the background.

Ralph laughed unexpectedly, his face shiny with sweat, the adrenalin still pumping through his swollen veins. 'That was mad!' he said, gasping for breath. 'Are you all right?'

'Yeah,' she said, her throat burning suddenly. 'I'm fine.'

'It had to be blink-182, didn't it!' he said recognising the band playing on the loud speakers, as if the song had been arranged just for them.

'You like blink-182?' she asked.

'Love them!' Ralph shouted over the din of voices. 'Have you heard "Adam's Song"? It's one of my all-time favourites!'

'Sure.' She smiled at his enthusiasm. She remembered getting into the band herself at college. She wiped the sweat from her face with a tissue. 'I need some water.'

'Well, we're in the right place! I think we should lie low in here for a while. Get a drink, see if our man turns up,' said Ralph. He was buzzing; still high from his endorphin rush due to the run. 'What do you think?'

'Fine with me,' said Clarissa, divesting herself of her jacket. 'Do you think there's a chance he could still be hanging around outside?'

'I doubt it. We did that pretty quickly. I'd be surprised if he saw us come in here.'

Together, they found themselves making their way through the throng towards the bar for temporary respite.

When Ralph asked for two bottles of water, he suggested they eat something at the same time to refuel themselves. Clarissa agreed. Ralph indicated an emptying table through the heaving mass of bodies, so Clarissa went off to claim it, giving him instructions to choose something from the menu on her behalf.

The pub was purring with the reassuring sound of idle chatter. It was soothing, calming. It was the sort of atmosphere she was reluctant to leave. She concluded that if Ralph had been right and they'd lost Fish Scar back at the Tube, what difference would half an hour make to their retrieval of the fourth Drop? She suddenly wished she'd asked Ralph to fetch her a beverage with alcohol in it.

Ralph appeared at her table with two beers as if he'd read her mind, announcing with a grin that their escape had to be: "a cause for celebration if ever there was one!". She smiled gratefully, thinking about the way he'd averted her panic attack on the train. She certainly owed him. How Charlie had expected her to follow this trail on her own was beyond her comprehension!

As they consumed pie and chips and sipped frothy beer from thistle glasses, Clarissa felt herself relax into the moment. She asked Ralph about his life.

He told her that he was from Dublin, that his parents were Irish, that his paternal grandfather was Spanish. Apparently his grandfather – a dedicated pianist himself – had been the driving force behind Ralph's piano lessons. Sadly, he'd died when Ralph was fourteen, so he'd not seen him reach his full potential.

'You ever played in a rock band?' she asked him.

'Sure, who hasn't?'

She recalled her own attempts at this at seventeen and smiled. For her, having been discouraged by her parents using gentle persuasion, she accepted that rock music wasn't her calling, but for him – with *his* talent and looks – she was quite sure he would succeed easily in the sector; he had the right fit. 'So why classical?' she was interested to know.

Ralph hesitated. 'I felt I owed it to my grandfather,' he said. 'I needed to carry on his legacy. I knew it was down to me to ensure that the Valero name lived on in the classical world. His DNA was in my blood. How could I ignore that?'

Clarissa held his gaze, but said nothing. She had never heard anyone speak with so much loyalty to family.

'He would have been proud of you,' she said earnestly.

Ralph nodded, a faraway look in his eye.

When they had finished eating, Ralph showed her a silver signet ring he carried around with him for good luck. He told her that it had once belonged to his grandfather. 'I never perform on a stage without it.'

Clarissa allowed him to drop the ring into her palm. She traced the engraved initials with her finger. 'A.V.,' she read.

'Álvaro Valero,' he said. '"An exceptional pianist for a man with such enormous hands!" That's what my ma' used to say, anyway.' He laughed. 'The ring's too big for me, really. I have to wear it on my middle finger. But it makes me feel close to him all the same.'

Clarissa handed him the ring back, touched.

'So, what led Álvaro to Ireland?' she asked.

'Love,' said Ralph, his eyes glistening with affection. 'Or my nan, to be more precise. Aileen O'Connor. She's passed on too now. She was an artist from Dublin. She went over to see La

Sagrada Familia – you know the Gaudí cathedral? – that's where she met him. He followed her back to Ireland.'

'Nice story,' she remarked, as Ralph tucked the ring back into his pocket.

'So why didn't you go to the Royal Irish Academy?' Clarissa asked, confused. 'Surely that would have been a closer option for you?'

'Because I wanted to go across the water,' said Ralph dreamily. 'See what all this fuss was about with a place called "London". Plus I wanted to escape my folks for a wee bit, you must know what I'm talking about?'

'And they were okay about that, were they?'

'Not at first. When I left school, my oul fella was dead set against me living anywhere outside The Pale, but they came around. My brother Johnnie helped them see sense.'

'You're close to your brother?'

'Not especially. I think he only did it because I said he could have my room!'

Clarissa smiled, absently caressing her cold glass of beer with her fingertips.

'Now, I want to know about you,' said Ralph eagerly. 'What can you tell me about yourself?'

'Well, my surname: "Belmonte" has Portuguese origins,' she offered.

'Really?' Ralph's eyes lit up with interest.

'But it was from quite far back, several generations. We have no connections abroad anymore,' said Clarissa, sadly, wishing that she could match Ralph's story with something equally as romantic. 'My parents live in Oxfordshire. I'm an only child. I'm as uninteresting as they come.'

'When did you start playing the piano?'

'When I was about five, I suppose,' said Clarissa. 'Mum and Dad both played. We always had a piano in the corner of our dining room. When I got into the Royal College, they were over the moon.'

'Then they must have been equally as devastated when you gave it all up!'

'But I haven't given it all up!' cried Clarissa. 'I still have a piano in my home – I bought a ground floor garden flat just to accommodate it – I just don't play...*publicly* anymore. That's all!'

'But you must have played publicly at the Royal College. It's a pre-requisite to admission,' said Ralph. 'So what's changed?'

Clarissa was horrified by his temerity.

'Look, Ralph. I know you're only trying to help, but I really don't want to talk about it.' She felt her grip on her beer glass tighten.

'It's got something to do with why you ran from the Academy today, hasn't it? Why you were upset? What is it you're running from Clarissa?'

'Ralph –'

'I just think you would feel a whole lot better if you –'

Suddenly Clarissa lost her grip on her glass and it fell, releasing its amber liquid with unexpected force. The resulting pool of beer crawled quickly across the table. Clarissa righted her glass and ensured her laptop wasn't in its trajectory.

'Ralph…. Perhaps, when I get to know you better, I'll tell you about…what happened,' she said irritably, reaching for her used serviette and mopping up the mess. 'But right now, I don't wish to discuss it.'

'I'm sorry,' said Ralph. 'I didn't mean to upset you. I just want you to know that when you're ready to tell me, I'm here for you, okay?'

He walked off to the bar.

When he returned, he produced a red and blue striped towel and began to wipe their table down silently.

'Listen, Ralph, I really appreciate your kindness,' said Clarissa. 'But I think we ought to go outside now and look for the Drop.'

He stood up. 'Grand idea,' he said smiling at her, but she picked up on the sulky undercurrent to his demeanor when he suddenly waltzed over to the exit without her.

Now that the serene atmosphere was broken, Clarissa was glad to leave the pub. Had she been on the verge of capitulation? The answer is undoubtedly no, but she *had* been touched by

Ralph's efforts to uncover her reasons for failing to pursue her career as a concert pianist. And try as she might, she couldn't recall Charlie probing for an explanation with anything like the same degree of tenacity.

Clarissa put her jacket back on and threw her laptop bag over her shoulder.

Ralph was waiting for her by the door.

Outside, the sky had started to darken and the street was busy. She thought it looked like rain.

They crossed the road.

'Well, here we are. Number 48,' said Ralph. 'Right next door to a strip club. I wonder what Chopin would have made of that! The actual building Chopin stayed in has long since been demolished of course. This one is used as an office space rental agency, apparently.'

They both began to search for the Drop.

Clarissa saw the black buffer sticking out of the kerb first. It was virtually identical to the one they'd discovered outside 64 Bryanston Square. She signalled it out to Ralph implicitly with her eyes and he nodded. Its position between two cars awarded her the privacy she needed.

'You do the business. I'll keep watch,' said Ralph. 'We're getting good at this don't you think?'

Clarissa removed the rubber barrier and proceeded to attach her laptop to the small rectangle of metal jutting from the kerb.

She pressed the keys softly to download the Drop, but she soon began to realise, with some unease, that nothing was happening.

'There's something wrong,' she said. 'It looks like the stick's been wiped.'

'Wiped? But I'm pretty sure we lost the man who was following us!' said Ralph. 'Have you attached it properly?'

'Of course. The stick's been detected, there's just nothing on it!'

'Here, give me a lash,' said Ralph, bending down.

She handed him the laptop and watched him replicate her actions.

'I'm right, aren't I?' she said.

'Aye' admitted Ralph. 'It's banjaxed, to be sure!'

'Great. So what do we do now?' said Clarissa, the disappointment engulfing her. 'Without this Drop, the trail to get to the others is broken!'

At that moment Charlie's phone started ringing from inside her bag.

She looked at its screen: *"Max calling"*.

Clarissa connected. 'Max?'

'You should have told me about the Dead Drops, Clarissa,' said Max reproachfully.

Clarissa closed her eyes and her mind experienced a hard, sharp flash of the woman on the train with the dark glasses and newspaper. 'Were you?.... You were following us. You've already downloaded the Drop, haven't you?'

'We need to meet up, Clarissa,' said Max gently.

'Well, have you got it or not?'

'I've got it.'

'So why call me?'

Silence.

'You want me to work the clue out for you as well, is that it?'

'That's it!' said Max dryly.

'What makes you think I can decipher it?'

'Because you've managed it with all the others, like. We've been watching you for a while. By the way, who's the lad?'

Clarissa felt her initial shock turn to rage.

'Are you watching me *now*?' She shot up from the pavement and began surveying the surrounding buildings anxiously. She felt Ralph's eyes questioning her.

'I'm close' said Max. 'But not that close.'

Clarissa put her hand to her forehead. 'Okay. What's the clue?'

Max laughed. 'Now what would be the sense in that? I twock the Drop before you get to it, then call you up and relay it to you over the phone! Do you think I'm stupid, like?'

'When did you download it?'

'While you were in the pub.'

'You can't be too far away, then.'

Silence.

'Tell me something,' said Clarissa. 'What do you intend to do with the manuscript once you've got it?'

'You need to meet up with us, Clarissa. Then I'll tell you. I can't tell you that over the phone.'

'Charlie doesn't want Roland Steed to get his hands on it. How do I know you're not going to take it straight to him?'

'*I* don't want Roland Steed to get his hands on it!'

'So how come you were at a party at his house?'

Silence.

'You've seen the photos,' said Max. Her shock was palpable.

'It was at *his* house, wasn't it?'

'…No. It wasn't.'

'Well, whose house was it, then? His brother's?'

'George Steed's place? You must be out of your mind! D'you think I'd socialise with the likes of him? I can explain the party to you, Clarissa, if you're interested. Can you meet us tomorrow? We can clear all this up then.'

'Why not tonight?'

'I can't tonight, I'm busy.'

'But you're *here*!'

'I *was*. Now, I'm paggered and I'm gannin yem. Listen, pet, I'm not your enemy here. I just don't like being cut out of the picture as if I don't matter, like. I'm just as much part of this as Charlie is. Surely you can understand that? I'll meet you tomorrow. Same place as before. Is 10 a.m. okay? …I'll take your silence as a yes. Text me from your own phone, to save using Charlie's. Call us if you can't make it.'

The line went dead. Clarissa threw Charlie's mobile back into her bag.

'What's going on?' asked Ralph.

'I'm afraid you only know half the story,' announced Clarissa. 'I think it's about time I filled you in on the rest of it. Shall we go back inside the pub?'

'So, what do I do?' said Clarissa, after relating everything that had happened since Charlie's disappearance to Ralph. She'd told him practically every detail, apart from the existence of the gun and the horrible photo of Charlie kissing the mysterious woman (as she hadn't been able to trust herself providing a decent description of the image without risking an embarrassing emotional outburst on her part).

She watched Ralph's face crease in consternation as he tried to understand it all, the equivocal jumble, the ambiguous tangle of chaos that had become her life.

'Bloody hell,' he said.

They were sitting at a table at the back of the pub. Ralph had bought them some more beers. She watched him take a swig.

She looked at the furrows in his brow, the creases around his eyes. She could see the effect her problems were having on his youthful face. She wondered how she could justify doing this to such a promising musical genius? Her unburdening had resulted in a delicious, ephemeral sense of relief on her part, but that was before the guilt set in.

'*Jesus*! You've got me caught up in a mess!' he said. 'Why is it that every time I like a woman, she has to come hand in hand with trouble?'

Clarissa blinked. This angered her more than it should have done.

I'm nothing like that child, she thought, that stupid little girl who passed drugs around a pub for money, feeding on people's addictions, contributing to their ill health, their wasting.

She tried to say nothing, but found herself incapable.

'How dare you liken me to her!' she cried, with a vehemence that surprised even her. 'Morgan brought all that stuff on herself! Passing packages for easy cash! Did she *have* to do that? No. But she chose to do those things! Whereas I've had all this thrown at me from a great height. Did I ask for any of this? No, I did not! But did I get the choice to ignore it if I wanted to, like her? No, I did not! And I also want to make it clear right now that *unlike Morgan,* I'm not asking you for your help. If you want to help, help. If not, walk away!'

Ralph looked embarrassed, offended. Shocked by her little tirade. 'Oh, come on. There's no need to be like that,' he said. 'I want to help you. Of course I do!'

'Well, help then, rather than comparing me to Morgan!'

Oh God, thought Clarissa, I didn't even need to mention the photograph of Charlie for an embarrassing emotional outburst to came tumbling out! But a small part of her knew that there was more to it than the photo. She was quite sure that she was still harbouring feelings for Charlie, and yet she found herself in the infelicitous position of being jealous of Morgan; of Ralph's bond with her, of Ralph's intimacy with her.

Ralph stared intensely into her eyes, which were now starting to burn from the threat of fresh tears.

'I *will* help,' he said benevolently, self-righteously. He was also wise enough not to mention Morgan again, or even point out the fact that he hadn't actually mentioned her in the first place.

'Let's think about this logically,' he said. 'Have you got a pen and a piece of paper?'

Clarissa took the notebook and a pen from her bag and put them on the table in front of Ralph.

'Thanks. Now, let's go through the clues we've had so far. Stop me if I'm missing something. Now, Drop One was in the keyring. Drop Two was at 64 Bryanston Square, London. Drop Three was at 8 rue Cadet, Paris and Drop Four was at 48 Dover Street. Right?'

Clarissa nodded.

'Well, with the exception of the first one, what's the connection between the sticks? What do they all have in common?'

'They're all connected to Chopin in some way.'

'More specifically?'

'They're all places where Chopin has stayed?'

'Good! So why don't we just make a list of everywhere Chopin has resided in London (as we're *in* London and not Paris at this precise moment) and go to as many of the addresses as we can, to see if any of them have a Dead Drop outside them?'

'I've already jotted that information down,' said Clarissa. 'Turn back a couple of pages, you'll see.'

Ralph looked through the notebook and found the list. 'That's grand! It's already done. Chopin didn't spend that much time in London, so it shouldn't take us too long to get through them.'

Clarissa got out her phone and headed to Maps.

'Okay. Let's start with 4 St. James's Place,' she said, with a little enthusiasm back in her voice. 'It's just around the corner. It was the last place Chopin lodged in London. It's certainly worth a shot. If it's a later clue, we might even be able to bypass a couple of Drops. Unless he's changed tactics of course, in which case, we're still stuck at Drop Four.'

'Do we know how many Drops there are in total?'

'Eight.'

'Okay. So we're halfway through,' said Ralph ruminatively. 'Wait. A couple of minor points. Are you working tomorrow?'

'No.'

'Good. Then, this is what I think you should do.'

Ralph told her to text Max and confirm their meeting for tomorrow. He pointed out that by doing this, Max would be more likely to call off anyone she'd paid to tail them when they left the pub. He offered to put her up for the night at his place, if it helped. Then he suggested that they hang about a bit so that anyone else who might be following them would assume they'd called it a night, and stop their respective searches.

Clarissa took out her phone and sent the text to Max.

'It's done,' she said.

'Grand,' said Ralph. 'Now, can I stand you another drink, while we wait for any vultures to fly? Then we can visit 4 St. James's Place and initiate the next phase.' He pulled a face of mock distress to try and elicit a smile from her.

She succumbed. 'Just one more, then,' she said. 'But, it's my round.' She made off to the bar.

'And best fetch another towel, while you're at it!' she heard him say in her wake. 'In case I upset you again.'

She rolled her eyes.

'Max was in our bloody train carriage the whole time, you know!' Clarissa said to Ralph fifteen minutes later. She took another sip of her drink, enjoying its effects. 'I still can't believe it!'

Ralph shook his head and asked Clarissa for a description of the Geordie, which she gave.

'We should have gone for the Drop *before* coming in here' he said. 'It was my fault.'

'It's a good thing we didn't, surely?' Clarissa replied, becoming agitated. 'Otherwise she'd still be following us and we'd be none the wiser. That would have been *far* worse!'

Ralph had to agree, albeit reluctantly. 'Incidentally though, if you do manage to complete the trail and find the manuscript, what will you do with it?'

'Oh, Charlie wants me to take it to someone,' said Clarissa. 'A Professor Kowalski.'

'*Kowalski*?' said Ralph, a flash of recognition on his face. 'Of King's College, London?'

'Yes. Do you know who he is?'

'Aye. Didn't he get a CBE last year?'

Clarissa suddenly began to feel the extent of her disassociation from the music world. 'Sorry. I'd not heard of him before any of this. I emailed him, but he didn't respond,' she said, disheartened. 'He probably thinks I'm some crackpot.'

Ralph smiled. 'Give him some time,' he said. 'These music professors are busy people, you know.'

Clarissa sighed. She was losing faith. 'Time,' she said, dejectedly. 'It's the one thing I'm fast running out of.'

'So now we've got *three* parties following us,' said Ralph, summarising their plight with a swig of his beer. 'Four if we count Slim and Silas.'

'Oh, God, I forgot about them!' Clarissa groaned. She could feel the beer softening the edges of reality. And it felt good.

'Now, Slim and Silas. They have got to be…the biggest pair of eejits I have ever –'

'Since when did you start using Irish slang?'

'I must have picked it up from you. Do you have a problem with that?'

Ralph shook his head. 'You know, you're completely different when you've got a drink inside you.'

'Different, how?' Clarissa was suddenly taken aback at how many shards of green and gold were radiating from the brown of Ralph's eyes. 'Did anyone ever tell you – '

'Different, as in less of a snob.'

'– you've got a very unusual eye colour? And I am *not* a snob, thank you very much!'

'A music student who's never busked is most *definitely* a snob!'

'Oh, don't start that again.' Clarissa knocked back some more of her drink. 'Oh, the Paris Drop!' she said suddenly. 'You didn't tell me what you said, to that couple?' Clarissa could feel herself loosening up. She was enjoying her senses slowing, her fear diminishing.

'Argh. I don't think it would be a good idea if I told you that, not at this exact moment anyway,' said Ralph.

'Why ever not?'

'Because if I were to tell you, you'll eat the head off me for sure!'

'What? Well, you've got to tell me, now that you've said that!'

'I'd rather not.'

'Oh, come on!'

'I don't think I should.' Ralph smiled at her with his eyes.

'Tell me! I'll eat your head if you don't!'

'You'll eat my head? Is that a promise?' Ralph laughed full-mouthed.

'What did I say?' Clarissa looked confused.

'I wouldn't use that one again, if I were you,' said Ralph, sniggering like a school boy. 'The "eejit" one was fine, but –'

'Well, what was it then? "Eat the head –"'

'"You'll eat the head off me"!'

Clarissa scrunched up her features from embarrassment.

'Listen. Just tell me what you said to that couple.'

'Okay,' said Ralph. 'But I must warn you. You're not going to like it, and I want you to know that I only said it to get the Drop. You understand?'

Clarissa nodded.

Ralph polished off his drink, for courage it seemed. Then he put down his glass and pulled his hair away from his forehead. Clarissa could see his veins pulsing away underneath his skin. Suddenly, she was afraid of what he might say.

Smiling, and mellow from the drink he'd consumed, Ralph looked at her and said: 'I asked the couple if they wouldn't mind leaving us alone because I said we'd met at the table they just happened to be sitting at, on this day exactly two years ago. I said we'd been alone and it had been raining, just like today, so I wanted to replicate the atmosphere exactly, so that it was identical to how it had been two years ago.'

Ralph stopped smiling. 'I said that I wanted us to be sitting in the exact same place, at the exact same table, as I wanted to tell you that ever since our first conversation, you have, unequivocally, been the most important person in my life and I couldn't live without you. I said that you couldn't speak any French so you had no idea what I was asking them right now, and if they would assist me by getting up and walking away, the look on your face would be priceless. I said that everything had to be perfect like this, because I was about to ask you to marry me.'

Clarissa was stunned into silence. Then she laughed.

10

When Clarissa and Ralph finally ventured out into Dover Street, it was dark and a light rain was falling. The effect was strangely refreshing.

'Apparently, Brown's Hotel isn't too far away from here,' said Ralph, pulling up the collar on his jacket. 'The place where Alexander Graham Bell supposedly made the first telephone call, in 1877.'

'Really? Mayfair. The playground of the rich,' said Clarissa, not meaning to sound so censorious. 'How do you know all this stuff? You're like a "walking encyclopedia"!'

'Was that supposed to be a compliment? I couldn't tell.'

Clarissa smiled.

'I guess I just like acquiring historical facts,' said Ralph, as they crossed the road.

'I wonder what Alexander Graham Bell would have made of the modern smartphone?' said Clarissa.

'Or Chopin. He didn't even know what a phone was!' Ralph remarked. 'Imagine that! How long could you go without using your phone nowadays? How things have changed. And then there's the pollution!'

'Don't get me started on that. It's my specialist subject, we'll be talking all night!' blurted Clarissa.

'I could talk to you all night,' said Ralph. 'Easily.'

She cut him a look.

They walked back along Dover Street into Piccadilly, past the Wolseley restaurant with its decorative iron arches; the alcohol in their blood and the velvety darkness that enshrouded them usefully blurring the edges of things, protecting them from the reality of their situation.

By the light of her phone, connected to Satellite Maps, Clarissa led Ralph into St. James's Street. They walked past business headquarters in grand buildings flanked by black and gold lampposts.

After a while, Clarissa caught sight of the Stern Pissarro Gallery on the corner with its bronze 1960's aluminium cladding. What an aberration it was! It was so shockingly incongruous with the rest of the period houses in the row, she suspected it fiercely divided opinion amongst the locals.

From there, they left St. James's Street and turned into St. James's Place.

The number 4 appeared a hundred yards in, on the right. A black iron lantern illuminated two window boxes brimming with flowers on the side of the old building. Ralph pointed to the blue

English Heritage plaque that hung above them. It read: *"From this house in 1848 Frederic Chopin (1810-1849) went to Guildhall to give his last public performance"*. They regarded the plaque silently, lost in deference for a moment for the great composer that had united them.

Then Ralph emitted the torch on his phone and began to search for the Drop. There was no one around which made things easier.

'Do you know what? I don't think he'd have planted a Drop around here,' said Clarissa suddenly. 'It's too near a blue plaque.'

Ralph inspected the area for a good ten minutes before he capitulated. 'I think you might be right.'

Clarissa found herself touched by his disappointment. 'Never mind, let's move on to the next one.'

'Wait a minute,' said Ralph.

She waited. The way the road was lit, she could easily have believed herself transported into a Dickensian novel, with its period lanterns and caged basements – although the effect was slightly ruined by the art gallery, which seemed to crouch on legs at the end of the street, resembling a recently-landed space craft. She wondered what Chopin would have made of that!

'Listen, Clarissa. If Charlie had devised a clue that led to 4 St. James's Place, he might have followed it with a single word command in French – like he did in Bryanston Square – in order to take you away from the blue plaque. Why don't *you* take this side of the road, while I take the other? Let's just walk to the end of the street. See if we find anything further afield?'

'Okay,' said Clarissa, doubtfully. She ran the light of her phone along the dark kerb. She was not hopeful.

They walked the entire length of the road and found nothing.

'Come, on. Let's try the next address,' said Clarissa, growing tired.

'Let's just follow it a bit further. Just around this corner,' said Ralph. The road widened suddenly, revealing a row of parking spaces, all but one occupied.

Ralph stopped at a black cast iron bollard.

She watched him run his long fingers around its base. Suddenly he got on his knees and held his phone torch to it. He called her over with swift jerk of his head, his hair falling into his left eye. She crouched down next to him. He took her hand and placed it on what felt like an angular metal stem.

Clarissa smiled.

It certainly felt like a Drop, but she refused to celebrate too early. They had made that mistake before. Silently, she took out her laptop and connected it to the protruding metal tab.

Her screen revealed a new file icon. She felt the excitement start to burn like a flame in her chest. She clicked on it eagerly.

They both stared at the screen with baited breath, both gasping at the exact same moment, when this appeared on it:

Stick No.6:38.R.D.L.C.38.N.OP.37.1.Paris

'Just call me a genius again!' said Ralph.

'I don't believe it!' exclaimed Clarissa. 'You are most definitely a genius, and look! It's the clue to stick six!'

'So, we've managed to bypass stick five altogether! Bloody brilliant!'

They stared at each other with conspiratorial excitement.

Clarissa downloaded the memory stick onto her laptop and deleted it directly afterwards, as was the procedure. Then she hesitated.

'Wait a minute, how about we now write our own clue for Max?' said Clarissa. 'That way, if she manages to make it here, we can divert her off to somewhere else. Any suggestions?'

'I like it, but we can't use a real Chopin address, as there might be a *real* Drop there, but I don't think we ought to put a random series of letters and numbers either,' said Ralph thoughtfully. 'Wait a minute, does Max know that all the Drops are either in Paris or London?'

'No,' said Clarissa. 'I don't see how she could.'

'Then how about we still use a real Chopin location, but somewhere else?'

'Warsaw?' said Clarissa, her green eyes sparkling.

'Aye. That's good. Err…what shall we…'

They both froze. They could hear footsteps.

'Hurry up, there's someone coming!' whispered Clarissa.

'Okay. Put: "K.P.20.Warsaw. Sens inverse!"'

'Is that French?'

'Aye, it means reverse.'

'Spell it for me, quick!'

Ralph sounded out the letters, while Clarissa typed them into her laptop hurriedly. The footsteps were getting louder.

When she'd finished, she slammed down the lid of her device and disconnected it from the Drop in one smooth action. Then she stood up. She had completed the procedure just in time before a man dressed in a long formal coat and red scarf rounded the corner. Ralph and Clarissa stood opposite each other, like lovers having just pulled back from an embrace.

They both eyed the man who glanced at them momentarily before moving briskly on. He must have been about forty, with milky blond longish hair and a goatee. Then they looked at each other and Ralph shook his head.

'Come on, let's get out of here,' he said, striding away from the bollard.

Clarissa followed him, experiencing a wonderful sense of gratification. She wanted to revel in the moment. Not only had they managed to jump two spaces in the trail, but she had set a trap for the unsuspecting Max. It was simply delightful!

'What did your clue mean?' she asked.

'I'll tell you when we're away from here,' he said, his face beaming with repressed elation. 'You never know who's listening. Come on, there's something I want you to show you!'

'Where are we going?'

'You'll see.'

Ralph led Clarissa back to the Royal Academy of Music. They passed through its main entrance, through its vestibule with its veined marble columns, and towards its rear staircase.

There were people milling about, talking, laughing, shuffling papers and removing instruments from cases. Ralph took her up some stairs, along a corridor and through another set of doors.

'Now close your eyes,' he said.

'What?'

'Close your eyes. You trust me, don't you?'

Clarissa did as she was told.

She could feel Ralph take her hand. They walked some more. They went through another set of doors.

'Now open!' he instructed.

She stared at the view in front of her. It was a red seated theatre. They had appeared on its upper balcony. A draped platform was immediately in front of them. The curtains had been left parted and a glossy black grand piano with gold castors stood centre-stage. They were surrounded by wooden paneling – carefully carved rectangles giving the appearance of book spines in a vast library. The walls curved into a horseshoe. The ceiling was a carved symmetrical circle with hundreds of fibre-optic teardrop crystal lights suspended from it.

'It's beautiful!' said Clarissa, genuinely overwhelmed. 'You can even smell the wood.'

'It's the new Susie Sainsbury Theatre,' said Ralph. 'It only opened last year. I didn't think you'd seen it. It's cherry wood, apparently.'

'How come it's deserted?' said Clarissa, realising that they were the only people in the vast space.

'They've just finished rehearsing,' said Ralph. 'Come on.' He led her down to the piano.

'Sit at it,' he said.

'What?' Clarissa looked horrified. 'Surely we shouldn't be in here?'

'It's fine,' said Ralph. 'I often come here on a Monday at around this time.'

Clarissa reached out and stroked the piano stool. Then she gravitated to the keys, which flexed as her fingers touched them.

'Sit down,' said Ralph. 'I want you to play something. There's nobody else here. It's just me.'

Clarissa gazed about her. The lights were truly beautiful; they had completely transformed the space, giving it an ethereal quality. The bulbs glinted like stars in a winter sky.

Ralph was right, the place appeared to be completely empty. The piano seemed to glow like a jewel in the rain.

Clarissa sat down on the stool and placed her fingers on the keys tentatively. Then she launched into Chopin's Nocturne in E-flat major (op. 9, no.2). She hadn't attempted the piece for years, but miraculously her fingers were still able to find all the right notes. As she played she felt like she'd been transported back to a place she hadn't visited for a very long time, not since her Royal College days. She made no errors.

As the piece concluded, Clarissa discovered tears in her eyes, and she began to stare at the lights in a sort of daze, constrained by a strange numbness.

Ralph said nothing but very gently brushed the little finger of her left hand with his own. This seemed to generate a spark between them.

She shot up, excited, but also deeply uncomfortable, waving her hand quickly over the glossy piano stool, gesturing for him to sit at it; keen to transfer the spotlight over to him.

'Now, will you play Etude, Opus 10, number 4 for me?' she said, her voice cracking unexpectedly, shocked by this new susceptibility that appeared to be consuming her. She did not welcome such feelings.

Ralph smiled irrepressibly, producing a curt nod. She knew it would please him to play something for her on a real piano in a real theatre. He removed his jacket enthusiastically and threw it onto the floor.

He settled himself at the instrument without saying a word. There were a few more seconds of quietude before he launched into the Etude.

The piece was fast. Clarissa felt that she did not have the skills needed to play such a piece; Ralph, on the other hand, did. Now comfortably seated, Ralph's feet were able to demonstrate their role in his creative process. In fact, she watched in fascination as his entire body took up the agenda; legs, torso, his long fingers dancing so quickly they seemed to blur in front of her eyes. It looked as if every muscle he had had become possessed by the music. She sensed his ultimate goal was to produce a masterpiece so rich in the texture of sound, words simply failed as a response; the body had to *feel* it.

When he'd finished, she said, 'You really have mastered it. It was perfect.'

'Oh *please*! I'm going to be sick in a minute!' said a woman's disparaging voice from behind them. They both turned, alarmed. Six rows back, Morgan was sitting in one of the red seats, her auburn hair tied back, her face pale and devoid of makeup. How long she'd been there was anyone's guess.

'Where the hell did you spring from?' asked Ralph, completely taken aback. 'Why aren't you in Paris?'

'I'm taking a break,' said Morgan.

'Don't tell me you've quit?' said Ralph.

'No. I haven't quit. I've not been well. Richard told me to return next week.' She jerked her head in Clarissa's direction. 'What's she doing here?'

'I invited her. She wanted to see the new theatre.'

'Is that right?' She flashed Clarissa a venomous look.

'Yes,' began Clarissa awkwardly. 'I wanted to see Ralph play on a proper piano, rather than one on the floor in an underground station.' The statement seemed to be a perfectly reasonable comment to make, but from the look on Ralph's face, it soon became obvious that it had been the wrong thing to say.

'What do you mean: *"on the floor in an underground station?"*' cried Morgan. 'You make it sound as if he's been busking! Ralph doesn't busk, not since the incident with the –'

'All right, Morgan! There's no need to bring that up,' interjected Ralph.

There was an uncomfortable silence.

'What incident?' said Clarissa, looking curiously from Morgan to Ralph and back again.

'It doesn't matter,' said Ralph.

'You haven't been busking, have you?' Morgan asked him.

Ralph just looked at her.

'You have!' yelled Morgan. 'I don't believe this. What on earth for?'

'As if you didn't know,' said Clarissa, unable to help the words falling out of her mouth.

Suddenly Morgan squeezed her eyes into small slits, lending her the appearance of a ghostly-looking Chinese doll. Clarissa watched the dancer's head tilt to one side like some sort of discarded puppet. She glared at Ralph. 'You've told her?'

Ralph said nothing.

'I can't believe you've discussed my private life with some woman you've only just met!' cried Morgan.

Clarissa noted her use of the word "woman" instead of "girl".

'Morgan, please,' protested Ralph, 'let's not do this here!'

The dancer began to shake her chin slowly. She looked strangely like she'd just received a blow to the mouth. While Clarissa waited for her to recover, something told her Morgan was getting ready to explode again.

The silence seemed to intensify, until it was finally broken by a stream of invective from Morgan, so elliptical, Clarissa couldn't understand what she was saying at all. Indiscernible words flew from her mouth, interspersed by expletives, in a garbled mess that seemed to drain the redhead to the point of exhaustion.

'Jesus, Morgan! WILL YOU JUST *STOP*!' Ralph shouted, cradling his head with his hands. 'Do you want an even bigger audience? The fuzz will be sure to turn up and arrest us all if you carry on like this!'

'But you said all that business was finished! You said you'd paid them off!' cried a frustrated Morgan. 'Well, have you paid them off, or haven't you?'

'I'VE PAID HALF OF IT!' Ralph yelled back, his voice so sharp and authoritative, it made Clarissa jump. 'I won't get the other half for a couple of weeks. Then I'll pay them the rest of it! Now, drop the subject will you. I'm tired of it.'

Clarissa stared at Ralph questioningly, but he wouldn't meet her eye.

'A couple of weeks?' asked Morgan, diffidently.

'A couple of weeks,' said Ralph.

'Then it's over? Then they'll finally leave me alone?' Morgan implored Ralph with tired eyes, her vituperative outburst having clearly taken its toll.

'Then they'll finally leave you alone,' repeated Ralph definitively.

This seemed to calm her right down. Clarissa watched Morgan close her eyes and a solitary tear leaked from her left one.

'You played for her,' said the redhead quietly, her eyes still closed. 'If you haven't slept with her already, it will only be a matter of time.' As Morgan's lashes flicked open again, a fresh animosity seemed to glow from her irises. Then she said: 'She's the reason you finished it, isn't she?'

Clarissa searched Ralph's face, confused, waiting for his explanation. Was she was referring to the show, or something else? She didn't understand.

'Answer me!' screamed Morgan.

'For God's sake! I've told you before, there's *nothing* going on between Clarissa and myself. Clarissa has a boyfriend!'

'Then why end our relationship?' said Morgan.

The silence that followed was so intense you could hear a pin drop.

Clarissa was staggered. If Ralph had finished with the dancer in Paris, why on earth hadn't he told her? She glared at Ralph, but found him looking intensely at the floor.

'You need me. Please don't do this!' said Morgan, as if Clarissa were no longer there.

'I thought I'd done it already,' said Ralph sarcastically. 'Don't make me keep repeating it. You're making a fool of yourself in front of Clarissa. Come on, we need to get you out of here. Sorry, Clarissa.'

'Don't apologise to *her*!' said Morgan, with renewed disgust.

'I should leave,' said Clarissa, her embarrassment intensifying.

'About to go back to his place, were you?' said Morgan, her mouth set into a rictus smile.

Clarissa just stared at her.

'Oh, my God, you *were!*' Morgan said sardonically. She looked so different without makeup, Clarissa was struggling to believe she was the same woman who'd been waiting for them, slouched against the taxi in Paris.

'Morgan. No more!' said Ralph, angrily. 'I've had enough of this now.' He jumped from the piano stool, grabbing his jacket and slipping it on deftly as he climbed off the stage.

He made his way towards her.

'BUT YOUV'E MADE ME ILL!' screamed Morgan. 'I can't dance anymore! When you finish with someone without giving them a valid reason, you make them ill! Surely you can understand that!'

Ralph shook his head as if the concept was alien to him, but Clarissa knew what she was talking about. She understood it exactly.

Ralph clambered up towards Morgan and took her arm before she could say anything else. She didn't resist, and allowed him to pull her from her seat. He flashed Clarissa a rueful look as he ushered Morgan away, subjugated.

Clarissa stayed where she was, seated at the beautiful black piano. For the first time in years she felt less like a flight attendant and more like a pianist.

In the distance she could hear Ralph still trying to placate the dancer, his Irish accent fluctuating up and down. She wasn't able to make out his words.

Then, as the two of them disappeared through the back of the theatre, Ralph shouted: 'Clarissa, wait here for me! I'll come back for you!'

He'd sounded as if he'd only be a few minutes. Then the door slammed shut.

'Okay,' said Clarissa, sitting back down at the piano. 'I'll wait,' she said to herself in the deserted theatre.

Surprisingly, she felt becalmed, sated. She attributed it to her performance. She hadn't played the piano like that for years. She expected somebody to come, ask who she was, ask what she was doing sitting on the stage of the Susie Sainsbury Theatre. But they didn't.

No one came.

She liked it here. It was the first time she had felt comfortable on a stage for seven years.

She had enjoyed playing the Nocturne, and now, perversely, she wished for an audience to perform it to.

Emboldened by her achievement at getting through the piece without a mistake, she considered playing something else.

She wanted to cure herself.

Clarissa looked at the red seats and tried to imagine them filled with people. She could not. It was just her, the teardrop lights and a glossy black piano floating in a sea of red velvet. But she was unable to play anything else, due to his absence. For she knew that she had played the Nocturne for him.

She must have waited for half an hour, but Ralph did not come back.

Eventually, reluctantly, she got up and left.

11

It had been eight days since Charlie had disappeared.

In her dreams Clarissa would return to the field near Perry Green where she'd found his car, and search for him. Again and again she would re-enact her frantic hunt for him on the evening of their break-up, charging through the pungent brown mud, ready to dive into the very cake of it to get to him. Sometimes she would discover him all confused and breathless, and she would take his hand and lead him back to her Fiat and drive him to her apartment. Sometimes she would find him injured – a twisted ankle or torn knee ligament – but somehow she would still manage to get him back to her car, and then on to a place of safety.

On the evening she'd played the piano on the stage of the Susie Sainsbury Theatre, Clarissa returned home feeling so exhilarated it had shocked her. She had not been expecting such a delicious tremor of excitement to overwhelm her senses. The intense physical thrill she'd experienced had been so strong, even Morgan's pernicious intervention hadn't ruined it. But that night, after Clarissa had fallen asleep and experienced yet another one of her recurring dreams searching for Charlie, she discovered that the outcome didn't play out in quite the same way it usually did. Charlie was nowhere to be seen, and when she ran to the place where she'd found his phone, she'd discovered only a bunch of twelve red roses with her name written on a small card beside them.

Now to any other person, a bouquet of red flowers may have hinted at something nice. But not to Clarissa. Their presence in her dream alluded to something terrible that had happened to her in the past, something she had been trying to forget for years, and she had been very frightened by it.

The following morning, when the piercing bleeping of her alarm clock woke her at 6 a.m., Clarissa prepared herself to meet Max as arranged, but her red roses dream had made her uncomfortable, as if it were somehow a portent, a warning that something bad was about to happen.

Something irrevocable.

The early train to London was packed as usual, and Clarissa found her mind riddled with paranoia. Her fellow passengers – as they read, typed or stared indifferently into space – suddenly all posed a threat to her, and she could only liken it to being surrounded by an unspeakable force of danger that only she could see. She tried to concentrate on her breathing, as Ralph had taught her, but she was finding it difficult to follow the task, and knew she was failing miserably to get on top of the situation.

Luckily, her phone rang from the depths of her bag, shaking her out of this horrible experience.

She swiped the glass expecting it to be Max, but it was Donna's voice that spoke, small and faraway: 'Hi, hun.'

'Donna?' said Clarissa. She glanced at her watch; it was still only 7:45 a.m. 'Are you okay?'

Silence.

Soon the clickety-clack rhythm of the train seemed to calm her down. She waited for her friend to speak. She hated talking on a crowded train, and it could only be bad news at this hour.

'Woody told his wife,' said Donna meekly.

'About you and him?'

'Yeah. About the affair, about the baby. About *everything*. It's all out. Out in the open at last!'

Clarissa shivered, convinced that her freshly-liberated friend should be sounding happier than this; something had to be wrong.

'Clarissa? Did you hear what I just said?'

'Yes! Wow! Well, that's good! *Isn't it*?' said Clarissa, genuinely stunned. She had expected this thing to go on and on; indefinitely, insidiously. She found the revelation of its clean-cut finale not only unexpected, but also most disconcerting.

Silence again.

'Donna?'

'Yeah.'

'Where are you?'

'I'm at the Herts and Essex Community hospital.'

'You haven't gone ahead with the –'

'No, of course I haven't!'

'Well, what are you doing there? Are you all right?'

There was no answer.

'Donna?'

'Woody's here,' said Donna sadly. 'I'm afraid his wife didn't take too kindly to our news.'

'What do you mean?'

'She stabbed him.'

'She *what*?' Clarissa was horrified. She glanced about, expecting some sort of reaction to her alarm from her fellow passengers, but they just continued to stare at their books and phones banally. Their obliviousness placated her. She lowered her voice: 'Where? When? Is he all right?'

'At their house. Last night. She took a knife out of the kitchen drawer and went for his chest,' said Donna in a somewhat strange, detached voice.

'Oh my God! Is he all right?'

'Yes and no. Luckily, he put his hand out to protect himself. It saved his life, but the blade went straight through it. The consultant says there's no reason for him not to make a complete recovery but it's bad, Clarissa. He's unable to move three of his fingers. They need to operate. There's even a risk he could lose them! I just wanted you to know. He'll be away from work for a while. He's going to tell everyone he was mugged, but I wanted you to know what happened. Well, I can't discuss this at work.'

'No, of course you can't,' said Clarissa, relieved that the incident was not fatal, for Donna's sake. 'Thanks for telling me.'

Clarissa had met Woody's wife on a couple of occasions; she had always come across as a petite, delicate little thing, so quiet and unassuming – what *was* her name now? She just couldn't remember. But Clarissa couldn't imagine her getting violent. She tried to play the scene in her head. Woody had probably delivered the news about his affair with Donna unsympathetically, brutally, even callously. She pictured his square jaw jutting out, his head cocked to one side, his arrogant blue eyes shrugging it off, the smugness in his voice. Then, just as the poor woman was coming to terms with this, he'd probably thrown in the news about the baby, crushing her, breaking her into little pieces. Confronted by similar circumstances, Clarissa was quite sure she would have stuck a knife in him herself!

'He tried to tell her gently,' said Donna. 'He was good with her; sensitive, considerate. He tried to say all the right things.'

Instinctively, Clarissa wanted to refute this, but held her tongue for Donna's sake. Instead, she tried to be pragmatic. 'Were you there? Did you hear what was said?'

'No.'

'So you can't be sure what actually happened then?'

'I can,' replied Donna, defensively. 'Because Woody told me what actually happened. He wouldn't lie to me about a thing like this!'

Clarissa shook her head despairingly and stared out of the carriage window. She looked at row upon row of terracotta tiled rooves slipping past the glass, and thought Donna had to be deluded to think like this. *The man was a snake!*

'And what about you?' asked Clarissa, suddenly feeling empathy for her friend. 'Are *you* okay?'

'I'm fine,' said Donna, with strained tolerance. 'We've decided to have the baby, together. Give it a go. But if he loses his fingers, he won't be able to fly anymore, and *he'll* have to get another job as well as me. Imagine that! Things will certainly be different then.'

Clarissa was so pleased that her friend had decided to keep the baby. 'I'm happy for you, Donna. I really am,' she said. 'When are you going to stop flying? Soon?'

There was a pause while she seemed to think this over.

'Not yet,' said Donna.

'But there's a health risk, surely? Can't you transfer to the ground or something?'

'I know I'll have to, eventually. But we're not ready to tell everyone yet.'

'Do you want me to come there? To the hospital, I mean?'

'What? No. Absolutely not!' said Donna, her voice slightly garbled. 'Sorry, I'm eating. No, you need to stick to your mission. Where are you anyway? You sound as if you're on a train.'

The mood had lightened. It was a relief. The old Donna had returned.

Clarissa told her friend that she was on a train heading towards Euston. She allowed Donna to probe into her progress with the Dead Drop quest for a while – answering her as succinctly as she could with 'yes' or 'no' answers – but the conversation stopped abruptly when she was asked if she was going to meet Ralph.

'…I think so,' replied Clarissa warily. But the truth was, she didn't know if she would be seeing Ralph in London because she hadn't heard a thing from him since he'd escorted Morgan home from the RAM last night.

'So, you two haven't forged a romantic connection yet, then?'

Yes, the old Donna had definitely returned!

'What makes you say that?'

'Sorry,' said her friend, amidst a sound like food packaging crumpling. It was unclear whether she was apologising for the sound or the comment. 'At the moment, I can't seem to stop eating,' she said, amidst more rummaging. 'So there's *something* there, then?' she asked brightly. 'Some chemistry between the two of you? Come on, fess up!'

'Donna, for God's sake. I can't talk about this, I'm on a train!' remonstrated Clarissa, her eyes roving around the faces in her carriage uncomfortably again.

'Okay, sweetie, but I can only take that as a "yes". I've obviously touched on *something*,' said Donna. 'This *is* exciting! But we'll have to resume this conversation tomorrow. I need to go. Face the wife.'

'The wife? She's there?'

'She wasn't. She was at the police station. But she's here now. She's asked to see me. I suppose I'll have to talk to her. Well, I can't just ignore her, can I?'

'I would,' said Clarissa, shuddering.

'But I'll have to face her sooner or later. Might as well do it now!' said Donna, feigning cheerfulness.

'I suppose you're right. But please, be careful. Make sure there's somebody with you, at least.'

'It's okay. She's diffused somewhat since last night,' said Donna reassuringly. 'Besides, I'm not the one she's angry with, it's *him*. So, don't worry about me, I'm perfectly safe. I wouldn't like to say the same thing for her though!' She laughed a faint disjointed laugh, and the two friends said goodbye.

Clarissa stared out of the window again. It looked like the train had reached the outskirts of London. They would be there soon, she thought. She was longing to speak to Ralph. She wished that he'd call. She'd intended to wait until he got in touch with her, but Donna's news seemed to throw a previously unconsidered danger into the mix: the possibility that Morgan could have turned on him last night. Soon, Clarissa began to imagine all sorts of things: Ralph lying in some hospital with a knife stuck in him; Ralph slumped on a street corner somewhere in need of urgent medical attention; the possibilities were endless.

But if something terrible hadn't happened to Ralph, Clarissa couldn't understand why he hadn't messaged her. His silence made no sense. Unless she'd imagined their connection last night, of course, or he'd decided to go back to Morgan after all. Or perhaps Morgan had threatened to hurt *herself* if he left her for good, so he'd been forced to stay with her? Whatever the reason, Clarissa thought she deserved an explanation; she only wanted to know he was safe, after all.

Clarissa pulled her phone back out of her bag and typed: *"Shall we meet up today?"* Then amended it to: *"Can we meet up today?"* and sent the message to Ralph.

Clarissa waited for ten minutes at the Marble Arch café before Max showed. She'd decided to play into the Geordie's hands; surrender, express her regret at having kept the Drops from her, and show willingness to help her with the clue she'd stolen. She just hoped that her compliance wouldn't arouse too much suspicion.

Max arrived out of breath. She was on the defensive, fully prepared for battle. She'd even brought in extra troops. She waved in her direction. Clarissa reciprocated the gesture, but stared disconsolately at the unknown dark-haired woman and blond man the Geordie had brought into the café with her. She watched carefully as Max ensured these strangers had drinks, signalling her out to them. Their presence made her feel confused, out of kilter.

'Morning,' said Max, producing a strained smile as she seated herself at Clarissa's small table, latte in hand. She wore dark combat trousers with a black faux fur coat, embellished with a silver scarf.

'Have you heard anything from Charlie?' Clarissa blurted.

'No, you?' asked Max.

Clarissa shook her head. 'Sorry. I wasn't expecting anyone else?' She indicated the strangers with her eyes.

Clarissa was wearing her leather jacket again, along with skinny black jeans and a cream polo-neck jumper; her hair had been left down. She had been worried that Max wouldn't recognise her dressed like this. But the Geordie appeared not to have even noticed.

'Err…I think there's a larger table over there we could use?' suggested the blond man, using the rolling dialect of the upper-classes.

Without consultation, Clarissa and Max got up and followed the strangers over to it.

'Clarissa, this is Jonathan Cavendish-Walton and Julia Manzanetti,' said Max, as they all sat down.

Clarissa exchanged smiles with the newcomers. Small talk was made; the odd joke proffered for comfort. Then, with all the familiarities out of the way, Clarissa flashed Max a glance of impatience, her fierce green eyes insisting on some sort of explanation to account for the couple's presence.

'Now, let's start by clearing a few things up!' said Max, responding to Clarissa's expression by cajoling her visitors to: "get down to business" as breezily as if she was about to open a garden party. 'Clarissa, you might have recognised Julia? She was the model we asked to kiss Charlie for the photograph I took on the 9th March. The one you saw posted on Instagram?'

Clarissa felt herself react to this by pulling all the muscles in her face into one quick and painful contortion. She inspected Julia for evidence of this, and decided to accept it as fact, not understanding why she had failed to see the resemblance on first encountering her. 'I see,' she found herself saying quietly.

'But just before you rip Julia's eyes out, you need to know that the photograph was a set-up,' said Max. 'Julia wasn't really involved with Charlie; Charlie just wanted to give that impression.'

Clarissa stared at Julia, then at Max. 'I see,' she said again.

'Jonathan was our party host,' Max went on, divesting herself of her jacket swiftly and placing it on the back of her chair. 'The gathering you saw on Instagram was at *his* house.'

'And why are they here?' asked Clarissa, rudely.

'Howay, man! Are you telling me that I stood a cat's chance in hell of convincing you that Charlie's kiss wasn't real, if you hadn't met them for yourself, like?'

'I wasn't seeing Charlie behind your back,' said the beautiful Julia, her Italian accent tumbling out of her like a waterfall on a June day. 'You have to believe me, Clarissa.'

Clarissa just stared at the woman, as if her presence in front of her was only a figment of her imagination.

'This is…this is all a bit hard for me to take in,' said Clarissa trying her best to smile.

'You're in shock. I can understand that,' said Max.

'We didn't even kiss properly,' Julia's mellifluous voice went on. 'I know it looks like we *did* in the photo, but we didn't. He was only able to do it when I told him to close his eyes and imagine that I was you.'

'Right,' said Clarissa. 'Well, thank you for clearing that up.'

'If you're still unsure whether to believe me,' said Julia. 'I've brought evidence.'

She placed a brown A4 envelope on the table.

'What's this?' said Clarissa.

'Open it,' said Max, her purple lips twisting in anticipation.

Clarissa pulled the envelope towards her tentatively. She ripped the seal apart. Inside, she discovered three photographs, all depicting the beautiful Italian model snapped in the same pose she had assumed with Charlie; although in each picture she was kissing a different man. The only thing they all shared was a strapline for Pernod.

'Charlie and I knew Julia through Jonathan,' said Max. 'Jonathan pointed out one of her advertisements to Charlie a few months ago. "Why not get Julia to replicate her Pernod shot?" he said, didn't you, Jonathan?'

'I hold my hands up to it, Clarissa! I did, yes.'

Clarissa looked at him, with his blond hair and slim nose.

'Are you a model too?' she asked him.

'Fuck, no! Julia and I are an item,' he gushed with his fast, tightly-clipped voice, smiling at the misunderstanding and winking at Julia salaciously. 'I'm an art dealer. I specialise in Mondrian; incidentally; if you're interested.'

Clarissa smiled, tight-lipped.

'Perhaps not. Anyway,' Jonathan continued. 'Look. I don't know exactly what's going on here, but Charlie's a good friend of mine. We've known one another for about five years. He said he needed a photograph to try and convince someone he'd been unfaithful to his girlfriend, and I suggested this.' He pointed at the images in Clarissa's hand. 'Julia agreed. It's as simple as that.'

Clarissa surveyed the three of them suspiciously. If this whole thing was an act, they'd certainly gone to town on it!

'Speak to us, Clarissa. Say you believe us!' said Max. 'Why would I go to these extremes to convince you, otherwise? Look, to be perfectly honest with you, I couldn't care less if Charlie dumped you for real that night, or not. What's it to me? But he *didn't,* and he'd be devastated if he knew that you'd spotted the photo and believed it and I hadn't put you straight, like.'

Clarissa glanced at Julia and Jonathan, before returning her gaze to Max.

'Okay, Clarissa,' said Max. 'Don't fret. I know we need to continue our little talk privately. Jonathan and Julia have to get off now, anyway.'

'We do indeed,' said Jonathan, taking his cue. He stood up, suddenly handing Clarissa one of his business cards. 'Look me up. There's plenty of photos of the house on the website, if you need any more corroboration. Check out my site!'

Clarissa read his card: *Cavendish-Walton Fine Art. Specialists in De Stijl.*

'Thanks,' she said. 'I will.'

The art dealer and the model seemed to bolt out of the café with a purpose, directly after this.

When they were safely out of earshot, Max said: 'So, did you believe them?'

'Isn't a friend who'll pose for a photograph to help somebody out, just as likely to sit at a table and *say* they'd posed for a photograph to help somebody out?' said Clarissa irascibly.

Max laughed her shrill bird-like laugh. 'Clarissa, I'm starting to understand why Charlie left the Dead Drop trail in your very capable hands! You think outside the box. I like that!'

Clarissa sighed. 'Don't worry, I believed them.'

'Howay man! She sees sense at last!' cried Max, quite visibly relieved.

'Now, you can tell me if you *really* have any news about Charlie,' said Clarissa seriously.

'We do have some leads to his whereabouts, yes,' said the Geordie hopefully. 'But you need to be patient and sit tight while we investigate them. Charging in like a bull in a china shop could make Charlie's situation worse, I'm sure you understand.'

'Who's "we"?' said Clarissa,' startled. 'And what sort of leads?'

'Clarissa. I can't tell you these things, for your own safety.'

'So you won't talk to me about it?'

'I *can't* talk to you about it.'

'Right.'

'But we're doing everything we can to sort this out, Clarissa, you've got to believe us!' Max implored.

Clarissa sipped her cappuccino and closed her eyes briefly. Although she did believe Max's explanation for the photo, beyond that she had difficulty trusting anything that came out of the woman's mouth.

'So, tell me who the lad is,' said Max. 'The one who's been helping you.'

'A friend.'

'How long have you known him?'

'A while.'

'How long's "a while"?'

'A few months,' Clarissa lied.

'And you've told him about the Dead Drops?'

'I wouldn't have *found* any of the Dead Drops if it hadn't been for him.'

Clarissa immediately regretted saying this. Besides, it wasn't even true. She'd only said it to wind the Geordie up, but in the process she'd inadvertently succeeded in making herself look incompetent.

'Is that right?' Max replied, clearly with a renewed interest in Ralph. 'Well perhaps it should be him sitting here, instead of you? You should have brought him along. I'd have liked to have met him.'

'What I meant was,' Clarissa started again, '*I* solved the clues, my friend helped me locate the Drops,' she said, trying to restore Max's faith in her. 'So, can I see it? The clue? It's the reason we're both here, after all.'

Max removed a piece of paper from her pocket and slid it across the table. Clarissa examined it with interest:

4SJP.48.UB.London

It was funny. When you knew the answer before you'd seen the question. It was like time was suddenly moving backwards.

'Thank you,' said Clarissa dropping the piece of paper into her bag. 'I'll need to think on it, of course.'

'How long does it normally take, like?' said Max.

'A few hours, maybe? I'll call you this afternoon.'

'And how do I know you won't decipher the clue and give the location of the Drop to your "friend", so that *he* can get to it before us?'

'You mean you haven't already paid someone to follow me as I leave here?' said Clarissa brazenly. 'I'd get a move on if I were you! But I can tell you now, you'd be wasting your time, and your money.'

'You're not making a good case for yourself here, Clarissa,' said Max, visibly irritated by her little joke.

'All right. How do you know you can trust me?' said Clarissa, starting to grow frustrated. 'I suppose you don't. *Not really.* But I've been thinking things through, and I want you to know that I don't blame you for taking the clue from under our noses like that.

I should have told you about the Drops from the start. I'm only sorry I didn't. For God's sake, Max, I'm trying to apologise here!'

Max looked at her speculatively. 'All right, Clarissa. Thank you for your apology. And now?'

'And now, I need to get back,' said Clarissa, suddenly concerned for Donna. 'Something's happened. My friend's boyfriend was stabbed last night and I need to see if she's all right.'

'Not fatally, I hope?' said Max, displaying concern.

'No. Thankfully. Look, all you have to do is give me a few hours to work out the clue, and if I do, *when I do,* I'll be happy for you to visit the next Dead Drop location without us. I accept that we'll need to start working on this together now, and I also accept how wrong I've been not trusting you. I just want Charlie to get out of this mess safely!'

Clarissa sat back. She'd done her best.

'All right Clarissa. One repentance speech was quite enough,' said Max dryly. 'I'll leave you alone. Give you some time to think about the clue. Wait for your call.' She stood up. 'It's all I want too, you know, to see that Charlie's safe.'

After Max had gone, Clarissa remained at the table in the coffee shop in quiet contemplation. The brown A4 envelope containing the "Pernod shots" had been left in front of her considerately – in case she wished to subject them to any further scrutiny. She did not.

She took out her phone.

Still nothing from Ralph.

She connected to the internet and typed in: *"Who is the model behind the Pernod advertising campaign?"*

She watched Julia Manzanetti's name come up with plenty of photos of her famous kissing shot.

Clarissa pressed her hands to her forehead and sighed.

Next she typed in: "Cavendish-Walton Fine Art". Hurriedly, she scrolled down the screen. She saw Jonathan Cavendish-Walton's image. There were pictures of a large house. She rolled her thumb down until she found a picture of a grand hallway. She found that she was looking at the same ornate staircase she had seen on Charlie's Instagram page.

She now believed beyond any reasonable doubt that the kiss between Charlie and Julia had been faked; what she failed to understand however, was why Charlie had gone to so much trouble falsifying evidence to suggest that such an intimate association with Julia had occurred in the first place. Surely she wasn't likely to be in *that* much danger, associated with him as "his girlfriend"?

Clarissa placed the envelope in her bag and removed her phone.

She decided the best thing she could do now was to return home and work on the clue to the sixth Dead Drop. She would have to find its location in Paris tomorrow without Ralph's help.

She intended to call Max with the destination for Drop Five at about 7 p.m., saddling her with the disadvantage of having to hunt for the USB stick in the dark. It was of course possible – they had found it under similar conditions themselves – just more difficult, and she thought it would do the Geordie good to get a bit hot under the collar for a change; after all, a little bit of frustration never did anybody any real harm, and it was the least she could do to thank her for the *indelicate* way she'd exposed the whole "Pernod shot" thing.

Clarissa considered Charlie's instructions again. They had been left explicitly for her, and her alone. He had expressed a will for *her* to find the manuscript, not Max, and there had to be a reason for that, thought Clarissa. Whatever happens now, she must not trust the Geordie.

Clarissa smiled as she prepared herself for the final leg of the trail. She felt confident. She had to believe that she could really do this (with or without Ralph's help). She had to believe that she could find the missing manuscript and deliver it to Kowalski, as Charlie had requested. It was possible, after all.

Max's scent: apples and cigarettes, was still lingering in the air when Clarissa finally got up to leave. As she walked out of the café, she took delight in deliberating how the Geordie would find the climate in Poland at this time of year .

12

'"Let's face it. We're done?", he really said *that*?' asked Donna incredulously, her dark eyes widening. 'That's vile.'

It was the following evening. After being paired together in business class for all of their flights that day (Edinburgh in the morning, Charles de Gaulle at lunchtime, and Malta in the afternoon) Clarissa had offered to make her pregnant friend dinner back at her Bishop's Stortford flat before she went on to the hospital.

Clarissa sighed as she loaded Donna's plate with pasta and placed a jug of steaming hot sauce before her.

'But Charlie didn't –'

'Charlie didn't really break up with you that night. I know,' said Donna. 'It was all an act. But for someone who didn't really want to break up with you, why did he have to use such brutal language?'

Clarissa sat down at the table. A heavy rain had started to pummel the window.

'Because he needed me to get upset, I suppose,' Clarissa replied irascibly. 'I guess I had to show real emotion in case we were being watched. I had to be seen as being genuinely affected, or they would suspect me of having the manuscript!'

'But they *did* suspect you of having the manuscript, didn't they? They went on to search your flat and your car!' said Donna.

Clarissa gave her an acquiescent stare.

'No wonder you were susceptible to the charms of a young, handsome, talented pianist!' said Donna, lacing her pasta with the thick red sauce in which chopped tomatoes, peppers and herbs bobbed tantalizingly. She tucked in.

'Donna. Do I need to remind you that nothing's actually happened between Ralph and myself?'

'Then why did he finish with his girlfriend?' cried Donna, stabbing her fork into a fusilli swirl. 'Oh, pass me another serviette would you, sweetie, I'll need to wear this uniform again tomorrow, I'm in the middle of taking my other skirt out.'

Clarissa threw her a napkin.

'Because she's insane?' Clarissa suggested. 'If you could meet her – you'd understand.'

Donna got up and walked over to the refrigerator. She returned with half a bottle of white wine and a stemmed glass that she'd plucked from the draining board on her way back to the table.

'I understand,' said Donna. 'Pour yourself some wine, hun. Don't mind me.'

'I couldn't drink alone,' said Clarissa, pushing the glass away.

'Sweetie, I insist!' said Donna graciously, her American accent exaggerated to intensify her point. She opened the bottle on Clarissa's behalf and poured it into the tall, stemmed receptacle. 'You go off it a bit when you're pregnant anyway.'

Clarissa didn't believe her. 'Really?'

'Honest to God. But you? You need to relax!' Donna went on. 'This Dead Drop business is getting too much for you!'

Clarissa accepted the wine willingly. It tasted good; especially after the day she'd had.

She cupped her brow, a tiredness coming over her. She was exhausted after having gone to bed far too late the night before. After communicating the destination of Drop Five to Max, as planned, she'd found herself working on the clue to Drop Six until she finally came up with its location in Paris.

It transpired that Charlie had continued the pattern. *"38.R.D.L.C.38.N.OP.37.1.Paris"* had translated into: *"38 de la Chaussée-d'antin, Paris"*. It was an address that Chopin had kept in 1838. And the reference Charlie had made to Opus 37, no.1, had turned out to be the Nocturne he'd composed in the same year.

Clarissa had once again, risked travelling into Paris between flights to retrieve the memory stick. This time she'd slipped on her trainers before leaving the airport, and she'd opted for the Metró instead of a taxi. At her destination, she'd found a clothing store encased in travertine (the original 38 de la Chaussée-d'antin had gone) but the sixth Dead Drop was there, buried inside a small hole to the left of the shop's fire-doors. The stick had been sitting in the wall waiting for her like a metal insect that had burrowed its way in out of the cold. And once again, her return to the airport to catch her flight back had proved breathtakingly close, but she'd managed it. Just.

Since they'd left Stansted (a good hour ago) Donna had talked endlessly about Woody and Woody's wife (whose name had been revealed as Amy). Apparently, at the hospital Amy had been all compunctious and maudlin about attacking her husband and broken down in Donna's arms. It had not been the reaction Donna was expecting. Once the scene had been related to Clarissa with astonishing clarity, Donna turned to her confidante with eager anticipation and encouraged her to talk about her progression with the Dead Drops.

'So, from the face on you, I take it you still haven't heard from Mr. Royal Academy then?' said Donna, between mouthfuls of pasta. 'Look, he's in his final year, you know what that's like. He's probably preoccupied with his musical commitments.' She continued to eat.

Clarissa just stared at her meal. It smelt good, but she ended up pushing it around her plate in silence.

'I just don't understand why he hasn't messaged me,' said Clarissa matter-of-factly. 'I mean, he's managed to find the time to send two random tweets *and* post on his Instagram, for God's sake!'

Donna raised her eyebrows. 'So, you've been keeping an eye on his socials? That's… pretty intense.'

'Well, after what happened to Woody, I was worried Morgan might have attacked him or something,' Clarissa ventured. 'He *knew* that the last time I'd seen him, he'd walked off with a lunatic and said he'd be right back. He could at least have told me he was all right!'

'My God. You have got it bad,' said Donna, making her feel like a teenager with a crush.

Clarissa stared at her with a furrowed brow.

'I think you need some more wine,' said Donna, filling up Clarissa's glass. 'Now, how are you doing with the next clue, or do you think you're going to need *his* help again?'

'I haven't examined it thoroughly yet,' said Clarissa, slowly devouring her pasta. But this was a lie. She had been turning the clue around in her head all afternoon and was utterly perplexed by it.

'But the next one's in London, right?' said Donna.

'Paris.'

'Again?'

'Yes,' said Clarissa, aggrieved. 'Again. It means I'll have to run for the Drop between flights one more time. I'm hoping the last one's in London!'

'Listen, hun, so far you've been so bloody lucky it's been unreal,' said Donna, with an admonishing point of her red fingernail. 'But going for it a third time, between flights like that? The odds have *got* to be against you! I wouldn't take the risk, if I were you. You'll be in big, big trouble if you miss your flight back! Carry on like this and all three of us will be out of a job: you, me and Woody!'

'I know,' said Clarissa ruminatively. 'I know.'

An hour after Donna had left, the rain abated. Clarissa was on her sofa with her laptop trying to decipher the clue again when her phone rang.

'It's not there,' said a disconsolate Max. 'I've searched twice.'

The Geordie had obviously not been shrewd enough to check under the bollard.

'It *must* be there,' said Clarissa. 'You can't have looked properly.'

'Or *you* haven't deciphered the clue properly! You'll have to come down here and help me,' said Max.

'But I can't! I'm about to go to bed. I have to be up at 4 a.m. for work,' said Clarissa, horrified that she was expected to just drop everything and run to the Geordie's rescue.

'What about that friend of yours, the lad who's been helping you? He lives in London, doesn't he? Can't you give us his number. Perhaps he can help me find it?'

'I'm sure he would,' said Clarissa wincing. 'But he's away at the moment, performing in a show in Paris.'

'Oh? Where in Paris?'

'Do you know what? I've forgotten where he said now. Listen,' said Clarissa, trying to take back control of the conversation, '"UB". Did you manage to figure out what that meant?'

'No,' said Max. 'None of the houses had plaques with those initials.'

Clarissa tried to coax Max in the right direction. 'Well, do you think it might stand for "under" something? Under something beginning with the letter "b" perhaps? Was there anything around that began with the letter "b"?'

'…Err…I'm not sure. Like: "under bush" or something like that?'

'Yes! Exactly like that!'

'Well, it's a possibility I suppose.'

'Perhaps if you were to go there again, something might become apparent? And is there any news on Charlie?' Clarissa asked hopefully. 'Are you any closer to finding out where he is?'

'No,' said Max, her voice softening briefly. She gave a respectful pause before snapping back to the task in hand. 'This new "UB" idea of yours? I think you might be onto something. I'll return to the location one more time and investigate. It's a shame Ralph isn't in London isn't it? I could really do with his help!' Max hung up dramatically, before Clarissa had time to respond.

Clarissa was sure that she'd been careful not to disclose Ralph's name in any of their conversations. If Max had found this out for herself, she'd probably already traced him to the Royal Academy of Music (she noticed that when she'd referred to his show in Paris, the Geordie hadn't probed into the nature of his performance). But just how far was she likely to go? Far enough to find out that he'd quit his show in Paris and was back at the RAM? Far enough to turn up there and demand his help?

I'll have to send him a message to try to warn him, thought Clarissa.

She was in the middle of composing a text to Ralph, when her phone rang. Then, as if by magic, the words: *"Ralph Valero calling"* began rolling neatly across the screen. She swiped right to accept the call in fervent anticipation: 'Hello?'

'Hey.'

As she waited for him to speak, the silence seemed to intensify.

'You're pissed off with me, I can tell,' said Ralph. 'And I don't blame you. The other night, I had to take Morgan all the way back to her place. It was unforgivable of me to leave you in the theatre like that, and I'm sorry. But Morgan went a bit crazy. She took my phone. That's why I haven't contacted you. I've only just got it back.'

'She took your phone?' Clarissa hadn't imagined this probability. 'I'm surprised she didn't delete my number!'

'Actually, she did, but I managed to retrieve it from the recently deleted file.'

'Then it was lucky she didn't delete it from there as well,' said Clarissa sardonically, not quite believing him. 'So, here you are!'

'So, here I am.'

Another silence.

'You played well the other night,' he said.

'Thanks. So did you.'

'Thanks,' said Ralph. 'We were having a good time until Morgan showed up, weren't we?'

'We were,' she said. 'Perhaps you should have put on Álvaro's ring before you performed.'

'Aye, to be sure. I guess I didn't realise I had an audience at the time!' He went on hesitantly: 'My invitation, to stay at my gaff, I'm sorry it got trodden on like that. I was looking forward to showing you where I lived.'

'Don't worry about it.'

'I have to ask you: Would you have come back with me and stayed over?'

'...I guess you'll never know that now, will you?' said Clarissa, deliberately adopting an enigmatic stance.

Ralph laughed, and she imagined his eyes sparkling as they creased together, his white teeth momentarily exposed.

'I've missed talking to you,' he said.

'Have you?' she said.

'Aye.'

Clarissa waited eagerly for Ralph's curiosity about the Dead Drop quest to return. She would wait for him to ask her for news of it. She refused to provide an account of all that had gone on as a matter of duty.

Ralph cleared his throat: 'So did you manage to find the sixth Drop in Paris?'

Clarissa smiled. His interest gratified her.

'I did!'

'Beautiful! And did you meet up with Max in London and throw her the dummy line?'

'Oh, yes,' said Clarissa. 'And she took it. Hook, line and sinker!' (She thought there would be little point in mentioning Julia and Jonathan, as Ralph knew nothing about the Instagram photograph). 'It all went according to plan; but she's visited the location twice now, and she still hasn't found the Drop. Her ineptitude is staggering! She's just called actually. She wanted me to give her your number.'

'*My* number? You didn't give it to the woman?'

'Of course I didn't! I said you were busy performing in Paris, but don't be surprised if she just turns up at the RAM and demands to see you. It's the sort of thing she'd do.'

'She knows where I'm studying?'

'Not from me, she doesn't! I've disclosed nothing about you, not even your name, but she took pleasure in letting me know she knew it, and probably a whole lot more besides!'

'Ah, that might explain something that happened today.'

'Why, what happened today?'

'I think she was waiting for me,' said Ralph. 'There was a woman standing outside the RAM watching me when I left this evening; dark curly hair piled on the top of her head, fur coat. I was with a large group of students. She appeared to follow us for a while, then she vanished.'

'So, while I was congratulating myself she hasn't been following *me,* it was because she's been following *you*!' said Clarissa, stunned.

Ralph laughed. 'Chill. It was just the once.'

'Are you sure about that?'

Silence.

When he spoke again, he changed the subject.

'Was it tight again? Getting the Drop? Did you risk leaving the airport between flights, like you did before?'

'Yes. I had to. It was close again, yes, but I made it.'

'You did well, then! And the seventh Drop? Has he put it in London?'

'No. It's in Paris.'

'Again? When are you next there?'

'Friday. It's my last return flight of the day. I'll be touching down at Charles de Gaulle at 3.45 p.m.'

'Great. I can meet you there if you like. How about the same place as before?'

Clarissa was shocked. It was the last thing she expected him to say. The man was inscrutable. He blew hot and cold like the wind. She just could not read him!

'But I don't expect you to come to Paris,' she said.

'But you do still want my help?' said Ralph, sounding crestfallen.

'Yes, but –'

'You just want me to help out with clues, not the Drops, is that it?'

'No, I like it when we find the Drops together, but –'

'I do too. Then I'll be there.'

'Wait a minute,' said Clarissa. 'The clue. I haven't been able to work it out yet.'

'Hence the reason for my call! Fire away, I'll see what I can come up with.'

'Okay,' said Clarissa, reaching for her laptop. She read from the screen: 'Stick No.7: MDLVR.AS.UP.Paris.'

'There's no numbers,' said Ralph.

'Of course!' said Clarissa, only just realising this fact for herself. 'That's why it looks so odd! Two Drops to go and he's decided to change tact. Incidentally, there aren't any letters from any of Chopin's Paris addresses in it either!'

'He's making it harder,' said Ralph. 'He's protecting the manuscript.'

Clarissa fell silent for a moment. She had just thought of something: 'Ralph? Has anything happened with Slim and Silas?'

'Happened? Like what?'

'It's just that back in the theatre, you said to Morgan that you'd managed to pay back *half* the money. Is that true?'

There was an uncomfortable silence.

'…No,' said Ralph. 'It's just something I said to calm the eejit down.'

'So, how can you afford to travel to Paris, when you still owe all that money? And…why was Morgan so freaked out to hear that you'd been busking?'

'Hey…okay. Nothing gets past you, does it?' Ralph made an effort to sound relaxed, but Clarissa picked up the tension in his voice. 'It's…sort of difficult for me to talk about that.' He went on. 'I will. Just not now, over the phone; like this.'

'Right.'

'Look. I'll make a deal with you. When you're ready to tell me why *you* gave up the piano, I'll tell you what happened to me while I was busking, okay?'

Clarissa was taken aback, even though Ralph had attempted to negotiate in this way before.

'Clarissa?'

'…Okay. It's a deal,' she said reluctantly.

'That's grand.'

'Ralph?'

'Aye?'

'Did Morgan really take your phone?'

Silence.

'Ralph?'

'…Ah, you've got me again! No. Morgan didn't really take my phone.'

His admission shocked her. Even though she'd suspected it to be the case, she didn't think he'd come clean about it, and so readily.

'So, why didn't you call me?'

'Because…'

Clarissa dug her fingers into the sofa's cold, soft pile.

'Because you do things to me,' he said.

Clarissa flinched. She could hear his breath clearly. She imagined him gripping his hair firmly in his fist. She imagined a lone vein pulsing wildly over his right eye. 'What things?' she said.

'Every time we meet…I feel a connection with you; it's like electricity. Tell me you've felt it too, or is it just me?'

Clarissa closed her eyes. *Yes.* She had felt it too.

'Ralph,' she said.

'Don't tell me. You're still involved with Charlie,' he said. 'I know.'

'We shouldn't be talking like this,' she said firmly. 'We have to focus on the Drops.'

'Aye. The Drops,' said Ralph. 'I guess I'll see you Friday then. At Charles de Gaulle?'

'Yes. But –'

The line went dead.

Oh, God, she thought.

13

The next day Clarissa woke early and pre-emptively switched off her alarm. With only two more Drops to go, she should have felt pleased that she was finally approaching the end of her quest, but she did not. She was jumpy, apprehensive and nervous. And it wasn't only due to her anguish over Charlie's whereabouts, or the new feelings she was struggling to repress for Ralph.

With Max well on her way to being successfully diverted to Poland, Clarissa had started worrying about the other two parties interested in the manuscript.

She had hoped that "the Pernod shot" had done its job and convinced Charlie's captors of the unlikelihood of a collaboration between Charlie and herself, and called off their spies. But she found herself unable to believe in this with any real conviction and could not rule out the possibility that this group could still be watching her.

Then there was Roland Steed.

She hadn't seen or heard from him since she'd eschewed his man with Ralph in Mayfair on Monday, and this fact in itself was proving to be a bit of a torment. His disappearance seemed to indicate that she was either still being followed by one of his men (so successfully she hadn't noticed) or that Steed had been quietly tucked away working on some other strategy that would inevitably lead to her downfall. Either way, she couldn't imagine a man like Steed walking away from a business like this without a fight, not if the things she'd read about him were true.

Clarissa had of course subjected Steed to the same online investigation she'd given the others. But as well as failing to find even one social media account for the silver-haired businessman, she'd discovered that very few photos existed of him either, which had surprised her. His name *had* surfaced however, in connection with a few other searches she'd made on the internet, including: "Chopin", "piano", "classical music", "the world's richest men", and her most shocking revelation: "theft". She'd discovered that while Steed had gained a reputation for himself as being a generous patron for the Arts (supporting a whole host of famous institutions), it turned out that the smooth-talking millionaire was also a bit of an obsessive art and antiques collector with a temper. In a *Times* article dated 2003 Clarissa had found the sentence: *"Roland Steed was reduced to storming out of Sotheby's yet again, at having lost his bidding war with Lord Bentinck over the last two Lots of the day"*. And when she'd dug even deeper, she'd made the startling discovery that Steed and his brother George had once been linked to a criminal investigation undertaken in Boston, USA during a holiday he'd taken there in 1990, when 13 paintings from the Isabella Stewart Gardner Museum (collective value $500 million) had mysteriously disappeared.

For some reason, Clarissa had not been surprised to learn that the Steed brothers had gained notoriety in this way.

Clarissa tried to ignore the scars in her mint Fiat as she inserted her key into its dashboard. She was restless, ill at ease. She switched on the two phones in her bag (hers and Charlie's), still intent on carrying his around with her, still hoping for some sort of breakthrough. Then she started the engine of her car and drove.

During the course of her journey to the railway station she heard three texts register, all on her phone: *ping, ping, ping.*

She waited until she was sitting comfortably on board her train to the airport before she read them. It looked like they had all arrived around the same time (10 p.m. last night).

The first was from Max, informing her that she'd found the Drop underneath the bollard. Her text, blunt and to the point, simply read: *"Got it. Ring me".*

Clarissa digested this quickly, and with a small sigh, moved on to the next. She was in no hurry to reply to the Geordie.

The second was from Donna: *"Thanks for tonight. Shouldn't have gone to the hospital. Felt faint, then threw up in my car. I'm calling in sick on Thursday. W's op at 11:30 a.m. Take care. D xxx".*

She responded to this immediately: *"Take it easy, hon. Don't let it put you off my cooking! I'm sure W. will be ok. Xxx".*

The third was from Ralph.

Clarissa found herself staring at her phone thoughtfully, savouring the anticipation of his reply, her index finger hovering tantalisingly above the blue bar that would turn the thick black font bearing his name into a thinner, less significant one as soon as she made contact with the screen.

She took the plunge.

She read: *"Clue de-coded. See you at the airport as planned. R."*

So the inscrutable Ralph Valero had done it again!

She pressed the part of her display that permitted her to reply and typed with pleasure: *"Great! See you tomorrow!"*

Of course, she did not know then, that their proposed Friday meeting would never take place.

Clarissa reached the airport in good time. She was briefed (she would take care of first class today). She performed her allocated checks on the plane along with the rest of the crew. Then she smiled and showed her passengers to their seats aboard her first flight, scheduled for takeoff at 5:45 a.m.

Then everything started to go wrong.

The fact that they were heading to Fuerteventura and not Charles de Gaulle should have put Roland Steed out of her mind for a while but it did not. The man worried her, and she found that very soon she was looking for him amongst her first class passengers, imagining that another impromptu visit from him was highly likely, suspecting that this was the sort of thing he would do for amusement.

Then, out of the blue, just as Clarissa was making her way towards her jump seat, Claire (the in-flight manager) called her name out, her voice biting through the hum of the air conditioning like a flute through a group of arco violins: 'Clarissa! Wait! I'd like you to change to economy to keep an eye on our new recruit. If you could switch with Vanessa, please.' The instructions non-negotiable.

Clarissa was a bit put out by the new arrangements, but she knew better than to question one of her superiors, so made her way to the economy section of the plane without completing her search for Steed.

The "new recruit" in question turned out to be a girl called Tara. She was young (about twenty), quite stunning in appearance with skin like snow, large green eyes and hair as black as coal, but her flying experience was limited.

Clarissa cringed as Tara made mistake after mistake. She'd seen the girl insistent on helping an elderly woman zip up her bag when the old dear had expressively told her not to, resulting in the bag's contents spilling out into the aisle and the woman taking umbrage. She'd also seen the young flight attendant pluck a child's dummy from the floor and hand it to a baby without washing it, which had caused the mother to shout. And when they'd encountered some turbulence over the North Atlantic, she'd heard Tara making a joke with a male passenger about: *"preferring that the plane went down now, (over the sea) rather than in fifteen minutes when they would be over land again!"* Unfortunately, this was also picked up by the antennae of an eight-year-old boy, who in turn had related it to his younger sister, and later on in the flight, when the engines started emitting a funny whirring sound, Clarissa heard both of them telling their mummy that: *"that stewardess said we were going to die!"*

The length of the flight was estimated at four hours and fifteen minutes and breakfast would be served approximately half way through this. It would constitute sausages, bacon, tomato, black pudding, hash browns, brown bread, butter, orange juice and a Lavazza coffee, all served in a plastic tray. The vegetarian option substituted the sausage with a veggie equivalent, and the bacon and black pudding with a banana, bagel and jam.

The first class breakfast would be far grander. There would be a fruit selection with cereals and yoghurt, then croissants and fruit conserve. This would be followed by black bean and scrambled egg wheat quesadilla with linguica sausage and tomatillo and apple salsa. Banana and buckwheat pancakes with berry compote and sweet syrup were optional to finish. Its vegetarian alternative was equally as impressive; the sausage being of a far higher quality than its economy/business counterpart and the scrambled egg decorated with a veggie version of the quesadilla with a garnish of salad and fresh herbs. The first class passengers could also enjoy the added luxury of china plates.

As all in-flight meals had to be pre-ordered beforehand, there were only ever the same number of meals as occupied seats. Everybody knew that for this reason, the meals couldn't be swapped or moved between classes. Everybody it seemed, apart from Tara.

When the breakfast distribution was well underway, Clarissa became aware of a bunch of youths who were becoming rowdy. She put it down to pre-holiday excitement. It was not uncommon, and the crew were used to having to deal with such groups, but one man in particular was proving to be a bit of a nuisance.

Just as Clarissa and Tara were distributing their final four breakfasts at the tail end of the plane, this man buzzed for a stewardess and Tara volunteered.

He was a cocky little devil of eighteen or nineteen. His head was as good as shaven, but for a small patch of hair about three inches in height that that stuck out of his crown like a utility brush. He had thin lips with slightly protruding buckteeth and a tattoo of a winged serpent on the small, hard bulge of his right biceps.

Clarissa heard him complaining that he was vegetarian and the meal he'd received contained meat. She watched Tara nod apologetically, before removing his food and head towards the galley. Unfortunately, she failed to reach it before another passenger intercepted her.

Attempting to rescue her new recruit, Clarissa started off down the aisle herself, but was stopped by a child spilling her juice at the back of the plane. 'Excuse me, stewardess!'

Clarissa turned and made her way towards the little girl who'd had the orange juice mishap. Luckily, she had a cloth on her and set about cleaning the fluid from the girl's seat. The girl thanked her, beaming sweetly, then whispered to her mummy with undisguised awe: 'She looks like a Disney princess. Is she Sleeping Beauty?' For a moment, Clarissa put the man's breakfast complaint out of her mind and smiled serenely back at the family, assuming her role. She chatted to the girl about the hotel they were heading towards with the promise of a giant pool with a flume, and Clarissa lost herself in the idea that the world was really a good place, where nice things happened and she was somehow part of that magic.

Five minutes later, just as Clarissa had finished clearing up the spillage, she looked up to find that Tara still hadn't managed to return to the vegetarian passenger, and very soon, the man in question started swearing with a passion.

Clarissa saw Tara acknowledge her error and sprint to the galley, so she hurried towards the thug herself to calm things down.

'Please, sir! Would you mind lowering your voice and softening your language? There are children present!' Clarissa cried.

The thug ignored her completely. Then Tara suddenly re-appeared.

Almost ceremoniously, Clarissa watched Tara smile sweetly and hand the undeserving thug her solution: A first class vegetarian alternative breakfast, complete with china plates.

Now if the man – who quite obviously had not been expecting such a splendid outcome – had just thanked her and eaten, Clarissa was quite sure that everything would have been just fine, (Tara would have received a ticking off from Claire once the passengers had exited the plane, but no great harm would have been done). But the man, buzzing with excitement at his newfound luck, proceeded to boast to his friends about the luxury breakfast he'd bagged, with great temerity.

In the meantime, Clarissa could see Vanessa and Claire, oblivious to what was going on, raising their arms at one another in the galley. She guessed they'd just become aware of the missing first class breakfast, so she started making her way towards them to explain.

Clarissa had remembered boarding the fat man with the squint and the funny little tortoise-shell specs who was sitting in seat 27D, as he'd had an exceptionally loud voice. She didn't know it then of course, but later she would blame this man and his loud voice for altering the sequence of events in her life.

The man, who must have been observing the saga with the forgotten food for some time, suddenly exclaimed with great gusto: 'It looks like all you've got to do to receive an upgrade on your food folks, is be rude to the cabin crew!'

This remark was met with an uneasy silence from the rest of the plane.

Then the thug's retort emerged like the in-flight movie had been turned up too loud: 'What did you say, man?'

'You heard!' the fat man replied, completely unfazed by the man's aggressive attitude and the jeering and whooping expounded by his friends.

'Do you want to come over here and say that?' the thug asked, struggling to turn in his seat to gain a clearer view of the man who had dared to express such an opinion.

Clarissa watched Tara's smile turn off like a light as she acknowledged that in her haste to correct one mistake, she'd inadvertently created another.

On catching a glimpse of the fat man, who was trying to continue with the consumption of his economy breakfast in peace, the thug then said perniciously: 'Oops! I'd be surprised if you can stand, mate, yet alone walk! The bloke's a monster! *Have you seen the fucking size of him*?' To this, his crowd began jeering like a pack of animals, and were soon rolling around in fits of laughter.

And that should have been the end of it.

But it was not.

The fat man could not let it drop. He hollered with disdain: 'YOU SHOULD BE ASHAMED OF YOURSELVES, THE LOT OF YOU! YOU DON'T DESERVE A NICE HOLIDAY!'

It didn't seem like much, but it was all it took to tip the thug over the edge.

First he stood up, visibly seething, still holding on to his breakfast. Then he raised his plate and brought it down with so much force it crashed into his tray violently, smashing into tiny pieces, his food splurging over his fellow passengers (friends and strangers alike), the messiest part being a curious red gloop swimming with limes that had once been the tomatillo salsa. As various parts of the matter hit sections of the plane, the china shattered in the most dramatic fashion, amidst cries of disgust and shock.

Immediately after this, Clarissa felt a shard of china enter her skin just below her right eye. The unpleasant sting of pain was so unexpected, any contingency plan seemed to allude her, and as she raised her hand to her cheek in disbelief, she saw a woman point at her and exclaim in horror, before covering her mouth. When Clarissa examined her fingers she found that she had pulled a tiny part of the plate out of her face, and that she was covered in her own blood.

The next thing she saw was the thug pushing past everyone to reach the fat man in seat 27D. The horrified man was then subjected to being punched squarely in the jaw, his spectacles vanishing so quickly, it looked like he was part of some spectacular magic trick. Directly afterwards Clarissa heard the man struggling to breathe, but he said nothing more.

The plane was stunned into a deadly silence, and this moment seemed to continue surreally for a few seconds longer than it should have done.

Then a commotion followed, and the youth was restrained by two helpful bystanders and dragged to the front of the aircraft amidst applause. His friends shook their heads and muttered to themselves. The thug then consented to being handcuffed to a rail in the galley by Claire and Clarissa (with blood streaming down her face) and the drama was over.

Upon landing, Clarissa was taken to the hospital in Fuerteventura where she was patched up. An hour earlier, just before the man had been escorted away by the Spanish police, she'd received a full and tearful apology from him. She discovered that, separated from his mates, the thug's former display of maleficence had diluted to practically nothing. This had both satisfied and amused her, and on the strength of it, allowed her to make the decision not to press any charges. The fat man, she had been told, had point-blank refused to see his assailant again, expressing the wish to prosecute at the earliest opportunity.

Clarissa was removed from further duties for the remainder of the day, and flown back to Stansted as a passenger, with four stitches in her cheek and a bloodshot eye.

On her flight home she found herself dissecting the dreadful incident repeatedly, as she tried to work out what the crew could have done differently. It was during this re-evaluation that she'd ended up recalling an incident that had occurred with Woody about six months ago, when a couple of men had engaged in a brawl upon one of his flights. She'd remembered how Woody had come out of the cockpit himself to put a stop to it. The men had been no match for their smug, laser-tongued captain, and he'd reduced them to grovelling wrecks in a matter of minutes.

Clarissa was forced to admit that she'd wished Woody had been flying their plane that morning. The thought surprised her, as previously she'd not had a good word to say about the philandering pilot, but she felt absolutely certain he'd have sorted the whole thing out far better than Josh, (their actual pilot) had.

So, there on a 12:15 p.m. flight from Fuerteventura to Stanstead – a flight she should never have been on – Clarissa had a thought she'd previously deemed herself incapable of: she'd longed for Woody's presence upon her plane that morning. *Woody!* Who'd have thought it? The man who was so deficient in restraining himself as far as the lure of a beautiful woman was concerned, was, and she had to admit it, highly proficient in maintaining law and order on board an aircraft (a quality she had previously overlooked).

She imagined the pilot in the hospital, residing pathetically upon some operating table whilst undergoing surgery on his wandering hand, and was prepared to admit that perhaps she'd been a little too quick to condemn her best friend's lover.

As soon as she landed, she took out her phone and typed: *"How did Woody's op go? Hope all is well xx"* and sent it to Donna, meaning every word of it.

It was 5:37 p.m. when they came to her flat, the sergeant and the constable. She'd not been expecting anyone of course because by rights she shouldn't even have been there. But as soon as she clocked that one of them was wearing a police uniform she assumed they'd come to question her about the incident on the plane.

'Alexa, stop!' she shouted. She was listening to: "Adam's Song" by blink-182. The music cut.

She opened her front door.

'Miss Clarissa Belmonte?'

'Yes,' said Clarissa, in a manner that suggested she'd not been that surprised to see them. 'Come on in.'

The men thanked her and entered her flat.

'I haven't changed my mind,' she said. 'About not wanting to press charges, I mean. The youth apologised to me before he left the plane, and as far as I'm concerned that was good enough for me. And *this* should heal up fairly quickly.' She pointed to the pad on her cheek. 'Or so I've been told,' she added. 'But I take it you need a statement from me to support the claims of the man who was punched?'

The sergeant, a thin man in his fifties smiled at her with wise eyes and said: 'I'm sorry to learn that you've been involved in some sort of altercation, miss, but our visit is unrelated to that. We're here about another matter entirely. I'm Detective Sergeant David Quinn of Hertfordshire Constabulary CID. This is Police Constable Jacob Risely.'

Both men proffered their credentials. The youthful face of Police Constable Risely smiled at her affably.

'We need your help with another incident, miss,' the sergeant went on.

Clarissa led the men into her living room. She beckoned to them to sit: the young constable taking the sofa, Quinn, the armchair; his legs spread wide, his elbows resting upon his knees, commanding a presence. He waited for Clarissa to join them before continuing.

She seated herself beside the constable.

'I'm afraid there's no easy way to say this, but the body of a man has been found,' said Sergeant Quinn, as gently as he could.

As Clarissa's green eyes registered the full implication of this, they flickered, then locked together with the sergeant's. She swallowed hard. 'Whose body?'

'Well, we were hoping you might be able to tell *us* that, miss. The man had no ID on him, you see.'

Clarissa sensed her heart rate quickening. She could feel the heat pulsing through her blood as it rode her veins. She was fairly sure that her trembling would soon become visible to them.

'The only thing he had on him was this,' the sergeant said softly, removing something from his jacket pocket and placing it on the coffee table before her.

Clarissa gasped in recognition. It was the paper aeroplane coaster she'd written her mobile number on, all those months ago when she'd first met Charlie. It had been carefully sealed in an evidence bag and appointed a number for reference.

14

There was a high-pitched humming in the mortuary that was strangely reminiscent of her former ear infection. It was also very cold, but she'd been expecting that.

The floor was grey and shiny; parts of it still gleamed with a wetness that suggested a recent cleaning; parts were pitted with small crevices. Clarissa was surprised to find a vaguely pleasant scent in the air as well, like detergent.

'It's the formalin,' said Sergeant Quinn, as if he could read her mind. 'The chemical they use for preservation. It can make your eyes sting after a while, so be careful.'

At that moment Clarissa wished that she'd taken the sergeant's advice and called someone, but she hadn't wanted to inflict this experience on anyone – particularly her parents or Donna.

When a man dressed in a blue gown wheeled the trolley in, she suddenly wished she'd called Max.

'Thanks Smithy,' said Sergeant Quinn, nodding again in that reassuring way he had. 'Are you sure you're okay to proceed with the identification, Clarissa?'

The cadaver was inside a black bag. It resided upon a silver trolley that bore smudges, tarnishes. She felt the trolley unworthy of its purpose.

'Yes,' said Clarissa, her response delayed, her voice unrecognisable due to the lack of fluid in her throat. 'Please go ahead.'

'Take this,' Smithy said, handing her a facemask. When she just stood there holding it, he said: 'I'd recommend you put it on.'

With trembling hands, Clarissa fiddled with the elastic of the face covering, struggling to hook it over her ears.

She couldn't take her eyes off the bodybag.

Smithy waited patiently for her to be ready before his fingers closed around the zip. Slowly, he began to pull it down.

When the face emerged, it was the colour of milk.

Clarissa thought his mouth seemed too small and his eyelids too deep, but there was no doubt about his identity.

It was Charlie.

In response, she felt a sound try to emerge from her mouth. It took its time but eventually it came out in the form of a low moan.

'Are you all right, Clarissa?' said Quinn.

The words took their time.

'...It's Charlie Davenport,' she said.

A sharp potent smell penetrated her nose suddenly, like someone had pumped an aerosol in her face, and the nausea came, filling her up as severely as if an invisible tube had been thrust down her throat.

'Where…was he found?' she said, with some difficulty.

'In a field out near Perry Green in Hertfordshire,' Quinn replied.

'No!' she cried, shaking her head aggressively. 'No, no, no.'

'He was shot once in the heart at close range. It would have killed him instantly. If it's any comfort, he wouldn't have suffered for long.'

'*Shot*?'

Clarissa knew that she was shaking quite visibly now, and a sensation like wire ravelling around a spool was taking hold somewhere in the frontal lobe of her brain.

'When?' asked Clarissa quietly. It felt like she was speaking in slow motion.

'It's difficult to say for sure, but the estimated time of death is approximately ten to fourteen days ago.'

'*Sorry*? Would you mind repeating that please?' said Clarissa incredulously. The sergeant's words seemed to be rolling around the inside of her brain like a thick oil, incapable of dissolving.

'Ten to fourteen days ago,' repeated Quinn.

'I see,' said Clarissa, digesting the full implication of this.

She stared at Charlie's pale face and was struck by an overwhelming sense of emptiness. She felt consumed by the paradoxical truth that Charlie was both there, and not there, at the same time.

There was a slight discoloration to the skin around his lips.

'What's wrong with his mouth?' she said.

'We think it might be duct tape residue,' said Smithy. 'But when we found him, his mouth was bare. It looks as if his hands had been tied together at some point too, but there was nothing on his wrists when we brought him in.'

Clarissa closed her eyes and visualised being back in the mud field on the evening Charlie went missing. Desperately, she began to replay it in her mind from the perspective she'd seen it from, all the time looking for inconsistencies. She wondered if he'd heard her calling him, but had been unable to respond because his mouth had been taped shut. Then she thought about the possibility that he'd managed to break loose from his captors, albeit briefly, freeing himself of the tape and whatever other restraints they'd had on him. She thought back to the conversation she'd heard from the two men by the side of the road referring to Charlie as having: "got away". In her mind's eye she imagined him running through the field. She pictured another man catching up with him and *bang*! She envisaged the bullet striking his chest.

She thought she was going to be sick.

An hour later, Clarissa stared at the plastic cup full of cold coffee on the table in front of her as if she were in a trance.

She'd made a statement to the effect that Charlie had invited her for a meal at the Hoops Inn on Sunday 10th March at 7 p.m. She'd told them that he'd ended their relationship as they'd been drifting apart slowly, and there hadn't been a scene. She'd explained that Charlie had driven off at approximately 8:15 p.m. and that that was the last time she'd seen him. Eleven days ago.

She knew that she would not drink the coffee and she had tried to tell them this, but they had insisted on giving it to her, leaving her by herself to recover from her shock in a small white room. She had felt bizarrely like she'd been trapped inside the cavity of a tooth.

While no one had been around, she had sobbed in loud angry paroxysms, the pain crawling around her insides like she was being attacked. Now, she was silent, staring at the wall in a daze whilst the dressing under her eye morphed from her tears.

She was shaken out of her reverie by the door opening.

A tall woman entered carrying a yellow notebook. She was followed by a young uniformed officer.

The woman's hair was set in small Bantu knots. She had sharp eyes and a Nubian nose. She gave off an air of importance.

'Hello, Clarissa. My name's Chief Inspector Onika Okoro,' said the woman in a low, deep voice. 'I'll be leading the investigation into Charlie Davenport's murder. This is Constable

Ryan Griffin. The constable acknowledged her by nodding, but he did not move away from the door and Clarissa soon realised that he must have been told to stand by it like some sort of guard.

'Is that in case I try to escape?' said Clarissa, intending to lighten the atmosphere, but the inspector just stared at her and said crisply: 'No. It's in case you turn violent.'

A noise, like a bone cracking, was issued by the policeman as he redistributed his weight.

Clarissa examined the inspector as she sat down. She was tall for a woman and well built. She wore a pale grey trouser suit which struck a sharp contrast with her black skin. She looked about forty years old. She had large, full lips and dark searching eyes.

After expressing her sympathy at Clarissa's loss and thanking her for her co-operation with the proceedings so far, the inspector opened her yellow notebook and smoothed back the pages carefully with long, bare fingers.

'So you met him on a plane,' Inspector Okoro began. 'You had a relationship with him for eleven months. The relationship began to fizzle out. He ended it.'

Perhaps she hadn't meant to sound so mordacious, but Clarissa flinched at the crudeness of this summary.

'That's *basically* it,' said Clarissa. 'Although, we err…had some good times as well.'

'I'm glad to hear it,' said Okoro, her top lip twitching.

'I loved Charlie,' said Clarissa, suddenly wanting this woman to know just how much pain she was in.

'Of course you did.'

Inspector Okoro wrote something down in her notebook with a scratchy pen. She smiled, revealing brilliant white teeth: 'How long have you worked as flight attendant, Clarissa?'

'About six years.'

'All for the same airline?'

'Yes.'

'How many times have you given your mobile number out to a passenger?'

Clarissa felt the tone of the conversation turn sour.

'That was the *only* time.'

'I see.'

The policeman by the door coughed.

'Did you suspect that Charlie was about to break up with you that night in the Hoops Inn?'

'No. It was a complete surprise.'

'Then you were upset?' The inspector used an upward inflection here and smiled. It seemed misplaced, insensitive.

'Of course.'

'But you didn't object to the split, ask him to reconsider?'

'No.'

'Why was that?'

'If someone doesn't want to pursue a relationship with you, they can't be forced into doing so!'

'I would beg to differ, in my experience,' said Okoro sanctimoniously.

Clarissa swallowed hard. This policewoman was tying her words up in knots.

'I accepted Charlie's decision,' said Clarissa sadly.

'What did you do after Charlie drove away from the venue?' asked the inspector.

'Well, it was raining. I just sort of stood there for a bit, in the carpark. I was in shock I suppose. Then a group of people came out of the pub and one of them, a man, came over to see if I was all right.'

D.I. Okoro looked up from her notepad, interested. 'Can you describe this man for me, Clarissa?'

'Well, he was white, tall. He looked like he regularly worked out at a gym. He was about forty years old, brown hair, dark eyes. He was wearing a white long-sleeved shirt and dark trousers, which was odd because it was raining quite heavily.'

'And did you speak to him?'

'Not really, I just said I was okay, and went and sat in my car.'

At this point, the inspector took down all the details of the Fiat. Then she asked curiously: 'And what happened next?'

'After a few minutes, the man came back and knocked on my window. This was at 8:20 p.m. precisely. I know this because I saw his watch. It was black; digital, with an orange display, and it read: "20:20". I remember this distinctly.'

'I see,' said the inspector in her low voice, writing something else down in her notebook. 'Do go on.'

'Well, the man asked me if I was all right again. I said that I was. I said I was waiting for someone. I wasn't, I just said that to account for the fact that I hadn't driven off yet, and he seemed to accept this. Then he nodded and said: "You take care, now," and got into a blue Jaguar and left. That was when I noticed he'd been alone, and I suspected that I'd been wrong about believing he'd been with others.'

Again, the inspector wanted as many details as possible about the car, but Clarissa could only say it was a two-seater Jaguar, and relatively new.

'Then what did you do?' said Okoro.

'I waited for the windows to clear, they'd all steamed up, you see. Then I drove home.'

'You drove straight home?'

'Yes.'

'Thank you, Clarissa. You've been very helpful. I'll give you my number in case you think of anything else that might be important.' The inspector threw her card upon the table. 'There's a protocol we have to follow in such cases, I'm sure you understand. So if you wouldn't mind waiting for Sergeant Quinn to finalise things, you can go home in one of our cars when he's finished.'

With this, the D.I. produced a large, white smile and left.

By the time Clarissa was deposited back at her flat by one of the squad cars, it was 8:35 p.m. On the approach to her building, she was convinced that she had seen someone loitering around beside her garden wall.

She unlocked her front door with trepidation and reconnoitered every inch of the place before she felt safe enough to settle there. She pulled all her blinds closed, but despite repeatedly peering out from beneath them, saw nothing else that caused her concern.

Ten minutes later Charlie's mobile received an incoming call. She let the phone ring out, then turned it off.

She knew that now Charlie was dead, carrying around his phone was not such a good idea, and was forced to confront the fact that by taking it from the mud field that night, she had inadvertently, removed vital evidence from a crime scene.

The phone was promptly hidden inside the bowels of her piano alongside the gun.

The task had given her something to do. But after this, the intense shivering she'd experienced in the mortuary seemed to return with a vengeance. Her stomach was growling like a caged dog. She was aware that she'd missed dinner, but eating seemed out of the question.

At the police station they had taken her fingerprints and swabbed her mouth for DNA. The experience had left her feeling like she was under suspicion of killing Charlie herself. She didn't know how to mitigate the tension that was building up inside her.

She settled upon tea.

Helplessly, she sat upon her blue sofa clutching a steaming mug of it with both hands, using its warmth to repress her trembling. This seemed to work until the liquid cooled.

Suddenly, she felt as though everything was getting too much for her again. She needed to talk to someone. She needed normality to return.

She called Donna.

No reply.

She called her parents' house.

No reply.

So she called Ralph.

He picked up.

'Hey,' he said, like it was any other ordinary day.

'…Hey.'

'You okay?'

'What are you doing?' she asked, trying to sound normal.

'I'm just walking home.'

'Ralph, I…' She faltered, struggling to get the words to form in her mouth. 'Something's…happened.'

'What do you mean?' He seemed miles away. He *was* miles away. She wished he were nearer.

'Charlie's been shot.'

'Jesus, Clarissa! Is he all right?'

'No. He's dead.'

She listened to the silence as he took this in, trying once more to take in the fact herself.

'What can I do?' said Ralph, with a sense of urgency.

She wanted to see him, but didn't know how to say it.

'I don't know,' she said. 'I haven't been able to stop shaking since I heard.'

'Where are you now?'

'I'm at home.'

'Is someone with you?'

'No. I haven't been able get hold of anyone yet. Only you.'

'Can I see you?' he asked, concerned.

She was relieved that he'd suggested it first, but then started to doubt whether it was the right thing to do, whether *he* was the right person to see.

'Well, I –'

'You really shouldn't be on your own at a time like this,' he said insistently. 'You need to be talking. You need to be with a friend.'

'I can be in London in just under an hour?' she offered.

'You want to come here?' he sounded surprised. 'Surely it would be better if I did the travelling?'

'It's okay,' she said, thinking about the person she'd seen by her garden wall. 'I'd just rather not be here right now. Where shall I meet you?'

'Do you normally get off at Euston?'

'Yes.'

'Take the Northern line to Tufnell Park Tube. I'll be there waiting for you,' he said reassuringly.

When she drove to the railway station, part of her was screaming: What the hell are you doing? You shouldn't be driving, not after a shock like that, and meeting up with Ralph in such a vulnerable state can't be a good idea! But she found that once she had started out on the journey she was incapable of turning back.

The station was busy. She felt a few people staring at her eye which was still very bloodshot, and the bruise around it was intensifying, despite her latest efforts to conceal it by leaving her hair down and switching to a smaller dressing.

She bought a ticket and sat by the window inside the train carriage hugging her laptop. The seat smelt of urine, but she didn't seem to possess the strength to get up and select another.

When she arrived at Euston the crowds swelling around her made her feel dizzy, and she fought the temptation to stop and rest awhile on an empty bench, but on she went, to find Ralph.

The Tube was hot and strangely comforting, unlike before, and nobody seemed the slightest bit interested in her eye, which was a relief.

As she passed through the underground passages of London she suddenly felt tired and consumed by the pulsing of a most unpleasant ache that appeared to be overtaking the frontal lobe of her brain. *Charlie is dead, Charlie is dead,* the ache seemed to say.

Ralph was standing waiting for her beyond the ticket barriers at Tufnell Park Station just as he'd proposed, his arms folded, black jacket and jeans.

Clarissa regarded him tenderly, touched by the anxious way he was pacing up and down waiting for her arrival, ready to escort her to a place of sanctuary. Then his eyes met hers and she saw horror consume his face; his handsome features adjusting as he took in her injury. It was only then that she'd realised she'd omitted to mention it.

'Jesus!' he cried. 'What happened to you?'

Her heart lurched as she reached his proximity. She was unsure exactly when she had started according him with such affection, but it was fast becoming evident that a new and unexpected resistance to it was in play on his part.

He was subjecting her to hard scrutiny, without emotion. It was making her feel uncomfortable.

At first, she blamed her injury. Without its distraction she was sure that he'd have opened his arms immediately, allowing her to run into the safety of his ginseng and musk embrace. But even after he'd long clocked the damage to her eye, he seemed to remain strangely detached from her, as if her suffering was not something he wished to assuage, and that something else far stronger was preoccupying him. Perhaps, she thought, he suspected she'd had something to do with Charlie's murder.

'What the hell happened to your eye?' he repeated, more aggressively this time, his expression fixed into what she could only interpret as disgust.

'Oh, I took a lesson on why china plates are forbidden in economy class onboard aeroplanes!' she said trying to make light of it, laughing at her own joke. But he just continued to stare at her, in a shocked, almost appalled way.

'Someone threw a plate at you?' he said, his mouth slightly ajar.

'Well, this idiot got angry and smashed a plate. I sort of got in the way of its trajectory,' she replied, humorously. Secretly, she was surprised she could even muster the effort to speak.

'Is it okay?' he asked. 'I mean, has it been examined by a doctor?'

'Yes. They took some debris out of it at the hospital in Fuerteventura, that's why it's a bit red, but it will heal,' she said. 'It might take a couple of weeks, but it will go back to normal.'

Again, she was surprised at her ability to relate all this to him so jauntily, as on the train she had been worrying that her voice would refuse to work at the sight of him.

'Jesus! Could your day have been any worse?' he cried, equally as blasé, as if he had run into an old acquaintance he hardly knew, or cared at all about, for that matter.

Clarissa shrugged and forced a tight smile for his benefit, waiting for him to offer his sympathy about Charlie, but this was not forthcoming.

Ralph pulled back his hair in his fist, as was his habit, and scratched his head. He'd obviously had a plan for them once he'd collected her from the station. This now appeared to be undergoing some sort of reconsideration. Clarissa listened to the pinging of the ticket barriers snapping backwards and forwards, as he deliberated his next move.

'Er... Shall we go somewhere for a drink?' he said, his hand reaching out for her arm, but for some reason his fingers just stopping short of reaching her.

She nodded her assent, feeling his absence like a physical pain, unable to understand his estrangement.

Ralph led Clarissa into a bar called Aces and Eights, its blue neon sign electrifying the black air like a fruit fly's nightmare. Clarissa asked for a brandy despite her headache (a mistake), and Ralph carried it, along with a pint of beer for himself, to a couple of vacant seats. The place was dark, and safe. They both sat down opposite one another and stared at the small red light in the middle of their table while a cluster of unthreatening, animated bodies generated around them.

He had made the right choice, coming here, she thought. The atmosphere was pleasant: the spilt beer smell mingling with waxed wood, the reassuring thump of the jukebox. It was helping her dissolve the image of Charlie's dead face held suspended in her memory.

'You okay?' he said, a bit more tenderly this time.

'I had to identify his body,' she said.

'Jesus.'

She then went over the sergeant's visit to her flat, running through the events of her afternoon, finally culminating with an account of her interview with D.I. Okoro at the police station.

'She sounds like a right bitch,' said Ralph, sipping his beer. 'Which police station did they take you to?'

'Welwyn,' said Clarissa, as a sort of hypnotic music pulsed in the background. 'I'm a suspect, I know I am. But I swear to you Ralph, I had nothing –'

'A suspect? Did they say that?'

'I'm the jilted girlfriend,' she said, staring into the red light. 'They must think I did it for revenge. I'm a suspect and I didn't tell them the most important thing.'

'Which was what?'

'That I was there. At the scene of the crime, directly before it happened. I picked up his phone. I found his car. I drove his car back to his flat the next day. I searched his flat. I took the gun out of his bedside drawer.'

Clarissa saw Ralph's expression change suddenly. She had forgotten that she'd previously refrained from mentioning the gun.

'You did *what*?' he looked indignant. 'There was a gun?'

'Ah. Yes. I –'

'And where is this gun now for God's sake?'

He seemed angry, furious, out of his depth.

'It's in my flat.'

'Jesus, Clarissa. You have to tell them about all of this!'

Ralph looked so distressed, she felt a deep and powerful crushing sensation overtake her.

'I know. But how can I?' she said desperately. 'I've already made my statement. I think Charlie would have wanted it told this way.'

'In the event of his death, I'm sure that Charlie would have wanted you to tell the truth!' he said, as if he were remonstrating a child.

Clarissa closed her eyes and her brow furrowed, but she shook her head. 'You don't understand. He gave me strict instructions not to talk to the police.'

'But surely *that* was about his disappearance!' Ralph lowered his voice. 'Things are a bit different now. I'm sure he didn't imagine in his wildest dreams that he wouldn't be able to get out of this thing alive!'

Clarissa felt a fresh stab of tears behind her eyes.

He saw it.

'Sorry, don't cry,' he said.

'I think we should complete the Dead Drop trail,' she said.

Ralph pulled his hair back in his fist violently. 'You can't be serious? *Sod the fucking trail*! You're perverting the course of justice, Clarissa. You could go to prison for not telling them what you know!'

'But it looks like Charlie got killed for the sake of this manuscript – whatever it is!' she cried emphatically, imploring him with her eyes. 'And it was Charlie's dying wish for me to get it to some professor at the Chopin Society in London. Ralph, we're *so* close, I can't give up now! I have to find that manuscript and take it to the professor!'

Ralph began to stare at her intensely.

'But there has to be a way you can tell the police you were there, in that field, without mentioning the Dead Drops. Surely?'

'There isn't,' she said irascibly. 'Don't you see?' She took a gulp of brandy. 'Look. Charlie breaks up with me. Drives off. I then find his car abandoned by the side of the road. Why didn't I report it to the police? Won't they think that was odd? I didn't report it to the police because Charlie told me not to, *because* he didn't want the police to intercept the manuscript. If I mention the field to the police, and don't mention the manuscript, what reason can I give for not calling them?'

'Okay,' said Ralph resignedly. 'I get your point. But there's another problem.'

'What?'

Ralph lowered his voice and leant in closer to her across the table: 'You returned to the field the next day to move his car. Now what on earth possessed you to do that?'

'Okay,' said Clarissa ruefully. 'I'll admit it. That was a mistake. But at the time, I did it because Charlie said he didn't want the police involved and I thought it would only be a matter of days before some farmer reported it.'

'But they're bound to find out that it was you who moved the car!' Ralph stared hard into her eyes. 'What with all the CCTV footage around on the roads. What if your image is picked up?'

'I wore black. I wore a hat and gloves. I wore dark glasses!' cried Clarissa defensively.

'And how did you get to the car?'

'I took a taxi.'

'Don't tell me you used your real name? And please don't tell me it picked you up at *your* address?'

Clarissa shot Ralph a crushed look.

'Jesus, Clarissa! They're bound to trace the moved car back to you! How long do you think it will take them to work all of this out? They'll piece all of this together in a few days!'

Clarissa knocked back the remainder of her brandy.

'Then we've still got time' she said.

'You still want to go to Paris and get the seventh Drop, don't you?' asked a stunned Ralph. 'With all this going on?'

'You said you knew where it was?'

'I do.'

'So we need to go and find it.'

'You want me to come with you.'

Clarissa shot him a disappointed glance. 'Well, you don't have to –'

'Of course I bloody have to! Do you think I'm going to let you go on your own? The mess you're in? These people have guns! You could very well be next. I don't think you quite understand the danger you're in here!'

Clarissa shivered and stared at him in alarm. They regarded each other silently for a few minutes before she spoke.

'It looks like you'll just have to come along and protect me then, doesn't it?' she said, enjoying the effect her ill-timed flirting had on his face.

They stared at each other again.

When he finally reached out and stroked her cheek tenderly with his thumb, she was taken aback. To her embarrassment, she responded to this by crying. Then she allowed herself to be swallowed up by his eyes and they both smiled, and she knew that she was starting to break through the barrier that he'd created.

Dreamily, she placed her hand on top of his, and said: 'You really have no idea how talented you are, do you?'

This did not go down well.

'Jesus, Clarissa. I'm no more talented that you are!' he cried irritably, pulling away from her.

'I wish that were true.'

'For God's sake, will you just leave off with the self-pity and tell me what happened, why you never play anymore?'

She flashed him an injured look.

'Not tonight, no. Haven't I been through enough today?'

'Okay,' he said with resigned commiseration. 'I'm sorry, you've been through hell today. I don't mean to make things worse for you. I'm just trying to understand, that's all.'

'I know,' she said. 'And I *will* tell you about it. But don't forget you still haven't told me what Morgan was going on about; why you stopped busking. Why don't you tell me about *that* first?'

Ralph sighed.

Clarissa smiled.

'Stay over at my gaff, and I'll tell you about it tonight,' he said. 'You can have my bed and I'll sleep on the couch. Then we can get a flight out to France tomorrow.'

'Hey, isn't that blackmail?' said Clarissa. 'And flying's out of the question I'm afraid. I've been signed off work for a few days, so I can't very well turn up at the airport. We'll have to go by train and I'll pay. Are you able to spare the time?'

'I'm free tomorrow,' said Ralph. 'I'm at your service. But will madam be requiring a bed for the night in Kentish Town?'

'Well, I –'

Clarissa tried to stand up, but found on doing so the room had started spinning violently.

'I'm sorry,' she said. 'I don't feel so good.'

She felt Ralph's strong arms supporting her.

'When was the last time you ate anything?' he said.

'I don't remember.'

'Come on, I think you need to eat. Lean on me. I'll take you back to my place. I live literally around the corner.'

'But I –'

'Don't try to talk.'

They started to walk through the pub, Ralph's warm arms still around her waist, but the room spun again and Clarissa felt herself go slack against one of the bar stools. She heard Ralph shout to the bartender: 'Excuse me, mate? Can I get a packet of salted nuts here and a bottle of water?' and she felt Ralph's strong arms lift her onto one of the bar stools, her head making involuntary contact with his chest.

In seconds, Clarissa felt the smooth end of a bottle reside on her lips and she swallowed back some water.

'You don't have a nut allergy do you?' he said.

She shook her head and the room spun again. Then she felt Ralph place a couple of peanuts in her mouth and a sharp spiky sensation followed as the salt hit her tongue.

'Chew. They'll make you feel better,' he said.

After half a bag of nuts and few sips of water, Clarissa started feeling more like herself again.

'Are you okay now?' Ralph asked. 'For a minute there, I thought you were well and truly banjaxed!'

'Yes,' said Clarissa. She touched his face in gratitude. 'Thank you.'

He regarded her dubiously, as if he were measuring her stamina, trying to determine whether she had enough energy to make it back to his place. Then she sensed the focus of his gaze fluctuating between her eyes and her lips repeatedly, the muscles in his jaw tensing, the vein in his forehead standing proud before he turned away.

She wondered if he'd been about to kiss her.

'Let's get going,' she said, sensing that she was winning him back.

When they emerged into the cool dark air, Clarissa felt better.

'Ralph Valero, you're my knight in shining armour!' she cried, as the traffic roared past them.

'Great. If anyone's following us, they now know my name.'

'There's nobody following us,' said Clarissa. 'I left whoever it was outside my flat.'

'What do you mean?' said Ralph, pushing back his hair and glaring at her. 'There was someone outside your flat? Why didn't you tell me about this?'

'Oh, don't worry, they didn't hang around for long, but I knew I had to get away from there. I don't think they've followed me here or anything.'

'Bloody hell, Clarissa!' Ralph cried, glancing around suspiciously. 'This is turning into a fucking nightmare!'

'I thought you'd had a drink?' said Clarissa. 'You should be more relaxed than this with a drink inside you!'

'How can I be relaxed? I'm with *you.* You make me unrelaxed.'

Silence.

'Your housemates. Will they be all right with me crashing? Hadn't you better call them and check with them first or something?'

'Nah,' cried Ralph, suddenly delighted that she appeared to be consenting to staying with him after all. 'They'll be cool with it. You look as if you've been in a punch up, admittedly, but it adds intrigue to your character. Don't worry, I won't tell them we could be harbouring a criminal, or anything like that.'

Clarissa flashed him a confused look. 'With one breath you're angry with me, saying I should be taking this thing more seriously, then in another you're making a joke of it! I don't understand you at all!'

Ralph averted his gaze.

'I'm sorry. I must have got a bit excited at the prospect of showing you my piano. Not that it's the right time. You should probably just eat something and go to bed. I hope you like beans on toast by the way?'

Relieved by his return to lighthearted banter, Clarissa began to feel more comfortable.

'Well!' she said, smiling at him warmly. 'Nuts *and* beans. You sure know how to treat a girl!'

'Oh, I wouldn't knock it if I were you!' said Ralph, flashing her one of his rare smiles. 'A portion of beans has enough protein in it to get you through a whole day. And *I* should know, I've fallen back on them many a time! By the way, would you object to me holding your arm? Just in case you keel over on me again? Just so that I'm right here, you know, if something were to happen?'

Clarissa stopped and extended her elbow to him.

Ralph took it gently.

'A wise choice,' he said.

'Lady Somerset Road. It looks nice!' said Clarissa, eagerly surveying the grandiose three storey town houses skirting the road in front of them.

'You sound surprised,' said Ralph. 'What were you expecting? A squat?'

'Well, nothing as eloquent as this, that's for sure! Who were you on the phone to just now, your house-keeper?'

'What?'

She'd made Ralph stop at a pharmacy on Fortess Road, not ten minutes ago, and while she'd stood in the queue with her toothbrush and cleansing wipes she'd seen the glass of his smartphone light up through the shop window.

He looked awkward all of a sudden, surprised to learn she'd been watching him.

'Sorry, I was only making conversation,' she said. 'You don't have to tell me.'

'You found me out,' he said, looking embarrassed. 'I just called the house to ask them to tidy up a bit, before we got back.'

Clarissa was so tired, they proceeded to walk the rest of the way in silence.

Ralph's house was a bit further away than she'd been expecting, so when he finally said: 'This is the one!' she was so relieved, she fought the urge to burst into tears.

Then his tone changed: 'Bloody hell! What the fuck?'

The two men positioned in his porch were a shock.

Clarissa quickly recognised them.

'Valero!' said Slim facetiously, his gold tooth glinting under the streetlamp. 'And we were just about to give up, weren't we Silas?'

Clarissa felt Silas look her up and down favourably, a cigarette wobbling on his lower lip. 'So it's true then? Morgan told us that you'd traded her in for the blonde!'

'I *am* here!' said Clarissa, offended.

Ralph was fuming. 'What the fuck do you two think you're doing loitering around here at this time of night?' he cried indignantly. 'I thought we'd made our arrangements for next week?'

'Ah! There it is, Silas! The acknowledgement we were seeking! I'm so glad you remembered, my friend!' said Slim. 'So, we're still on for next week then, for the other half?'

'Are you deaf or something?'

'Now, now, Valero! There's no need for that! We just had to make sure, you see. What with you deciding to dump Morgan out of the blue like that. We needed to be sure you hadn't any illusions about "dumping her debt" along with *her,* if you know what I mean?'

Silas smiled his ugly smile and blew smoke in Ralph's face.

'Her debt is my debt,' said Ralph. 'I thought I'd made that clear?'

'Do you know, Valero, I didn't think you'd say that? That's very noble of you my friend. You dump the girl, but you keep her debt! We're satisfied. Say no more. Come on Silas,' said Slim, walking away. 'It's time we left these two to it.'

Silas stared at Clarissa and smiled: 'Morgan's handiwork was it? Your face?'

'No,' said Clarissa. 'It was not.'

'I believe you! Thousands wouldn't,' he said, sniggering like a child.

15

Ralph's house was warm and homely. It smelt like a mixture of cooked dinners and scorched washing.

It was also strangely deserted.

Clarissa noticed that it was already half past nine. Having consumed their evening meals, she presumed Ralph's housemates had made themselves scarce.

Clarissa was divested of her coat and taken into a long living room that had been lavishly furnished. She was shown the John Broadwood and Sons' piano that resided at the far end of it, with the distinct impression that Ralph would have been a lot more enthusiastic if Slim and Silas hadn't freaked him out with their impromptu visit. She also sensed with dismay that Ralph's initial shock at finding the two thugs on his doorstep was staying with him, threatening to return him to the former detached version of himself she'd encountered earlier when they'd met at Tufnell Park Tube.

It was all a bit odd. The room was so large, their voices seemed to reverberate through the space making her question whether she was really there at all and not still trapped in her cavity at the mortuary, indulging in some sort of fantasy about where Ralph was likely to live (she certainly couldn't have dreamt up a nicer house for him). She wondered what sort of rent he paid. She was also confused about the comments he'd made last week suggesting Slim and Silas had targeted him because he'd been "poor". (After seeing where he lived, she couldn't understand how such a conclusion had been drawn). And it hadn't escaped her attention that Slim had alluded to Ralph bringing him: "the other half of the money", when Ralph had explicitly told her that he'd lied about having paid off that much of the debt.

Her questions came and went like a torrent in her brain, with no time for answers. She knew that something was amiss here, but she couldn't quite determine what it was.

After a few minutes, Ralph set about making them something to eat in the kitchen, leaving her alone on the living room sofa.

She closed her eyes and tried to relax there, putting her concerns down to "overthinking". Then she tried to purge these irritating inconsistencies from her mind once and for all by diverting her attention to her laptop.

Resignedly, she perused: "Eurostar train times" on the internet, exchanging her wild notions of speculation with the practical pre-occupation of securing their means of travelling to France.

She booked two return tickets from London to Paris.

Their train was set to depart from St Pancras at 9:22 in the morning and they would return at 6:45 in the evening. She thought that at least this way they could retrieve the Drop, get some lunch, and return to London without being in too much of a rush.

Once they had eaten their beans on toast, Clarissa ran through her plan to Ralph. With a mild frown, he nodded along to it, then said: 'I'm sorry you had to encounter those eejits again.'

She shrugged and said: 'No matter,' then promptly changed the subject to enquire where everyone was.

'Upstairs. Around,' he said flatly. 'You're bound to bump into one or two of them sooner or later. Your eye is looking far less inflamed now,' he added, smiling, 'which is good.'

Clarissa took this to mean that her eye wouldn't shock anyone quite as much now if they were to chance upon it, and she smiled and nodded in a vague manner.

She suggested they should rise early tomorrow and get to St. Pancras by 8:30 a.m. He told her that he'd set his alarm for six.

'How much did the tickets cost?' he asked with an inquisitive tilt of the head.

'£170 each.'

'I'll pay you back,' he said intransigently.

'I told you, there's no need.'

'There's every need,' he said. 'By the way, what did you think of our piano? You didn't comment.'

'Well, it's very beautiful, obviously,' she replied.

'It sounds good too.'

'You're not going to ask me to play it, are you?' she remonstrated. 'I'd rather hear you.'

'Not now,' he said, smiling, repressing the urge to perform for her once again. 'I want to show you something else. Come on.'

He led her out of the living room and up the stairs to the first floor.

Awkwardly, he showed her into his bedroom, which smelt of his ginseng and musk scent mingled with sweat. It was a large and sparse room, with a king-size mattress on the floor adorned with a plain white duvet. A wardrobe, a modern desk and a swivel chair flanked one side of the room. The only things upon the desk were a laptop and an anglepoise lamp. The floorboards had been stripped bare and the large expanse of wood dominated the room.

'You don't have much stuff,' she said.

'I prefer minimalism,' he said, with a small, low laugh and pulled the chair out from the desk so that she could sit on it.

She stared at the chair as if it were alien to her.

'Please,' he said, gesturing, 'sit.'

'Surely it's more comfortable downstairs?' she said, pushing a lock of blonde hair behind her ear.

'More comfortable, perhaps. Less private,' he said. 'I want to show you something.'

She perched on the edge of his swivel chair.

To her surprise, he began to take off his clothes, stripping to his waist in front of her, his eyes downcast. She was subjected to his fine pectoral muscles and taut abdomen for only a few seconds – shiny with perspiration under the fierce light of a solitary ceiling bulb – when he promptly turned around.

'Oh, my God!' she cried, taking in the state of his back. She stood up.

A richly defined eight-inch pink scar ran diagonally across it from one side to the other, the flesh puckering around the laceration, creating a ridge where stitch-scars latticed down it like a child had attempted to draw a ladder.

'Eighteen months ago I got knifed by two nasty fuckers outside Kennington Tube,' he said, by the way of an explanation.

'They stuck a blade in your back?' she said, her features troubled. 'What for?'

He kept his back to her. 'My busking money.'

'What happened?' said Clarissa.

'I was playing at the foot of the escalators in the station,' he began, his voice unexpectedly charged with emotion. 'I used to live down there. In those days I busked at night – it must have been about eleven o'clock I reckon – when these two fellas decided to jump on me and take what they could. I made the mistake of chasing after them. When we got to the top of the escalators I managed to pull the one who'd swiped the cash to the ground. The fall did something to his knee. He then called back to his accomplice who proceeded to pull a knife. While the one with the injured knee jumped on me, the other one took a slice out of my back. I was in hospital for two weeks. The blade punctured my lung. It took me about eight weeks to recover from it. Physically, I mean. Mentally, I guess I'm still battling with it.'

'Oh, my God that's horrific,' said Clarissa shaking her head, unable to help drawing a comparison between this, and what had happened to her that morning on the plane. Her brief encounter with the brush-headed thug had resulted in a shard of china driving a three-centimetre gash in her left cheek. She could not imagine a metal blade carving a twenty-centimetre crevice into the flesh of her torso, nipping her lung in the process.

'The pain must have been excruciating!' she said.

'Aye,' he said quietly. 'It was. For quite a time afterwards I experienced panic attacks. I couldn't perform publicly. I began to think it was the end for me.'

Try as she might, Clarissa was unable to visualise Ralph in such a dark place. Then she remembered the conversation they'd had in the Paris taxi, when Ralph had gone all quiet on her, and she recalled that it had happened directly after she'd mentioned Chopin's "failing lungs".

'But you can perform publicly now,' she said, resisting the urge to touch his back. 'How did you overcome it?'

'I haven't yet,' said Ralph. 'But I'm better than I was. I use a few coping strategies: meditation, relaxation, mindfulness. I saw a medical professional who specialised in PTSD for a while. It all helped.'

'I would never have thought –'

Ralph turned around and stared into Clarissa's shocked eyes. 'You think you're the only one who's going through this? You've no idea how many people go through it every day. And with the right help, you can get over it. You don't need to be imprisoned.'

Clarissa said nothing, taking a minute to fully absorb Ralph's words. She understood what he was trying to say, but for her, the counselling had not worked.

Suddenly everything was beginning to make sense. The confidence that this man exuded was part of his "coping strategy". The way that he'd helped her with her panic attack on the train – regulating her breathing and massaging her neck – it had all been learned from his time in therapy.

Ralph turned away from her again, causing her to stare at his scar, an indelible memento of the torment he'd endured, permanently fused into his flesh for all to see. He had been brandished both mentally and physically. There were no such tell-tale marks on her flesh to represent *her* suffering. But she felt her pain had been irrevocably synthesized into her in very much the same way.

'And what happened to the men? Did the police catch them?' she asked.

'*Nothing* happened to the men, Clarissa. They got away with it, scot-free,' said Ralph, disparagingly.

'What? They just ran off?'

'Into the fucking night.'

The injustice of this seemed to produce in her a real physical pain. His attempts to heal her had filled her with an overwhelming sense of compassion.

Tentatively, she placed her hand on the cicatrix on his back and ran her fingers down its angry bubblegum pink groove, her blood fizzing from the contact with his flesh. Then she kissed his shoulder.

He turned and stared at her unblinkingly, his hazel eyes sharp with unleashed passion.

Slowly, she felt his fingers navigate their way across the dressing strapped to her cheek where he cupped her jaw. Then she felt the softness of his lips as he kissed her mouth.

Clarissa took Ralph's hand and led him over to the bed, pulling him towards her.

He kissed her again, harder this time, his incipient stubble caressing her cheek. 'I didn't bring you up here to seduce you, I swear,' he said.

'I know,' she said.

He motioned to lean towards her again, but she turned away, drawing her knees up into her chest suddenly. 'Christ, you're so young!' she said in a derogatory way.

Ralph glared at her, confused. 'So you're a few years older than me, what's the big deal?' he said.

'How old *are* you?'

'Twenty-three,' he said.

So, she was six years his senior. Abstractly, she remembered that George Sand had been six years older than Chopin. She would have told him of the coincidence (he'd have liked it), but he'd already started a stubborn display of refusing to show any further interest in the subject, so she decided to leave it at that.

'Did you end your relationship with Morgan because of me?' she said instead, her curiosity regarding this little bombshell finally getting the better of her.

Ralph smiled and placed his right hand upon his left shoulder creating a 'v' with his arm. His muscles tightened as he appeared to baulk from the question.

'The relationship was winding itself down anyway,' he said, his Irish accent accentuating the word "anyway" in a colourful, buoyant way that seemed to imbue it with a different meaning.

'Is that a "yes" then?'

'Does it matter?' he said, surprised.

She found his reluctance to repudiate her suggestion touching.

'Look,' said Ralph awkwardly. 'After spending some time with you, I realised we had *something,* a chemistry. I've never felt anything like it before. With anyone. And I wanted more of it.'

Clarissa laughed mirthlessly. It sounded cruel, as if she were mocking him or something, but she hadn't meant it to sound like that.

Ralph was stunned. 'So much for sincerity,' he said. 'Remind me to conceal my feelings next time.'

'I'm sorry,' she said lightheartedly. 'It must be the shock of seeing…' her expression changed to one of solemnity, 'what I saw today.'

Ralph put his T-shirt back on and assumed an embarrassed but slightly disconnected countenance.

'If you want to talk about it, go ahead,' he said.

She knew by 'it', he was referring to her feelings for Charlie, but she didn't want to talk about Charlie. Not now. Even though the image of her dead boyfriend's face was still haunting her, flashing up in front of her intermittently like she had been staring at the sun too long; she didn't want to talk about that. She wanted to keep her end of their deal and tell Ralph what she had promised. She wanted to tell him why she had stopped playing the piano. She *needed* to tell him why she had stopped playing the piano.

Carefully, she re-arranged her legs on the mattress and took a fierce intake of breath:

'My piano teacher used to come to our house. Edward Letterton was his name. He'd always come on Saturday afternoons. He was bald, twitched like a bird. An ugly man, missing a tooth in the front – I used to think that was funny. Well, one day he came in, and we were engaged in a lesson when my mother announced that she needed to pop out to the shop. "You'll be all right won't you, Edward? I won't be a minute". That's what she'd said to him before she left. His reply had been: "We'll be fine,".'

Clarissa closed her eyes briefly, then opened them again.

'As soon as my mother had shut the door, he invited me to sit on the floor with him. I consented, thinking that it was some sort of new relaxation exercise he wanted me to try (we used to do that sort of thing at school). But I had been wrong."

She coughed suddenly and wished that she'd brought some water up with her, bracing herself to relive the trauma she'd been hiding from for so long.

This is not going to be easy, she thought, as she prepared to recall the memory, as if she were about to enter some sort of time machine that would take her back there: the 3rd October, 1998. It was like ripping a scab off a wound. Inevitably there would have be pain, but she knew that it was the only way she could initiate a more substantial healing process.

'Do you think you can dim the lights?' she said. 'I'm getting a bit of a headache.'

'Sure,' he said, igniting the anglepoise lamp on the desk and turning off the ceiling bulb as adroitly as if he'd been rehearsing the manoeuvre for weeks.

'That's better,' she said, her voice beginning to sound quite different, a little hoarse, fractured. She continued with some unease: 'Where was I? Oh, yes. Sitting on the floor with Letterton. Well, after a couple of minutes I felt his hand land on my knee. Then up it moved, onto my thigh; then suddenly his fingers were inside my knickers. I was so surprised by this I didn't know how to react. Then I felt his other hand clamp my mouth. When I went down, my head struck the carpet with so much force I felt dazed. Then he…' she floundered. It was even more difficult than she had imagined. Getting it out. Releasing it from festering inside her. The words emerged jagged and muddled. 'Then he…he raped me.'

She had said it fast, as if the words could be made less harmful that way, with hot tears smarting in her eyes.

Ralph began to stare at her with undisguised horror, a wave of solicitude revealing itself in his body language.

'He did *what*?'

'I won't say it again,' said Clarissa, trembling. 'It was hard enough saying it the first time.'

'You don't have to. Sorry,' said Ralph. 'How old were you for God's sake?'

'Nine,' said Clarissa, trying to control the tremor in her voice.

Ralph squeezed his eyes shut and opened them again, shaking his head, as if his vocabulary was failing him. His shock was evident.

'When he'd…finished,' Clarissa struggled on, 'he saw that he'd made me bleed a little and do you know what he said? He said: "Never mind. That can happen sometimes, but you mustn't worry. Your mother can give you something for that." Then he said that I would probably need to find a new piano teacher. Then he walked out.'

'Jesus. Nine?' Ralph exclaimed, as if he'd only just processed the information, as if his reactions had been delayed.

'Afterwards, I wondered why I had let him do it without a fight,' said Clarissa. 'I mean, why hadn't I kicked him, bitten him, *anything*? Why had I just let him do it?'

'He overpowered you! You were a child!' Ralph cried pitifully.

'The shock of it was overwhelming,' she said. 'I couldn't react to it properly. It was like I had been hypnotised or something.'

'The sick *bastard*!' Ralph spat the words out like poison. 'The man was a mentally ill paedophile!'

He moved closer to her, but refrained from any contact. 'I'm sorry, Clarissa. I had no idea.'

She stared at nothing; her vision had been reduced to a blur. She could hear Ralph's voice asking her repeatedly if she was okay, but she felt as cut off from him as if she were in another room.

'CLARISSA?'

Snapping back into herself, she jumped.

Her voice cracked slightly, but she went on. 'Sorry. I need to… I need to carry on.' She swallowed hard. 'When my…when my mother came home from the shop, she found me crying in the corner of my bedroom. I couldn't speak for an hour. Then I told her exactly what had gone on and she started sobbing and called the police. But his story was very different. He said my period had started suddenly and I had been hysterical about it and blamed him, but that he'd never laid a finger on me. But they examined me, you see, took samples. There was a trial. Two other girls came forward and said he'd touched them inappropriately during their piano lessons. He was found guilty of raping a minor, and two counts of indecent assault.'

'How long did he get?'

'Twelve years.'

Ralph nodded sombrely. 'You stopped him from repeating the abuse. You did a good thing.'

She searched Ralph's face as if she were trying to convince herself that this were true. But in reality she had always denied herself any consolation from this, due to her mother's subsequent mental collapse.

'My mum never forgave herself for leaving me alone with him,' said Clarissa agonisingly. 'She had a complete nervous breakdown; she was never the same again. Her anxiety and depression got worse over the years. It made me wonder if our family would have been in a better place if I'd kept the whole thing to myself! At least then, I'd have had a normal mother. Our relationship was difficult. She sent me to a counsellor for a while, but my therapy was…less successful than yours,' she smiled wanly. 'Anyway, I didn't give up the piano. I had a succession of piano tutors after that, always female, and always chaperoned. I got over it in my own way. I became quite good I suppose. Good enough to win a scholarship at the Royal College of Music anyway. Then…' She felt herself falter.

'You okay?' Ralph asked.

She nodded.

'Then, I was given the opportunity to play Chopin at the Royal Festival Hall,' she resumed. 'Given my own dressing room and everything. I was treated like royalty! I received some flowers before my performance. Twelve red roses were sent to my room with a card. They were from *him*. He'd just been released from prison. The card read: *"Dearest Clarissa. Please know that I sincerely regret my conduct that Saturday afternoon in your family home and despise myself for it. I do not expect you to forgive me, nor do I seek your forgiveness, but I want you to know that I am truly sorry. I am now free from my incarceration after twelve long years and send you a rose to represent every year I have caused you suffering. Recently, I have become aware of your progress with your music and would like to congratulate you on everything that you have achieved. Your success fills me with*

great joy! It is my one and only consolation, to know that I have
helped to create a star in the black sky that has been my life."

Clarissa stared at Ralph, her eyes full of tears and pain. 'Do
you like the way I've managed to memorise the bastard's note
word for word?' she said trying to hold back her tears. 'I suppose
it's my equivalent to the scar on your back.'

She felt Ralph's fingers brush her hand, but she pushed them
away.

'Please don't,' she said in her tightly clipped way, 'I need to
continue. Stop wallowing in my own self-pity once and for all,
right?' She saw him flash her a look of contrition, his hair pulled
back so that she could see the pulsing vein in his forehead.

'Clarissa, I don't –'

She held up her hand to stop him, and went on:

'Well, I got as far as the wings of the stage,' she said, noting
with some embarrassment that she was now trembling as well as
crying, but she tried not to be deterred.

'I peeked around the curtain, half-expecting to see him there,
in the front row, with his bald head and his missing front tooth,
looking exactly the same but older. He wasn't there of course –
well, I didn't see him – but he might as well have been, if you
understand my meaning. Anyway, I was still determined to
perform, when my introduction came. It was all down to a case of
a most unfortunate choice of words, you see. I think that's what
did it. The announcer said: "Please welcome *Clarissa Belmonte,*

our latest rising star!" And that was it. I froze. I was quite literally immobilised by fear; unable to move a single muscle. I could not perform. I never even made it to the stage. I gave up my career as a pianist shortly after that. You see, if my musical success was a comfort to *that* man, I decided that *I DID NOT CARE* for musical success. I decided that I would give it *all* up, be something else instead; something that didn't involve him!'

As Clarissa concluded her story, a fresh deluge of tears streamed down her cheeks. She felt Ralph touch her arm and she fell against his chest. She felt relieved but confused. She'd repressed her feelings about Letterton's assault for so long, she couldn't understand why the stopper on her emotions had chosen *this* moment to work itself loose. She guessed there had to be a limit to how long anyone could withstand this sort of pressure, and that hers had been reached.

Ralph wrapped his arms around her protectively as she wept. He kept repeating over and over that none of this had been her fault and that she'd done the right thing by disclosing the incident to her mother that afternoon. Eventually, she found herself believing him.

She had dealt with Letterton's release from prison absurdly, she knew that. Enrolling as cabin crew for a large airline – it was hardly the obvious choice. But it had helped somehow: barricading herself in the fuselage of a speeding plane, learning how to conduct herself differently, perfecting her external appearance, the uniform. This way, she had been able to seal herself into a disguise, making herself impenetrable. Once the mask was on, it had made it easier for her to live again. Easier because nobody could see the real "her" anymore. And nobody had wanted to dig any deeper beneath her carefully polished exterior, until she met Charlie. But even *he* didn't delve deep enough when he'd had the chance.

With Ralph it had been different.

When her sobs finally began to subside, she stared at him. He looked like he was trying to rescue her with his eyes, hanging onto every word that emerged from her mouth, encouraging her to extricate her pain. He'd been the only person who'd wanted to see her as she really was, without the camouflage. He'd been the only one who'd tried to save her.

She spoke in a controlled but highly charged voice: 'It should have been Letterton's rotting corpse lying there on that trolley this morning, not Charlie's! If anyone deserved to die, it was him!'

Ralph began to caress her shoulders with a tenderness she found endearing; showing her that he understood, letting her know that he was on her side. She nestled herself into him, fresh tears falling. This time her distress was for Charlie, whose life, she now realised, she knew nothing about, but whose ultimate punishment smacked of unjust exploitation.

'I always thought prison was too good for that bastard,' she said.

'What a fucking piece of scum!' said Ralph. 'If I ever encounter him, I'll kill him for you, I swear. I'll *fucking* kill him!'

She could see that he meant it.

Their respective stories exchanged, Clarissa sensed that a new intimacy was now forging between Ralph and herself. She allowed him to manoeuvre her backwards onto the mattress, where he pulled the duvet up around them, and with an overwhelming sense of relief, she fell asleep in his arms.

At 3 a.m. Clarissa awoke to find Ralph staring at her, his eyes alert and glistening in the moonlight.

'You okay?' he said.

'Much better,' she said. 'You've opened the blinds.'

'I wanted to see you,' he said.

He moved towards her, then stopped. The house was silent. He was looking at her ardently.

She realised that she had awoken with a strong physical desire for him too. But she needed to check on her wound and freshen up a bit.

She got up. She saw his eyes cloud with disappointment as she did so, but start to glitter once again when she asked him for directions to the lavatory. He laughed gently before answering her.

She opened his bedroom door swiftly, taking her bag with her and ventured out onto the landing.

The bathroom was white with powder blue tiles. Clarissa shrank away from her reflection in the mirror. She thought she looked simply dreadful; her cheeks covered in dissolved mascara, and the dressing under her eye had all but come away, resting upon her face like a crumpled leaf. She pulled it off, relieved to see that her wound was now fusing. Her white sutures were barely visible, but their presence was announced by two rows of four, smudgy pink dots at the points where they met her skin. The soft tissue around her eye's periphery was now a rich and solid black.

Clarissa used the toilet. Then after cleaning her teeth and refreshing her face with the cleansing wipes, she returned to Ralph's room.

He was laying prostrate, exactly where she'd left him. He flipped onto his side when she climbed back onto the mattress and reached for her hair. Gently, he stroked her face with his thumb and forefinger and she climbed on top of him. He flashed her a look of surprise, then smiled.

'Are you sure…?'

She placed her index finger across his lips to silence him, and he took the end of it in his mouth seductively. She ran her fingernail down his stubbly jaw and she felt his soft warm mouth clamp onto hers.

They kissed slowly, then more fervently. She realised that she was squeezing his flesh with an inexorable hunger.

This encouraged Ralph to sit up and remove his T-shirt, and she found herself responding by lifting her arms to allow him to undress her, which he did with savage gratification. When they were both naked, they seemed to pause in mutual admiration of one another. He, entranced by the way the moonlight struck her pale skin. She, mesmerised by his sinuous, flexing muscles; the only thing he'd left on was his silver neck chain. She continued to press her body passionately against his, running her fingertips tenderly across the vestiges of the knife wound on his back.

'You were *so* brave,' she said, dimly aware of an urgent admonitory voice in the back of her head trying to shake herself around to the fact that they were about to have unprotected sex, trying to find the words to ask if he had a condom.

'*Foolish,* more like,' he said in his strong Irish accent, referring to the way he'd pursued the men relentlessly in order to claim back a few measly coins.

'Talking of being foolish,' she said. 'Do you...'

Ralph stared at her, his beautiful eyes glittering in the subdued light, distracting her.

'Do you...have anything?'

'Err...no,' he said, understanding exactly what she meant. 'Do you want me to stop?'

She didn't answer.

'Clarissa?'

She couldn't speak.

I don't want you to stop, she thought.

She shook her head and felt her long hair cascade around her shoulders. Ralph combed his fingers through it to find her nipples, and his quick, dexterous hands began an immediate, passionate inspection of her breasts, moving down across her stomach, then onto the curve of her hips.

When he reached the inside of her thighs, he stopped. His reluctance to continue suggested a concern that she might still be suffering from issues connected to her violation by Letterton.

In order to reassure him, Clarissa put her lips to his ear and said: 'Please don't think about what happened to me, I've long since recovered.'

But she knew that this was more wishful thinking than anything else. For, if she *had* recovered, why hadn't she returned to the world of music again, where she inevitably belonged? She half-expected him to say as much, but of course he didn't. He didn't want to have a conversation with her. He wanted to be inside her.

'Please,' she said. 'Don't stop!'

'I wasn't as brave as you,' he whispered.

Eased by her supplication, he resumed his urgent exploration of her, maneuvering his hips to fit hers; a new hard, wet presence ascertaining itself on her left thigh. Then he rolled with her, their bodies entwined, so that *he* was the one in control, and gazing down at her, he penetrated her yearning body, emitting a low moan of sweet gratification. Happily, she drank him in, her senses singing, both of their bodies moving in harmony, their breathing accelerating. At first, they moved quickly. Then more slowly. Then quickly again, until the fulfilment they both sought so desperately was finally and dramatically realised.

Her release was delicious, *glorious*. She allowed herself to be absorbed by it fully and completely as she floated, yes, *floated,* her nerve endings fizzing away, into a truly beautiful place where she felt nothing but contentment.

Then she returned to reality with a crash. Back to his room and his mattress and her complete mess of a life.

Physically exhausted, her happiness cruelly flooded by the immutable guilt that always seemed to be lurking within her somewhere, she felt a tear slide across the wound on her cheek.

She looked at him and smiled.

He smiled back, pushing his hair away from his damp forehead, the sweat oozing down his neck. Then he rolled away and padded off down the corridor towards the bathroom.

16

The following morning Clarissa and Ralph awoke to the bleating sound of the alarm on Ralph's phone. He kissed her on waking as if he were demonstrating how easy it was for him to slip into his new intimate role with her, and jumped straight into the shower.

When he went downstairs, Clarissa took a shower herself, using Ralph's gel and towel. She pulled on the same clothes she'd worn yesterday, her flesh now infused with his scent, listening to the tread of new voices echoing around the house. Then, relieved to see her makeup bag and hairbrush, she hurriedly set about making herself presentable to venture out of the bedroom.

Before she took the plunge, she switched on her phone to check for messages and saw that her parents had tried to return her call. Her mother had left a voicemail asking if she was home this weekend or at Charlie's, and she flinched when she heard Charlie's name mentioned as if he were still alive. She planned to call them as soon as she could to explain.

The door slammed when she was half-way down the stairs alerting her to the fact that she was too late to meet *one* of Ralph's housemates, but she found another one in the kitchen – a tall, blond-haired man with black rimmed spectacles in a bathrobe – who was introduced to her as James.

James was pleasant enough and stood with his back to the cooker munching cereal, proposing his day to them as if Clarissa often frequented their kitchen. He also completely ignored her black eye with an impartiality that made her think that Ralph had told him not to mention it. This seemed unnatural as she was quite willing to discuss it, and even *wanted* to discuss it at one point, but James just went on and on about himself. Then Ralph wished him good luck for something, using expressions such as "you'll walk it, mate" and "piece of cake!" which sounded odd, as she'd never heard him speak like this before, and James left the kitchen shortly afterwards.

When they walked to Tufnell Park Tube (which thankfully didn't seem quite as far as it had done last night), Clarissa teased Ralph about his language in front of James. She thought it was funny how people adjusted their vernacular to suit the company they were in (and in this, she did not exclude herself). But their conversation did not flow, and she attributed this to her resistance to immerse herself fully in this new arena they had both found themselves in. It was a realm she had been only too willing to explore last night, but now, in the cold light of day, she was starting to feel somewhat uncomfortable.

The air was crisp and fresh but still resembled inky water, and when Ralph reached out for her hand, Clarissa was reluctant to take it, as if their union would somehow be under threat if exposed out in the open.

'You okay?' he said, shunting his rucksack up a little higher on his back. 'How are you feeling?'

She hesitated. It was difficult to explain exactly how she was feeling. The rows of identical, subtly illuminated Victorian townhouses stretching on for miles were making her feel depressed, but she gripped Ralph's hand and said: 'Alive. I feel alive.'

It was not a lie. She *did* feel alive and grateful to be so. She was allowing herself to become absorbed by the physical sensations of breathing (how the air smelt as it entered her lungs) and walking (how the ground resonated with soft noise when she slapped it with the soles of her trainers) and how Ralph's skillful pianist's fingers, hot with blood, felt within her own. She didn't want to think any deeper than that. Not for the time being anyway.

The Northern Line took them to King's Cross St. Pancras, where they followed the signs to St. Pancras International and below a monstrous arch of steel girders they boarded their 9:22 a.m. train to Paris Gare du Nord.

Their journey to France was comfortable. They spent most of it turned to face one another in their seats, Clarissa with her knees pulled up. They did not touch but instead stared into each other's eyes with a wonderment familiar to new lovers, and Clarissa began to feel the temptation to succumb to her new predicament with a delicious sense of abandonment.

Half an hour into their trip, Ralph went to the buffet car and returned with croissants and coffee. Clarissa removed the lid of her drink and watched the steaming brown liquid tremble to the motion of the train. Her ambivalence about her feelings could not be expressed. She felt both desperately melancholy and joyously exhilarated at the same time and a little ill by the dissonance. She felt on the verge of crying about how happy she would have been if she had hadn't been so sad.

She asked Ralph to explain how he'd arrived at the destination for the Dead Drop clue and she noticed that when he answered her he was now speaking in a very different way. The fabric of his voice had softened to a lover's pitch and his repeated smiling and touching was distracting her from understanding his words. She tried to pretend that she was indifferent to this, but found that her skin was almost trembling with pleasure from the new way he was regarding her.

'I think "MDLVR" stands for "Musée de la Vie romantique"', said Ralph softly, 'and "AS" are the letters of the initials of Chopin's friend's name: the painter Ary Scheffer'.

Neither commented on how strange it was that they were on their way to The Museum of Romantic Life, when they had just begun a new romantic life of their own.

When they had finished their breakfast, Ralph showed Clarissa a photograph of a painting on his phone.

'Ary Scheffer's portrait of the great man, painted in 1847,' he said, handing his mobile to Clarissa.

Clarissa stared at Chopin's face, the high forehead and soft full lips; the pain behind those deep-set eyes. She calculated that he must have been about thirty-seven years old.

'Two years before his death,' she said.

'It was also the year his relationship with George Sand dissolved,' said Ralph, as he pressed all their breakfast waste neatly into a paper bag.

Clarissa took a moment to reflect on this. After Chopin and Sand's nine year relationship, the attention Chopin paid to Sand's daughter Solange (then, nineteen) became too much for Sand to bear, and she accused him of having an affair with her. From what she'd read, Clarissa thought Solange had simply been so jealous of Sand's bond with her brother Maurice, she'd flirted with Chopin to irritate her.

'What's Chopin's connection to the museum?' she asked.

'Well, it's only been a museum since 1982,' he said. 'In the 1830s it was Scheffer's home. He used to host weekly salon evenings there so that everybody connected to the Romantic Arts scene could get together. I suppose it must have been one of the places where Chopin and Sand socialised.'

Ralph put his phone back into his pocket.

As the windows blackened and their train slipped down below the English Channel, Clarissa enjoyed the idea of being beneath the huge expanse of ocean with her new lover. She imagined the Atlantic waves crashing fifty metres above their heads.

Two and a half hours later, their feet on French soil, Clarissa spun around in the gigantic Gare du Nord terminus, its ceiling reminding her of the pylons she'd seen in the French countryside during their anxious taxi journey, its globular lamps lining the platforms like miniature floating suns.

'It's so huge,' she said. 'Where do we go from here?'

'Montmartre. We need to go to 16 rue Chaptal. It's in the ninth arrondissement!' cried Ralph into the vast vacuum of noise.

'Shall we take the Metro?' Clarissa asked, fumbling for their tickets.

'There's a bus apparently. Line 54. Takes about ten minutes. I think it might be quicker.'

Clarissa nodded her assent and off they went to find it.

The Musée de la Vie romantique was a cream building with pale green shutters surrounded by roses and lilacs. It was lit beautifully by the sun, but it did not blend in well with its surroundings. It was rather like coming across a corner of Aix-en-Provence off an alleyway from a Parisian street, but its displacement only added to its charm. One minute they were on a busy road beside a row of parked motorbikes, the sun igniting stalked wing-mirrors like stemmed leaves, the next, they were standing in a tranquil courtyard opposite a fairytale mansion buzzing with insects.

On the bus, Clarissa had seen the Eiffel tower in the skyline. It had looked almost magical, emerging from the mist like some sort of enchanted monument. When she'd pointed it out to Ralph, he'd reached for her hand. As Ralph escorted her across the Musée de la Vie romantique's courtyard, he gripped her hand in a similar way.

As the two of them walked together across the irregular cobblestones, they were encompassed by visitors taking their lunch alfresco on the chairs and tables assembled there. In her mind's eye, Clarissa imagined George Sand charging up to the house adorned in gentleman's clothing, puffing away on a cigar (as it had often been said). Such outrageous behaviour must have been considered shocking at the time. She pictured Chopin watching his new muse intently, at first glance a little repulsed by her audacity, but at the same time strangely turned on by it. She wondered what Chopin and Sand would have thought if they'd been told that a hundred and eighty years from now, this building, the place they'd socialised in, would become a museum dedicated to the memory of their romance. She suspected that Chopin would have been both horrified and amused at the same time.

As the museum was free, Ralph suggested they might as well take a look inside as well as out, whilst they were there. It consisted of two buildings. One had a temporary exhibition space and the other housed two floors of artefacts. They explored the temporary exhibition first, then proceeded to the historical part.

Inside, the old museum smelt like an ancient library. The leaded glass warped their view of the garden and the floorboards creaked as they wandered. There was a lock of Sand's hair (taken at the end of her life, when she was grey and ageing) and some watercolours that she'd painted. She had been more prolific with her writing than Clarissa had realised, and aside from a recurring theme of a suppressed female protagonist seeking freedom from a violent husband, it seemed that she had drawn much of her inspiration from ancient folk tales, as Chopin had done.

Clarissa stopped beside a glass display cabinet where a plaster cast of Chopin's left hand seemed to be reaching out for a plaster cast of George Sand's right hand. Between them lay some love letters and a pen.

'Look at this,' she said to Ralph, fascinated.

'It's a miracle they survived,' he said, referring to the letters.

'Yes,' said Clarissa. 'People will go to extraordinary lengths to preserve documents if they consider them important enough.'

On leaving the museum, they looked at one another.

'So, where do you think he's put it?' said Ralph.

'Surely he wouldn't have buried it anywhere near a place like this?' said Clarissa.

Together, they walked the periphery of the grounds, scrutinising every possible nook and cranny Charlie could have had access to, but found nothing.

'It's no good,' said Clarissa, dejectedly. 'It isn't here. Perhaps Charlie didn't even complete the trail?'

'We'll find it,' said Ralph.

She followed him down the alleyway leading to the building's entrance. 'Come on, let's look down here,' he said, hopefully.

Clarissa joined Ralph running her flat palms around the base of a small brick trough full of plants, then along the latticed fence that flanked it. Whenever they got strange looks from the museum's visitors, Ralph would mutter something in French and they would be ignored.

'What is it you keep saying?' she asked, as they continued their search along the side wall.

'I'm making out we're checking the soil consistency.'

Clarissa flashed him a strained look. 'Is that even a thing?'

'The French take their gardens very seriously.'

At that moment two elderly women started out down the alley, Ralph winked at her and they continued their little charade. The women smiled at them politely. Once they had passed, Ralph leaned across to Clarissa and kissed her full on the mouth. When he pulled away, he said: 'I think I might be falling in love with you, Clarissa.'

She glared at him, first in mock horror, then in amusement, before suggesting casually that they go and find somewhere to have lunch.

The museum coffeeshop was a small greenhouse-like construction with naturalistic walls and blond furniture.

Ralph bought them both tea, quiche, green leaf salad and fruit tart. At the checkout, he spoke to a pretty girl behind the counter in French and their conversation seemed to cover far more than the items on his tray. Clarissa noticed the way the girl was smiling at him – she noticed the effect he had on women in general. She thought that if she were to enter into any kind of relationship with Ralph, this was the sort of thing she would have to get used to. Part of her predicted a romance with such a charismatic music student was not likely to last long.

She tried to shake these thoughts away.

'Come on, let's go and sit outside,' she said brightly, leading Ralph away from the girl. 'It's such a nice day, it would be a shame to waste it.'

Ralph agreed, and allowed her to escort him to a vacant table in the garden, where they found some more blond furniture and visitors chatting away in various tongues.

It was during this lunch that it began to hit her. Up until then, she had allowed herself only to feel grateful to be alive, enjoying all of its sensations with a sensitivity that was predominately pleasant. Now she realised, with a slight sickening feeling, that her mind was starting to warp things into a slightly different perspective. She still felt grateful to be alive but she was now starting to feel guilty about it; guilty she'd slept with Ralph so quickly after hearing about Charlie's death; guilty she hadn't called the police immediately the night Charlie disappeared; and guilty she'd been galivanting around Paris and London with Ralph – her heart pumping blood around her body – when all the time Charlie had been lying in a field, dead!

Guilty, guilty, guilty.

Suddenly she could hear the tread of Ralph's voice in the background, but not what he was saying.

'Clarissa?' Ralph cut in more loudly.

'Sorry, what was that?'

'I was asking her about the grounds,' said Ralph, offering an explanation for his conversation with the coffeeshop girl. 'She said there's another entrance around the back. There's a gate apparently. It might be worth a look.'

Clarissa nodded, hurriedly wiping away the tears that were fast streaming down her face, allowing herself to return to their Dead Drop problem, but she found remaining there difficult, like a swimmer treading water aware of the pull of an invisible undertow.

She felt Ralph sense her disquiet and squeeze her hand.

'Hey, it will be all right,' he said, gently. He bent to kiss her, his lips tasting of strawberries and pastry, and she felt herself revel in the comfort that this produced, like a dry dam being struck with a fine rain.

It was then that she jumped as if struck by an invisible lightning bolt.

A woman's voice – Geordie accent, said: 'Well, fancy meeting you two here!'

Clarissa glanced up in horror, expecting to see Max charging towards them with some semblance of recognition on her face, but she was relieved to see that the voice belonged to a large russet-haired woman considerably older than Max. Clarissa could clearly see that this woman was making her way towards another couple, and that this woman was *not* Max. But its effect produced a horrible reaction in her and she found herself trembling.

'I wonder if Max knows about Charlie?' she said hurriedly to Ralph, her green eyes sparkling with fresh panic.

Ralph shrugged. Without ever having been exposed to the Geordie's distinctive voice, he could not have made the connection, and remained unperturbed.

Clarissa reached for her bag and took out her phone. She saw that Max had messaged her again about the sixth Drop in Warsaw. Hesitantly, she began tapping the screen of her mobile.

'Are you texting her?' asked Ralph.

'I'm telling her to go on to Poland without me, then suggesting we could meet up in London to discuss the clue. I'll leave it to the police to tell her about Charlie,' she added, wincing.

'That ought to keep her quiet for a while,' said Ralph.

As soon as the message was sent, Clarissa jumped to her feet. A small spark had taken hold of her eyes. 'I think I know where the Drop is,' she said.

Ralph followed Clarissa back to rue Chaptal. They stood on the busy street beneath the blue road sign beside the motorbikes; the walls opaque and crack free, the kerb an unmolested smooth lip. Ralph glanced about in confusion, wondering where she could possibly be referring to.

Clarissa indicated the black, skinny bollards with a small inclination of the head. He understood and started out towards them, but just as he was about to begin his investigation, a man turned up. He was in his mid-fifties, overweight, with long grey dreadlocks and a salt and pepper beard. His shabby fringed leathers glinted in the sun.

From their respective vantage points, Ralph and Clarissa both watched him mount one of the bikes and remain defiantly there, scrolling through his phone.

Ralph returned to Clarissa, wrapping his arms around her waist from behind.

'So you think he's used the old bollard trick again?' he said. 'Although drilling into cast iron without attracting attention couldn't have been easy.'

'I bet he did it around three in the morning or something,' suggested Clarissa.

'There's a source of light coming from the one at the end,' said Ralph starting to smile. 'I think you might be right.'

'Is there? Why doesn't he leave?' she said impatiently, referring to the man. 'We can't wait around here all day!'

The biker glared at them formidably.

'Look at your watch,' Ralph whispered to Clarissa, before saying something to her in French.

'Are we making out we're waiting for someone?'

'You've got it.'

Clarissa saw that the time was 3:07 p.m.

The man did not move for a full ten minutes. Then he slipped on his helmet, fired up his bike and thundered off down the road.

Clarissa wasted no time. She raced over to the bollard, crouched down and ran her fingertips around the base of the metal.

The Dead Drop was there. She could hardly contain her excitement. She smiled at Ralph, but he shook his head. She backed off.

Somebody else had come to retrieve a bike. A woman this time, young and sexy. A brunette wearing leather trousers and knee-high boots. She was incredibly curvy with red lips and long black eyelashes. She smiled at Ralph and he smiled back. Clarissa bit her lip and rolled her eyes whilst she waited for her to leave.

The woman said something in French to Ralph and he replied.

Oh, here we go, thought Clarissa.

Then the woman laughed and flicked back her long mane of hair seductively, before going on to say something else.

What happened next wasn't planned. Clarissa strode over to Ralph and kissed him long and hard on the mouth. Then she stared at the girl in an admonitory way, as if she were forcing her into some sort of remission.

The girl climbed onto her bike sulkily. Suddenly, it growled into action and she sped away.

'That was mad!' cried Ralph, his face breaking into one of his beautiful white-toothed grins and his laughter escaping in an almost shocked manner. 'Mad, but I fucking loved it!'

Clarissa looked at Ralph, embarrassed. She wanted to say something, but she was distracted by a man at the entrance to the alleyway staring at her. He was holding a cigarette in his mouth but the second he locked eyes with her, he promptly discarded it and hurried back in the direction of the museum.

'What is it?' said Ralph, who'd turned to see what Clarissa was looking so serious about, and saw nothing.

'Download the Drop!' Clarissa instructed, as she pushed the laptop into his hands.

'But where are you going?'

'Just do it!' She saw Ralph's shock at her peremptory reply.

She left in pursuit of the man, hearing Ralph's protesting cries fall away as she moved swiftly towards the museum.

As she rounded the hedge into the alley, she could just make out the man's back in the courtyard. But by the time she reached the cobblestones she had no idea whether the man had entered the house or snuck around the back of it. She addressed some people milling about asking them in English if they'd seen which way he'd gone, but all she received were blank stares. She stood for a minute, confused, her heart racing, unable to decide whether to go back into the museum or slip around the side of the building, knowing that every second she delayed making this decision was a second lost. Finally, she went back into the museum, racing through the house as fast as the crowds would let her, the smell of the ancient artifacts engulfing her. She took the red spiral staircase to the first floor, and spun around trying to spot him, but it was no use, she sensed he'd given her the slip.

When she got back to the motorbike parking bay, Ralph wasn't there. She imagined that he'd probably returned to the museum to look for her so she called his phone.

It was engaged.

Then she wandered to the mouth of the alley, where the man had been watching her, and tried to see if she could spot Ralph making his way back. But there was no sign of him.

A glint of light from the floor suddenly diverted her attention to her feet and she saw something silver lying on the ground. Bending down to retrieve it, she saw that it was a lighter. She quickly realised that the man who'd been watching her must have dropped it in his haste to get way.

Exhausted, she slumped down against the wall, a couple of metres from the alleyway and waited, turning the lighter over in her hands, delighted to find it engraved with the initials: "D.P.D." A few minutes later, she rang Ralph again, but he was still engaged.

After about ten minutes Ralph emerged from the alley, her laptop bag on his shoulder together with his rucksack, and their eyes met. He looked relieved.

'What happened?' he said.

'Did you get the Drop?' she said.

'Aye.'

'And you remembered to delete it afterwards?'

'Of course.' Ralph flashed her a confused glance. 'Who did you see?'

'I don't know who he was,' replied Clarissa, 'but I'm sure I've seen him somewhere before.' She looked bewildered. 'He definitely ran from me, but I lost him.'

'What have you got there?' said Ralph catching a glimpse of silver in her hand.

'His lighter,' said Clarissa rather proudly. 'He must have dropped it when I started chasing him.'

'You look like the cat who got the cream.'

'That's because I've got his initials,' she said, holding it out to him.

'D.P.D,' said Ralph, smiling. 'Good work, Sherlock.'

'It might come in useful, you never know,' said Clarissa, dropping the lighter into her bag.

Ralph offered her his hand and pulled her from the dusty floor. She stood up and took back the laptop. 'Thanks,' she said. 'Come on, we'd better head back to the station. We can figure out the new clue on the train.'

'Err...this one's a bit more than a clue,' said Ralph. 'It's a personal message addressed to you.'

'*Really*? Did you read any of it?'

'I couldn't.'

'I wouldn't have minded, you know.'

'No, I mean I physically couldn't. It was encrypted,' he said, his Irish accent rolling the word "physically". 'Apparently, the password to open it is the last thing Charlie said to you. "Unlock, by entering my parting words to you", that's what he put in the Drop. Can you remember what he said?'

'Err…' she said. 'Maybe. I'll need to think about it.'

But she knew that she didn't need to think about it. Not really. How could she forget Charlie's parting words? He'd even chosen to address a letter to her with them – the one he'd slipped onto the music stand of her piano – in order to make sure they were infused firmly into her memory. "Good luck baby" was the password. It was only now that his strange valediction made any sense. And Clarissa knew that no one else could possibly know this password but her. So, Charlie had taken extra measures to ensure that she was the only one who could reach the final Dead Drop. And because of this, she felt it only right that she should read this message alone. Clarissa trusted Ralph implicitly, but she planned to go and find the public conveniences as soon as they reached the station so that she could read Charlie's message in private. Then they could head back to London to find the final Drop.

As they made their way towards the bus stop, Clarissa couldn't resist turning back, to see whether the man who'd been watching them was still around, but there was no sign of him.

'By the way, I tried calling you a minute ago, but you were on the phone,' she said casually, as they crossed the road. 'Morgan hasn't been hounding you again, has she?'

'Thankfully, no,' said Ralph, as they walked.

Clarissa waited for his explanation as to why his phone had been engaged, but he offered her nothing more.

17

The following day the police bashed emphatically on the door of Clarissa's Bishop's Stortford flat at 2:35 p.m.

She was alone. She'd called both her mother and Donna that morning and told them about Charlie. They'd been very sympathetic and she'd done a lot of crying, but on the whole, she felt that a huge weight had been lifted from her shoulders. She'd left Ralph at St. Pancras Station at 9.30 p.m. last night and headed home alone, despite his objections. He'd tried his best to get her to return to Tufnell Park with him but she'd declined. She'd read Charlie's message in the Eurostar toilet. When Ralph had asked her if she'd looked it, she said that she hadn't. She'd said this because she couldn't quite believe what Charlie was asking her to do in it. When she'd arrived back at Bishop's Stortford station she'd discovered a £100 fine taped to the windscreen of her Fiat. She was staring at the ticket again, wondering how long she had to pay it, when the police started their relentless pounding.

Clarissa opened the door to find Detective Inspector Onika Okoro and a uniformed officer.

'Hello again, Clarissa,' said the detective, in her deep, masculine voice. She gave her credentials as was customary. She gestured towards the policeman standing beside her. 'This is Constable Rice. We need to have another little chat with you.'

Clarissa froze. Then she opened the door a bit wider, expecting her visitors to enter. But they did not. Clarissa squirmed under the penetrating gaze of Inspector Okoro, whose dark eyes seemed to be boring into her like skewers. Suddenly Clarissa felt very frightened.

'I'm afraid we're going to have to insist that you accompany us down to the station,' said the inspector, her face hard and unflinching.

'But I made a statement. Is there a problem with it?' asked Clarissa starting to panic.

'No. It's not about what you told us, Clarissa. It's about what you didn't tell us.'

Inspector Okoro looked really serious now.

'You see,' she went on, 'some new evidence has come to light in Charlie Davenport's murder case, and we now need to ask you some more questions. We've a car out the front. If you choose to co-operate, it shouldn't take too long.'

'I'll get my coat,' said Clarissa.

Clarissa was shown into a small white room, similar to the one she'd been taken to the day before yesterday, but the atmosphere was notably different. She sensed that she was now being treated with a higher degree of suspicion and no allowances were made for her grief.

Sergeant Quinn and Inspector Okoro sat down opposite her at a rectangular wooden table and the inspector set about arranging a brown folder, a single sheet of typed paper, a yellow notebook, a small plastic tub and a laptop upon its surface with a quiet sensibility. The laptop's screen was open and facing the inspector. Clarissa imagined an artist setting up a still life with a similar decorum.

Okoro ran through the preliminaries of her position with a bored expression. First, Clarissa had to sit through the inspector's "official caution", then it was explained to her that even though she had not been "arrested", she was still entitled to free legal advice if she so wished.

Clarissa refused this outright.

'Okay,' said the inspector, rubbing her hands together. 'Let's not waste any more time.' She pressed some buttons on a panel in the wall and announced that Clarissa's interview was being recorded. After reciting the time, date and full names of all the persons present, she turned to Clarissa and said: 'I have to remind you that this interview is voluntary, and as such, if you wish to remain silent or answer "no comment" you may do so. Do you understand?'

'Yes,' replied Clarissa.

'For the benefit of the tape, I am showing Clarissa CCTV footage: 15941J,' said the inspector flippantly.

The laptop was turned around so that Clarissa could clearly see it, and she cringed when a grainy image of herself behind the wheel of Charlie's Audi TT appeared in front of her. Then she watched herself tapping a code into the keypad to elevate the barrier underneath Charlie's flat; her dark glasses having been removed, one of their plastic arms residing in her lips.

'I'm showing Clarissa footage recorded at the entrance to the carport of the Gabriel Square apartments, St. Albans, on Monday 11th March at 10:37 a.m.,' said Okoro. 'This was the day *after* you supposedly last saw Charlie. Now, there are no prizes for guessing the question we're going to ask you next, Clarissa. In the statement you filed with us the day before yesterday, you failed to mention that you had driven Charlie's Audi TT into his parking space underneath his flat the day after you last saw him. Why was that?'

Clarissa did not know what to say. The sight of her image captured for all to see in the carport underneath Charlie's flat filled her with fear. Even though Ralph had warned her that something like this would happen, she hadn't really expected it. She found herself inwardly berating herself for her naivety. Clarissa looked at the inspector with a pained expression, unable to speak, trying to work out the best way forward without exacerbating things further. She hoped she was imagining it, but the detective seemed to take pleasure in watching her squirm, and allowed the silence to ensue for far longer than was necessary.

Finally, Inspector Okoro relented and said: 'Okay, Clarissa. Let's approach this from a slightly different angle. Do you admit to driving Charlie's car into his carport on the morning of the 11th March?'

Clarissa shuffled in her seat and swallowed. 'Yes.'

'Where did you take the car from?' asked Okoro.

'A field just outside Perry Green.'

'The field where Charlie's body was recovered?'

'Yes. But I didn't know they'd killed Charlie then.'

'Who's "they?"'

'I don't know,' said Clarissa. 'I *genuinely* don't know! But Charlie believed that someone was after him.'

She went on to explain that she'd seen Charlie's car abandoned there on her way home the night before. She described the conversation she'd heard from her car between the two men who appeared to be looking for him.

'So why didn't you tell us any of this on Thursday?' said Sergeant Quinn, unable to suppress his irritation. It was the first time he had spoken since the interview had started.

Clarissa looked at him. 'I know I should have done,' she said. 'I guess I was in shock. I had just seen…Charlie's body. My mind was all over the place. I'm sorry.'

Inspector Okoro looked unimpressed. When she spoke again, her tone was different, sarcastic, thick with irony: 'Well, perhaps you would care to go over the events of the evening of the 10th March again for us, Clarissa, *without* leaving anything out this time. What do you say?'

'Yes. Of course,' said Clarissa.

So Clarissa related the entire episode of the evening of the 10th March again, telling the police the full story this time, relaying everything exactly as it had occurred, apart from three things: any mention of the Dead Drops, the manuscript or the gun.

When asked again, why she hadn't revealed any of this information the day before yesterday, she repeated that she'd still been in deep shock about Charlie being found dead, and referred to Charlie's instructions about not involving the police.

'And do you still have the "letter" that Charlie left for you?' asked Okoro.

'No,' said Clarissa. 'Charlie requested that I destroy it after reading it.'

'I see,' she said sardonically. 'And there's nothing else you've omitted to mention?'

'I don't think so,' said Clarissa quietly.

'Where's Charlie's phone?'

'In my flat.'

'So. Let's recap. You go for a drink with your boyfriend. He ends your relationship. You're in shock. You've been drifting apart for a few months but you still weren't expecting the relationship to end. It's raining heavily. Charlie drives away in his Audi at approximately 8.15 p.m. Then six people come out of the Hoops Inn. A man asks you if you're okay. You say you are, but he comes over to the car and knocks on the window to check again. You see his watch. It says 8.20 p.m. You say you're okay again. You wait a few minutes for your windows to clear, then you drive away. You intend to go home. Is everything correct so far, Clarissa?'

'Yes,' said Clarissa.

'Great. Now, we get to the bit you *didn't* tell us about. You told us that you drove straight home but this, you now tell us was a lie. Let us resume. You attempt to drive home, but you see Charlie's car abandoned beside a field, about a mile from the inn. The driver's door is open, so you park your car about a hundred yards from the TT and go take a look. Charlie's keys are still in the ignition. You take his keys. You lock the car and venture out into the nearest field to look for him. You find his phone. You search for him but it's too dark to see anything so you return to your car. Then you hear two men talking about him "getting away". Let me ask you something, Clarissa. At this point, why didn't you call the police?'

'I was going to,' said Clarissa truthfully. 'I really was. But I was scared. I just wanted to get out of there!'

'So you drove all the way back to your flat, without stopping?'

'Yes.'

'So why didn't you call the police when you reached your flat?'

'I was about to. Then I saw Charlie's note telling me not to.'

'I see. Let's go back to Charlie's phone. Was the phone on?'

'Yes.'

'Did anybody call the phone whilst it was in your possession?'

Clarissa hesitated.

'Come on, Clarissa. Anything you don't tell us now, we'll find out for ourselves once we're in possession of Charlie's mobile.'

'I'd been home for about ten minutes when it rang.'

'And did you answer it?'

'Yes. It was a man called....' Clarissa did not want to reveal Steed's name, but felt that she had no choice. She had been backed into a corner. 'His name was Roland Steed,' she said.

Clarissa went on to relate the conversation she'd had with Steed.

Inspector Okoro wrote something down in her yellow notebook. As she did this, Clarissa thought she saw the flicker of a smile travel across her mouth.

Sergeant Quinn sighed heavily.

'We appear to be getting somewhere, at last!' she said, happily. 'We go on. The following day. You book a taxi. You ask to be dropped off near Charlie's car. You wander back into the field again but you don't see anything, you don't hear anything. You find the Audi TT. Is this all correct so far?'

'Yes,' said Clarissa.

Inspector Okoro stopped briefly and glared hard at Clarissa. 'Did you notice anything different about the TT?'

'…No.'

'Was there any damage to the outside of the vehicle?'

'No. I looked. There was nothing that I could see.'

'Did you open the car boot?'

'No.'

'How did the car sound when you were driving it?'

'Sound?' Clarissa looked at the detective blankly. 'I don't know what you mean.'

'Did you hear anything unusual during your drive back to St. Albans? You must have been in the car for what? About an hour?'

Clarissa nodded.

'Did the car sound different to you?'

Clarissa was confused. She didn't understand where the inspector was going with this.

'Well, I remember thinking the engine sounded loud. But that's all,' said Clarissa. 'Why? What's this got to do with anything?'

'Let us continue,' said Okoro, with strained tolerance. 'You get into the Audi, you don't notice anything different about it, although you do notice that: "the engine sounds loud". You drive to Charlie's flat. Charlie has previously supplied you with the code to the barrier of his carport and the alarm to his flat. You park the car at 10:37 a.m. You go up to Charlie's flat. Did you see anybody between parking the car and entering the flat?'

Clarissa described the young couple she'd seen on the balcony, the man who'd been talking on his phone and the elderly woman who'd been cleaning her windows.

The inspector wrote something else in her notebook and frowned long and hard before she continued with her summary. 'So. You go into Charlie's flat. You prepare to enter the alarm code, but you discover that the alarm was not set. You find the contents of the flat disturbed. Did you take anything from the apartment?'

There was another silence. Clarissa knew that it was her last chance to tell the police about the gun, and her mind swam with confusion as she deliberated on her answer.

Inspector Okoro repeated the question, this time choosing to remove all traces of her former sarcasm and replace it with a sort of bored indifference.

'Did you take anything from the apartment?'

'Yes.'

'What did you take, Clarissa?'

'I took a phone charger and a Beretta 9mm hand gun from the drawer beside Charlie's bed.'

Inspector Okoro and Sergeant Quinn looked at one another, then they both stared at Clarissa intensely.

'I'm sorry. Can you repeat that? You took…a *gun?*' said Okoro, her eyes suddenly alert and glittery.

Clarissa went over the details of the gun for them. The fact that she'd known about it, that she'd seen it there before, that she'd overheard Charlie on the phone late one night saying that it was loaded. She tried to explain that she'd taken it for safe keeping, but in reality, she knew that she hadn't really had a logical reason for taking it all. She had simply responded to her instincts.

She could see that the detectives were now arching their necks and staring at her with rapt attention and that both of them were reluctant to take their eyes off her now, just in case they missed something in her body language.

'Was Charlie in possession of a firearm's licence for this gun, Clarissa?' asked Sergeant Quinn.

'Well, I always thought he must have been. But of course, I never knew for sure. I never actually saw one.'

Quinn continued this line of questioning:

'Do you know how much ammunition was inside the gun, Clarissa?'

'I didn't open it. So, no.'

'Was Charlie aware that you knew about the existence of this gun?'

'...I don't think so, no. But I suppose he could have hidden it better.'

'How did you get back from Charlie's flat?' Inspector Okoro cut into the conversation suddenly.

'I...took the train to Euston, then back out to Bishop's Stortford.'

Okoro pulled a face of mock horror.

'Did it ever occur to you, Clarissa, that by boarding a public train, in possession of a live firearm, licensed or un-licensed – however, it's quite clear that you are *not* the licensee of the afore-mentioned weapon – that you were in fact breaking the law?'

'I err...I'm sorry,' said Clarissa. 'I obviously didn't think it through properly. I just wanted to get it out of harm's way.'

'So,' the inspector continued. 'You removed a gun, you suspected was loaded, but that you did not check, from a locked, empty flat in order to carry it aboard a crowded passenger train heading towards central London "to get it out of harm's way"?'

Clarissa buried her head in her hands.

'Do you see the problem we're having here, Clarissa?'

Sergeant Quinn cleared his throat.

'And where is this gun now, Clarissa?' asked Inspector Okoro, with fresh alacrity.

'It's inside the piano in my flat,' said Clarissa. 'Alongside Charlie's mobile.'

At this point the inspector said: 'Inspector Okoro is leaving the room. Interview suspended at 3:44 p.m.'

The machine in the wall was stopped and Okoro stormed out.

'What's happening?' Clarissa asked the sergeant.

Quinn rubbed his jaw and re-adjusted his position in his chair. 'I think we're about to go back to your flat,' he said.

'Oh, my God,' said Clarissa, suddenly struck by a fact so blindingly obvious, she was shocked that it hadn't crossed her mind before. 'You think the Beretta I found in Charlie's flat was the murder weapon, don't you?'

Sergeant Quinn just shook his head and remarked that he was unable to comment.

Before Clarissa could digest this piece of information further, Inspector Okoro returned to the interview room, slamming the door shut behind her, and Clarissa saw that the detective had suddenly come to life. She was highly animated, unable to sit still and starting the recording device again, she said in her low, but now distinctly excitable voice: 'Interview resumed at 3:51 p.m.'

Inspector Okoro was now a different woman. She paced up and down, her eyes squeezed, her lips twisting back to reveal her brilliant white teeth.

Then she turned her attention to the plastic tub on the table, pulling something out of it in a transparent bag.

'For the benefit of the tape, I am showing Clarissa evidence bag: 14112.'

Clarissa looked down at the plastic wrapper. She could see that it contained a piece of jewellery. A watch. It was black with an orange digital display. She recognised it at once.

'Have you ever seen this before, Clarissa?' said Okoro.

'Yes! I think so. It looks just like the watch I saw on the wrist of the man who knocked on my car window just after Charlie left the pub!' exclaimed Clarissa, shocked. 'Where did you find it?'

'It was retrieved from the field near Perry Green,' said Okoro, 'two metres away from Charlie's body.'

Clarissa eyes grew huge. 'The man I saw. He was...'

'He was what?' said Okoro aggressively.

'Now I remember!' cried Clarissa. '*He* was the man I saw outside the Musée de la Vie romantique yesterday! He's been following me! Do you think this man could have killed Charlie?'

'Isn't that in Paris?' said Quinn, with undisguised astonishment. 'Are you telling us that you were in Paris yesterday?'

Clarissa had not intended divulging this piece of information. She was on the verge of producing the silver lighter she had picked up outside the museum, when Inspector Okoro said: 'We believe that the watch belongs to a man by the name of Daniel Paul Darlington. Have you ever come across this name before, Clarissa?'

Clarissa's mind was racing. D.P.D. Yes, the initials matched! It was proof that it had been the same man who'd been following her, and they already knew his identity! She couldn't believe it.

'No,' said Clarissa. 'The man, yes. The name, no. But if you know who he is, why haven't you arrested him?'

'Up until know, his whereabouts have been unknown to us,' said Quinn.

'So why was Daniel Darlington following *you*?' asked Okoro.

'I have absolutely no idea!' cried Clarissa.

Inspector Okoro looked disappointed.

'I'm intrigued,' said Quinn. 'What on earth were you doing in Paris yesterday? The airline told us you've been signed off for four days. Were you there alone?'

It was an involuntary reaction. An oversight. A blip. She had not meant to mention Paris or Ralph. Now she was bitterly regretting it, but could not take any of it back. She'd wanted to keep Ralph's name out of all this. She'd wanted to show them Darlington's lighter to prove that he'd been following her. It was bound to have his prints on it. It might be useful to them. But they already knew his identity, so they must already have his prints. When it came down to it, she was unsure how much use the lighter would actually be. And now she was being steered in a completely different direction, and she was faltering badly, and she knew it.

'Clarissa?' Inspector Okoro's voice was insistent. 'Can you answer Sergeant Quinn's question please?'

'Err…I went there with a friend. He suggested it, as he thought it might be a bit of a break for me. I was upset after identifying Charlie's body. It was a sort of spur of the moment thing,' said Clarissa waveringly.

The moment she'd uttered the words, she knew they'd sounded awful, insensitive, *inhuman* even. Revealing she'd visited a museum associated with romance with a man, the day after identifying her ex-boyfriend's body, what was she thinking? She was making herself look guilty again.

'And this friend's name?' said Okoro.

'Ralph. Ralph Valero.'

'I'm sorry. Is he a boyfriend or a friend?' Inspector Okoro was suspicious of her now, she could sense it.

'…I don't see how that's relevant.'

The inspector smiled a horrible smile.

'It's relevant because your "ex-boyfriend" was found dead two days ago. The man you told me you *loved.* Now suddenly, you have another boyfriend?'

'No. Ralph isn't my boyfriend.'

'So your relationship with Ralph is purely platonic?'

Clarissa felt as if she'd been stung. Surely this line of questioning was wholly inappropriate. To make matters worse, she thought she could see a smile appear briefly at the vestiges of Okoro's lips.

'…No comment.'

'How long have you known "Ralph?"' said Okoro.

'Err…Twelve days.'

'Twelve days?'

'Yes.'

'So you met Ralph, what? A couple of days *after* you and Charlie broke up?'

'Yes.'

'Did you pick him up on a plane as well?'

'No!'

'So how did you meet Mr. Valero?'

'He was busking on the Underground. He was playing an electric piano. I recognised his piece and we got talking.'

'I see. And in which London underground station was he playing?'

'Baker Street.'

'And why were you going to Baker Street?'

She should have seen this one coming, but the inspector was too shrewd. She was running rings around her and she seemed to be enjoying the fact.

'I was…I was going to Regent's Park.'

'To meet someone?'

'No. It was where I used to go when I lived in London, when I was upset. I wanted to walk through the park.'

'So, you took a train from Bishop's Stortford into central London, in order to walk through a park, on your own?'

'Yes.'

'Okay, Clarissa. Thank you.'

Inspector Okoro lifted the brown folder from the desk. She positioned it carefully in front of Clarissa with her long, deft fingers and stared at her.

'What's this?' said Clarissa, confused.

'For the benefit of the tape, I am showing Clarissa photographs: 761,762 and 763.'

The photographs were of a man's face. In the first two his eyes were closed, his hair dark brown. He had a slim nose and full lips. In the last one he was looking at the camera with baby blue eyes and a smirk across his lips. She had never seen the man before.

'Do you recognise this man, Clarissa?' said Okoro.

'No.'

Okoro sat down and stared at her.

'Who is he?' said Clarissa.

The inspector leaned towards her sergeant and whispered something into his ear.

Clarissa cleared her throat.

The two detectives continued to stare at her, saying nothing.

'Look. What's this about? I can see they're photos of the same man, but who is he?'

Inspector Okoro took a deep breath before she said: 'He's the man we found dead in the boot of Charlie's Audi TT in the carport of Gabriel Square, St. Albans.'

Clarissa felt the room waver around her.

'*What*?'

'When you took Charlie's Audi from Perry Green to St. Albans on the morning of the 11th March it seems you had a passenger, Clarissa,' said Okoro.

Clarissa thought she was going to be sick.

'But...I had no idea!' she cried, defensively. 'You *have* to believe me! Wait a minute. Are you saying he was alive when he was put in there?'

'That's what we're trying to establish,' said Quinn. 'Someone had certainly gone to a lot of trouble tying him up and gagging him.'

'Who was he?' asked Clarissa, a pained expression on her face.

'His name was George Steed. I believe he was Roland Steed's younger brother,' said Inspector Okoro.

Clarissa was taken to a police cell. She sat upon the thin bed and buried her head in her hands. She could not believe what she had just heard. *George Steed*! Surely there had to be some sort of mistake? She couldn't have driven for an hour with George Steed in the back of Charlie's car. Could she? The consequences of this were unthinkable. She could only imagine what Roland Steed would do to her if he got wind of this.

She'd been in the cell for forty-five minutes when Inspector Okoro's face appeared through her barred window.

'Let's go, Clarissa,' she said. 'I've organised a car. You need to show us the location of the missing gun and phone. Now!'

Clarissa rose carefully, trying not to let the detective see how much she was trembling.

On leaving the room, Clarissa was marched back through a series of magnolia corridors, a tangible display of eager anticipation empowering Inspector Okoro like some sort of predatory animal. Clarissa could hear a phone ringing through the sound of muffled talking.

As they exited the building, the phone's insistent bell rose in volume and Clarissa watched the inspector acknowledge it as hers, and raise it to her ear.

'No, okay…*What*?' she said, as she gestured for the car to be brought round and a blue and yellow checkered BMW 3 series pulled up, its lights flashing.

Clarissa was shown into the backseat of the squad car and Sergeant Quinn got in beside her. A uniformed officer she hadn't seen before got in the driver's seat, and Inspector Okoro sat beside him still talking into her mobile. 'You must be bloody joking!' she shouted as the car slid into reverse. 'Call his bluff. Do it! Got to run.' She turned off her phone. 'Come on, let's hear some noise,' she said, and Clarissa winced in horror as the car's siren was applied, and they sped back to her flat with the utmost urgency.

Clarissa could hardly contain her shock. To be escorted in a speeding police car with its lights blazing like this; the traffic parting before them like metal syrup. Who'd have thought it! She really was starting to feel like a criminal now. It was humiliating.

To her relief, the whooping and squealing was deactivated about two hundred yards before they turned into Chantry Road.

When they pulled up outside Clarissa's flat, Inspector Okoro announced their arrival into a radio and a woman responded amongst the crackling.

After a small commotion of voices and car doors slamming, they all walked briskly to her flat, Inspector Okoro cutting a particularly striking figure due to her size and her Bantu knots; she was leading the way like a revolutionary in a revolt.

Clarissa glanced about surreptitiously, embarrassed in case any of her neighbours were watching, but she saw no sign of life, apart from a frightened cat making a run for the bushes.

Once inside the apartment, Okoro snapped blue plastic gloves onto her hands and strode straight over to the piano, as if she'd visited the place many times before.

'Now. What's the best way to do this, Clarissa?' she said, her fierce brown eyes glinting with expectation.

Clarissa was shocked to see that the detective was taking on the task of removing the items herself. There must be a separate team for this sort of thing, she thought. Perhaps it had been impossible to assemble them at such short notice?

'Clarissa?' repeated the inspector, insistently.

'Err…There's a screwdriver in the top drawer in the corner,' said Clarissa, sounding nervous. She didn't feel like her lungs were receiving the right quantity of air, but she couldn't seem to adjust her breathing to rectify it. 'It should just break away from this seal, here,' she said, gesturing at her line of recently applied wood glue with the back of her wrist, her voice cracking under the strain of speaking, her ears suddenly only aware of the sound of her own heartbeat.

Inspector Okoro prised the wood glue seal apart with quick, incisive movements. She seemed to take on the task with a queer mixture of excitement and patience fluctuating between the two states like an archeologist about to unearth a much-revered artifact. Once she had diligently broken the periphery of the piano – and Clarissa was grateful for the care she exuded here (it would have been easy to have bashed the instrument to pieces) – she watched Sergeant Quinn come forward, and together, the two of them began to pull the structure apart. They looked like they were lifting the lid off a coffin.

Suddenly the detectives backed away from the objects like they were dangerous, and the room was filled with an explosion of light.

A camera flash. It was unexpected.

Clarissa watched a young, thin policeman take photos of their find.

Inspector Okoro waited for him to do his job before she returned to the piano. She paused briefly, before dipping both of her blue-gloved hands into the instrument.

Then out they came. The 9mm Beretta gun and the smartphone.

Inspector Okoro produced a small whistling sound as her eyes skimmed the firearm's metal barrel. She seemed to forget herself for a moment. 'Ooh, it's an old one!' she exclaimed excitedly. 'Looks like a Second World War weapon. Did Charlie have any Italian in his family by any chance?'

Clarissa shrugged. 'I don't know,' she said, realising that when it came down to it, she hadn't really known that much about her boyfriend at all.

The items were placed in separate evidence bags with the upmost caution and promptly taken away.

As the tension in the room dissipated, Clarissa was relieved to find that she was able to breathe more easily again. 'What happens now?' she said, addressing Sergeant Quinn.

'We wait for ballistics,' he replied.

'How long will that take?'

'About forty-eight hours.'

Inspector Okoro returned to the flat, her blue gloves still on, her gaze triumphant.

'So, while you wait for the ballistic report, am I free to do as I please?' said Clarissa, addressing Sergeant Quinn again.

Her reply came from Okoro.

'Yes, Clarissa,' she said. 'As long as you stay in the country. There can be no more excursions to France, or anywhere else for that matter, you do understand that, I suppose?' She produced one of her sly smiles.

Clarissa nodded submissively. 'And if the gun turns out to be the murder weapon? Will I be arrested?'

'If you killed Charlie, you'll be arrested,' said Okoro with a categorical coolness that made Clarissa shiver. 'It's as simple as that.'

When everyone had gone, Clarissa slammed her front door shut and locked it. Then she sat down on her sofa and stared at her piano, decapitated once again. What a pitiful sight it was.

After a few minutes, she reached for her laptop and opened the message Charlie had concealed in the seventh Drop. She read it again, still not quite believing what he was asking her to do. Then she checked her emails in a bit of a daze, as if everything that had happened in the last two hours had been a figment of her imagination.

To her surprise, she saw that Professor Kowalski had replied:

23.3.19, 2:47 p.m.

Dear Clarissa,

Apologies for the delay in responding to your email. I have been in Poland. I am sufficiently intrigued! I have a lunch appointment at the Shard tomorrow. This should conclude around 3:30 p.m. after which I shall be quite free. Perhaps we could share afternoon tea?

If you'd care to join me, I'll be in the Aqua Shard until 4.30 p.m.

Kind regards,

Nikolai Kowalski

Clarissa took the professor's decision not to include his title and post-nominals as a good sign. She responded at once.

23.3.19, 5:17 p.m.

Dear Professor Kowalski,

Delighted to hear back from you. I'll be there.

Thank you.

Kind regards,

Clarissa

Ten minutes later, Clarissa's phone rang. She saw with relief that it was Ralph.

'Are you all right. Has anything happened?' he said, concerned.

'You could say that.'

She filled him in on her visit from the Hertfordshire Constabulary CID. She explained that she'd changed her statement to say she'd moved the car, and she admitted that he'd been right about disclosing the gun and the phone.

'I've handed them both in,' she told him, knowing that he'd be pleased to hear her say this. Then she held her breath. 'But there's something else.'

Ralph listened to the tragic story of George Steed.

'And they didn't arrest you?' he said, horrified, as she concluded.

'Not yet,' she attempted a small laugh, but it seemed to get stuck in her throat. 'They think the gun might have been the same one used to kill Charlie. But they need forty-eight hours to confirm it.'

Silence.

'And how do you think Roland Steed's brother ended up in Charlie's boot? Do you think Charlie locked him in there?' asked Ralph.

'Your guess is as good as mine.'

Clarissa went on to tell Ralph about Daniel Paul Darlington's watch being found beside Charlie's body.

'And you think *he* was the one who shot Charlie?' he said.

'It had to be him.'

'But wasn't it Charlie's gun?'

'Yes, it was,' said Clarissa. 'So Charlie must have taken his gun out with him that night after all. Perhaps George Steed had been the one to tape Charlie's mouth shut and tie his hands that night, but somehow, he'd managed to break free, transferring his restraints to George Steed and locking him inside the boot of the TT? Then when Charlie ran, Darlington could have caught up with him, got his gun off him somehow, and shot him with it.'

'It's a probable theory,' said Ralph, 'but mere speculation. Charlie's assailant could have been anyone. We don't know who else was lurking in those bushes!'

Clarissa shivered, reminding herself that she had not been too far away from those bushes herself just before all this supposedly kicked off.

'You're right,' she said. 'The only way we can ever know what actually happened that night is by talking to someone who was there.'

Ralph did not speak for a while. If she hadn't been able to hear the slow measured rhythm of his breath, she'd have disconnected the call.

She waited for him to speak.

When he eventually broke the silence, he said: 'What about Charlie's message? Did you unlock it?'

'Yes,' said Clarissa. 'He left instructions for the final Drop. I know where it is, Ralph.'

'Where?'

She hesitated.

'I can't tell you that. Not yet.'

'*What*? Don't tell me you don't trust *me* now?' said Ralph, aggrieved.

'Don't be ridiculous, of course I do!' said Clarissa. 'There's just something I need to do first, that's all. Are you able to meet me in London tomorrow morning, at 10 a.m. at the Angel Tube Station?'

Ralph assented willingly, then returned to pressing her about the contents of Charlie's last message again.

Clarissa bit her lip.

'He gave me some special instructions for the eighth Drop,' she told him. 'I'm not sure I agree with them, but he gave them to me all the same –'

'What sort of instructions?'

Clarissa paused. She knew that Ralph would not like the next part.

'He wants Max there,' she said quietly.

'*You can't be serious?*'

Clarissa repeated herself amidst Ralph's protestations.

'I've been thinking about his reasons,' she said pensively. 'Perhaps he didn't trust Max when he started the Dead Drop trail. But then something happened and he changed his mind?'

'Well, it's a possibility,' said Ralph, sounding unconvinced. 'I wonder how she took the news about Charlie.'

'I don't think she *knows* the news about Charlie!' said Clarissa.

'Don't get her involved again, Clarissa,' Ralph insisted.

'But I have to. Charlie's requested it!'

There was an awkward silence.

'Well, it's not like he's going to *know* now, is it?' said Ralph.

'I suppose not, but –'

'You could be walking straight into a trap!' Ralph warned. 'What if Max intercepted the seventh Drop before we got to it and replaced the message with a new one to ensure that we walk her with us to the eighth Drop?'

'…But that's impossible!'

'Why?'

Silence.

'Well, firstly, how would she have got to the seventh Drop? She was thrown off at the fifth! Secondly, Charlie's letter was coded, and *I'm* the only one who could possibly have known that code. And thirdly, let's just say she *did* know the password. Surely, she'd just take the clue and go to the last Drop alone. Why would she need us there?'

'For the clues?'

Clarissa clutched her forehead. This thing had started to give her a headache.

'Okay. I admit it,' she went on. 'Max isn't the brightest bulb in the box. And she certainly needed our help before. But how would she have known the last words Charlie uttered to me? She wasn't *there* at the Hoops Inn with us!'

'No. But Daniel Paul Darlington was,' Ralph reminded her. 'What if they're in on it together?'

Clarissa had not thought of this possibility before. Her mind swelled with it. Max and Darlington in a relationship? She supposed it was feasible, but something stopped her from buying into the idea. Besides, she was quite sure that nobody was around when Charlie had uttered his fateful last words to her, and she was also quite sure that Darlington hadn't come out of the pub until after Charlie had driven off.

'No,' she said. 'If Max and Darlington are in this together, they definitely wouldn't need us around complicating things. They'd tackle the clues themselves, I'm sure of it! And if we *were* both there with them, what would they do with us once we'd worked out the clue for them?'

'I could hazard a guess,' said Ralph. 'Charlie's already been disposed of for the cause. Two more deaths wouldn't make that much of a difference. It's just another couple of bullets to them.'

Clarissa was horrified.

'A couple more bullets? But no gun! Don't forget it was Charlie's gun. Darlington took it off him, remember?'

'Yes, and that's another thing I don't understand,' Ralph continued with fresh gusto. 'If Darlington killed Charlie with the Beretta, why did he then think it was a good idea to return the weapon to Charlie's flat? It doesn't make any sense. Surely it would have been easier to dump the thing in the canal or something. Why take it back?'

'For the same reason I took the car back, I suppose,' said Clarissa. 'To return everything to its prior order?'

She sensed Ralph chewing this one over, but she knew that he had a made a good point. The gun could easily have been removed from the scene of the crime; the killer's fastidiousness to return the gun to Charlie's flat *was* illogical.

'I don't think it was Charlie's gun that killed him,' Ralph concluded.

'Then how did Darlington get implicated in all of this? I'd assumed they must have seen CCTV footage of him returning the gun to Charlie's flat, like they'd seen of me returning the car. But I still don't think he has any connection to Max.'

'But you can't know that for sure!' Ralph remonstrated. 'Surely it's better not to take that risk. Once you do, it's too late!'

Clarissa hated disagreeing with Ralph, but she was intransigent about the matter. She had to follow Charlie's instructions exactly as he had set them out, and she was not about to change her mind.

'I'm sorry, Ralph, but we *have* to involve her,' she said definitively. 'You're just going to have to trust Charlie on this one.'

To her relief, Ralph finally backed down and left the subject alone. After switching to small talk for a few more minutes, she ended the call.

Clarissa placed her phone on her coffee table and took one last look at her poor piano. Then she put her jacket back on and threw her laptop bag over her shoulder.

It felt good to be outside, on her blue seat in her garden. Her flowers looked and smelt nice. After taking a moment to admire her forget-me-knots with their tiny blue flowers, her pink and white hyacinths with their fluffy heads and her red and yellow tulips fluttering backwards and forwards in the afternoon breeze, Clarissa took out her laptop and opened up its screen.

18

S unday morning, 9:55 a.m. Clarissa was waiting outside the Angel Tube Station. She felt tired. She had not slept well. She had arranged to see Ralph alone before they met up with Max.

Both Donna and her mother were sending regular texts, asking if they should come round to the flat, checking on her almost hourly; she didn't know how to respond to them. She told them that she just needed some time to get her head around things. She said that she was fine (a blatant lie). She implored them to stop worrying, and promised that she'd be sure to let them know if "anything happened" good or bad. She hoped that her communications had projected a confident and composed demeanour on her behalf, but in reality, she felt like she was walking on precarious ground; an uneven surface that was likely to swallow her up any second.

Ralph had sent her a few texts as well. His messages were considerate, affectionate. He did not make any further attempts to try to convince her to call off their meeting with Max. He wanted her to see him perform at the RAM later (he was opening a concert in the Duke's Hall, scheduled to start at 8 p.m.). He wanted her to spend the night with him. She'd replied that she would like to do both of these things.

Standing still had made her cold. She'd been waiting outside the Tube station for fifteen minutes now.

Her mind returned to the night she had last seen Charlie alive, as it often did. In fact, she was getting sick of it, the interminable replaying of the evening inside her head on a loop, forcing her to endure her conversation with Darlington over and over again. It was torturous and it wasn't helping; and she really didn't know why she was doing it. She suspected that she was desperately trying to remember something about the evening that she'd perhaps previously overlooked, but her regret at not having detained Darlington for: "just that little bit longer" was tormenting her deeply. She knew that the things she'd chosen *not* to do that night had changed the course of the evening rather dramatically. Her biggest mistake – she now realised with excruciating pain – was failing to call the police on her first sighting of Charlie's abandoned car, and she could not forgive herself for this lapse of judgement.

She tried to control her breathing and stop these awful thoughts. But their dissolution only brought about an image of Letterton's ugly, toothless face bearing down upon her innocent body; the smell of him, the weight of him, the overwhelming sense of fear that she had willed herself to recollect in order to explain things to Ralph. She had conjured it all up again in an attempt to finally extricate it all from her aching soul, but she was now forced to concede with horror that the images were stubbornly refusing to leave her. She wondered if she would ever be free of Letterton's hold. She sincerely doubted it now.

Unexpectedly, Clarissa thought of Chopin, and what she'd read about the great composer freezing in the middle of a performance of his own. It had happened on a stage in Paris in 1848 (the year before his death). He'd later attributed his abandonment to "another sighting of those cursed creatures". The same "creatures" that had appeared to him whilst he'd been staying in the Carthusian Monastery in Majorca. But he'd dealt with them like the professional that he was, waiting patiently until they'd dispersed, returning to his piano to conclude his piece the moment they'd left his side. So with this in mind, Clarissa willed her own cursed creature away, trying to dissipate Letterton's lecherous form from her head.

Looking at her watch, Clarissa saw that it was now 10:20 a.m. She couldn't understand why Ralph was so late. She was starting to think he wasn't coming.

She glanced about expectantly. She wanted to see his approach, his swagger, the way his feet graced the pavement. She had been looking forward to it. But when Ralph finally arrived, it was with an abrupt and instant materialisation, causing her to nearly jump out of her skin. His hand was upon her shoulder and suddenly he was there.

She felt cheated; she'd barely had time to take him in. Then he kissed her passionately and desperately, as if he had cause to believe that the privilege wouldn't be awarded to him for that much longer. Clarissa didn't know why his voraciousness disturbed her. But it did.

She pulled away.

'How are *you* this morning?' he said, sporting one of his beautiful full-mouthed grins, his hair smelling good, his orange and black jumper peeking out from underneath his leather. But she sensed that all was not completely well with him, as she detected in his eyes the tiniest glint of a disturbance, almost like they were defying the rest of him by trying to communicate an implicit message to her.

'You're late,' she said, watching him inspect her wound with tender concern. She waited for his explanation.

'It looks better,' he said. 'God, I've missed you.'

'I've missed you too, but why are you so late?'

'There was a delay on the Northern Line. Don't look so worried!' he said breezily. 'Where are we meeting her then?'

'Moorgate,' said Clarissa, leading him down the concrete steps into the Angel Station. 'And we'll need to get a move on, or she'll be gone by the time we get there!'

Ralph nodded in quiet acknowledgement as they ran on, slapping their Oyster cards on the touchpads of neighbouring gates simultaneously and slipping through the barriers.

So he had chosen to play it cool, thought Clarissa. He was trying to carry on as before. Part of her was grateful to him for not questioning her decision to meet Max all over again, but part of her thought he was acting out of character, which was unsettling.

'We're heading towards Guildhall, aren't we?' he said, as they mounted the descending escalator.

Clarissa threw her blonde hair back and glared at him in astonishment, her instinct to probe further into his wellbeing temporarily repudiated. 'How on earth did you know?'

'November 16th, 1848. Chopin's last public performance. It seemed fitting that Charlie would end it there. What was the clue?'

'Err. Well, there wasn't really a clue this time. It was just stated.'

'Really? That's strange.'

'Why?'

'Well, it's not exactly a small place, you know!'

Clarissa flashed him a slightly worried look as they joined the belt of moving pedestrians navigating their way through the passages of the Underground.

'But he's given you an indication of where to go, right?' said Ralph as they moved along with the crowd.

'Err…not exactly.'

'Jesus! We'll be there all day! And where's your laptop?'

'I won't be needing it this time,' said Clarissa.

'I don't understand.'

Clarissa tried to find the right words as they followed the signs for the Northern Line, Southbound.

'What's going on?' said Ralph as they stepped onto the platform for Moorgate, the heat in the tunnel suddenly overwhelming them. 'There *is* another Drop, right? The last one, the eighth?'

'Yes.'

'So how do you propose to download it without your laptop?' He was looking at her as if she had lost her mind.

'Our brief for this Dead Drop is to find it, not download it,' said Clarissa ominously. 'At this moment I can't be any more specific than that.'

'O…kay,' said Ralph hesitantly. 'So I'm still not allowed to know what's going on?'

'All will be revealed when we find the Drop,' she said.

Max was standing just inside the ticket barriers at Moorgate Tube. She had picked up Clarissa's phone call on her third attempt. She had not heard that Charlie had been killed, but she had not seemed that upset when Clarissa had broken the news to her either. Her first reaction had been to remain silent. Then she had simply said: "But it doesn't make any sense."

There were several pedestrians clustered around the mouth to the underground station, waiting in the void between the ticket barriers and the escalators. It was a space where everything seemed to have black edges, and the metallic, dirty smell of the Underground was rich, almost fibrous in its consistency. Clarissa could taste it in her mouth as she walked; it made her want to retch.

'Do you see her?' asked Ralph anxiously.

'Yes,' replied Clarissa.

'Where?' he said surprised, as if convinced that no one around matched the description of the woman he'd seen waiting for him outside the RAM.

'Grey joggers, hands in pockets,' mumbled Clarissa.

Ralph identified her, standing with her back to a map of the Tube.

'Jesus! She looks rough,' he observed.

Clarissa knew from the moment she saw her that Max had taken Charlie's death badly. She realised that her response to the news of his shooting on the phone must have been impeded by her failure to comprehend it through shock, and that the full force of the impact couldn't have registered until later. Now, Max looked as though she'd suffered mightily under the weight of death's punch, both physically and mentally, and the ultimate effect had, most alarmingly, rendered her unrecognisable. She was a mere shadow of her former self. The faux fur coat had been exchanged for a khaki parka, her hair had been tied back in a low ponytail and was concealed. Gone were the heels (she'd opted for blue jeans and trainers). And even though she'd made up her face, her eyes were puffy and hollow-looking; her lips, the colour of dried blood.

Max smiled on their approach. Seconds later, she adjusted her gaze to Clarissa's black eye and frowned, but passed no comment. Then she turned her attention towards Ralph.

'Max,' she said, holding her hand out to him. 'We meet at last! You're Ralph, right?' Her thick Geordie accent was emphatically projected. For a moment she lit up, her sudden voracious energy revealing a snapshot of the old Max within. Then her light went out and she seemed consumed by her grief once again.

Straight-faced, Ralph shook her hand and said: 'Hi,' but he refused to enhance the gesture with even the slightest hint of warmth; remaining indifferent, heavily guarded; so completely distrusting of her, she must have been aware of it.

But she seemed so open and keen, convincing Clarissa that she had absolutely no idea she'd been duped by their fake Dead Drop clue. Clarissa's request for her to attend the eighth Dead Drop location had seemingly been accepted without suspicion or interrogation. Clarissa had told her that they had discovered a pattern in the clues, enabling them to bypass the Warsaw Drop altogether and reach the seventh Drop in Paris. The Paris Drop had, in turn, led them *here,* to the final drop location in London. Max had gone along with this explanation quite readily, and if she suspected even a hint of duplicity from them, Clarissa saw no indication of it.

Clarissa directed them both back towards the escalators – Max sandwiched between Ralph and herself like some sort of hostage. Clarissa was not remiss of the fact that Ralph kept checking behind them and looking around distrustfully. She also noticed that he had clocked that Max was wearing a laptop bag.

The three of them got back on the Northern Line and continued south. There were empty seats in their carriage, but they all remained standing.

As their train sped through the tunnel, Clarissa couldn't get over how frail and crushed Max looked.

The nearest stop to Guildhall was Bank. When the red and blue "Bank" signs started rolling past their windows, Clarissa announced that it was time for them to get off, and both Ralph and Max motioned towards the doors in her wake.

Emerging from the station into the open air, the sun struck Clarissa's face with a fierce gold incandescence, and she was grateful for the feeling of warmth on her skin as they reached the top of the Underground's concrete steps.

The Royal Exchange with its eight columns, was truly resplendent in the morning sun. A statue of the Duke of

Wellington on his horse was also bathed in a shard of light, as he gazed down at the three of them commandingly from his plinth.

They all glanced around in silence, taking in the dramatic panorama; sixteenth-century pillared architecture surrounding them on all sides, with only a thin slither of modernity in the form of a skyscraper – sharp and incongruous against the scudding clouds – to remind them of the real century in which they stood.

Clarissa connected to her satnav, and looked at the little map on the screen of her phone. 'Come on, it's this way,' she said, indicating Princes Street.

They walked towards a large yellow box junction where two roads crossed, and Clarissa directed them to turn left onto Lothbury. Finally, they veered around the corner into Gresham Street with all its fancy restaurants and bars.

When the pavement turned to bricks, they diverted into Basinghall Street and after a short walk, encountered the start of the building known as Guildhall, with its rough weathered bricks and gothic window arches.

'Guildhall!' announced Clarissa, indicating its presence with one arm extended. 'Built in 1440. It's Grade I listed, so Charlie won't have buried the Drop anywhere near it. I suggest we inspect all the walls, kerbs and bollards in the surrounding area from around ten metres, starting on this corner and working our way around its entire construction, avoiding the courtyard.'

'Yes, ma'am!' said Ralph.

'Do we split up or stay together?' asked Max.

'As long as we can still see one another, we can space ourselves out a bit I suppose,' Clarissa replied. 'We get to cover more ground that way.'

They all agreed and off they went, looking for a glint of metal that might suggest the end of a USB stick, whilst navigating their way around the periphery of the building.

After ten minutes, Max said: 'Aren't there the remains of a Roman Amphitheatre here somewhere?'

'Aye. It's in the basement underneath the Art Gallery, but stay away from it,' instructed Ralph. 'We're not sight-seeing here. Charlie wouldn't risk damaging any part of a historic public landmark. Stick to the perimeters.'

Max rolled her eyes.

As Ralph disappeared up some steps into a narrow stone walkway around the side of one of the buildings, Max said: 'Couldn't the same be said of the surrounding passages? Surely Charlie wouldn't have defaced any of those either? You don't know what you're doing, man!'

Clarissa heard Ralph mutter an expletive in response to this.

After a good hour of searching, they reconvened in Guildhall yard outside the central tower. Sight-seers were clustered everywhere. There was a lot of excited chatter and a tour guide was delivering a talk to a group of teenagers within earshot.

Max pursed her lips, her frustration slowly consuming her features. 'This is ridiculous. I'm paggered! And we've searched everywhere!' she cried, exasperated.

'I think we should go back to Basinghall Street,' said Ralph.

'Howay, man! We've already searched there!' shouted Max.

'We've already searched everywhere!' cried Ralph. 'Now we're going to need to start all over again! Maybe check out the other sides of the roads this time.'

'But I *was* checking the other sides of the roads!' protested Max.

'Well, obviously not well enough, or we'd have found it!' admonished Ralph, marching off in the direction of Basinghall Street.

Max shouted after him: 'Who put *you* in charge, man?'

Ralph stormed off around the corner to get away from her.

Clarissa went after him.

This is not how it's supposed to work, thought Clarissa. All this arguing. *This is not going to help us find the Drop!*

As she caught him up he turned and, acknowledging the fact that she was alone, received her with tender affection, reaching for her jaw and kissing her slowly.

'We'd better not,' said Clarissa. 'She might see.'

Ralph looked at her despondently. 'Don't kid yourself. You think she doesn't know about us? She was probably not that far behind us when we walked back to mine, Thursday night!'

'Oh, come on. Now you're just being paranoid! Well, I'd still rather we didn't, in front of her,' said Clarissa gently.

'Fine. As you wish. But I don't know how much longer I can stand this,' he said. 'She's beginning to get on my nerves. I vote we give her the slip.'

'Now, you know we can't do that.'

'Then in God's name, tell me why we need her!' demanded Ralph. 'I just wish you'd enlighten me with whatever it is we're doing!'

'Look. There'll be plenty of time for that later,' she said, taking his hand. 'Come on, I think you're right. Let's head back to where we started, and work our way around again.'

'Okay. But we'd better go back and fetch her first,' said Ralph. 'She's probably calling Darlington this very second! You mark my words; he'll be turning up here in a minute.'

Clarissa flashed him a look of mock alarm. 'I don't think so.'

'Well, let's not leave her alone, just to be sure,' he said. 'I don't trust her.'

Clarissa sighed, and turned to face Max's direction.

'I don't think she even knows who Darlington is,' she said. 'Come on.' She pulled on Ralph's arm, but he let go of her hand.

'You go,' he said. 'I'll be searching around the corner. The less time I spend with her the better!'

Clarissa nodded. 'Fine,' she said. 'But when we find it, you've got to promise to go along with whatever I say – no matter how strange it sounds – okay?'

Ralph stared at her.

'Sure,' he said. 'I daren't do anything else.'

Max was standing at the top of some steps, one arm folded, the other hand sporting a cigarette which she sucked and tapped a couple of times whilst she waited for Clarissa to reach her.

'What happened to your face?' said Max, when she did.

'Oh, somebody threw a plate at me on one of my flights,' said Clarissa, taking in the redness around Max's eyes.

Max's lips twitched ruthlessly as she fought to suppress a smile. 'Service that bad, was it?'

'Did Charlie know how you felt about him?' said Clarissa, and Max's smile instantly obliterated.

As Clarissa waited for a response, Max shot her a discomfited glance but continued to ignore her question, smoking her cigarette through her dark lips in the strained silence.

A couple of minutes later they both watched a group of elderly tourists amble past them carrying leaflets and guidebooks, wearing matching red caps and smiling at them vacantly. When they had all trundled on, and their various conversations had faded into a distant murmur, the two women regarded one another afresh.

'That obvious, is it?' said Max taking another drag from her cigarette.

'It is now,' said Clarissa.

'And the answer is "yes", by the way. He knew. He didn't reciprocate it though.' She smiled. 'He only had eyes for you.'

Clarissa looked embarrassed. 'You and Charlie. Did you ever …Have you…?'

'Been intimate?' said Max.

Clarissa nodded.

'Once.'

Clarissa's eyes widened from the shock.

'There's no need to look at us like that! It was about two years before you came on the scene, like,' said Max. 'We fucked. It was a stupid, drunken thing.'

Clarissa was taken aback. 'Why did it…not continue?' she asked, her voice cracking a little.

Max discarded her cigarette on the cobblestones and stamped it out angrily with her foot. She arched her neck and jutted her chin forwards, trying to take back control of her composure and the terms of her confession. 'I suppose the simple answer is: business and pleasure don't mix. *Can't* mix. But I might as well be honest with you. I wanted him. He didn't want me. Or our baby.'

'You got pregnant?' Clarissa felt sick.

'Yep. It was the result of our one intimate night. Can you believe that?' Max smiled at her.

'And what happened to…'

'To the bairn, you mean? Abortion. It was what *he* wanted, but I can honestly say, I've regretted it ever since. Especially now. *Especially* now!'

Clarissa turned away, unable to take any of this in.

'When he met you, he was crazy about you. I was so bloody jealous sometimes I wanted to scream!' Max cried, her savage eyes smarting with tears.

'Please. Don't.'

'Makes you feel guilty does it? You certainly didn't waste any time finding somebody else. And I thought you believed Julia's explanation. I wish I'd never even bothered with that one, man!'

'It wasn't like that. And for what it's worth, I *did* believe Julia,' said Clarissa earnestly.

'This Ralph. How long have you *really* known him, Clarissa?' said Max. She bent in closer, her pupils dancing wildly, like fruit flies on rotting meat; her beauty temporarily abandoning her, savagely extirpated by the grief that was slowly seeping through her blood.

'I thought I'd already told you that. A few months,' said Clarissa.

'That's what you said, yes. But for some reason I didn't believe you then. And I still don't believe you now!'

'What does it matter, a couple of months, a couple of weeks!'

'For your sake, I sincerely hope it isn't a couple of weeks.'

'What are you talking about?'

'Well, if you met him after Charlie dumped you, the likelihood is he's probably only after the manuscript!'

Clarissa took a couple of steps back from Max's belligerent glance.

'Now you're just being ridiculous. He didn't know anything about the manuscript until I met him!' she retaliated.

Max produced a high peal of laughter. 'Oh, yeah? And how exactly *did* you two meet?'

'I refuse to lower myself to engage in –'

'Oh, get off your high horse, you doylem, and wake up! Do. Not. Trust. Him.'

'Do you know, it's almost funny,' said Clarissa slowly. 'But he says exactly the same thing about you.'

'I bet he does!' said Max. 'I wonder which one of us you believe?'

In the distance they could hear shouting. Ralph was running towards them, his arms flailing. 'GET OVER HERE!' he cried excitedly. 'I'VE FOUND IT!'

The two women ran towards him as if their lives depended upon it, as if their horribly uncomfortable conversation had never happened.

Ralph led them to the point where the last black bollard met the start of the Guildhall building on Basinghall Street. The bollards had been painted black with red and white crowns and he indicated one of them to Clarissa with his eyes as a group of German tourists wandered by.

Clarissa knew what she had to do next.

She could not allow herself to be distracted by the magnitude of Max's revelation.

She turned to Max. 'It's all yours,' she said.

The Dead Drop was located at the base of the bollard. As Max approached it, Clarissa stared hard at Ralph, imploring him with her eyes to look on while the Geordie carried out this task. He responded with a tacit nod, implying that he understood.

Max removed her laptop from her bag and crouched down at the base of the bollard. Clarissa saw the feverish glint in her eyes, and despised the woman for all she was worth.

The USB stick was acknowledged and downloaded, then Max shut her laptop with a slap, making Clarissa jump.

The three of them looked at one another.

'It's done,' said Max.

'Now all we need to do is see the next clue,' said Ralph.

Max seemed to hesitate at the request, staring at him with obdurate eyes. Then she smiled and cocked her head to one side.

'I don't think so, do you?' she said, with a fulminating scowl.

Ralph glared back at her in horror.

2

'What's *that* supposed to mean?' he snapped.

Clarissa took hold of Ralph's arm, as if to hold him back.

Suddenly a car growled in the distance. Max seemed distracted.

Ralph exchanged concerned glances with Clarissa.

Max started to shuffle backwards, all the time maintaining eye contact with the two of them, back and forth, as if one of them could go for her laptop at any time. She looked at Clarissa. 'Sorry, pet, but I'm afraid the two of you won't be seeing the next clue.'

Clarissa frowned.

'What are you talking about?' said Ralph, confused.

At this moment a black Mercedes began to roar towards them, and Max started to run in its direction.

Ralph broke away from Clarissa. 'What's going on?' he cried.

'WAKE UP, PIANO BOY! IT MEANS *YOU'RE NO LONGER FUCKING REQUIRED*!' Max yelled, as she caught up with the Mercedes.

As the car drew up alongside her, Max pulled its passenger door open, and managed to jump inside and lock it before Ralph got to the window.

Clarissa screamed as the car executed a hurried three-point turn threatening to knock Ralph to the ground as he furiously slammed his fists against its rear window. Finally, he was forced to back away from the vehicle altogether for his own safety, and the driver sped off up Basinghall Street emitting one final high-pitched screech.

Ralph was left standing in the middle of the road, his hair pulled dramatically away from his face, the vein in his forehead pulsing frantically, as he watched the Mercedes disappear.

'Are you all right?' shouted Clarissa, sidling up to him.

'I'm fine.'

'Did you see who was driving the car?'

'Some black guy. Never seen him before in my life.'

'So it wasn't Darlington then?'

Ralph shook his head. 'Correct me if I'm wrong, Clarissa, but you don't look *that* pissed off by what's just happened. Please tell me you were expecting something like this, or have we just lost the manuscript?'

Clarissa smiled at him. 'I knew she was a traitor, yes! But to be honest, I didn't think she would show her true colours quite this quickly.' She touched his arm. 'I'm sorry, Ralph. But I couldn't tell you about any of this before, or it wouldn't have worked.'

'*What* wouldn't have worked?' said Ralph impatiently.

'Well, when I phoned Max last night, I told her that both of us had had our laptops confiscated by the police, which is why we needed hers,' Clarissa explained. 'I bet she couldn't believe her luck! But what she doesn't know, is that the USB stick she's just downloaded isn't the eighth Drop.'

'It's not?' said Ralph, still trying to get over Max's sudden departure.

'It's not,' said Clarissa matter-of-factly.

'And it is?'

Clarissa felt herself bristle with excitement. She had been waiting for this moment. 'It's an encrypted file. With a password question that only *Max* would have the answer to. Charlie's configured it so that as soon as she enters it, a virus will seep through her device, scrambling everything in it!'

A smile began to argue with Ralph's mouth.

'It's brilliant, isn't it?' cried Clarissa emphatically. 'She betrayed him, Ralph. It was all in Charlie's coded letter; although, I didn't really understand why until just a few minutes ago. Charlie discovered that she'd been planning to escape with the manuscript all along. Apparently she'd found her own buyer behind his back. She'd arranged her own deal, set up her own transport, even set up a secret bank account to receive the money. Charlie discovered it all on her computer!'

Ralph searched Clarissa's eyes hard. 'So, in the last Drop, Charlie asked you to lead Max to a stick he'd laced with malware, so that she'd open it up on her laptop causing her little clandestine operation to collapse?' he said.

'Exactly,' said Clarissa.

Ralph took his head in his hands, and squeezed his eyes shut. 'But why did she do it?' he said.

Clarissa looked at the grey cracked pavement briefly.

'She had her reasons,' she said.

'Unrequited love?' offered Ralph.

'Now, how on earth did you know that?'

Ralph stared at her. 'Have you ever been in love, Clarissa? It's not a force to be reckoned with.'

She waved his words away with her hand. 'After a betrayal, love inevitably turns to hate,' she said solemnly.

Ralph still looked as though he was trying to process what had just happened. 'So when Max turned on Charlie and decided to cheat him out of the manuscript,' he began, scratching his head ruminatively, 'he enacted revenge on *her* by destroying her plans with the malware, a task he managed to execute – with your help of course – even after the event of his own death. I must say, I'm impressed!'

Clarissa stared absently at a group of people enjoying their day sight-seeing. 'So am I,' she said, with tears forming in her eyes.

Suddenly distracted by something in the distance, Clarissa detected a dark face peering at them from a shadowy area behind some trees.

'What is it?' said Ralph, sensing her disquiet.

'I think I've just seen Steed's man,' she said. 'The one with the fish scar.'

Ralph swore.

'We should go back into the Underground,' she told him. 'Head for the Circle Line, Eastbound.'

Once they were safely on a train, Ralph's mouth found its way to hers and they kissed, the train vibrating through them as they connected.

'I think we've successfully given old Fish Scar the slip!' Ralph gloated.

Clarissa touched the delicate area below her own eye. 'People will be calling *me* that soon.'

'In a few weeks, you won't even know yours is there,' said Ralph reassuringly. '*He* probably got knifed in the eye or something.'

He kissed her again, more slowly this time, rolling his thumb underneath her injury.

'So, where's the real eighth Drop?' he said as he released her, a tired smile upon his face. 'We can't be going after it now because you don't have your laptop. So what's the plan?'

Clarissa was scrutinising the row of passengers on the moquette seats in front of them. She examined them one by one: a businessman in a suit with an umbrella, two teenage girls in plastic jackets, a young man with glasses listening to music. She determined the threat level low.

Carefully, she rested her chin on Ralph's shoulder. 'I don't need my laptop,' she whispered, 'because I've already downloaded it.'

She felt Ralph's body react to this like a hammer in a cocked gun. He turned to look at her. '*When*?'

'Yesterday afternoon.'

'Without me?'

'Unintentionally without you,' she said ruefully. 'You see, it was buried in the wall of my garden.'

'You're kidding me!' He gave off a sort of wild, astonished laugh. 'So we've been racing all over Paris and London, when the final Dead Drop was literally "outside your flat" the whole time?'

She nodded, barely able to comprehend the thing herself.

'But that's totally mad!' said Ralph.

'I know,' she said, the bright glare in their carriage suddenly making her feel like she was looking at him through a sharp lens, the blueness of his veins strangely visible through his soft skin. It had the effect of intensifying his vulnerability.

'I wonder when he planted it there,' he said.

'He must have let himself into my flat whilst I was at work,' she said.

She could just imagine this: Charlie Davenport sauntering around her garden, confident and self-assured, examining her wall with his shrewd blue eyes. Her key dangling from his back pocket, a pot of adhesive ready his hand. Presuming, like we all do that life was laid out before him like an open book, that he would travel to a thousand more places, that he would grow old. It made her feel so desperately sad.

'It's almost like he didn't create the Dead Drop trail to lead you to the manuscript at all, but to alert you to the presence of anyone who might be following you for it,' said Ralph speculatively.

'Yes. It certainly had that effect,' said Clarissa.

Their train began to slow. She suspected they were approaching St. Paul's.

'So did the eighth Drop reveal the manuscript's location?' asked Ralph, suddenly buzzing with renewed energy.

'Yes.'

'Was there a clue?'

'No.'

'So it was encrypted again?'

Several passengers started to navigate towards the sliding doors.

'Err…yes, sort of,' said Clarissa. 'You'll see what I mean when we get there.'

'So, do you know *what* it is yet? This mysterious manuscript?'

The train ground to a halt. The two girls in the plastic jackets got off. An elderly couple took their seats.

'I do,' said Clarissa. She took a deep breath. 'Yes. I finally know *where* it is and *what* it is.' The doors bleeped and sealed shut.

The train started to move.

'It's in London,' said Clarissa staring at Ralph, his eyes hungry for her answer. 'And it's a piece of music Chopin wrote for Sand in 1838.' The steady click-clacking of the train cut through her voice.

'Bloody hell!' Ralph threw his head back as if he'd been struck. 'Then it has to be fake!'

'What makes you say that?'

'Come on.'

Clarissa shook her head fervently. 'I have every reason to believe it's genuine,' she said. 'Charlie and Max had it authenticated by three independent bodies. And the reason it's so valuable is that the piece has *literally* never seen the light of day! It's an unpublished score thought to have been buried by George Sand in the grounds of the Carthusian Monastery in Valldemossa, Majorca.'

Ralph was staring at her as if she'd lost her mind. 'Surely it would have rotted?'

Clarissa glanced around their carriage self-consciously. The man wearing the headphones caught her eyes briefly, then looked away. 'Providing the paper is safely sealed in a container that has been kept away from light, humidity and insects, it can last for centuries,' she said, relating the information that Charlie had given her in the eighth Drop.

'But if it's genuine, it must be worth millions!' said Ralph.

She glared at him, imploring him to lower his voice.

He read the hint. 'But didn't Chopin request that any unpublished works discovered after the event of his death were to be destroyed?' he said, more softly. 'When was it found?'

'2015. In a secret passage underneath the monastery. I don't think even Charlie knew who removed it originally. It's changed hands quite a bit on the black market since then.'

'So it was stolen from the monastery?'

'Yes. Charlie and Max weren't hired to investigate and transport the manuscript until the 11th of February this year, so it had been circulating on the black market for four years before they got involved. God knows how many thieves have handled it in that time!'

One of the inter-joining carriage doors suddenly snapped open. A homeless man shuffled along the walkway asking for change.

'But if it was stolen from the monastery, surely that's where we should return it?' said Ralph, irascibly. 'Why should Professor Kowalski take precedence here?'

'That's the Spanish in you talking,' said Clarissa.

The homeless man was asking everyone for change repeatedly in the background.

'Well, if it was stolen from Spanish soil, surely it should be returned to Spanish soil?' said Ralph.

'In theory, yes,' agreed Clarissa. 'But I have to fulfil Charlie's request. I have to take it to Professor Kowalski!'

'I thought you might say that,' said Ralph, sitting back in his seat, observing the hard coloured lines of the Tube map in his eye-line.

Clarissa glanced at her watch. It was 1:20 p.m. She was wondering if the manuscript could be retrieved in time for her meeting with Kowalski at the Shard. It was certainly workable.

'So, are you going to tell me where it is?' said Ralph.

'Actually, we're heading there right now,' said Clarissa, in an understated way, trying not to induce too much excitement.

Ralph turned to face her. She watched his features react to this with feverish anticipation, but he said nothing. Then he kissed her suddenly.

On breaking away, he said: 'So when do I get to play it?'

'Got any spare change, missis?' The homeless man's red face lunged in front of Clarissa's startled eyes without warning. His pungent stench of alcohol and unwashed skin wrestled with her senses.

Ralph reached into his jacket pocket and pulled out several pound coins. He piled them into the beggar's hands and the man smiled, revealing a missing tooth. Clarissa was suddenly reminded of Edward Letterton. She shivered at the association.

'God bless ya, governor!' the man muttered appreciatively to Ralph.

'It's the only way to validate its authenticity,' Ralph continued, as the man shuffled away to badger somebody else. 'I *have* to play it.'

'But I am in no doubt of its authenticity,' said Clarissa censoriously, trying to extricate the horrible image of Letterton's mouth from her mind.

Ralph flashed her an injured look, as if he found her certitude irritating. 'Charlie says it's genuine, so it's genuine, right?'

'But it's not about what Charlie believed. It's about what the experts believed!' Clarissa countered, correcting him.

'But it's not enough! You've got to let me play it!' Ralph implored. 'It's the only way we'll know for sure! If that piece of music was written by Chopin, I'll be able to *feel* it in my blood.'

Clarissa looked at him, sensing the tenacity in his voice and the thirst for truth his eyes. She knew that what he was saying made sense.

'Okay,' she said, resignedly. 'Let's go and get it.'

19

'It's *here*?' said Ralph in utter disbelief.

'It's here,' said Clarissa definitively. This was followed by a palpable stab of disappointment as she took in the building's black windows and lack of life. 'But it's closed!'

As the Museum of the Royal Academy of Music's pillared entrance came into view, Clarissa slowed her pace.

'I could have saved you the time, if you'd told me where we were going!' exclaimed Ralph. 'The museum's always closed on a Sunday.'

Clarissa closed her eyes briefly. 'This is going to be a problem.'

'He's put it inside one of the pianos hasn't he?' said Ralph excitedly.

'Yes,' said Clarissa, trying her best to keep calm, but Ralph's eyes were sparkling furiously, inviting her to share in his thrill of nearly completing their quest; something she was reluctant to do, when she could see no way of tackling the most difficult part of it: getting the manuscript out of a piano, locked inside a museum.

'I'm impressed,' said Ralph. He lifted his hands to his temples. 'I wonder *how*…and when?'

'Never mind that,' Clarissa gripped his arm. 'Can you get us inside?'

'What? No way!' he remonstrated. 'I just study here. I don't have the run of the place!'

'But there must be another entrance?'

'Are you serious? How about we just come back tomorrow when the museum's open?'

'Because I might be somewhere else tomorrow, like a *bloody police cell*?' she retorted sharply.

Ralph stared her full in the face. 'If we gain access to the museum without permission, you've got a good chance of being taken to that bloody police cell today! Is that what you want?'

His recrimination brought her up short.

'You're right,' she said. 'We'll need to think of another way to get inside.'

Ralph cupped his forehead and sighed.

'You play in there sometimes, right?' Clarissa asked suddenly, starting to pace around a bit, as if stretching her leg muscles could in some way influence her brain to formulate a better plan.

'Aye. We demonstrate the pianos for visitors.'

'When was the last time you were in there?'

'Err…Thursday morning?'

'Okay. What would you do if you'd left something in there? Something you needed for your performance tonight? Some script music maybe? Who would you ask to gain access into the museum?'

'Why can't I just print off another copy of the script music?'

Clarissa groaned. 'Let's just say it's set out just the way you like it, with special notes and everything. You don't have access to another copy of it and there's no time to prepare another. Or your grandfather's ring? You would have to have *that* for your performance, wouldn't you? What if you'd dropped the ring in the museum? What would you do?'

'Contact security, I suppose.'

'Then let's do it!' She glanced at her watch with mounting frustration, painfully aware of her impending appointment with Kowalski. Of course, she hadn't expected to arrive at their meeting with the manuscript on her, but if they could obtain it now, she *could;* and the manuscript would not only be safe, but it would also be exactly where Charlie wanted it: in Kowalski's hands.

'And where exactly *is* the manuscript?' said Ralph.

'Well, according to the Dead Drop in my garden wall, it's "concealed inside the instrument I liked so much in B.P"'.

Ralph screwed his features into a frown.

'Don't even bother trying,' said Clarissa. 'You'll never get this one. It's designed just for me. "B.P" is Buckingham Palace. I think Charlie was referring to: "The Music Lesson" by Vermeer. Last summer, we took a tour of the palace and I pointed the painting out to him. It depicts a young woman playing –'

'A virginal,' said Ralph, finishing off the sentence for her.

'That's right,' said Clarissa. 'Now, how many virginals are there in the museum?'

Ralph was silent for a moment. Then he said: 'There's just the one.'

'Fantastic!' Clarissa cried, relieved. 'We have just the one to search then.'

Ralph backed away from her, his brow furrowing. 'But the manuscript can't be *inside* the virginal. The instrument's far too shallow for that! I've had it open myself, many times. And if Charlie had placed anything inside it two weeks ago, it would have long been discovered by now!'

'Maybe it's concealed somehow,' suggested Clarissa. 'We've got to at least check, otherwise the Dead Drop clue makes no sense, don't you agree?' Clarissa tried to look as if her interpretation of the clue could not be refuted, even though she was now wondering if she had somehow managed to misinterpret it. 'We'll need some inspection gloves though,' she added.

'There's a drawer of them in the corner of the gallery,' said Ralph. He scraped back his hair. 'Okay. Supposing they let me into the museum – and I don't think they will by the way – but supposing they do, how am I going to explain the fact that I'm opening up one of the oldest and most precious instruments in the gallery? Do you think they're going to just stand there and let me do that? You'll have to come in there with me. It's the only way. I'll have to distract whoever escorts us in there while you head for the piano.'

'You think they'd let me in?' Clarissa cut him a doubtful look.

'If you're with me, they might,' said Ralph. 'I'll show them my ID. Tell them you're my girlfriend.'

Suddenly a voice could be heard in the distance. 'Miss Davenport?'

Clarissa winced and turned around.

There could only be one person who would call her that.

There, across the courtyard, was Professor Ward. She was ambling towards them, waving enthusiastically, her ivory waterproof jacket glowing like a beacon.

Clarissa mumbled under her breath: 'Listen, just to fill you in, she knows me as Charlie Davenport. If you call me anything, you must call me Charlie.'

'*What*?' cried Ralph.

Clarissa set her face into a smile and waited for the professor to reach them. Clarissa greeted her with bright, nervous twitches, absently tucking her hair behind her ear, forgetting about its dual purpose as a curtain for her injury.

'So, what brings you back here?' gushed Professor Ward, slightly out of breath, the afternoon sun dancing on her mass of grey hair. 'And your eye! My Goodness! What happened?'

'I err….' Clarissa touched her face briefly. 'I dropped a mirror in my flat. A shard caught me.'

'Crikey! How unfortunate!' The professor drew away from her as if she were contagious.

'I'm sorry. I didn't get the chance to apologise for the other day,' said Clarissa.

Ward bunched her lips. 'These things happen. I take it Max filled you in?'

'She did. Thank you. Yes.'

'And I see you've become acquainted with our young Mr. Valero here!' Clarissa noted the emphasis on the "young". 'Do you two know one another then?'

Ralph started to say something, but Clarissa cut him short. 'Not really. We've literally just bumped into one another in the foyer,' she said diffidently. 'I was enquiring about the museum. I didn't get the chance to have a proper look around before. It was stupid, I didn't think to check the opening hours. I thought most museums were open on Sundays these days.'

'Are you going into the museum now, Professor?' asked Ralph, suddenly eager to show willing for the cause.

'Yes. I left something behind.'

Ralph beamed in response to this, flashing a recondite twinkle in Clarissa's direction. 'Snap!' he said. 'I've only gone and left my sheet music for tonight's concert in there!' he said, bristling with charm. 'I couldn't just pop inside and get it could I? I know exactly where it is.'

Ward cut Ralph a sharp stare. 'Mr. Valero! Since when have *you* needed sheet music during a performance?'

Awkward laughter followed.

A lost ring would have sounded better, thought Clarissa.

'I'm not as confident as you think I am,' said Ralph.

'What is it that you're playing tonight?' asked Ward.

'Chopin's Nocturne in E-flat major, op. 9, no.2,' Ralph replied.

Clarissa looked at him, her eyes raised in soft questioning. It was the piece she'd played at the Susie Sainsbury Theatre.

'Splendid!' The professor nodded. 'Any particular reason for the choice?'

'It's become a bit special to me recently,' said Ralph, his eyes briefly brushing Clarissa's.

She felt a lump appear in the back of her throat.

'All right. Where did you leave it? I'll go and fetch it for you,' Ward offered enthusiastically.

'Err…. Well I….'

'Actually, if you're opening the door, I don't suppose *I* could take a quick look in the piano gallery, could I?' said Clarissa, sensing the need to step in. 'There's a particular instrument I'd really like to see.'

'You said you wanted to see the Heichele piano, didn't you?' said Ralph spontaneously, looking grateful for the life-line, and showing her he could take it to the next level.

'I did,' said Clarissa, going along with the improvisation. 'I'd hate to leave without seeing it.'

Ward removed a large bunch of keys from her pocket. 'Yes. It *is* rather special, isn't it Ralph?'

'Aye,' he agreed avidly.

'Very well,' said the professor amicably, alternating her gaze between Ralph and Clarissa, a bemused expression on her face. 'Well, it's not as if I don't know both of you. The thing is, I can't really hang around for long. Will ten minutes suffice?'

After this, Ralph and Clarissa immediately launched into their own excited speeches of appreciation while the professor smiled and unlocked the door, her ivory waterproof crackling as the lock snapped undone.

As soon as the three of them had shuffled across the threshold, the professor locked the door again and placed the keys in the pocket of her waterproof. There would be no fast escape if they needed it, thought Clarissa.

In semi-darkness, they walked through the violin gallery in silence.

When they reached the stairs, Ralph turned to Ward. 'I can show our visitor where the piano is, if you like, if you need to do something,' he said helpfully.

Clarissa was grateful he'd refrained from addressing her as Charlie.

'Go on then, Ralph!' said the professor winking at Clarissa conspiratorially. 'Play Charlie some Chopin. I think she'd appreciate that.'

Ralph led Clarissa hurriedly up the stairs.

The piano gallery was impressive. Clarissa had seen it before, but it was so long ago she could hardly remember it. The pianos were remarkable. But she knew that this wasn't the time to appreciate them.

She twitched her feet as she waited for Ralph to turn on some lights and fetch her a pair of cotton gloves from a small chest of drawers.

The Italian virginal had been positioned against a crimson wall at the far end of the gallery. Clarissa located it at once and stared at Ralph. He handed her some gloves and went and seated himself at the Heichele, giving her the nod to go ahead and begin her search.

Within seconds Chopin's Fantasie-Impromptu (Opus 66) blasted from Ralph's fingers, filling the gallery with its rich and powerful sound.

Clarissa scanned the space anxiously, checking the door for any sign of Professor Ward. She experienced a jolt of panic on detecting a CCTV camera in the far corner of the room, but on closer inspection, found it pointing in a different direction to the virginal. She breathed a sigh of relief.

Clarissa approached the instrument with a reverence. She knew it was theoretically incorrect to categorise it as "a piano", as its strings were plucked as opposed to being struck by hammers, but found herself unable to refer to it as "a harpsichord". It *was* however, indisputably beautiful. She slipped the cotton gloves onto her fingers and imagined all the musicians who must have played it over the centuries.

A warm glow seemed to emanate from the virginal's ancient wooden keys; each one held a half-moon of split wood like a section of a snail's back beneath its veneered outer layer. There was a petrol blue beaten shell encompassing the whole instrument that bore weathered markings like an ancient language. Clarissa ran her gloved hand across it gently.

She glanced towards the door. She could feel her heart rate quicken. She had to make herself believe that Professor Ward would leave them undisturbed.

After folding away its music stand, Clarissa opened and inspected the instrument's innards as Ralph played.

Inside, it was small and neat, with a single set of strings laid crossways to the keyboard. It was also completely empty, as

Ralph had predicted. The wooden cavity was shallow. And as nothing could lie within it and go unnoticed, Clarissa began to feel her way around looking for secret holes.

After about a minute, just as Ralph's melody slowed to a largo, Clarissa's fingers came across a moving panel in the wood. She began to apply pressure to it, biting her lip with anticipation. Suddenly, it slid back revealing a secret dip. It was impossible to see anything down it apart from a black space, but with three fingers inserted Clarissa managed to make contact with something hard and tubular. It had been positioned in the corner and was completely invisible from the outside.

Clarissa pulled it towards her feverishly, and with trembling fingers extracted it from its hole.

It was an old metal tube about twenty centimetres in length. It was rusted to hell, brown and corroded.

Clarissa dropped it into her handbag. Then she closed the lid of the virginal and reassembled the music rest, her heart now thumping at such an astonishing rate, it was as if someone had set a metronome at the wrong speed to the music.

She raced over to Ralph, removing her gloves and placing them in one of her jacket pockets. The piece he was playing had become animated again and she watched his feet dance across the instrument's six pedals. She waited for him to conclude the piece, before she whispered in his ear: 'Mission accomplished.'

Ralph pulled down the lid of the Heichele and smiled at her.

Professor Ward was waiting for them downstairs.

'Any joy?' she asked, referring to the missing sheet music, as they drew alongside her.

'No sign of it,' said Ralph. 'I must have left it somewhere else.'

'Really?' She didn't look at all surprised. 'Never mind. I'm sure Charlie appreciated the Heichele demonstration.'

'Oh, yes. It was superb!' Clarissa chimed in collaboratively. 'I've been treated to my own private show! I feel very privileged.'

'You know me, Professor. I'll do anything for a beautiful woman!' cried Ralph, getting into the full swing of his role.

Ward chuckled and enquired if he'd remembered to turn out all the lights. Ralph said that he had, but he'd go back to check just to be sure, and disappeared upstairs.

Clarissa had the feeling that the professor wanted to talk to her alone. She followed her back past the violins suspended in their glass coffins.

When they reached the main entrance, Professor Ward gave her a long, hard stare. 'This manuscript of yours? I trust it's in a safe place?'

'Of course. Why?'

'You are aware of its current value I presume? My estimate is at least ten million, perhaps more.'

'That much?' said Clarissa, drawing her bag tighter on her shoulder.

'Oh, yes.'

The professor unlocked the museum's external door and smiled. 'And you really needn't have lied,' she said.

Clarissa felt her heart lurch. 'Excuse me?'

'About Ralph,' said Ward.

Clarissa looked confused.

'I saw you earlier. Holding hands?'

'Ah.'

'A bit of a dish, isn't he? And gifted too. He'll break a few hearts in his time. I'd be careful if I were you; you've got some bad luck heading your way.'

Clarissa flashed the professor a questioning glance.

'They say it's seven years for breaking a mirror, don't they?'

'Oh, yes,' said Clarissa, suddenly understanding.

Just then, Ralph bounded up to them. The three of them smiled and a polite laughter resounded.

'All the lights are most definitely off,' he said.

'You used Charlie's identity?' said Ralph, as they marched back towards the Royal Academy of Music's front entrance. 'Are you mad?'

'I know. It looks bad *now,* but I was trying to find out about the manuscript. Where are we going?'

'Practice rooms.'

Ralph led her into the Academy. They cut through the foyer, past the entrance desks and towards a staircase. A knot of students was standing around chatting.

'So Professor Ward was one of the experts authenticating the manuscript?' said Ralph.

'That's right.'

They ran down a corridor.

'And you spoke to her from Charlie's mobile?'

'Yes?'

'Then it's only a matter of time before the police get in touch with her,' said Ralph. 'She'll say that Charlie was female. She'll say that she's seen you with me!'

'Then we'd better hurry!' cried Clarissa.

Ralph took her into a small room with a number '5' on its door. It contained a piano, two chairs and a modest amp. He looked at his watch.

'James has booked it, two thirty till four. He'll be here any minute. We've got to hurry.'

Clarissa removed the inspection gloves from her pocket and put them back on. Then she took the old tube out of her bag. The corroded metal glittered under the lights.

They were both transfixed.

'It's a bit stiff!' said Clarissa as she struggled to prise the container apart. She offered it to Ralph.

As he strained to break it open, the lip of the metal shunted back a bit from its central join but would shift no further. He swore.

He persisted, Clarissa egging him on.

'It's moving,' she said. 'Keep going. You're doing it!'

'It's a good job these cubicles are sound proof,' said Ralph, with a smirk.

Clarissa winced at his ill-timed levity. 'Come on, you're nearly there.'

A few seconds later, Ralph succeeded in opening the tube. He brushed a sprinkling of ground metal dust onto the floor and they smiled at one another.

Clarissa inserted a gloved fingertip into the tube cavity and extracted its contents slowly. Curled around her finger, she drew out a sheaf of brown paper.

Once removed, Clarissa unrolled the bundle, an ancient smoky scent pervading the room like the breath of an imprisoned spirit.

There were three pieces of paper inside. On the first one, written at the top in black ink were the words:

Ma Chérie Aurore,
Une composition faite uniquement pour toi.
Votre Frédéric Chopin.

'My Dear Aurore. A composition made purely for you. Your Frédéric Chopin,' Ralph translated.

Clarissa felt a wave of wonderment trickle through her body as she examined the words.

Hand drawn staves followed. Three pages of them, filled with music notation.

'This is incredible!' shouted Ralph. 'Bring it over to the piano.'

'It's beautiful,' said Clarissa, her eyes round with wonder. 'I can't believe I'm holding a piece of Chopin's original work in my hands!'

She carried the sheaf towards the music stand.

A sudden thumping on the door made them jump, followed by shouting, severely muffled by the sound proofing.

'It's James,' said Ralph. 'We'll need to find somewhere else.'

Clarissa rolled the manuscript back up quickly and returned it safely inside its tube. Once she'd got it back into her bag and removed her gloves, Ralph threw open the door.

It wasn't James. It was one of the receptionists from the foyer.

'Ralph Valero and Charlie Davenport?' he said.

'Yes?' said Ralph.

'Professor Ward called. She'd like you both to pop back to the museum as soon as you can.'

'Right. We'll be there in a minute,' said Ralph.

The receptionist left.

'There's something's wrong,' said Ralph. 'Come on, we need to get out of here!'

He led Clarissa along the corridor and back down the stairs. They ran past the reception desks and through the glass doors out into the street. They encountered a group of students huddled immediately outside the entrance.

'Hey, Ralph?' said a girl. 'Do you know what's going on? There's a lot of police outside the museum.'

The words sent a shiver down Clarissa's spine. Things were progressing fast.

'No idea!' cried Ralph to the girl, as they zipped past them.

They ran in the direction of the Tube.

Clarissa looked at her watch. It was 2:35 p.m. They were in good time for her meeting with Kowalski; they could be at the Aqua Shard for 3.15 p.m.

'Come on, this way!' she called leading Ralph towards the signs for the Jubilee Line South.

'Where are we going?' cried Ralph.

'London Bridge!' shouted Clarissa.

She slapped her Oyster card on a barrier pad and hurried through the gate, leaping onto a descending escalator, the identical digital billboards producing a strange vertiginous effect as they rolled and flashed in the periphery of her vision.

They boarded the Tube. They had to ride through five stops so they sat down, Clarissa hugging her bag to her.

'Where are we heading?' said Ralph.

'Kowalski's waiting for me in the Shard,' she said.

'What? Now?' Ralph gave her a wounded look. 'You're going to hand it over already? Without me having played it?'

Clarissa flashed him a look of contrition.

'I want it to be safe.'

'Can I at least photograph the pages?'

'You want me to get it out on the Tube?'

'Don't be stupid.'

Exiting their train, they followed a network of passages until they found the connection that ran under the bridges to the outside.

When they emerged they found themselves at the base of the Shard, its magnificent glass and steel structure looming up into the bright March sky.

People were congregating around the circular door beside the Shangri-La hotel, where identical shard-topiaries were lined outside its entrance. Clarissa and Ralph fell in behind them.

They entered the building.

'It's on the 31st floor,' said Clarissa.

She marched towards the lifts. A silver button stood proud of the wall with a chevron cut into it pointing skywards. Clarissa pressed it. A group of people were milling about: a loved-up couple in their twenties, two young men, a middle-aged couple with their two children. They all piled into a lift leaving no room for Clarissa and Ralph. Clarissa indicated that they'd wait for the next one.

'When did he reply to your email?' said Ralph.

'Yesterday,' said Clarissa.

A couple of minutes later, the lift door slid open again and they got in alone. They were greeted by themselves, as a large mirror stood opposite. A male voice announced from a speaker that they were not required to press anything, that they would automatically be taken to their destination, and that it would take fifteen seconds. The door closed. They rode in silence, a blue screen counting them up to thirty-two.

The door opened again.

They were confronted by an illuminated map of London looking a bit like a stained glass window, the lift lobby dimly lit to extenuate the beauty in the map. They walked across the wooden floor towards some glass doors where they were greeted by a woman in black with a clipboard.

'Table for Kowalski?' said Clarissa to the woman. She felt Ralph instinctively pull back.

'Look, I'm sorry but I really need to pee,' he said. 'Wait here for me?'

Clarissa nodded.

He disappeared.

The woman with the clipboard smiled and directed Clarissa down some stairs to an intermediary viewing platform halfway between floors 32 and 31, where she waited, the Aqua Shard restaurant clattering and humming gently immediately beneath her.

Clarissa surveyed the London skyline. It was breathtaking. The iconic buildings, the Thames threading through them. It all looked so different from up here.

She could smell the food from the restaurant. It was making her fully appreciate how hungry she was. She shuffled about nervously, preparing for her meeting with Kowalski. She was excited. The manuscript would soon be where Charlie had asked her to put it: in Kowalski's possession. Then all this would finally be over.

Suddenly a man's voice said: 'Amazing, isn't it?' She assumed he was referring to the view.

She turned.

She jumped when she saw who was standing beside her. She was unable to believe that he had the nerve!

Charlie's killer bent in closer to her, so that she could see the lines around his brown eyes, the grey patches in his hair, but he was not smiling this time. He looked rough, like he had been on the run. He smelt of sweat and the Tube. His large, muscular arms worried her.

'Daniel. Paul. Darlington,' she said slowly, her voice a low vibrato.

'You know who I am?' he asked, surprised.

'I know who you are and what you did. And so do the police,' she snapped. 'They found your watch next to Charlie's body.'

'Now, you need to listen to me, Clarissa,' said Darlington. 'Whatever you think has been going on here, you haven't got a fucking clue.'

She looked around for Ralph; he was nowhere to be seen.

'You're here to meet Kowalski, right?'

Clarissa just stared at him, wondering how on earth he knew.

'Allow me to disclose something you should know. That man down there in the booth claiming to be Kowalski?' – he made a general gesture towards the restaurant even though individual diners could not be seen from their vantage point – 'Well he *isn't* Kowalski. He's an actor paid by Roland Steed to pose as the professor so that they can get the manuscript off you.'

'Ha! Is that the best you could come up with?' spat Clarissa. 'It's laughable!'

'It's also true.'

She was unconvinced.

'Prove it,' she said.

'I don't have time for games, Clarissa. We have to get out of here. You don't know the danger you're in!'

'What are you talking about? Why would I go with you? *You're* responsible for…what happened to Charlie.'

He lowered his voice to a whisper, gripping her elbow. 'Clarissa, *I* didn't do it! You've got to believe me. He was my friend. I was trying to protect him. He asked me to keep an eye on you while you were following his Dead Drop trail! Roland Steed was the one who shot him. I was running *with* him not *after* him!'

Clarissa shook her head in disbelief. 'I don't believe you!'

'I was supposed to lie low. You weren't supposed to know I was there, but Charlie said that if things got difficult and I needed to reveal myself, there was something I should say to you to prove my dependability.'

'And what was that?'

'"Good luck, baby."'

Clarissa froze.

This changed everything. She had told absolutely no one about the significance of this, not even Ralph.

Clarissa searched Darlington's eyes, seeing him differently. He coaxed her away from the glass.

'I believe you,' she said. 'But I can't just go! My friend's in the toilet. I need to wait for him to get back.'

Darlington threw her an embittered look. 'You mean Valero? *A friend*! He's one of them! He's been working for Roland Steed from the start. He was the bait he used to reel you in! Steed paid him to busk in the Tube until he picked you up!'

Clarissa felt herself waver as she took on the full meaning of this.

'What?' she said.

Darlington was pulsing with impatience for them to leave. 'Look,' he said. 'I'm sorry for the brutal wake up call, but it's about time you knew. Leave Ralph and come with me!'

Clarissa felt the part of her brain responsible for speech fail miserably. She looked out at the view of London, then back to Darlington's imploring eyes, trying to understand what was going on here. Suddenly nothing seemed to make sense anymore.

She allowed Darlington to escort her body from the building, while her mind blurred, lost in confusion, refusing to believe that Ralph had betrayed her.

When they got outside, Darlington led her across the road, then up a narrow street flanking a hospital. When they passed an undulating wall that looked a bit like hundreds of bulbous lumps of molten mercury, Clarissa felt pain rise up within her. When she felt she was unable to contain it any longer, she opened her mouth and screamed.

It came out loud and fierce, the sound a wild animal might make if unexpectedly caught in a snare. It was accompanied by a flashing mess of confused images in her mind. She saw Ralph playing Chopin's Raindrop Prelude outside Baker Street Tube. No coincidence; but a very deliberate set up. The melody carefully selected by Steed, who must have known somehow that she'd be incapable of walking past a busker playing Opus 28, number 15 – the same score she should have played at the Royal

Festival Hall that fateful evening, after receiving Letterton's flowers. Charlie had known this. Perhaps Steed had somehow extracted this information from him. If not, her debut performance at such a prestigious theatre must have been documented somewhere. Perhaps Steed had done his homework and dug it out? Steed must have known about her meeting with Ward. He must have told Ralph to play the Prelude repeatedly until she arrived. It had all been a trap of the most sophisticated, underhand kind.

As she stood there by the side of the road, the strong safety net Ralph had woven around her in tatters, she sensed herself falling, careering aimlessly, unsure of her trajectory.

She knew that Darlington could have been lying, but somehow everything seemed to make sense: the itching inconsistencies she could never quite fathom; it was as if they had all been pulled into one sharp, tight focus. Suddenly she could see everything in astonishing clarity: the way Ralph had instantly got half of Slim and Silas' drug money; the mysterious phone calls he'd clammed up about; why he'd suddenly tried to distance himself from her when she'd given him the news about Charlie's death.

She returned to her physical self again at the sound of Darlington's voice repeating her name.

She glared at him.

He was looking at her like she was pointing a gun at him. It made her wish she still had the Beretta.

'Are you okay?' he said, edging towards her.

She nodded, tasting the salt from her tears. She saw his hand reach for her arm.

'Don't you come near me!' she warned him, thinking of the manuscript in her bag, knowing that it wouldn't take much for him to whip it from her and disappear, leaving her reeling.

Suddenly she felt very unsafe.

He backed off, lifting his arms to indicate his compliance.

At this moment, a family walked past with young children. She caught sight of a young girl, around six, staring at her with large, frightened eyes, her parents anxiously pulling her away from this crazy woman with a black eye screaming in the middle of the road. What had become of her? She felt she had been cruelly transformed from a Disney princess into some sort of monster who put the fear of God into small children; a Sleeping Beauty who had just woken up in hell.

Abruptly, Clarissa's phone started ringing from the inside of her bag.

She removed it.

The little screen said: *Ralph Valero calling*. She accepted the call.

'Hello?'

'Where are you?' came Ralph's apprehensive reply.

Silence.

'Clarissa?'

'Is it true?' she said, her voice cracking.

'Is *what* true?'

'That Steed paid you to pick me up in the Tube?'

A shocked silence.

'IS IT TRUE?'

'Yes. But I can explain –'

'Oh, my God.'

Clarissa felt something fracture deep inside her.

There was some commotion at Ralph's end. Clarissa could hear him talking to someone else.

'Hello Clarissa.' A different voice. A deep cockney tongue. 'Darlington there, is he?'

Clarissa put her phone on speaker and held it out so that Darlington could listen.

'Who is this?' said Clarissa, but she knew the answer already. It was Roland Steed's voice. It had a profound effect on her. The sound of it made her skin crawl.

'Oh, come on, Clarissa. You know who I am, surely?' said Steed playing the game. 'But I bet you can't guess *where* I am. I'm here at the Aqua Shard along with your new friend Professor Kowalski and your old friend Ralph. The professor wants to know why you stood him up. I think Ralph here, wouldn't mind having the answer to that question as well!'

'You must be mistaken. I don't have any friends there,' replied Clarissa, trying to stop herself from trembling.

'Oh, come now, Clarissa. You mustn't be too hard on the boy. I can assure you, his loyalty to you is one hundred per cent genuine. He's been feeding me a pack of lies from the moment he met you. The thing I didn't take into account was how strong your attraction would be for one another! You see, I thought that you and Charlie were, how shall I put it, unbreakable. But Charlie's love for you was so great, he tried to protect you by dumping you and faking his allegiance to another woman. This, as he tried to explain to you, was not real, but he'd done such a good job of it, even *you* bought into it in the end! So, in your broken state, you found a hero in my pianist. A pianist who was so besotted with you, he decided to switch sides! A big mistake. As he will very soon realise. But for now, I've discovered a way to use it to my advantage.'

'What do you mean?'

'You see, Ralph and myself, we have this one thing in common. We're both *very* driven. We both know what we want. Ralph here, wants a career as a professional pianist and a composer, and he is, as you know, a very accomplished musician with potential.'

'And what do *you* want?' asked Clarissa, already anticipating the answer.

'The thing I've always wanted, Clarissa. The Chopin manuscript. And you have the power make both of us happy. It would seem.'

'What do you mean?'

'A little birdie told me that you have the aforementioned manuscript in your bag. Whereas, I have Ralph's right hand taped to a board with a machete hovering a few inches above it. Now, it's really very simple. You bring me the manuscript, and I'll spare Ralph's hand.'

Clarissa felt sick. She looked at Darlington. His eyes were still fixed on the glow of the screen. He turned to her and nodded. 'Tell him we'll go back,' he said.

'Where do you want to meet?' Clarissa asked Steed.

'Good girl,' said Steed. 'Come to the reception desk of the Shangri-La hotel at the base of the Shard with the manuscript, and I'll get someone to bring you up to my suite.'

'Okay,' she replied, her voice weak.

'But listen carefully,' warned Steed. 'There's a few ground rules. Daniel Darlington is the only one who can accompany you. Tell no one else about this. If I see anyone else with you or detect a police presence, I shall break one of Ralph's fingers. Secondly, no trickery. Don't try and be clever and substitute the manuscript for anything else. If I see any evidence of this, I shall break another one of his fingers. And, finally, no sudden moves. You and Darlington move slowly. You both keep your hands where I can see them and do exactly what I tell you to do, or, well, I'm sure you can guess what I'm likely to do. Do you understand the rules, Clarissa?'

'Yes,' she said. She was shaking.

'Take your time, we'll be waiting. It's half past three. I'll give you half an hour. If you don't show by 4 p.m. I'll cut off all the fingers on Ralph's right hand with my machete and it's goodbye to his promising future.'

He hung up.

Darlington was staring at her sympathetically. 'Are you all right?' he said.

'Ralph is just as much a victim in all of this as I am,' she said, rummaging around in her bag. 'I can't let the bastard get away with this!'

'What are you doing?'

'I know who can help us.'

Clarissa pulled Inspector Okoro's card from her bag.

'But you're disobeying the first rule!' protested Darlington.

'Inspector Okoro will know how to handle this. She won't make herself visible,' said Clarissa confidently.

'Listen, I wouldn't mess with him if I were you. He'll break one of the pianist's fingers for sure!' said Darlington, confused.

Suddenly Clarissa said: 'Did you know that I was there? In the field where Charlie was killed?'

'You were?' said Darlington, shocked.

'Oh, yes. And I'm convinced that if I'd called the police that night, Charlie would still be alive right now! And I'm also convinced, *convinced,* that if we don't bring the police in at this point one, or both of us, will also end up dead. Probably me, because he needs you to remain alive so that you can be framed for killing Charlie, and he needs Ralph to remain alive so that he can feel the effects of his hand, his ultimate punishment for betraying him.'

Clarissa suddenly had a flashback of the night of Charlie's murder. Steed had called Charlie's phone asking for Charlie, knowing that Charlie couldn't possibly have answered. He must have known all along that Clarissa had been there in that field, and that *she* had taken Charlie's phone! Steed had also made a point of saying that he'd been waiting for Charlie at his home: "just outside London" and he'd been careful to provide her with his name, thereby cleverly extricating himself from the murder scene. He must have expected her to pass this information on to the police sooner or later, and of course, she had done just that. It was only now that she could see what he'd really been up to: he'd been exonerating himself from suspicion! And his plan had very nearly worked.

Clarissa cast her eyes over Darlington, standing diligently beside her, patiently waiting for her to say that she was ready to head back to the Shard. Now Darlington, on the other hand, had been kind to her. He had been unable to walk past her in the carpark of the Hoops Inn without checking that she was all right, despite being told by Charlie to lie low and conceal his cover. She had seen the concern in his eyes. How could she have thought him capable of murder? She realised now that she had got everything the wrong way round, that it had all become twisted somehow. Things were starting to make sense to her at last, and she knew that she would have to explain all of this to Inspector Okoro before Darlington got arrested for Charlie's murder.

Clarissa dialed the policewoman's number with her heart in her mouth.

To her relief, Inspector Okoro's voice answered straight away, stating her name and rank. She was efficient. She was on the ball. She wouldn't fuck things up, thought Clarissa. She was her only hope.

Clarissa spoke quickly before she could change her mind. 'Hello, Inspector. It's Clarissa Belmonte here.'

Bleep!

Silence.

'Shit, it's an answerphone!' said Clarissa. 'What are we going to do now?'

Suddenly Inspector Okoro's real voice interjected. She'd have known it anywhere.

'Clarissa? Is that you?' The inspector couldn't have sounded more surprised. 'Where are you? Are you all right?'

'Inspector Okoro? It's me! It's Clarissa Belmonte. I think I can lead to you to Charlie Davenport's killer. But you have to come now, to the Shard. You have to come now or someone is going to get hurt!'

20

L evel 34, the Shard. Light flooded into the Shangri-La's sky lobby through its enormous windows transforming its veined floor into a mirror. It resembled a vat of oil into which reflections ran, long and deep like chasms of molten silver. Two marbled reception desks had been set off beautifully with an oriental floral display, and two black-suited women were looking busy behind it.

Clarissa and Darlington emerged from the lift and glanced about anxiously.

There were a few people milling about. Darlington was getting some disapproving stares. He not only resembled a homeless person: unshaven, dishevelled, with a hole in his crumpled suede jacket, he smelt like one too. Clarissa began to worry that the hotel's security would soon escort him from the premises.

Clarissa scrutinized the cluster of bodies around the reception desks while they walked on towards the windows.

Two empty grey armchairs were positioned in front of a low coffee table covered in books. Opposite was a sofa. Scatter cushions had been excluded so that nothing disturbed the fluidity of the modern furniture. Upon the sofa sat Inspector Okoro. She was dressed in jeans with a copy of the *Metro* on her lap. Her dark eyes met Clarissa's briefly as they passed. She was positioned exactly where she said she would be, looking like any other ordinary paying guest at the hotel. Clarissa was suddenly grateful that not many police officers looked the way she did.

Behind Inspector Okoro, the view of London loomed.

Clarissa and Daniel Darlington walked towards an open descending staircase leading to another viewing platform.

They waited. Clarissa pulled her bag close; her fingers were damp with sweat and she was trembling. She had removed the manuscript from its metal canister and it was lying directly underneath the zip of her bag which had been left partially open. Beside it was her smartphone. Its screen was black, but she had turned on her recording app and she hoped it would be able to pick up all of Steed's threats.

Suddenly, Clarissa's phone pinged with a message. She unzipped her bag and gazed at it briefly. Her mother. *"Ring me as soon as you get this. I have news! x."*

Clarissa drew the zip on her bag back to a half-closed position. Looking up, she found Darlington staring at her expectantly. She shook her head, indicating that the message was unrelated to what they were about to do.

They watched a man in a suit climb the stairs: Asian, dark-haired, muscular, about forty, with heavy stubble. His eyes danced with distorted reflections. The amount of light that was flooding through the tower's windows was overwhelming.

'Come this way,' he said, his voice low and direct so that they could be in no doubt that this was a command, not a request.

'Which suite are we going to?' asked Clarissa. This was for Okoro's benefit, whom she hoped could hear their exchange, but their guide did not reply.

The man led them down to another viewing platform where several small circular tables with transparent chairs had been positioned next to the view. A few of these were occupied. Clarissa spotted Sergeant Quinn at one of them. Their eyes brushed for a fraction of a second as Clarissa walked on past him.

They were taken up another flight of stairs, where leather seats looked out upon the view, and shortly after this, led into one of the mirrored lifts, all in deadly silence. They emerged on Level 37 where they were ushered down a long corridor, a spot-beam of light pooling onto the marble floor.

Steed was in the Westminster Suite. The door swung back as soon as they reached it. The man with the fish scar smiled at her as they entered as if he were an old friend.

The luxurious suite was furnished in metallic colours with flashes of a rich peacock blue accent. They walked through a vestibule cut with storks in flight, preparing the way for the oriental theme.

The air in the room felt restricted. A sofa and two armchairs, chunky and bow-legged, resided on a plush copper carpet. A coffee table held a white china tea-set, a selection of biscuits and a wooden chopping board. Clarissa could see steam spiralling out of the pot, indicating that the tea had been freshly made.

Steed was sitting in one of the armchairs, surrounded by a panoramic view of London. He wore a grey suit with an ice-blue tie and handkerchief to match. He was completely still, apart from his eyes that flicked between Clarissa and Darlington like he was deliberating on which one of them would betray him first.

There was no sign of Ralph or a Professor Kowalski look-alike.

'Thank you, Imran,' Steed said to their guide.

Clarissa felt her blood run cold from her proximity to him.

'Blimey! That's some shiner!' he said, clocking Clarissa's eye. 'Please. Take a seat. Let's be civil about this. Have some tea.'

'Where's Ralph?' Clarissa demanded. 'Ralph!' she called out despairingly.

'Hello, Daniel,' said Steed, ignoring her and turning his attention towards Darlington. 'You look as if you've been kipping in a doorway. I must say, I'm impressed you got her to trust you, seeing as *you* were the one responsible for her boyfriend's death!'

Steed nodded to the man with the fish scar. 'Zack. Tell Simon to bring the pianist out now.'

'It was *you* who shot Charlie, you bastard,' said Clarissa, glaring fiercely at Steed, refusing to believe that Daniel Darlington had had anything to do with the killing. 'You tied him up and gagged him, but he got away, didn't he? So you chased him. Ran him down like an animal and shot him dead!'

'Now, *you* can calm the fuck down, or they'll be consequences!' ordered Steed.

Clarissa was shocked by his sudden change of tone.

'Just remember, there are two sides to every story,' he growled, using a more measured voice. 'I'm guessing Daniel was the one who told you about me hiring Ralph?'

Clarissa nodded.

'And how do you think he knew that?' said Steed. 'He knew that because *he* was the one who bloody hired him! He was working for me. I paid him to kidnap Charlie, not to kill him. But he got shot by accident because of *his* mistake!'

'He's lying, Clarissa,' said Darlington.

Suddenly the door of the adjoining bedroom burst open and Ralph was paraded before them, held by Zack and a thick-set, bald-headed man she presumed was Simon. Ralph's hands had been tied behind his back. He'd received a blow to the eye and another to the jaw; the two pink swollen lumps on his face alarmed her. He stared at her forlornly through his hair.

'I've done everything you've asked!' Clarissa protested. 'Why have you hurt him?'

'You may have. He didn't,' said Steed. 'We wouldn't have touched him, but the fool tried to take on Simon here.'

Clarissa looked Simon over. Butch, un-shaven, suited and rippling with muscles like Imran. There wasn't a mark on him.

'Ralph?' cried Clarissa.

Ralph was deposited on the sofa. He folded like a doll.

Clarissa attempted to rush over to him but Simon put his hand out to stop her.

'We've had to drug him,' said Steed. 'As a precautionary measure you understand. In case he tried something else.'

'What have you given him?' spat Clarissa, contemptuously.

'Oh, just a mild sedative. It's nothing to worry your pretty little head about. A few hours and he'll be as right as rain,' said Steed, smiling at her with his steely eyes.

This news came as a blow. It would certainly scupper her plans; she was relying on Ralph running with her when the time came.

Clarissa went to remove the manuscript from her bag, but Zack prevented this: 'Keep your hands where I can see them!' he cried, producing a gun from somewhere and pointing it in her direction.

'Look, do you want this manuscript or not?' said Clarissa growing frustrated, unable to take her eyes off the gun. It was much bigger than Charlie's, and it looked more powerful. She doubted very much that he'd actually use it, until she saw him produce a silencer and calmly screw it onto the barrel.

'Get Valero into position,' said Steed.

Simon cut the restraints from Ralph's wrists and placed his right hand across the chopping board on the coffee table. Imran began to fasten Ralph's hand to the board with duct tape.

'There's no need for this!' said Clarissa. 'I'm handing over the manuscript! Let me get it out of my bag.'

'Slide the whole bag over to me,' demanded Steed.

'No way,' said Clarissa. '*I'll* remove it or I'll rip it in half right now!'

Steed called off his advancing men with another curt nod. 'Alright, Clarissa. Keep calm,' he said. 'What a little firecracker you are! No wonder they all fall for you!'

'I think she's informed the police,' said Imran. 'The hotel was packed. It didn't look right.'

'That's not true!' Clarissa objected.

Steed poured himself a cup of tea, seemingly ignoring the suggestion and consequent denial, drawing the hot brown liquid from the teapot in slow and pensive consideration. Then he said: 'Start with his little finger. But better shut him up first.'

Clarissa watched Simon stuff some sort of fabric into Ralph's mouth and duct tape was applied to his lips. He looked at her through languid eyes.

Then, to Clarissa's absolute horror, Simon produced a claw hammer from nowhere, its metallic gleam shooting up through the air as it rose. Then it came down hard on the last finger of Ralph's right hand, claw-side down. Ralph's pain was expressed plaintively as a muffled falsetto broke the silence of the room. There was blood everywhere.

Steed threw him a white napkin.

'You bastard!' shouted Clarissa.

'You knew the rules,' said Steed.

Steed nodded abruptly to Zack.

'Now take the fucking manuscript out of your bag,' said Steed.

'Slowly,' said Zack, jerking the gun at Clarissa.

The atmosphere in the room was so tense, Clarissa could hear the sound of her own breath coming out in irregular shaky bursts.

Steed's eyes were locked on her fingers.

Clarissa unzipped her bag all the way and dipped her hand inside.

She whipped the manuscript from her bag along with something else: Darlington's lighter. She held the rolled manuscript aloft in her left hand, the lighter in her right. Clarissa flipped its silver lid, igniting an orange flame that licked the air menacingly.

Imran edged towards her.

'Come any closer and I'll set light to it!' she threatened.

Steed's smug smile disappeared.

'I mean it!' shouted Clarissa, emboldened by her anger, her heart drumming furiously. 'Now back off!'

Steed produced a curt nod and Imran slunk back.

'Now, tell me who killed Charlie or the manuscript goes up!' cried Clarissa.

Steed looked indignant. 'Threatening me is *not* a good idea, Clarissa.'

'Who fired the gun?' Clarissa felt a runnel of sweat run down her forehead. 'I need to know what happened that night and I want the truth!'

Steed lifted his hands in submission. 'Alright, Clarissa,' he said. 'Keep the flame away from the fucking manuscript.'

'What happened?' Clarissa repeated.

'I'll tell you what happened!' roared Steed, his voice simmering with fresh annoyance. 'Charlie Davenport killed my fucking brother!'

'How do you know that?' asked Clarissa.

'Alright, Clarissa, I'll explain it to you,' said Steed perniciously, his top-lip curled into a canine snarl. 'George stopped Charlie's car. There was fisticuffs. Then George chased

Charlie into the woods. Daniel and I searched for them for nearly half an hour, didn't we, Daniel? But with no luck. Then we found Charlie back at his car, but he couldn't get inside it because his fucking keys had gone missing.'

Clarissa felt her face blanch. In her mind she was back with the thug on the plane the moment the breakfast plate shattered. She felt the air drain out of her lungs.

'He came back to his car?' she said incredulously. She was reeling. She could almost see slimy in-flight food slithering down the walls of Steed's pristine suite.

'He was on his hands and knees, looking for his keys,' said Steed oblivious to her reaction. 'When he saw us, he legged it back towards the woods again.'

The truth was sharp and unyielding. It had taken her unaware. If she hadn't showed up and removed the keys from the ignition of the TT, Charlie might have been able to escape that night! If she hadn't blundered so clumsily into the proceedings, Charlie might still be alive!

Clarissa found herself struggling to breathe. It had all been her fault! As she continued to hold the manuscript and the lighter aloft, she imagined the sensation of the plate fragment entering her cheek: sharp and painful, her brain conflating the memory with the aftershock of Steed's revelation. Desperately, she tried to calm herself in order to ride through the shock; refusing to be taken out by a panic attack when she needed to find composure; refusing to lose control when she had come this far.

'Daniel and I took off after him,' Steed went on. 'Then Charlie slipped. When he got up he pulled a gun on us. Strange thing was, we searched him before and he'd been as clean as whistle.' He cut Darlington a reproachful look. 'Funny that, eh, Daniel?' He returned his gaze to Clarissa.

To her relief, Clarissa found that her breathing was returning to normal. She was taking back control. She only hoped her recording app was picking up all this.

'Daniel here then treated me to a fine display of his rugby tackling skills, bringing Charlie down,' Steed continued. 'The gun fell. I picked it up. I asked Charlie where George was and do you know what he said? He told me to go and look for his fucking corpse in the woods! So I pressed the gun to his fucking chest and shot him.'

Clarissa felt her eyes burn with a fresh onslaught of tears.

'I had him on the ground!' cried Darlington, with unexpected emotion. 'There was no need to pull the fucking trigger! I had him and you knew it!'

Steed glared at Darlington, his pale eyes suddenly acquiring malevolent resonance. 'Cut the fucking pretence. You must think I was born yesterday! My only regret is that I didn't shoot the pair of you. My appetite for retribution was only half-satisfied.'

Steed motioned to Zack.

Suddenly Zack grabbed Darlington by the neck, pressing the gun against the side of his head.

Steed stared balefully at Darlington.

'I did nothing to harm your brother!' Darlington insisted, wriggling in Zack's grasp.

Uninterested, Steed raised his hand to silence Darlington's futile supplication. 'You'll get what you fucking deserve later!' He returned his attention to Clarissa. 'The manuscript. Give it to me.'

Clarissa looked at Ralph. With his mouth still sealed with silver tape, he was trying to stem the flow of blood from his finger unsuccessfully. His new slow drug-induced perimeters were making it virtually impossible for him to do anything.

'Let Ralph leave the room,' she said.

Steed shrugged and nodded his assent.

Clarissa watched Ralph try to stand. She was horrified to see the extent to which they had drugged him – he could not maintain his balance – and he collapsed back down on the sofa, all knees and elbows.

Clarissa brought the fulvous paper scroll dangerously close to the flame again. 'You'll get the manuscript,' she said, her voice faltering, 'but first, you must let Ralph go.'

Steed's gravelly laughter filled the room. 'So the demands keep on coming!' he announced. 'But he *can* go, Clarissa! Nobody here's going to stop him,' he said, knowing full well that the drugs had rendered Ralph incapable of going anywhere. He smiled at his ineffectual efforts. 'If you're expecting us to help him, you can think again. Why don't you put that lighter down and give your fucking lover a bit of assistance?' he said smugly.

Clarissa's pupils were darting frantically between Ralph, Steed and Darlington.

Clarissa stood still, her eyes bearing the reflection of the lighter's flame.

Zack had the gun firmly pressed into Darlington's throat.

Ralph was trying to speak.

Clarissa glared resentfully at Steed: 'Take the tape off his mouth, for God's sake!'

Stead motioned his consent to Simon, and the duct tape was ripped from Ralph's lips in one swift action. He spat out the ball of fabric. He flinched, but made no sound.

'Are you okay, Ralph?' Clarissa cried, with urgent concern.

'Clar…issa,' he mumbled, his voice strained. 'Set…light to…it.'

A loud rap on the door startled everyone.

'Leave it,' said Steed.

The knock came again, more persistently this time.

Steed walked towards it.

'Who is it?' he called.

'Room service!' sang a female voice.

'We don't require any,' said Steed in his commanding way.

Silence.

Steed tilted his head expectantly.

Nothing.

It was the calm before the storm.

Then everything happened quickly. Darlington suddenly broke out of Zack's grip, dived over to the door and threw it open. Zack's gun fired, the bullet entering Darlington's arm.

Steed reached for the manuscript. At the same moment Ralph stood up and threw himself onto Imran.

The shot had triggered the armed response unit waiting outside, and uniformed police quickly started infiltrating the suite.

Steed had taken hold of the manuscript but it was engulfed in flames – it had gone up like touch-paper as soon the lighter had brushed it.

Several voices could be heard, all shouting the same instruction, their overlap simulating an echo: "LIE FLAT ON THE FLOOR WITH YOUR HANDS ON YOUR HEADS!"

Through a screen of smoke, Clarissa saw Inspector Okoro's Bantu knots fly past. Across the room Steed was trying in vain to stop the fire that was fast devouring the precious sheaves. 'You stupid cow!' he cried. 'That's a five million pound note you've just lit!'

'The last I heard, it was ten million!' Clarissa screamed back, hunkering down on the plush carpet. 'I thought I'd show you my firecracker skills!'

All eyes were drawn to the flames. It felt to Clarissa as though Chopin himself had appeared before them in disembodied form, preventing them all from taking possession of his manuscript by turning it into a wild, vermillion blaze.

The musical score was reduced to smoke in front of their eyes, dissolving its secrets; its crackling like an ache.

Steed swore and emitted a loud, guttural cry as the flames took hold of his sleeve. Within seconds a policeman had thrown a wet towel over his arm and a ball of fire fell to the carpet where it was promptly stamped out.

Armed police were everywhere. An injection of black and white mingled with smoke. The room filled up with them, disturbing the clean metallic lines of the space. There was a lot of shouting and Zack, Imran and Simon were all cuffed lying flat on their stomachs, then they were slowly pulled to their feet and led away.

Darlington remained on the floor. The bullet had entered his left elbow; his grubby crumpled jacket was now also soaked in blood. Clarissa watched a policeman radio for the paramedics to enter the room.

Steed was swiftly wrapped in a blanket, a policeman on each arm. It was the first time Clarissa had seen him lose his composure. She thought he suddenly cut a pathetic figure with his white head bent down, his grey eyes wincing in pain.

Clarissa pin-pointed Inspector Okoro through the chaos and rose to a crouch, keeping her hands firmly on top of her head.

'It was him!' she cried, jerking her chin in the direction of Steed's back. 'He's Charlie's killer! Roland Steed!'

Inspector Okoro hurried across to her. She called off the nearest two police officers and beckoned Clarissa to stand. Behind her, some paramedics were transferring Darlington onto a trolley.

'It's okay, Clarissa,' said the inspector reassuringly. 'We've got him now. Rest easy.'

In the distance she could hear Roland Steed being read his rights by Sergeant Quinn. The sound of his arrest was like music to her ears. Clarissa watched as they led him from the suite. He flashed her a venomous look as he passed by her. Brazenly, she returned his gaze and stared him out.

Once he had gone she caught the detective staring at her hands. They had assumed a strange claw-like stance since she had been told to lie on the floor. It looked as though she were still clinging fast to the carpet despite no longer having any carpet to hold onto. They were also trembling forcibly. She waved away Okoro's concerned words, maintaining that she was all right.

'Do you know what happened to George Steed now?' Clarissa asked her, folding her arms in a desperate attempt to stop the shaking.

Inspector Okoro assumed a more serious tone. 'We think so, yes. The post mortem report confirmed that he died from asphyxiation due to strangulation. There was no evidence to suggest suffocation, which means you're in the clear. We believe he was strangled by Charlie Davenport. We think it was self-defence. We also found numerous texts on Charlie's phone suggesting George Steed had made plans to target you. As Charlie's girlfriend, you were in great danger, Clarissa. It could be the reason he ended your relationship the way he did.' She produced a small tight-lipped smile.

Clarissa shivered. 'And Darlington?'

'Charlie and Darlington were old friends, they went to school together. Charlie knew that the Steed brothers were after him. We think he must have hatched a plan to get Darlington into their circle. The Steed brothers hired Darlington three weeks ago. But when George Steed went a step too far and Charlie ended up killing him in the woods, Darlington tried to cover it up. We found traces of soil in George Steed's mouth and ears. It's now our understanding that Darlington removed Charlie's restraints that night and transferred them to George Steed before burying him. We believe he must have returned to retrieve George Steed's body later that night and transferred it to the Audi.'

'But how could he have opened the boot?' said Clarissa, confused. 'I had the key.'

'He had one too,' said Okoro.

'He did?'

'We hadn't been able to locate his whereabouts, until you told us about seeing him in Paris, but we'd searched his flat previously. We'd already found a spare key to Charlie's car in his living room.

'Oh my God.'

Okoro shook her head sympathetically. 'It wasn't your fault, Clarissa. You did what you thought was right. The only person responsible for killing Charlie was Roland Steed.'

Clarissa nodded. She wanted so hard to believe this.

'Although,' Okoro continued, adjusting her tone, 'it would have helped us considerably if you'd mentioned the Chopin manuscript during one of your interviews. We've had a team investigating the whereabouts of the document for months. Apparently the group who hired Charlie Davenport and Maxine Siskind had stolen the Chopin score from the Steed brothers. George Steed was trying to retrieve what he believed was rightfully his.'

'But the Steed brothers couldn't have had any legitimate claim on the manuscript, surely?' said Clarissa, startled. 'I presume the only reason they had it in the first place was because they'd stolen it themselves?'

'You presume right,' said Okoro. 'They'd stolen it from a professor of music at King's College, London.'

'Nikolai Kowalski?' said Clarissa.

'That's right! So you knew about Kowalski?' The inspector looked shocked, her dark eyes blinking rapidly.

Clarissa nodded. She was having difficulty digesting a new fact that was fast materializing: that Charlie's involvement with the proceedings had been within the confines of the law. A surprise. She had always assumed that Charlie's role had been one of an underhanded criminal. She stared hard at Okoro. 'Charlie wanted me to get the manuscript back to Kowalski. I'd arranged to meet him here, at the Shard. There was a man claiming to be him waiting for me, but Daniel Darlington told me it was a set-up.'

'Professor Kowalski was found bound and gagged in his Richmond apartment about half an hour ago,' said Okoro. 'It seems Daniel Darlington told you the truth.'

Clarissa shook her head as she tried to take this in. 'Was the professor all right?'

'Apart from the shock of it, he endured no physical injuries,' said Okoro in her tight professional manner.

A radio crackled loudly close by and a female voice could be heard issuing more instructions in a coded tongue. It reminded Clarissa that her phone was still recording.

She reached into her bag and stopped it, explaining what she'd attempted to achieve to the inspector. Nervously, she played the beginning of the transcript back to her, revealing Steed's confession to Charlie's murder. To her relief, she found it quiet but perfectly audible. Okoro appeared impressed and said that they could certainly use it in court. Despite a fierce dislike of Okoro's brusque manner, Clarissa couldn't help but feel a shot of satisfaction at having pleased her.

'Darlington will be trialed for his part too, of course,' Okoro said, walking away, 'but he's bound to receive a far leaner sentence when the court hears he tried to protect you.' She flashed Clarissa an unexpected smile. This time it was large and white. 'I think you need to take a breather, collect yourself and when you're ready, Sergeant Quinn will take a statement from you.'

The detective nodded at her once, then hurried away to issue some fresh instructions to a group of officers.

Suddenly Clarissa became aware of Ralph sitting on the floor being attended to by a paramedic. She half-expected to see a piano residing on his knees, but all she could see was blood.

She sighed, swallowing back the bitter taste of guilt, knowing full well that the claw hammer had been brought down on his hand because of her actions. With great sadness she conceded that Ralph had been the one who'd paid the real price for Roland Steed's arrest.

She went to him.

He stared up at her.

'How's your finger?' she said.

'I'll...live,' he said, through the effects of the drugs.

'I'll come with you to the hospital,' she said, worried.

'I didn't…' Ralph struggled to speak, still reeling from the drugs they'd forced into him. 'I wouldn't have taken the manuscript from you…to give to *him*. I wouldn't…have gone through with it. You have to believe –'

'I believe you,' said Clarissa, searching his hazel eyes and finding nothing but good in them.

They both looked at the black stain on the copper carpet, the ubiquitous presence of the police buzzing around them.

The manuscript had been reduced to a fine powder. Dead; like its composer.

'I'm sorry you didn't get to play it,' she said sadly. 'But I'm not sorry I destroyed it.'

'It's…what Chopin…would have wanted,' said Ralph.

Clarissa agreed.

Guy's Hospital waiting room was busy with patients. Clarissa was holding out for the verdict on Ralph's hand when her phone indicated an incoming call.

"Donna Calling" was rolling across the screen.

'Hi hun, how ya' doing?' said Donna's cheery voice.

'Hi!' said Clarissa. 'How are you?'

'Well, I've not vomited over anyone today, which is a bonus!' she laughed. 'How are you? Anything to tell me?'

Clarissa swallowed hard. 'How long have you got?'

She gave Donna a brief version of what had happened and her friend listened intently. After a few solemn exchanges, Donna tried to make light of the situation.

'Hey! How's this for a "role reversal!"' she giggled. 'Now *you're* the one sitting in a hospital waiting to hear about your boyfriend's hand and I'm the one doing the consoling! Weird or what?'

'Oh, how's Woody?' asked Clarissa, keen for an update on the pilot's recovery.

'He's doing great, thanks hun!' Clarissa could hear the relief in Donna's voice. 'The operation was a complete success. And don't think I didn't notice your reaction there.'

'What are you talking about?'

'I referred to Ralph as your "boyfriend" and a denial did not immediately follow! I'll take that as a good sign.'

'Donna. Ralph and me. It's all a bit complicated. You don't know the half of it.'

'Well, how about we meet up tomorrow evening and you tell me?'

'Okay,' said Clarissa gratefully. 'I'd like that. Thanks.'

Clarissa saw Ralph emerge from the consultant's room.

'Listen, Donna. I've got to go. Ralph's just come out from seeing the doctor. I'll be in touch tomorrow, okay?'

'Sure, sweetie. Text me.'

Clarissa disconnected. She looked up at Ralph expectantly. He was walking slowly towards her, as if his youthful body had suddenly become inhabited by that of an old man; it pained her to see it. All that self-confidence and swagger, that furious focused energy: gone.

The consultant accompanied him down the corridor. As Ralph's speech was still slurred due to Steed's sedative, the consultant offered to relate his news to her on his behalf. He was a sympathetic man with kind eyes. He told Clarissa that Ralph's finger had been temporarily splinted, but due to the nature of his injury he would need to return in two days for it to be pinned. He went on to say that he saw no reason why Ralph shouldn't make a full recovery and resume his rightful place at a piano again in six weeks' time. The drugs, he said, should wear off within the hour. The relief brought tears to Clarissa's eyes.

When Ralph left her briefly to organise his next appointment, Clarissa called her mother – her former text, instructing her to get hold of her urgently playing on her mind.

Her mother started crying as soon as she heard Clarissa's voice. 'Something significant has happened,' she said. 'I think it's good news!' Then she went on to tell her that Edward Letterton, the bastard who had raped her sweet innocent child twenty years ago, had finally succumbed to a heart attack. The man who had ruined her daughter's life was dead. The news felt like a monsoon on Clarissa's shrivelled, neglected plant-like soul.

When Ralph returned, the two of them went to refuel themselves in the hospital café and Clarissa told him about Letterton.

He said only one thing in response: 'You're free now.'

Clarissa surveyed the red lumps on Ralph's face with tender concern. He really had endured the most terrible beating. She recalled his assailant, with his muscly build and bald head.

'Whatever made you think you could defeat Simon?' she asked. 'Did you have a death-wish or something?'

Ralph grinned with one side of his mouth. 'I needed to…get to you. I thought you…were in danger.'

'But there were three of them, and then Steed *himself* to get past. What were you going to do, fight your way through them all?'

'I guess I was…thinking with my heart, not…with my head,' Ralph replied earnestly, in his new constrained manner. 'I wish I could…bloody speak properly.'

They both laughed, before falling vacantly silent again.

Clarissa found herself examining Ralph with renewed attention. Suppressing the urge to touch him was proving more difficult than she'd imagined, but she was painfully aware that what she'd once had with him had been irrevocably altered.

At a loss to understand where they needed to go from here, both physically and metaphorically, Clarissa and Ralph sat in silence for several minutes, their new reticence with one another strange and unnatural. Then, shortly after glancing at his watch, Ralph said: 'I know what we have to do.'

21

It was 7:25 p.m. when Clarissa and Ralph reached the Duke's Hall at the Royal Academy of Music.

It all felt a bit unreal as they walked past the gathering musicians talking animatedly, dressed in their finery and preparing to mount the Duke's Hall stage. Ralph beckoned to a woman with a messy bun, in jeans and a black blouse. 'Kate!'

'Bloody hell, Ralph! What happened to you?' she exclaimed at the sight of him. 'I take it you're not performing?'

'Don't worry, Clarissa here will be taking my place,' Ralph informed her, almost in his normal speaking voice, the effect of the drugs now fast wearing off. 'But she'll need something to wear!'

It had been Ralph's idea. A man with a broken finger could not play the piano, he'd said to her sadly at the hospital, but he'd gone on to suggest with a fierce glint in his eye, that this did not mean his 8 p.m. slot to play at the Duke's Hall should be cancelled.

'*Who?*' A startled-looking Kate was casting her a dubious glance.

Suddenly a crowd began to assemble around them and Clarissa realised that she was the main focus of it.

'Are you sure? She doesn't look that much better off than you,' said Kate, glaring at Clarissa's black eye.

'She's fine. More than capable,' said Ralph. 'Trained at the Royal College. Can somebody get her…something to wear please? We've got what? Twenty-five minutes? Come on!'

When they'd discussed it in the hospital only a couple of hours before, Ralph's plan had made perfect sense, that *she* should perform the Nocturne instead of him – his premise: with no time to generate any reluctance for the task, she would be in a better frame of mind to carry it out. Now that it was actually happening, Clarissa felt the throb of fear pulsing hard through her body.

'You look like a ten, yeah?' said a tall girl in a green velvet dress. 'Come with me!'

'You're all just going to take Ralph's word for it and let me play? Just like that?' cried Clarissa, trying to keep up with the girl's pace along a narrow corridor.

'Ralph's a bit of an authority around here,' the girl replied. 'If he says you're good enough to take his place, we trust him.'

Clarissa found herself whisked into a small room that smelt of hairspray and metal polish. She was handed a black velvet dress which she put on hurriedly. The girl introduced herself as

Marlena. She told her that she'd been unable to decide between the green or the black, so she'd brought both with her.

The black dress fitted Clarissa well, hugging the curves of her body in all the right places. She left her blonde hair down.

Marlena nodded her approval, politely ignoring Clarissa's black eye. 'Come on, you've got fifteen minutes,' she said.

Clarissa was ready, but she couldn't find Ralph anywhere. Marlena and a few well-intentioned bystanders helped her search for him.

When she finally located him in the foyer by the reception desks, he was not alone. Slim and Silas had crawled out of the nearest gutter and were standing confrontationally in front of him. Their timing was extraordinary.

As she reached him, he threw a bundle of cash at their feet.

'It's all there,' said Ralph. 'Now get the fuck out of my life!'

'Bloody hell, Valero, you've surpassed yourself!' cried Slim.

'We're gonna need to count it, of course,' said Silas, scooping the wads of money off the floor like a greedy child let loose in a sweet shop; it was almost comical.

'I said it was all there,' said Ralph firmly.

Slim shot Silas a look, then returned his gaze to Ralph. 'Much obliged to you, Valero.'

'If it's a penny short, I'll be back for it!' Silas threatened.

'Just take your money and piss off,' said Ralph.

Clarissa noticed a security guard edging his way towards them.

Slim and Silas looked from Ralph to the security guard, then back to Ralph again. Clarissa saw the gold of Slim's tooth wink at her as it caught one of the foyer lights.

She observed the almost imperceptible smile on Ralph's lips as the pair began to walk away in submission.

'Hey, Silas! You forgot to give me my *lesson in physical damage*!' he shouted.

Silas stopped, his ugly mouth pulling back into a smile. 'Looks like you've already had that from somebody else, mate,' he said resignedly.

Clarissa watched them leave.

When Ralph turned around, he seemed surprised to see her. 'Wow, Clarissa! You look –'

'So Steed still coughed up the cash?' she interjected, shocked. 'I don't believe it!'

'Like hell he did,' said Ralph. He lowered his voice: 'I took the money from his suite in the hotel before they drugged me. Hid it in my clothes. They had me locked in the bedroom for twenty minutes. I found three cases of cash in a safe in the wardrobe. The eejits had only gone and left it open! There must have been a hundred thousand pounds in there at least! I just took enough to pay off Morgan's debt, I hope you don't mind.'

'Mind?' she said. 'Why would I mind? It's money well spent, if you ask me!'

'Well, I wish I'd taken a bit more of it now. Enough to get your piano repaired, at least,' he said, the regret in his voice palpable.

Clarissa smiled at him. 'Oh, I wouldn't worry about that. It's nothing a line of wood glue won't fix, I'm getting quite skilled at it now. Have you told Morgan?'

'I'll text her later. You look wonderful, by the way,' he said, admiring her dress.

'The black eye really adds to the look, don't you think?' she said sarcastically.

Ralph grinned.

'Listen, Clarissa, I would never have agreed to work for Steed if I'd known what he was really asking me to do,' said Ralph ruefully.

'I know,' Clarissa replied. 'You don't need to explain.'

The hum in the foyer softened.

'It must nearly be time for you to go on,' he said.

Clarissa experienced a hard jolt of nerves.

'I'm not calm, Ralph. I don't know if I can go through with it.' Her eyes were large and afraid.

'Yes you can. Just concentrate on your breathing and clear your mind of everything but the Nocturne, and you'll be fine,'

Ralph said reassuringly. 'Besides, Letterton's gone now. The days when you could use him as an excuse are over.'

'Yes,' said Clarissa. 'You're right.'

Ralph unzipped the pocket of his leather jacket and removed his grandfather's signet ring. He lifted the chain from around his neck and attempted to thread the ring onto it, struggling with his broken finger. She helped him with it.

'For good luck,' he said, placing Álvaro Valero's talisman, now rolling around on his silver chain, over her head. The ring fell into the velvet of her dress. Then Ralph left his fingers where they had landed on the nape of her neck, and kissed her gently on the lips.

When he pulled away, he stared deeply into her eyes.

'Just perform the piece like you did in the Susie Sainsbury Theatre,' he said, with gentle affection. Then he flashed her one of his beautiful full-mouthed smiles and said: 'Imagine you're playing just for me!'

Clarissa nodded and watched him go to find a seat for her performance.

Once he had gone, she said: 'I am.'

Clarissa didn't look directly at the audience in the Duke's Hall, but she could feel them whispering in confusion as she walked out to the grand piano residing on the stage.

The Dead Drop quest is over, she thought, as she sat down upon the red velvet piano stool, and *nobody* has ended up with Chopin's precious manuscript. She did not regret destroying it – it meant that she had done the right thing by Chopin – but she couldn't help wondering if any copies had been made.

Charlie would always have a special place in her heart, she reflected sadly. She now believed that he had always loved her, but his plan to protect her had gone horribly wrong, just like her plan to protect him had done.

Letterton's death had been a shock, but its timing had been providential. Clarissa knew that the hold he had on her could no longer exist. Ralph had been right, she had brooded on this for too long. There was nothing to stop her performing now, she just had to do it. So here she was, about to give her first public performance in seven years!

Clarissa tucked Ralph's grandfather's ring inside her dress to prevent it from obscuring the keys. The feel of the cold silver upon her chest provided her with a source of unexpected comfort. She had connected with Ralph in a way previously unknown to her. The trace of his last touch sent a shiver up her spine before it ebbed away.

She took a deep breath.

She sensed the hall fall silent around her. She placed her hands on the cold white keys of her beloved instrument, acknowledging that she was close to the edge of something new, and played the piano.

AUTHOR'S NOTES:

Aram Bartholl (b.1972 -) is a real artist who lives and works in Berlin, Germany. In 2010, he launched a new art manifesto to the world entitled *The Dead Drop Manifesto*. In it he encourages the public to share information by cementing USB drives into walls in public spaces. Bartholl describes a beautiful Dead Drop as revealing only the connecting part of a USB stick's metal sheath (the rest of it being fully submerged inside a wall, step or kerb). Since then, hundreds of Dead Drops have appeared in various cities around the world. They are sought and explored by a large diversity of people and contain data in many languages. Unlike Charlie's Drops, these Dead Drops should never be deleted, so that numerous people can continue to enjoy downloading their contents again and again.

Frédéric Chopin (1810-1849) was one of the world's greatest composers of solitary piano. He wrote 59 mazurkas, 27 études, 27 preludes, 21 nocturnes and 20 waltzes for the instrument. He was born in Poland, but came to Paris at the age of 21, where he lived until his death at the tender age of 39. He left explicit instructions in his will that in the event of his death, any previously unpublished manuscripts later discovered in his hand should immediately be destroyed. He was famously romantically involved with the French novelist Amantine Lucile Aurore Dupin – best known by her pen name George Sand (1804-1876). She wrote 58 novels (nine of which have become internationally renowned) and 13 plays. To this day there is no known piece of music that has been officially recorded as having been composed by Chopin for Sand.

ACKNOWLEDGEMENTS

I would like to express my sincere thanks and gratitude to my family and friends for their support during the writing of this book. A special mention must go to my husband Peter Denman, for putting up with my regular late night writing stints (repeatedly waking him at 3 a.m. when I tried so hard not to); my mother, Pamela Howard for providing me with fresh hope whenever I lost confidence in my ability to write; and my brother Steven Howard, for his encouragement to get this novel published, no matter what! I would also like to thank my friends: Belinda Cahill, Sally Edwards and Julia Ludgate. Your continued interest in this project from start to finish has helped ensure its completion!

I would like to thank Aram Bartholl for providing me with the initial inspiration for this novel; Elizabeth Ward, my editor for ensuring my words flowed together as they should; and Gabrielle Gale (Museum Curator of the Royal Academy of Music Museum) for assisting me with my research. I am extremely grateful to Benoît Puttemans (Director of Books and Manuscripts, Sotheby's Paris) and Graham Bignell (Conservator-Restorer), for their respective information regarding nineteenth-century paper conservation; and I would like to thank Peter O'Dell, for sharing his expert firearm's knowledge with me, and for providing useful information about the Beretta handgun. I would also like to take this opportunity to thank the award-winning Film Director Stuart Wahlin, who consented to creating a cinematic book trailer for this novel (available to watch on YouTube).

Finally, I would like to acknowledge my debt to the composer Frédéric Chopin and the author George Sand. These two sharp, creative minds have each left a legacy of their own behind, and I hope that this story will encourage my readers to explore their work.

Made in the USA
Coppell, TX
04 June 2023

17685424R00256